WHO MADE STEVIE CRYE?
WHO MADE STEVIE CRYE?
WHO MADE STEVIE CRYE?
WHO MADE STEVIE CRYE?
WHO MADE STEVIE CRYE?
WHO MADE STEVIE CRYE?
WHO MADE STEVIE CRYE?
WHO MADE STEVIE CRYE?
WHO MADE STEVIE CRYE?
WHO MADE STEVIE CRYE?
WHO MADE STEVIE CRYE?
WHO MADE STEVIE CRYE?
WHO MADE STEVIE CRYE?
WHO MADE STEVIE CRYE?
WHO MADE STEVIE CRYE?
WHO MADE STEVIE CRYE?
WHO MADE STEVIE CRYE?
WHO MADE STEVIE CRYE?
WHO MADE STEVIE CRYE?
WHO MADE STEVIE CRYE?
WHO MADE STEVIE CRYE?
WHO MADE STEVIE CRYE?
WHO MADE STEVIE CRYE?
WHO MADE STEVIE CRYE?
WHO MADE STEVIE CRYE?
WHO MADE STEVIE CRYE?
WHO MADE STEVIE CRYE?
WHO MADE STEVIE CRYE?
WHO MADE STEVIE CRYE?
WHO MADE STEVIE CRYE?

WHO MADE STEVIE CRY?
WHO MADE STEVIE CRY?
WHO MADE STEVIE CRY?
WHO MADE STEVIE CRY?
WHO MADE STEVIE CRY?
WHO MADE STEVIE CRY?
WHO MADE STEVIE CRY?
WHO MADE STEVIE CRY?
WHO MADE STEVIE CRY?
WHO MADE STEVIE CRY?
WHO MADE STEVIE CRY?
WHO MADE STEVIE CRY?
WHO MADE STEVIE CRY?
WHO MADE STEVIE CRY?
WHO MADE STEVIE CRY?
WHO MADE STEVIE CRY?
WHO MADE STEVIE CRY?
WHO MADE STEVIE CRY?
WHO MADE STEVIE CRY?
WHO MADE STEVIE CRY?
WHO MADE STEVIE CRY?
WHO MADE STEVIE CRY?
WHO MADE STEVIE CRY?
WHO MADE STEVIE CRY?
WHO MADE STEVIE CRY?
WHO MADE STEVIE CRY?
WHO MADE STEVIE CRY?
WHO MADE STEVIE CRY?
WHO MADE STEVIE CRY?
WHO MADE STEVIE CRY?

A NOVEL OF THE AMERICAN SOUTH BY

Michael Bishop

WITH PHOTOGRAPHIC ILLUSTRATIONS BY

Jeffrey K. Potter

ARKHAM HOUSE PUBLISHERS, INC.

Library of Congress Cataloging in Publication Data

Bishop, Michael.
   Who made Stevie Crye?

   I. Title.
PS3552.I772W5   1984   813'.54   84-9251
ISBN 0-87054-099-8

Printed in the United States of America
First Edition

For Jim Turner

Seeking to contrive a way both to have one's cake and to eat it is undubitably a shameful activity; but human, too, I fear, so very, very human.

—A. H. H. LIPSCOMBE

WHO MADE STEVIE CRYE?

I

Stevenson Crye—her friends called her Stevie—was nearing the end of her feature story on detection-and-diagnosis procedures at the West Georgia Cancer Clinic in Ladysmith when a cable inside her typewriter snapped and the machine began emitting a sound like an amplified raspberry. The disc on which the type characters were embossed refused to advance, and the angry blatting of the stalled element grew perilously louder. The typewriter seemed to be threatening to blow apart, a seven-hundred-dollar time bomb.

Stevie jabbed the on/off key and pushed her folding chair away from the desk, her entire body trembling as if the scream of an emergency vehicle had riven her peace of mind. She wanted to scream herself.

Instead she murmured, "Shit," and exhaled a despairing sigh. Although that word was forbidden the lips of thirteen-year-old Ted, Jr., and eight-year-old Marella (the penalty for bad language being the forfeiture of a week's allowance), ever since her husband's death in the hospital next door to the clinic about which she had just been writing, Stevie had found plenty of occasions to use the word herself. Bills falling due, deadlines missed, and now her expensive PDE "Exceleriter" breaking down and proclaiming its failure with a mechanical Bronx cheer. Shit. Thank God the kids were still at school.

Stevie went to the window of her second-floor study and leaned her face against the cold glass. The naked limbs of cork elms and dogwoods could not conceal the silver struts and lofty unpainted belly of Barclay's water tower four blocks away. The town looked uninhabited. Who did you turn to on a bleak February afternoon when the instrument you and your children depended on for nearly every necessity went on the fritz? Dr. Elsa was fine at setting bones and incinerating warts, but probably not so handy at doctoring broken typewriters. You could romanticize small towns all you liked, but sometimes they were pretty damned inconvenient. Lots of work for a plumber and electrician like Ted, though. He had loved this place. . . .

The Exceleriter, meanwhile, reposed in the middle of Stevie's rolltop as if nothing much were wrong.

Her cheek still against the glass, Stevie stared at it. The typing element was canted at an unfamiliar angle, but otherwise the machine looked okay. Ted had given it to her for her birthday two and a half years ago, not long after she had decided to develop her latent writing talent and shortly before Dr. Elsa had diagnosed his gastrointestinal cancer. Ted was gone, but his gift remained, providential and indispensable. Maybe if she switched it on again, the type disc would click back into place and the machine obediently resume its lovely rotary-engine purr.

Worth a try, Stevie thought, leaving the window.

The typewriter, however, responded to her touch with a voice like a robot magpie's. In self-defense she gouged the on/off control. In helpless anger she pounded the machine's dark-blue hood. When she had finished, the only sound in the world seemed to be the propane hiss of her Dearborn space heater, that and the faint mockery of the winter wind clicking the leafless branches of the trees.

"Shit!" cried Stevenson Crye. "Shit! Shit! Shit!"

Downstairs, her tantrum spent, Stevie sought to remedy the situation in a rational way. When a problem presented itself, Ted had always cautioned her, you didn't spout curses, pound inanimate objects, or tear your hair. No, of course not. You made a list of possible solutions, either on paper or in your head, and you tried each of these solutions in turn until everything was hunky-dory again. Otherwise, according to this consummate handyman-for-hire, you went rapidly and counterproductively bonkers.

So be it. She would take her late husband's advice.

Too bad you didn't practice what you preached in bookkeeping and financial matters, thought Stevie involuntarily, with a twinge of the old resentment she had been trying to exorcise for months. She administered a reproving slap to her own forehead and put the thought out of her mind.

What to do about the broken Exceleriter? First, Stevie decided, she would try to borrow the clunky old Smith-Corona at the Barclay medical center to finish her article. So that she need not transport the typewriter back and forth in her van, Dr. Elsa would probably agree to let her work in an empty examination room. It might even be fun to turn out a story in a building where you could hear other human beings moving about.

Second, she would telephone the offices of Pantronics Data Equipment in Ladysmith to see about having her Exceleriter repaired. The last time something had gone wrong with it (a minor glitch in its timing), Ted had taken care of the matter while the machine was still under its original warranty. Really, then, she had no right to accuse PDE of marketing an unreliable product. In the twenty months since her husband's desertion—*death*, rather; she didn't mean *desertion*—she must have run nearly a half-million words through the Exceleriter. By that standard, it had been a bargain, the most astute investment in her future security Ted could have possibly made—with the inarguable exception of a decent insurance policy and a growing savings account. A good hand with a measuring tape and voltage meters, he had never been able to balance his checkbook. . . .

Although eighteen miles away, Ladysmith was a local call for Barclay residents. Stevie found the PDE number in the directory, dialed it, and began explaining her trouble to a secretary who interrupted her anxious spiel to connect her with the service department. This time a man answered, and Stevie began again.

"Give me directions to your place of business," the service employee interjected. "We'll send someone over."

"I'm self-employed. I work at home."

"Do you carry a service agreement with us?"

"At three hundred dollars a year? Are you kidding?"

The man gave an ambiguous harrumphing laugh. "Well, we make house calls even for private individuals without service agreements."

"For a price."

"No different from anybody else, Mrs. Crye. You don't work for free, I'll bet. Neither do the folks at Pantronics Data Equipment."

"Okay, okay. Apart from repair costs, what *do* you charge for a service call?"

"Just a minute." Stevie heard the pages of a loose-leaf manual turning and the serviceman muttering half-audible computations. "It's a mileage thing, Mrs. Crye," he said a moment later. "To Barclay and back . . . well, about twenty-three dollars."

"I'll bring it in."

"Fine with us."

"That's better than a dollar a mile," Stevie accused. "Fine by me if I don't pay your extortionist rates."

"Actually, ma'am, it's *less* than a dollar a mile."

"You're figuring this on a PDE calculator, I take it."

"Not at all, Mrs. Crye. You used the Ladysmith directory to call us, but you're talking to a Columbus exchange. PDE headquarters in South Georgia happens to be in Columbus, that's where I am, and that's where you'll have to bring your typewriter. See how helpful we are? The magic of electronics has just saved you the cost of a long-distance call."

Stevie's sense of frustration mounted. South on I-185, Columbus was over forty miles away. Although she did not mind driving there on weekends for the grocery specials and some rueful window shopping, today was Tuesday. She could hardly put off the repair that long. She would have to gas up the VW microbus and drive down there tomorrow, forfeiting a large part of a valuable workday. Indeed, if they asked her to leave the Exceleriter, she would have to waste a portion of another day fetching it home. The mock-affability of the man on the other end of the line heightened her frustration.

"Your thoughtfulness is a model for us all," she told him.

"Thank you, ma'am."

"How much to replace the cable on my ribbon carrier? Can you give me an estimate, to sort of cushion the shock before I get down there?"

"Our hourly rates went up at the first of the year."

Oh, no, thought Stevie. The PDE man had made this announcement as if declaring a stock dividend. From his point of view, maybe he had. Maybe he was a working-stiff shareholder with a vested interest in soaking the company's clientele.

"Are you afraid to tell me to what?" Stevie asked.

"From forty-four dollars an hour, Mrs. Crye, to fifty-two. We don't prorate that amount, either. Fifty-two dollars is the *minimum* charge for whatever may need to be done."

"Fifty-two dollars to replace a goddamn carrier cable? Even if it only takes five minutes?"

"That's not a ladylike way to talk, Mrs. Crye."

"Listen, in January it only cost me thirty-five dollars to get complete physical checkups for both my kids, tests and lab work included. You don't really think servicing an Exceleriter ought to cost more than examining two living human children, do you?" Her indignation gave her voice a murderous, unappeasable edge.

"Kids aren't our specialty, ma'am."

"Do me a favor. Never tell the American Medical Association what you're charging, okay? If Dr. Sam and Dr. Elsa ever

decide they want parity with you overpaid gadget fixers, I'll
have to start treating my kids with chicken-noodle soup and
Band-Aids, no matter how bad they hurt. Really, Mr. Who-
ever-You-Are, this is outrageous.''

"Smith," said the man, amiably. "John Smith."

"Yeah, I'll bet. Listen, I'd have to be out of my mind to
bring my machine to you two-legged piranhas. You've made it
very clear what PDE stands for. It's not Pantronics Data
Equipment, either. It's—''

"—Pretty Damned Expensive," said the man in the service
department. "We hear that all the time." And he hung up.

"Arrrgggghhhhh!" cried Stevie, slamming her own receiver
into its cradle. Then she covered her face with her hands and
hunched forward over the breakfast bar wondering how Ted
would have handled that smart-alecky company shill. Better
than she had, probably. Far better than she had. Ted had been
good at handling problems, and in his work around Barclay he
had encountered dozens of ticklish ones every day. The only
problem he had not known how to deal with, money worries
aside, was his illness. To his illness he had turned belly-up
like a yard dog beset by a pack of vicious strays. Why, in the
one conflict where resolve really mattered, had he proved so
weak. . . ?

Stevie abruptly uncovered her eyes and lifted her head.
"The typewriter's the problem," she admonished herself.
"Not Ted; the *typewriter*. Stop this rotten sniveling."

She dialed the telephone again.

With Sam Kensington, her physician-husband, Dr. Elsa
worked alternate days in the medical centers of Barclay and the
nearby Wickrath community. Being in Barclay this Tuesday,
she had no objection to Stevie's popping over to commandeer

the ancient Smith-Corona in the rear examination room.

"Come ahead, honey," the older woman had said. "You might want to wear a surgical mask, though."

Indeed, Stevie found the tiny facility's two waiting rooms (once upon a time, whites had sat on one side and blacks on the other) teeming with flu victims, lonely pensioners in need of either prescriptions or official reassurance, and worried mothers with colicky babies. February always overburdened the Kensingtons, but, marvelously panic-proof, the fiftyish Dr. Elsa gave Stevie a smile from the doorway of one of the examination rooms up front, motioned her down the hall to the spare typewriter, and apologized for not being able to stop for a chat.

"Do whatever you've got to do, Stevie."

"Thanks. I'll try to be out of your hair in an hour or so. Marella expects me to be waiting for her when she gets home from school."

Pounding out the final four paragraphs of her article for *The Columbus Ledger,* Stevie felt acutely uncomfortable. She had no real fear of catching a flu bug from one of the sufferers out front, but she did regret preempting the use of this room for the examination of patients. The little clinic was bursting at the seams, and here she was occupying space that rightfully belonged to the sick. Had Dr. Sam been on duty today instead of Dr. Elsa, she would never have thought to impose. Although she was taking advantage of the older woman's friendship for several cogent reasons—the imminence of her deadline at the *Ledger,* the care and feeding of her family, the furtherance of her uncertain free-lancing career—she could hardly justify intruding a second time this week. Maybe she should simply take the Smith-Corona home with her. The Kensingtons, after all, had another typewriter, and she would be closer to her reference books, her files, and her telephone.

Unfortunately, Stevie *despised* the Kensingtons' old machine. Frequent occurrences of type clash cut down her speed, the platen was loose, and ten minutes of playing the damn thing at the requisite energetic fortissimo reduced her arms to limp, sodden rags. Besides, the *c, q, u, o,* and *e* produced by the dilapidated Smith-Corona all looked like miniature bowling balls or piratical black spots, so greasy were the raised characters on the typebars. You came to such a machine only in an emergency. Because the Kensingtons put their other typewriter (a newer electric model) to regular daily use, Stevie could hardly ask to borrow that one. She had to get her Exceleriter repaired as soon as possible.

But where? And by whom?

At ten minutes to three Stevie shuffled her manuscript pages together, made more than a dozen hurried corrections with a leaky Bic pen, and prayed that her editor at the *Ledger* would forgive her the unconscionable messiness of the final few paragraphs. After arranging a dust cover patched with grimy strips of masking tape on the boxy machine, she bumped into Dr. Elsa in the clinic's narrow hall.

"You've been a lifesaver, Elsa. I've got to drop this off at the post office and get home to meet Marella."

"What about Teddy?"

"Oh, he's got basketball practice at the middle school. Thirteen years old and Dr. Sam measured him at five feet seven last month, half a head taller than You-Know-Who. Seems like yesterday he was in swaddling clothes. Crap-laden Pampers, anyway. I don't expect him until six-thirty or seven."

Dr. Elsa, her habitual haggard cheerfulness giving way to a penetrating concern, gripped Stevie by the shoulders. "You all right, kiddo? Every time I see that vein tickin' in your temple I want to take your blood pressure. Kids aren't the only ones need checkups, you know."

"All I'm sick about's my typewriter, Elsa."

"If you're in a real bind, take ours. Not that clunker in there, the good one Sherry's usin' up front."

"No. I couldn't. I'm not going to." Grasping one of Dr. Elsa's bony red hands, Stevie squeezed it companionably. "I need someone to talk to, though. You think you could come by this evening? Drop in for some wine and cheese dip? I've had the wine since Christmas, but the cheese dip's new—I promise."

"You're on. Look for me around eight. I'll leave Sam home.

This'll be our own cozy little hen party.''

"Teddy'll be there, Elsa."

"That's all right. He's not a rooster *yet*."

During her time in the clinic, it had begun to drizzle, a depressing histamine mist from on high. Barclay huddled beneath this drifting moisture like a toy city in the hollow hemisphere of a paperweight.

Back in her VW van, Stevie stifled a sneeze, swung past the post office to deposit her article in a curbside box, and eventually, behind a pair of yolk-colored buses, pulled into the elementary school's oily-looking parking lot to pick up her daughter. Marella did not need to walk home in the rain. She was a willowy girl with a delicate constitution, a lively ballerina of a third-grader if you overlooked her occasional indispositions. Stevie usually did. Before Ted's death she had smothered the child with affection. Since then, however, she had adopted a more levelheaded approach to raising her daughter, primarily to keep from spoiling her. Gratifyingly, Marella had never shown any signs of resenting this deliberate change in tactics. She appreciated whatever Stevie or anyone else did for her, and she would be pleasantly surprised to find her mother waiting for her outside the school in this icy mistfall.

Or so Stevie believed.

Perversely, then, Marella climbed into the microbus as if it were a taxi tardily arrived from the dispatcher's. She slumped sideways in the seat next to Stevie's and let her notebook drop to the floorboard with a rude resounding thump. Her eyes had the hungry cast of one of those children in a television commercial for the Foster Parents Plan. You came because you felt guilty, they seemed to say. Then they filmed over and seemed to say nothing at all.

"Marella, sit up!"

"Mama," the girl managed. "Mama, I'm sick. I've been sick since lunch. Didn't tell anybody, though."

Stevie put her hand on Marella's forehead and found it alarmingly feverish. "You didn't tell anybody? Why in the world not?"

"So you could work, Mama."

So I could work, Stevie mentally echoed her daughter. You didn't tell anybody so your typewriter-poundin' mama wouldn't have to forsake her rolltop to fetch you home. The girl's selfless, foolhardy bravery annoyed as well as touched Stevie, evoking the terrible suspicion that for mama to ply her semireputable Grub Street trade in her upstairs study, maybe her children had to sacrifice more than she did. She ought to go back to teaching. Her hours would correspond to the kids', she'd have summers off, and the local board of education would guarantee her nearly two weeks of sick leave every year. Most important, Teddy and Marella, not to mention Dr. Elsa, would no longer have to treat her like an emotional invalid just to keep her from falling apart over the slightest unforeseeable reverse in her daily schedule.

Like the snapping of an itty-bitty typewriter cable.

"Oh, baby," Stevie crooned. "Oh, my silly, thoughtful baby."

Once home, she lit the space heater in the den, folded down the sofa bed, and arranged Marella on its lumpy mattress with three or four quilts and a paperback copy of Beverly Cleary's *Runaway Ralph*. (Now there was a woman, Stevie reflected, who had made a successful career of writing; unfortunately, Theodore Crye's widow seemed to have no talent for fiction, not even the sort children might like.) Stevie also spread some newspapers on the floor near the sofa and positioned a yellow plastic bucket atop them in case Marella found her gorge rising faster than she herself could scramble to the bathroom. This was the quintessential winter ritual in the Crye household, and Stevie carried it out to the letter.

Thank God it wasn't leap year. If February had had even a single extra day this year, she would have probably used it to take a header from the rustic stone viaduct up in Roosevelt State Park.

"Didn't know this was going to be a house call, kiddo. Thought you asked me over for a party."

"Sorry, Elsa, I really am. I didn't know she was sick until I picked her up at school. Give me credit for not running her by the clinic while you were swamped with other patients, though. I did have *that* much sense."

"What's sensible about failin' to take a sick child to her doctor?"

"*I'm* her doctor." Stevie placed a basket of Tostados and a plastic container of cheese dip in front of Dr. Elsa, then filled her champagne glass with a domestic burgundy. A small wine-red shadow danced on the countertop beside the glass. "I've done this so many times I'm practically infallible. Look, she's sleeping, Elsa, gathering strength before your very eyes."

From their vantage at the breakfast bar they could see Marella's inert form lying sprawled in a jumble of quilts in the den. She did seem to be resting comfortably. Stevie's bucket-carrying labors had ceased shortly after six when she had disinfected everything in sight with Lysol before attempting to prepare dinner for Teddy and herself. The pungent smell of that commercial product had not yet completely faded.

"I hope I don't get what she's got," Teddy said from the kitchen table, where he was supposedly doing a social-studies assignment. "Three guys at B-ball practice was out this afternoon on accountuv the trots."

"That's a lovely sentence," Stevie remarked.

"Diarrhea, then."

Stevie grimaced. "Come on, Teddy!"

"Try Montezuma's revenge," Dr. Elsa advised the boy. "It's not exactly what you mean, but it sounds a whole lot prettier."

"Teddy, why don't you just go upstairs to finish that?"

"It's cold up there, Mom."

"Turn on your electric blanket. You'll be going to bed in

another hour or so, anyway. Give it a chance to warm up.''

Wearing one of his father's hand-me-down fishnet sweaters, Teddy entered the cold dining room and closed the door behind him. Then Stevie and Dr. Elsa could hear him clomping toward the front foyer, there to begin the climb to his chilly bedroom. You couldn't afford to run every space heater in the house, but Teddy would hardly risk freezing to death giving Dr. Elsa and Dear Old Mom ten or fifteen minutes to themselves. He was a smart boy. He knew why she had sent him upstairs, and he would fiddle around up there blowing breath balloons and tracing the furry rime on his windows with a fingernail—until, Stevie hoped, they had had time for at least one meaty confidential exchange.

''I'm thinking of quitting this ulcer-making business,'' she said, swirling the wine in her champagne glass. ''I'm thinking of going back to teaching.''

''Because your stupid typewriter broke?''

''Lots of things besides, Elsa. Marella being sick, Teddy growing up, their daddy surrendering to his disease—surrendering in spite of everything he used to tell me about tackling the future head-on.''

''Get your typewriter fixed.''

''I feel like he ran out on me, Elsa. That's a horrible thing to say, I know, but he just stopped trying. You told me he had cancer—Dr. Sam did, anyway—and he started acting like somebody confined to Death Row with no hope of pardon. Overnight he was a different person, a stranger.''

''Get your typewriter fixed.''

''Damn it, Elsa! I told you this afternoon I wanted to talk. Why are you trying to shut me up?''

Dr. Elsa rolled the burgundy in her mouth as if it were Lavoris. ''I'm not a shrink, Stevie, just a small-town lady doctor who doesn't know Sigmund Freud from Freda Stimson.'' Freda Stimson ran a florist's shop on the Alabama Road just west of town.

''You're a friend. Friends *listen*, Elsa.''

''I'm listenin'. Besides, one way or another you've told me all this before. Ted was a wonderful fella who didn't face death in a way you could admire. The last year of his life spoiled your good opinion of the previous fifteen or so you'd known him. You resent him for doin' that to you, and you feel guilty for not bein' able to get past your resentment to the fella he was before I diagnosed his cancer."

"Exactly."

"A hotshot shrink in Atlanta would charge you fifty dollars for that little analysis. Then he'd ask you back for nine more sessions."

"That's why I asked you over, Elsa. You see through all the crap to what's really important."

"Get your typewriter fixed."

"*Elsa!*"

"Listen, honey, you couldn't admire Ted because he seemed to give up, right? Right. So your solution to a problem a whole lot less troublesome than his—a broken typewriter, for Tilly's sake—is to hoist your slip up a broomstick and holler, 'Uncle!' Now *that's* admirable, I take it."

Stevie poked her little finger into the cheese-dip container, licked it clean, and closed her eyes against the merciless irrefutability of her friend's logic. Right through the crap to the core of the matter . . .

Finally she said, "Fifty-two dollars to replace a cable, Elsa. I just don't have it. Just like I can't afford a hotshot Atlanta shrink. Even if I had fifty-two dollars, I wouldn't give those jerks at PDE the satisfaction."

The older woman took a prescription pad from her purse, tore off a sheet, and began writing on it with a pencil. "Here's the address of an office-supply company in Columbus with a typewriter service in the back. Hamlin Benecke and Sons. Sam swears by 'em. He swears by anybody who's cheap, but we knew the Beneckes socially some dozen years back. Don't see 'em anymore except when we've got a typewriter problem— they sold their lakeside cottage up this way in '70 or '71—and it was one of their boys got that manual you was wrestlin' with this afternoon in something like workin' order. Last autumn they gave us a discount on our electric machine. I'll give 'em a call in the morning to let 'em know you're comin' in. Tell old

Hamlin you can't afford to be kept waitin' till Memorial Day to get your typewriter back, either. That okay by you, Mrs. Joyce Carol Shakespeare?''

Stevie indicated her consent by laying one hand on Dr. Elsa's wrist.

A knock on the heavy wooden door connecting the kitchen and the unheated dining room startled both women. " 'S all right if I come back in now?'' Teddy shouted from the other side. "I'm freezin' my buns off.''

Because of Marella's illness, Stevie spent most of Wednesday at her desk in the den preparing a longhand first draft of a manuscript proposal she intended to submit to the Briar Patch Press in Atlanta. This company had published and successfully promoted collections of miscellaneous nonfiction by three of the columnists on Atlanta's two major dailies, and Stevie figured that her book—she intended to call it *Two-Faced Woman: Reflections of a Female Paterfamilias*—would slot into this popular format as easily as a penny into a parking meter. Already she had thirty or so 750-word columns around which to assemble her own collection (pieces she had originally sold either to local newspapers or to several different specialty magazines with regional distribution); and if the editors at the Briar Patch Press liked her proposal, she could expand these early columns or add to their number with a signed contract as warranty that any future work on the project would not be wasted. She desperately coveted such a contract.

As for Marella, the child had improved steadily throughout the day. By midafternoon she was begging permission to eat a peanut-butter-and-jelly sandwich (too oily, Stevie told her) and to watch a soap opera called "Ryan's Hope" (equally sticky fare, Stevie disapprovingly pointed out). By way of compromise, then, the child nibbled at a package of stale Nabisco saltines and thumbed through a two-year-old issue of *Cosmopolitan*. She also slept some more.

At 3:40 P.M. Polly Stratton, a sophomore at Wickrath County High, came in to babysit Marella until Teddy got home from basketball practice, freeing Stevie to lug her PDE Exceleriter 79 down the stairs from her study and outside to the VW microbus. The machine was about the size of a breadbox, but a breadbox laden with bricks or iron ingots. Maybe, thought Stevie sardonically, returning to the den to give Polly her final instructions and to kiss Marella goodbye, Dr. Elsa can come over again this evening to treat my aching back. Then she was off.

The trip to Columbus down I-185 took only forty-five minutes, but the rush-hour traffic inside the city itself kept her from reaching Hamlin Benecke & Sons, a green brick building not far from the television studios of the local CBS affiliate, before 5:30 P.M. In another half hour they would close, and Stevie despaired of explaining her problem and having her machine repaired in so little time—even if Dr. Elsa had assured her that, before you could say, "Exceleriter's Excellence Exceeds Every Exacting Expectation," young Seaton Benecke could *build* a typewriter from the space bar up. And Dr. Elsa had so assured her.

Indeed, before Stevie could lift her machine from the passenger's seat to carry it inside, a pudgy blond employee in white coveralls and rubber-soled shoes intervened to assist her. He had the unblemished complexion of a baby, blue eyes so bright they looked lacquered, and a nap of velvety peach fuzz on his jowls and dimpled chin.

"I've been expecting you all day," he said, backing through the door of the office-supply company.

"You're Seaton?"

"Yes, ma'am. Seaton Benecke. You're Stevenson Crye, the writer. I read all your stuff. I even go to the library and work through past issues of the *Ledger* looking for your stuff."

"Goodness," Stevie said. No one outside Barclay had ever professed any interest, either big or small, in her competent but obscure canon, and she really did not know what to say. Was this dumpy, squeaky-clean youth trying to impress her? If so, what for? Dr. Elsa had supposedly been quite forthright in telling the Beneckes that Stevie was bringing her Exceleriter to them because of the outrageous service charges at PDE Corporation. She certainly couldn't afford to *tip* Seaton for his unexpected flattery. Was that what he was futilely wangling for?

The boy—actually a man in his ambivalent midtwenties, suspended between the senior-class prom and full membership in the Jaycees—led her through the stacks of office supplies (typing paper, file cards, manila folders, staples, address labels, and lots more) to an immense work area with a concrete floor and unit after unit of modular metal shelves. One of these Erector Set towers housed typewriters, a veritable parliament of typewriters, some in their dust covers, some with their insides exposed and their platens lying beside them like carbon-coated rolling pins. Each typewriter had a tag wired to its carriage or its cylinder knob. Seeing so many machines in so many different states of disrepair, like bodies in the impermanent mausoleum of a morgue, Stevie feared that Seaton Benecke would place her Exceleriter on a shelf and promptly forget about it. She was surrendering her typewriter to a kind of high-tech cemetery.

"Are all these others ahead of mine?"

Seaton put her machine on a workbench and wiped his hands on his coveralls. "No, ma'am. I've got the cable you need. I'll have it installed in a jiffy. You *need* your typewriter."

"Don't these other folks need theirs?" She made a sweeping gesture at the broken, cannibalized, immobile relics behind the workbench. "Is this where superannuated typewriters come to die?"

"Some people just leave them here, Mrs. Crye. Abandon them or trade them in. I fix the ones that *need* to be fixed." He did not look at her when he talked, but of course he was busy peering into the guts of the Exceleriter and affixing a new ribbon-carrier cable to the element on which the type disc moved. A shock of white-blond hair fell across one eye, but his pudgy fingers went about their intricate task with unimpeded speed and deftness, a miniature screwdriver flashing spookily from the dim cavern of the machine. "I enjoy fixing typewriters for people who *need* them."

An icicle of apprehension slid through Stevie's heart. Why, though, she could not really say. She probably should have asked for an estimate before letting him start work. Or was it something else? Seaton Benecke's handiness and his blasé, vaguely patronizing manner intimidated her on some basic level. He seemed unaware of the effect he was having on her, though, so maybe she was reading too much ulteriority into his irritating emphasis on the same word. He was a young man without much grip on others' reactions and sensibilities. His work must frequently isolate him in this echo-prone typewriter's graveyard.

"That's good," Stevie said belatedly, just to make conversation. "You like what you do."

"I'd rather do what you do. I'd rather be a writer."

By sheer dint of will Stevie kept from laughing. She had seldom met anyone who seemed so ill-suited to the occupation. Seaton Benecke would not look you in the eye, his speech was repetitious and remote, and his awareness of his surroundings seemed limited to whatever he happened to be working on. His fingers loved her Exceleriter—she could see that—but otherwise he impressed her as having all the passion and tenderheartedness of a zombie in a George Romero flick. A cruel, uncharitable judgment, but there it was.

"You probably make more money fixing typewriters."

"People don't respect you, though."

Alternating currents of guilt and self-contempt surged through Stevenson Crye. Her pudgy-fingered Lancelot apparently had enough people-savvy to assess her unspoken opinion of him, even as he gallantly rescued her from distress. She deserved to be horsewhipped. Judge not lest ye be judged, and all those other astute Biblical injunctions about loving thy neighbor without coveting his ass. Yass.

"I admire anyone who's handy," she said penitently, meaning it.

Seaton Benecke neither looked at her nor spoke.

"What kind of writing do you want to do?"

"I don't know. Stories, I guess. Stories about the way people go about trying to figure themselves out."

"Psychological stories?"

Seaton Benecke shrugged. "I don't know. I guess. I can't do it, though. All I can do is fix typewriters. That's as close as I get. That's why I enjoy doing it for people who really *need* them."

The same grating litany. Stevie wished that she could like the young man, but his pitiable remoteness and his doomed ambition put her off. Unless he developed some management skills before inheriting his share of the family business, he would fix broken typewriters until his retirement. That was all. Stevie could not even imagine him marrying and fathering more little Seaton Beneckes. He would probably have the same skim-milk complexion at sixty-five that he had today.

"I'm just about finished," he volunteered a moment later. "And it's only going to cost you ten bucks and a few pennies tax for the cable."

"That's wonderful. I'm delighted. I really am."

He nodded. "You can get back to work. That's good because I like what you do. It's personal experiences or feature stories instead of, you know, made-up stories, but I like it anyway. All you lack is getting really deep into the way people try to explain who they are to themselves. What their most frightening worries are and so forth."

"Sorry," said Stevie banteringly, giving young Benecke a smile he did not look up to see. "I guess I'd rather be Erma Bombeck than Franz Kafka."

"Sometimes writers don't have a choice," he countered. "But you'll get better at it. I've read your stuff, and I can see it happening. You know, the personal-experience columns in the *Ledger*—sometimes they get close to what I'm talking about, when you exaggerate things to make them deeper, when you sort of *confess* your feelings." He stared contemplatively over the top of the Exceleriter. "Deepness is what I really like. Not being afraid to write about fears and dark desires. Nitty-gritty stuff."

"Seaton—" His first name sprang to her lips unbidden. "Seaton, most feature columnists exaggerate for humorous effect. They confess, as you call it, for the sake of pathos. That's what I'm usually trying to do in my *Two-Faced Woman* series. Get people to identify. 'Deepness'—whatever that is—well, it's not usually what I'm after. Only sometimes." Why was she arguing the aesthetics of writing for the popular press with this blond obsessive-compulsive? Their conversation had grown more and more surreal. "I'm grateful you've been following my work, though."

Despite having told her the repair was nearly complete, he had bent to the task again. Was he dallying? Was his apparent concentration a sham? His tiny silver screwdriver whirled in his fingers like a Lilliputian camshaft.

"Is everything all right?"

"Oh, yes, ma'am. I'm just giving it a special twist here. You need your machine in tiptop shape, don't you? I'm putting a little extra in. So you'll be able to get a little extra out."

"Extra?"

"Free of charge, though." For the first time Seaton Benecke looked directly at her. Although his expression held neither animus nor threat, Stevie was chilled by the penetrating knowledgeability of his lapis-lazuli eyes. Flustered or sated (Stevie did not know which), he finally dropped his stare, wiped his hands on a rag, and closed the Exceleriter's hood. "There we go," he said. "Maybe the extra you get out—the times when your writing goes really deep, I mean—maybe that'll remind you of me. I can't do that really heavy writing stuff, but you and this typewriter can."

Stevie softened again. "That's sweet, Seaton. You've saved me time and money both. I'm grateful."

At the young man's awkward insistence she sat down at the machine and, to demonstrate that his repair work had succeeded, typed several lines of quick brown foxes jumping over lazy dogs. No more stalled typing element. No more raucous blatting. Stevie put her thumb to her nose, waved her fingers in the air, and gaily unburdened herself of her own Bronx cheer.

"That's not for you," she told Seaton quickly. "That's for

the jerks over at PDE.''

He smiled a bemused, feckless smile that soon evaporated. However, it did last long enough to convince Stevie that Seaton could occasionally drop in on the Real World from his fog-shrouded hideaway in Never-Never Land, and she felt much better about him. Standing at the glass counter in the front of the store writing out her personal check for $10.67, she felt much, much better about Seaton. In fact, she left a five-dollar tip for him with the office-supply company's cashier.

On the twilight drive back home Stevie fell into playing a funny sort of game. Calling up an image of Seaton Benecke's face, she would slide this phantom around the inside of her windshield as if it were a big transparent decal too moist to stay in one spot. Then she would try to superimpose the remembered faces of people who vaguely resembled him on the restless outlines of Benecke's features. The headlights of oncoming vehicles played continual havoc with this bizarre game, but on a deserted stretch a few miles below the Barclay exit she succeeded in obtaining a ghostly match. Startled, she blinked. She blinked to disrupt and banish both phantasmal images.

Seaton Benecke, she had just realized, looked a great deal like the unfortunate young man who had tried to assassinate the President early in his term. This eerie coincidence probably accounted for her uneasiness in Benecke's presence, her uncharitable first impression of him. A weight lifted from Stevie's mind. She was pleased to have found a semirational basis for her initial antipathy toward the young man. Moreover, she was glad she had triumphed over this silly aversion before leaving his family's store.

For the remainder of the way home Stevie thought about Marella and Teddy, her unfinished book proposal, and the money she had saved by heeding Dr. Elsa's advice. Besides that, her generous tip to Seaton had salved her conscience without unduly diminishing her savings on the repair. PDE, after all, had wanted five times as much. All in all, a highly satisfying trip.

The next day, even with Marella back in school and the Exceleriter in perfect repair, Stevie's work did not go well. She typed the first paragraph of her book proposal for the Briar Patch Press at least seven times, screwing words into and out of the tangle of her sentences as if she were testing Christmas tree bulbs and finding nearly every one of them either forlornly lackluster or completely burnt-out. Nothing seemed to work. Her proposal had no intellectual festiveness. Whoever ultimately tried to read it would conclude by tossing the whole shebang into a wastebasket.

"Yippee," said Stevie. "What fun."

She rolled her seventh clean sheet of paper into the machine, stopped about midway down its length, and typed a string of abusive upper-case epithets at herself:

> CALL YOURSELF A WRITER, STEVIE CRYE? YOURE AN INCOMPETENT HACK WHO CANT HACK IT. A GRUB, A DRUDGE, A DULLARD, A PENNY*A*POPPER. YOU HEARD ME, A PAUPER. AND NO WONDER, POOPSIE. ALL YOUR BEAUTIFUL THOUGHTS COME OUT ON PAPER SCREAMING THE STENCHFUL STIFFNESS OF BULLSHIT, BULLSHIT, BULLSHIT!!!

Stevie banged the on/off key with the side of her hand and yanked the page out. She could not unclog her brain. This string of alliterative raillery represented her most productive burst of the morning. If only she could achieve such fluency typing news stories and feature columns . . . and, yes, book proposals. Some writers sat down and let their fingers fly, but she . . . well, this morning she could not unclog her brain. Shitting bricks, Ted had called this kind of labor, but he had always stayed with the struggle until victoriously spent.

It's the typewriter, Stevie suddenly thought. Typewriters are passé.

This thought amused her. She knew she was rationalizing her failure to get going, using the typewriter as a scapegoat—

but, at the moment, the rationalization, irrational as it was, appealed to her. She threw away her last botched proposal page, along with its codicil of free-associational abuse, and left her desk.

At the discolored Dearborn heater, she warmed her back, her hands clasped behind her, her eyes fixed on the recalcitrant instrument of her *stuckness.* It was working perfectly, but it was also frustrating her every effort to overcome her block. It exuded a smug fractiousness. It grinned a bleak analphabetical grin. It withheld the words it had an innate power—yea, *obligation*—to surrender.

"Typewriters are passé," Stevie informed the machine.

Over the last few years lots of writers—some of them only mildly affluent—had begun using word processors, computer systems with display consoles and printer hookups. The *Ledger* newsroom in Columbus, which Stevie occasionally visited to discuss free-lance assignments with the managing editor, now had more video consoles than typewriters. Reporters could emend their copy by deleting errors, opening up their texts for insertions, and even moving entire paragraphs from one place to another, all without recourse to strikeovers, ballpoint pens, Liquid Paper, or flaky little tabs of Ko-Rec-Type. Word processors willy-nilly permitted a writer to overcome blocks and increase production. Although these nifty systems cost about three thousand dollars (at least), you could take investment and depreciation write-offs and so bid a tearless permanent farewell to your typewriter. Stevie envisioned a day when only die-hard sentimentalists and penniless beginners would sit down at their Remingtons, Royals, Smith-Coronas, and PDE Exceleriters. Those poor souls would seem as backward and disadvantaged as a court stenographer with a Venus No. 2 lead pencil. And that day was probably not far off, either.

A fantasy. Stevie did not really believe that a word processor would solve her problem. She was stuck. Whether working with a goose-quill nub or an Apple computer, she would be just as stuck. Dickens, Collins, Eliot, Trollope—all the great Victorian novelists—they had never even seen a typewriter, much less the blank unblinking eye of a word processor, and yet they had produced staggering quantities of work, some of it brilliant. Her problem was not technological, it was emotional and mental.

I'm stuck, damn it, I'm stuck. And I'm stuck because I don't have any confidence in this stupid proposal. It's a dumb idea for a dumb book, and no matter how I dress it up or attempt to prettify it, it's going to remain a dumb idea. A word processor could not possibly play 'Enry 'Iggins to my illiterate Eliza Doolittle of an idea. . . .

Or could it?

Stevie returned to her Exceleriter, rolled in a clean sheet of paper, and imagined the touch of a single button lifting several paragraphs of text right out of the machine's (nonexistent) random-access memory. Another touch and an instance of muddy diction gave way to just the right word. Yet another and the sequence of her arguments rearranged itself in the most forceful and convincing pattern. Her basic idea was not at fault—think of all the dumb ideas that had giggled or panted their way to bestsellerdom—but rather her *presentation* of that idea, and she was having trouble with its presentation precisely because this damn machine had no reliable capability for error correction. A word processor would supply that lack.

Impatiently Stevie jabbed the on/off control and let her fingers speak her disillusionment:

TYPEWRITERS ARE PASSE.

The Exceleriter had no key for accent marks, and the word *passé* looked funny to her without the necessary diacritical symbol. (Did the keyboards of word processors have this symbol? She did not know.) Stevie advanced the paper and tried to think of a synonym that would not require an accent mark. It took her only a moment.

TYPEWRITERS ARE OBSOLESCENT.

There. Very good. Happy with this choice, Stevie typed the sentence twice more, releasing much of the anxiety occasioned by her block. What a gas, belittling the heretofore unhelpful Exceleriter through its own stupid instrumentality.

TYPEWRITERS ARE OBSOLESCENT.
TYPEWRITERS ARE OBSOLESCENT.

Of course it was a foolish rationalization, but it was also a form of therapy, and, by indulging herself, maybe she could coax herself back into a productive frame of mind. Scapegoating an innocent typewriter made more sense than going after the president of Pantronics Data Equipment with a .22-caliber Röhm RG-14. And no one need ever know, either.

TYPEWRITERS ARE OB

Blaaaaaht! protested the PDE Exceleriter 79. The noise horrified Stevie. Reflexively she lifted her hands from the keyboard and gripped her shoulders. Before she could untangle herself to turn the machine off, however, the type disc reeled off eight more letters and a period without her even touching the Exceleriter. She stared at the result.

TYPEWRITERS ARE OBNIPOTENT.

Omnipotent, it undoubtedly meant. The mechanical hangup —the brief Bronx cheer—had not taken place quickly enough for the machine to substitute the requisite *m* for the *b* left over from *obsolescent.* In fact, the Exceleriter had failed to demonstrate its assertion. What it *had* done, though, afflicted Stevie with an incredulous fear and curiosity. It had typed several letters by itself, and it had somehow managed to type them in a meaningful sequence. These letters refuted her own self-serving claim and held the implicit promise of an even wider power. No typewriter could perform such a feat without prior programming, of course, but she had just seen it happen.

"No, you didn't," Stevie said aloud. "You saw no such thing."

The pleasant low-level purr of the Exceleriter seemed to confirm this assessment. It was eerie, though, and Stevie shut the machine off. The declaration on her paper—TYPEWRITERS ARE OBNIPOTENT—did not disappear with the hum. It remained, a ridiculous joke and a threat. An accident, surely, with a sub-conscious impetus.

What had happened, Stevie realized, was that she had quickly and inadvertently typed NIPOTENT just before the type disc's noisy revolt and the machine had obediently printed out these letters after the element righted itself. The Exceleriter had only seemed to be operating independently of her control. As for that particular sequence of letters, it clearly embodied a sardonic Freudian gloss on her failure to get going this morning. She was tweaking herself for her pride, her indecisiveness, her readiness to elude responsibility.

Or maybe the space heater had used up so much of the oxygen in her little room that she had hallucinated the entire episode. Don Willingham at Barclay Builders Supply had advised her to vent the heater, but Stevie had resisted because of the inconvenience and expense. Maybe, though, the propane fumes and the depletion of oxygen in her upstairs study were combining to play tricks on her mind. Had she really heard that raspberry? Had she really seen the type disc spin out those last eight strident letters by itself?

Whether she had or hadn't, the fact of what she, or it, had written would brook no disbelief. It was there to touch and look at, twenty-some bright, black characters, a graffito as perplexing and impersonal as any scrawled obscenity:

TYPEWRITERS ARE OBNIPOTENT.

"Mom's in a grumpy mood because she didn't get a lick done all day," Teddy said.

"Is that why we're having chicken potpies?" Marella asked.

"The grumpiness I admit to," Stevie said testily, stooping before the oven to peer at the potpies dripping beige lava on the burnt-black baking sheet. "What that has to do with our evening menu, though, escapes me. There's nothing wrong with potpies, for God's sake. They're inexpensive, and reasonably nutritious, and you've both told me you like them."

"Once in a while," Teddy said.

"*I* don't like them," Marella corrected her mother. "*I* never told you I liked them."

"And you always fix 'em when you're in a grumpy mood, Mom. If you were feelin' great and somebody served you one, you'd *turn* grumpy. That's the way it is with you and potpies."

"Listen, buster, if anybody in this house served me *anything,* I'd turn a cartwheel for joy. As soon as basketball season's over—*season*'s a great word for it; you never even play any games—anyway, as soon as these nightly practice sessions are over, *you* can take over the chef's duties." One hand hidden in a padded glove, Stevie carried the baking sheet to the table and upended a potpie on each plate. "Beggars can't be choosers, and fanny-sitters can't be grousers. My alleged grumpiness does not revoke these hallowed rules, and I'm damn tired of hearing about it."

"It's not *alleged,*" Teddy said. "You admitted it yourself."

Stevie gave the boy a long withering look, and they ate for a while in silence. Marella, Stevie noticed, toyed with her dinner, plunging a fork into each tidbit of chicken and revolving it skeptically in front of her before either eating it or dislodging it from the tines beside her salad. Had she fully recovered from her virus? Her face looked drawn, almost transparently pale. As for the potpies, well, they would probably never elicit a rave review from Julia Child or *Gourmet* magazine, and Stevie began to feel a little sorry for the girl.

"Why couldn't you get anything done?" Teddy suddenly asked. "I thought those people Sam and Elsa know fixed your typewriter for you."

"The typewriter wouldn't cooperate," Marella said. "It's fixed, but it wrote Mama a nasty note."

"I was being facetious, Marella. It just seemed to me that the silly thing was acting up, resisting me. That's the kind of day I had. Of course, being told how grumpy I am and having my delicious dinner insulted has improved my spirits so much that I may try to do some work this evening.''

"Oh, Mama," said Marella, unfeignedly crestfallen. "Please don't."

"Why not? If you'd like to see sirloin strip on this table again, or even prime ground round, Mama's gotta grind it out. Otherwise it's vitamin bars and chicken tripe forever."

The children stared at her uncomprehendingly.

"That's a sort of a joke, just to prove I'm not all that horrendously grumpy. Bars and tripe forever. Stars and stripes forever. See?"

Marella, ignoring this explanation, said, "I wanted you to help me memorize my lines for our Fabulous February skit."

"You were home all day yesterday," Stevie pointed out. "Why didn't you mention your skit then? This is the first I've heard about it."

"She was having too much fun pretending to be sick."

"I was not!" Marella responded, glowering at her brother. "I forgot about it. Miss Kirkland reminded us today."

"Now who's the grump?" Teddy wondered aloud.

Lord, thought Stevie. Spare me this persnickety hassle. I was almost coming out of it, but if these two get going I'm liable to lapse and dump my potpie right into somebody's lap. . . .

Blessedly, the telephone rang. Teddy left the table to answer it. "It's for you, Mom," he said, bringing her the receiver on its curly elastic cord. "Long distance, I think. Sounds sorta echoey, anyway." Stevie took the receiver and murmured a hesitant hello.

"Mrs. Crye," came the familiar monotone. "Mrs. Crye, this is Seaton Benecke. In Columbus. I . . . I called to see if your typewriter was working okay. I'm the person who fixed it. I'm just checking up for the company. It's our policy to do that a day or two after a repair."

"Oh," said Stevie, nonplused by both the caller's identity and the inquiring looks on her children's faces. "Oh, it's fine. It's working just fine. It's me who needs a tune-up, I'm afraid. My brain's a little muzzy. The work didn't go well today. The typewriter, though, it worked just fine."

"That's good."

The words simply hung there, awaiting Stevie's disagreement or concurrence. "Yes, it's good," she obliged the young man. "I'm lost without that machine, even when I get exasperated with myself for not using it very well."

"Yes, ma'am."

"Well," she said, "is that all? I'd talk longer, but we're right in the middle of dinner."

"I wanted to thank you for the five-dollar tip. My dad gave it to me yesterday afternoon."

"Oh, you're perfectly welcome, Seaton. You earned it. I'm sorry it couldn't have been more."

"I think a writer's machine should be in tiptop shape." Again, an annoying pause designed either to prompt her response or to let Benecke think. But before Stevie could mutter another broad hint about their dinner hour, he found his tongue again: "So if you ever have any trouble, Mrs. Crye, I'd be happy to ride up there to fix it. It wouldn't cost much. I have a motorcycle." His next pause was briefer. "Probably, though, you won't ever need to call me."

"I appreciate your concern, Seaton."

"Good night, Mrs. Crye."

"Good night. Thanks for calling." When Seaton broke the connection, Stevie gave the receiver to Teddy to hang back up. The boy returned to the table wearing a Cheshire cat grin. "What's that for?" Stevie demanded.

"I guess it's about time you had a gentleman caller, huh? I guess Marella and me wouldn't mind havin' a new dad."

"Ugh," said the girl. "Yuck."

Stevie shuddered. Marella had succinctly articulated her own feelings about the prospect. Especially, she was afraid, about *this* woebegone prospect (a word altogether unacceptable in its application to Seaton), who was almost a decade younger than she.

"You're way off base, young man. Way off base."

"I'm basketball, Mom. You've got the wrong sport."

"I probably do," Stevie acknowledged. "I probably do."

VIII

After the children were in bed, snuggled beneath their electric blankets against the damp mid-February cold, Stevie returned to her study and lit the space heater. Marella, as usual, had already learned her part in Miss Kirkland's corny but well-intentioned skit, and the mandatory rehearsal session after dinner had not taken long. Unfortunately, the temperature in Stevie's study had dropped twenty or thirty degrees since late afternoon, and she doubted she could raise it enough to make sitting at the Exceleriter for an hour or so a bearable enterprise. Her feet had gone numb inside two pairs of socks, and her breath was spilling from her nostrils and lips like smoke from a burning building.

This is no place to keep an expensive typewriter, Stevie scolded herself. No wonder you've had trouble with it.

The machine did require a long time to warm up in the mornings. Even though she lit her Dearborn and turned the Exceleriter on before going downstairs to prepare the kids' breakfast, on really cold mornings the machine might not accelerate to top speed until she had finished a page and a half of double-spaced copy. A good thing she had not mentioned *that* to the jerks at PDE. They would have told her she had reaped just what she had sown, breakdowns being the natural consequence of improper storage and skimpy maintenance, blah blah blah & blah.

Shivering, Stevie slid into her chair and removed the typewriter's dust cover. The page bearing the "nasty note" was still on the platen: TYPEWRITERS ARE OBNIPOTENT. Well, not quite. Cold weather and their operators' disobedient fingers often sabotaged them, even when a giant corporation like PDE supposedly stood behind them.

Stevie pulled the typed-upon page from the Exceleriter and wound in a clean sheet. Although she had pretty much decided to get a fresh start tomorrow, this visit to her study was a necessary step in reasserting her dominion over a mere assemblage of pulleys, levers, wires, keys, and cams. She would not do any real work, but she would call the electric demon's bluff. Mockery was a time-honored form of one-upmanship. She would mock the Exceleriter's presumption as it had earlier mocked hers. At the top of the clean page, then, Stevie energetically lampooned the monster:

TYPEWRITERS ARE OBNIPOTENT.
TYPEWRITERS ARE OBNIXIOUS!
TYPEWRITERS ARE OBNOXIOUS!!!

So there. Without removing this page or replacing the machine's dust cover, Stevie hit the on/off control and leaned back to admire her handiwork. Later, her authority reestablished, she shut off the flow of propane to the space heater, doused the room's overhead light, and tiptoed into her bedroom to crawl beneath her own electric blanket. It was warm, luxuriously warm, and once her feet had thawed, she forgot the frustrations of the past two days and fell into a heavy sleep.

IX

Stevenson Crye could never remember her dreams, but this one, as she endured it, lashed her with a multitude of familiar anxieties and a few completely fresh ones. Groping for a handle on her whereabouts, chagrined that the ghastly imagery of her dreams had again eluded her, she awoke in a bath of sweat. As usual, she had washed ashore ignorant of the size and number of the nightmarish jellyfish whose stings had scourged her. She kicked aside her blankets and lay in the frigid gloom trying to recover her wits. Her sweat began to dry, her body to convulse. She grabbed her shabby housecoat from the bottom of the bed and hurriedly snugged it about her shoulders.

At which point she heard the Exceleriter in the next room, her study, clacking away like a set of those grotesque plastic dentures you could buy in novelty stores. Or, for that matter, like her *own* chattering teeth.

"No," Stevie said. "It's something else."

After all, your ears *could* fool you. The whine of a vacuum cleaner in another room could sound like an ambulance wail, bacon sizzling in a skillet like rain on a summer pavement. Maybe this typewriterly clacking was nothing but tree branches scraping her study window or squirrels clambering through the uninsulated walls. But, as Stevie well knew, neither of these sounds came accompanied by the distinctive *ping!* of a margin-stop bell or the smooth *ker-thump!* of a returning carriage. Her ears had not deceived her. The Exceleriter was working independently of human control, percussing out its alien derangement.

I left it on, Stevie thought. I forgot to turn it off, a key was accidentally depressed, and it's been stuck like a broken automobile horn ever since I fell asleep. A mechanical explanation for a simple, although weird, mechanical problem. Of course this explanation still doesn't account for the thumping regularity of the carriage reflex—but it's got to be *close* to what's going on in there. It's *got* to be.

Stevie realized that she did not want to go into her study to check. She wanted the Exceleriter to stop of its own accord. She wanted to slide back into her bed and forget the whole incident. The night—especially a winter's night—imbued even the simplest phenomenon with mystery. In the morning she would be less prone to extrapolate nonsense from her muddled senses. But the Exceleriter did not stop, and Stevie was now sufficiently awake to know that its possession—its maddening midnight activity—would seem no less mysterious in the bleak light of dawn. Eventually, either now or later, she must cross her study's threshold.

When she turned on the hall light, the typing abruptly ceased. Quick glances into Teddy's and Marella's rooms assured her that the children had heard nothing; they lay huddled under their GE blankets, hot-wired for sleep, mercifully heedless of her apprehension. Thank God for that.

Sighing her relief, Stevie pushed the door to her study inward. In the light filtering in from the hall she saw that the page carelessly left in the typewriter had curled back over the cylinder almost to the full extent of its length. The Exceleriter had advanced it that far. Phalanxes of alphabetical characters covered its pale surface. Stevie proceeded cautiously to her rolltop and switched on her brass desk lamp. Then, her breath drifting in puffs through the halo produced by the lamp, she fumbled the page from the top of the machine, lifted it into the light, and began to read. . . .

Tomograms, thermograms, sonograms, mammograms, and fluoroscopic "movies."

Although this catalogue reads like a list of options that some futuristic Western Union might provide its customers, these exotic-sounding "grams" are in reality an integral part of the detection-and-diagnosis procedures at the West Georgia Cancer Clinic in Ladysmith.

Stevenson Crye, 35, of nearby Barclay—her friends call her Stevie—came to know the sophisticated machines that perform these vital diagnostic functions during her husband's unsuccessful treatment. Although the clinic also has an arsenal of machines designed to cure as well as to diagnose cancer, Mrs. Crye's husband rejected the possibility of hope in favor of a noble despair.

"He simply gave up," said Mrs. Crye Tuesday. "He ran out on us."

Early this morning Theodore Crye, Sr., who died in 1980 at the age of 39, answered this charge. Forsaking the family plot in the Barclay cemetery, Crye returned to the Ladysmith clinic to meet his wife in the same downstairs treatment room where he once underwent radiation therapy beneath the tumor-destroying beam of the Clinac 18.

downstairs treatment room whe
apy beneath the tumor-destroyi
Swollen-tongued and eyeless,
he floor-to-ceiling unit and p
res for his horrified wife.
veloped by the Varia
its manufactu
aid Crye.

J.K.POTTER

Swollen-tongued and eyeless, Crye put one decomposing hand on this floor-to-ceiling unit and painfully detailed its various features for his horrified wife.

"Developed by the Varian Co. in Palo Alto, Calif., the Clinac 18 is known by its manufacturer as a 'standing-wave linear accelerator,'" said Crye. "It speeds electrons around an interior track to shape a beam that eventually generates X-rays.

"Only X-rays of one intensity must come out of the machine and hit the patient," Crye continued. "Certain organs can tolerate only so much radiation, and people vary in their tolerance to radiation, just as some people get sunburns more rapidly than others."

Clad only in her sleeping gown and a pair of powder-blue mules, Mrs. Crye appeared distraught and inattentive through her dead husband's recital. Dr. Elsa Kensington, director of the West Georgia facility, said that her friend would probably have bolted from the treatment room if not for the calming presence of clinic dosimetrist Seaton Benecke, 26, of Columbus.

"Every morning I run a series of 'output checks' on the Clinac 18 to make sure its dosage emissions are constant and controllable," Benecke told Mrs. Crye. "I also make 'patient contours'—images of the abdominal region outlined on graph paper with a piece of wire—to determine the proper dosage of each patient.

"I plot this amount with a radiation-therapy planning computer. We once did dosage plotting by hand, but it took hours and the need to be exact is so great that the job could be truly nerve-racking."

"You're not Ted," Mrs. Crye accused her husband's corpse. "You don't talk like Seaton Benecke," she accused the clinic dosimetrist.

Ignoring his wife's objections, Crye said, "Benecke discovered that I had a very low tolerance to radiation. Ionization occurred in the tissues through which the Clinac 18's beam had to pass to reach my tumor, and my body began to fall apart from the inside."

Crye then invited his wife to lie down under the movable eye of the Clinac 18. When she refused, he and Benecke firmly placed her on the pallet beneath it. The facility's space-age acoustics kept her screams from being heard beyond the treatment room.

"I'm just giving it a special twist here," Benecke said, turning on the accelerator. "Deepness is what I really like. A beam from the Clinac 18 can go down as deep as fifteen centimeters before 'exploding' through the tumor-bearing area. That's what I really like."

"I fell apart down deep," Crye said, a dead hand on his wife's forehead. "If I appeared to give up, Stevie, it was only because

XI

Dr. Elsa was working on Friday in Wickrath's tumbledown clinic. Although Dr. Sam plied both pills and solace in the Barclay branch of the Kensington practice, Stevie, who had spent the tag end of the night trying to rediscover the gateway to unconsciousness, did not believe she could confide in him. Therefore, after seeing Teddy and Marella off to school, she drove to Wickrath and signed the patient register like any other flu victim or hypochondriac day laborer. Her head ached, but her heart, which barely seemed to be beating, preoccupied her more. The calm of exhaustion had not yet had a chance to settle upon her.

"Keep showin' up this regular," Dr. Elsa told her ten minutes later, pointing Stevie to an examination table, "I'll have to start givin' you a volume discount. Typewriter break again?"

"Read this, Elsa."

" 'TYPEWRITERS ARE OBNIPOTENT. / TYPEWRITERS ARE—' "

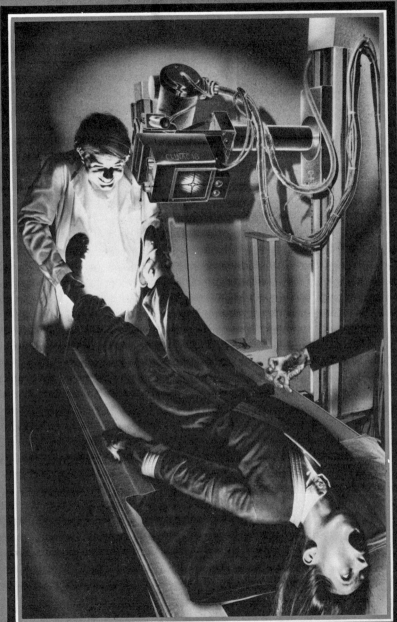

J.K.POTTER

"No, not that, Elsa. The single-spaced story under it. Read it to yourself and tell me what you think."

A minute or two later Dr. Elsa passed the page back to Stevie. "Well, I don't think Dr. Curry up in Ladysmith's going to be too thrilled to see I've got his job."

"Besides that, Elsa."

"Can't afford to alienate my colleagues, kiddo. I'm not the cancer clinic's director. You're not plannin' to send this little ghost story to the *Ledger,* are you?"

"Elsa, what do you *think* of it?"

"Morbid? Obsessive? Paranoid? I don't know. You keep tryin' to get me to play head doctor, but most of what I see is furred tongues, bunions, and broken bones. I haven't got the lingo, Stevie." She touched the younger woman's close-cropped hair. "You're madly in love with a dead man you don't respect. The psychological term for that escapes me."

"Necrophilia?"

Dr. Elsa raised an eyebrow. "Not quite, Mrs. Shakespeare. I don't think that's a spiritual affliction. What you've got probably is. Partly, anyway. And that's all the Sigmund Freuding I'm going to do."

The scuffed linoleum in the examination room, the stoppered bottles of Q-tips and alcohol, the entire rustic ambience of the Wickrath clinic, worked on Stevie's mood. So did Dr. Elsa's intelligent folksiness, which perceptibly allayed her depression. She scooted backward on the paper-covered examination table and propped herself upright in the corner. How could you be fearful in a place so cozy, so sloppily antiseptic, so downright old-fashioned? If only she could stay here . . .

"Did you notice the opening?" Stevie asked. "The lead?"

"Very clever."

"Well, the first two paragraphs are verbatim from the article I mailed to the *Ledger* Tuesday afternoon."

"Self-plagiarism's a forgivable crime, I guess."

"Do you know what the rest is, though?"

"A paid advertisement for the Clinac 18?"

"I wish." Stevie handed the page back to Dr. Elsa. "Look at it again. The rest's an exact rendering of a nightmare I had last night, but in a deliberately journalistic style. It's the way Joseph—the Biblical one—would have reported a dream if he'd spent a year or so at *The New York Times*."

"Okay," said Dr. Elsa noncommittally.

"I never remember my dreams. The Exceleriter wrote this, Elsa. It picked my brain and organized what it found there in the form of a news story."

"Lots of writers think like that, Stevie. They sit down at their typewriters, and when they're rattlin' along at a good clip, it's as if they're takin' *dictation*. They're an instrument through which the words splash themselves down on paper. That's the subconscious mind workin'. Same thing's true of people who speak in tongues, and estate auctioneers, and most of the lawyers you're likely to hear in the Wickrath County Courthouse on Thursday morning."

"That puts it in perspective," said Stevie wryly.

"I don't mean to take you down a notch, kiddo. Just pointin' out that you needn't give your typewriter *all* the credit. The receptor-conductor's important, too—essential, in fact. I couldn't be one if I tried. It takes talent and training."

"Elsa, I wasn't even *sitting* at the typewriter when it did this. I was in the next room. It typed that page by itself."

"Seaton Benecke's a wizard, all right." Releasing the miraculous page, Dr. Elsa let it waft back into Stevie's lap. "Typewriter repairman and part-time dosimetrist."

"You don't believe me?"

Dr. Elsa squinted at her visitor. "You're *serious?*"

Stevie held up her evidence. "It stops in the middle of a line of Ted's dialogue—just as he's about to explain why he surrendered—because it ran out of room. Alibi interruptus. That makes me as crazy, Elsa, as the crazy way it all got down on paper in the first place."

Thoughtfully Dr. Elsa hoisted her ample lower body to the edge of the examination table. "What do you want me to do, honey?"

"Tell me you believe me."

"I believe you believe the typewriter wrote that by itself. That okay for now? The other's liable to take me a while."

"Okay for now," Stevie said quietly. "You think I'm ready for the funny farm?"

"Kiddo, they're not ready for *you.*"

Both women laughed. Whether she or Dr. Elsa moved first to abandon the examination table Stevie could not have said, but they bumped shoulders and hips on the way down. Stevie apologized, mentioned their common need to get back to work, and then found herself gazing pensively at the broad strip of shiny white paper on the table.

"Where do you get this stuff?"

"This? From a medical-supply salesman who comes through here every couple of months. Why?"

"Could I buy a sheet or two when I'm paying my bill?"

"What bill? And hell, no, you can't buy any of this slippery sausage wrap. I throw a sheet away every time somebody puts her fanny to it. You can have this piece and a half-dozen more if you want." Dr. Elsa folded the long sheet from the table into Stevie's arms and fetched several more from the bottom of an aluminum cart. "Enough?"

"Plenty, plenty."

"What you gonna do with it? Turn your minibus into a float for the Barclay Easter parade?"

"Shelving paper," Stevie improvised. "I never remember to buy shelving paper. Don't you think it'll do?"

"Sure," said Dr. Elsa. "Cockroaches *love* to go skatin' on this stuff. Turn your shelves into a regular cockroach roller rink."

XII

She knew what had happened. She was not insane. She had heard the Exceleriter typing and had actually found the unfinished product of its labor. If her machine had been functioning as the printer in a word-processing system, she could have attributed its performance to prior programming—but her typewriter was a desk model, with no expensive hookups or modifications, and it should not have been doing what she had seen it do. Telling Dr. Elsa, dumping her impossible discovery into the minor maelstrom of her friend's workday, had not shown good judgment. Although their friendship had spanned ten or twelve years, Stevie could hardly expect Dr. Elsa to embrace a report as unlikely as the one she had ill-advisedly sought to foist upon her.

All you did, Stevie chided herself, was make her worry about you. She thinks the pressure has finally worn you down. She thinks you typed that page during an episode of fugue and no longer remember doing it.

Or else she thinks you're crazy, kiddo.

Stevie wondered if her insanity lay in failing to . . . well, to fear the machine. An electric typewriter that suddenly began to churn out highly detailed versions of your dreams warranted a certain awe. It could remake your life. It could reveal your most shameful secrets. It could destroy you. Cataloguing these melodramatic possibilities, Stevie smiled at herself.

In point of amusing fact, a typewriter—no matter how voluble, vulgar, and malicious—had no forum unless you conceded it one. It could not saunter from room to room rummaging through your belongings, or go to the chief of police to denounce your private appreciation of smutty books, or even creep over a few inches to upset the bottle of Liquid Paper next to your latest manuscript. A typewriter sat where you put it. If you kept your study door closed and forbade anyone else to enter, it became your absolute captive.

Stevie intended to make use of these undeniable facts. Why, then, should she fear her typewriter? Although burdensome to lift, it was not otherwise physically imposing. Its grimy platen knobs and complacent keyboard grin conveyed not a flinch of menace. Besides, before visiting Dr. Elsa, Stevie had ruthlessly defanged the machine by the simple expedient of unplugging it. If it wanted to get rid of her or ruin her reputation, it would have to wait until she obligingly restored its power. When she did, she fiercely believed that Stevenson Crye rather than the

PDE Exceleriter would occupy the driver's seat. She would turn the machine's intermittent self-sufficiency to her own advantage.

That was why she had asked Dr. Elsa for those long sheets of slippery white examination-table paper. Since returning from Wickrath, she had not set foot in her study. She had spent the morning scissoring Dr. Elsa's "sausage wrap" into streamers about eight inches wide—so they would fit into the Exceleriter. These virgin scrolls lay about the kitchen—on the breakfast bar, the circular oaken table, the seats of her wobbly captain's chairs—as if she were trying to convert the place into a medieval library. All her manuscripts lacked were words and meticulous illuminations. The words, at least, would come later.

Teddy came in, dragging his expensive winter jacket and matter-of-factly eyeing the paper-filled kitchen.

"You're home early," Stevie said, baffled. The clock on the stove showed only a few minutes after noon.

"It's the beginning of a teachers' in-service weekend, Mom. We only went half a day."

"Oh." She had forgotten.

"The elementary school let out early, too. Isn't Marella home yet?"

The day's plans—some of them hastily formulated at breakfast while she was still trying to absorb the implications of her strange discovery—began to take focus again. "Tiffany McGuire's mother picked her up, Teddy. Marella's supposed to spend the night over there."

"She well enough to go?"

"Claimed she was this morning. If she can go to school, I guess she can go to a friend's house, don't you?"

"'Sno skin off my nose." Before she could tweak Teddy for the slovenly offhandedness of this remark, he added, "I thought you'd be upstairs workin', tryin' to make up for yesterday and all."

"Afraid you'll starve?"

"No, ma'am." He looked genuinely taken aback, and Stevie regretted snapping at him. The guilt of the neglectful breadwinner had just triumphed over maternal solicitude.

More tenderly she said, "In a way, I *am* working."

"Somebody ask you to do decorations?"

"I'm going to type on this, Teddy. I'm halving the strips so they'll roll into my machine."

"I thought you typed on typing paper."

"I do. These are for rough drafts. From now on I'll be using long strips like these for almost all my preliminary drafts."

"What for?" Teddy picked up one of the tightly wound scrolls and began thumping it absentmindedly against his chin.

"It's a psychological thing," Stevie told him. "When I get to the bottom of a page, I want to stop. If I've got a sheet of paper four feet long, though, it'll take a while to get to the bottom and I won't be tempted to stop working so often. Do you see?"

"Yes, ma'am, I guess."

"Maybe I'll increase my productivity."

Teddy began to grin. " 'N' if you don't, at least you won't have to buy us a flyswatter this summer." He bopped an imaginary fly on the breakfast bar, tossed the dented scroll into his mother's lap, and declared that he was going over to Pete Wightman's house for a patio scrimmage. He had eaten lunch at school. She didn't need to worry about him.

After the boy had left, Stevie glanced about the kitchen at her handiwork. The real reason she wanted long strips of paper, of course, was so that the automatic activity of the Exceleriter did not henceforth automatically cease at the bottom of a standard eleven-inch sheet, stranding her in the middle of a crucial, maybe even a revelatory, text. The machine was her captive, her slave, and she was going to put it to work in the service of her own vital goals. No one she had ever known had ever owned a Ouija board of such awesome potential, and if it could help her plumb her own dreams or establish a spiritual contact with her dead husband, then it *must* be put to that use.

She would never mention the Exceleriter's capabilities to Dr. Elsa again. She would never tell Teddy or Marella. She would never tell anyone. She knew what had happened, and she was not insane. . . .

XIII

For most of that afternoon Stevie worked with the Exceleriter as if the complications of the past four days had never arisen. Human being and machine met across the interface of their unique quiddities (Stevie *liked* the metaphysical thrust of that Latinism), and copy poured forth on Dr. Elsa's butcher paper at a rate of almost six hundred words every thirty minutes. Anthony Trollope had written a good deal faster, of course, but this speed wasn't too shabby for a gal who had recently been suffering a debilitating block. Indeed not. Stevie took a tranquil pleasure in her recovered—even augmented—fluency.

By three o'clock she was within a paragraph or two of completing her submission proposal for *Two-Faced Woman: Reflections of a Female Paterfamilias.* A shrill buzzing ensued. Stevie's hands jumped away from the keyboard, but the noise had its origins not in another broken typewriter cable but at the doorbell button downstairs. Thank God for that. She never liked being interrupted at work, but the doorbell was better than a repetition of Tuesday's debacle. A jingly SOS, the doorbell rang three more times, and Stevie shouted over it that she was coming, hold on a second.

At the front door she found herself face to face with Tiffany McGuire's mother, who, gripping Marella supportively at the shoulders, favored Stevie with an apologetic smile. "I'm afraid she's not feeling too good, Mrs. Crye. The other girls wanted her to stay, you know, but I'd hate it if she brought everyone down sick. I've got Carol and Donna Bradley, too."

"Of course, of course." Stevie could see Mrs. McGuire's Pinto station wagon under the Japanese tulip tree at the foot of the walkway, a bevy of third-grade girls sproinging about energetically in the backseat. "I appreciate you running her home."

But when Marella came into her arms, her heart sank. The child turned back a face so drawn and translucent that Stevie could see the blue veins in her cheeks and eyelids, the mortal jut of bone beneath her brow. February was a bad month, of course, but during this past year Marella had frequently come down sick. (Of late she had tried, valiantly, to disguise or mitigate the degree of her discomfort.) It was probably nothing more, this time, than a nervous stomach. Tuesday she had contracted a touch of the flu, but today the excitement of spending the night with Tiff—or maybe the small trauma of an argument with Donna Bradley, with whom she had trouble getting along—had caused her upset. A nervous stomach was a funny ailment. Almost any emotional disturbance could trigger it. Stevie wondered, in fact, if Marella had registered her mood that morning at breakfast; the child's present illness might be a delayed reaction to the disbelief and helplessness that Stevie no longer felt, a kind of sympathetic aftertremor.

"Oh, you poor kid. Come on in."

Mrs. McGuire having retreated out of hearing, Marella said, "I didn't want to come home. I could have stayed. *She* got scared, though." Her frail voice encoded the hint of a forbidden *nyah-nyah* taunt. "*She* was afraid I'd throw up on her carpets."

"That's a legitimate fear, daughter mine. I don't blame her."

Marella began to cry. "I've done it again. I've done it again, haven't I, Mama?"

"It's all right. Hush."

Stevie folded down the sofa bed in the den, settled Marella in with her faithful upchuck bucket and some maze books, and went back upstairs to finish her proposal. Surprisingly, her nagging awareness of Marella's nervous upset notwithstanding, she was able to resume work with some of her former enthusiasm and effectiveness, and in only twenty minutes she had completed the job. Look out, Briar Patch Press, Inc. She used a pair of scissors to separate her draft from the long strip of paper in the machine, rolled out the abbreviated piece, inserted another uncut one to receive whatever the Exceleriter might compose in the hours after midnight, and blew a puff of air at her bangs. She did not unplug the machine.

The remainder of the evening she spent caring for her

daughter, cleaning up the dinner dishes, and thumbing through a battered paperback from Ted's little library of science-fiction novels, something called *The Grasshopper Lies Heavy*. Long before tucking the kids in, she began to anticipate, to build expectation upon expectation. By the time she climbed into bed, Teddy and Marella long since asleep, she understood how hard it was going to be to join them in slumber. Was the Exceleriter really plugged in? Did it have enough paper? Would she hear it when it began? What would it tell her?

In her flannel nightgown, then, she arose and went into her study to check the setup a final time. She resisted the temptation to turn on the Exceleriter's electricity; last night it had done that by itself, and if it were going to perform again, it would undoubtedly emulate the pattern it had already established. If not, not. Beyond setting the stage, she really could not prescribe or direct its untypewriterly behavior.

Nevertheless, her parting instruction to the machine was, "Tell me about Ted. Let him finish his confession. I need to know."

XIV

Awake or asleep? Awake, surely, for in the next room the resourceful Stevenson Crye, mistress of her fate, tamer of typewriters, could hear the businesslike rattle of the Exceleriter's typing element, a concert muted slightly by the intervening plaster walls. She sat up in bed. By canny prior arrangement her robe lay within easy reach, and she quickly put it on. Her powder-blue mules she found beside the bed exactly where she had left them, and after slipping into these hideous knockabouts she went lurching over her carpet into the hall, not pausing to turn on a light.

Her clumsiness Stevie charitably attributed to her excitement, her failure to illuminate either bedroom or hall as an attempt at stealth. In truth, she was afraid to catch the Exceleriter unhandedly clattering away, and her emphatic "Oh, shit!" as she stumbled into her study door obligingly sabotaged any last hope of surprising the percipient machine.

It stopped typing.

Stevie hesitated a moment. Maybe it would start again. She wanted to catch the typewriter in the act. *In flagrante delicto,* lawyers called it. Or maybe she wanted no such thing. A kind of prurient ambivalence plagued her—much as a curious child may be of two minds about trying to witness, even from a secure hiding place, its transmogrified parents engaged in an instance of strenuous lovemaking. But the Exceleriter did not resume its unassisted labors, and before Stevie could steel herself to enter her study, she heard a high pathetic moaning from Marella's room.

"Hot, Mama. Oh, Mama, I'm so hot. . . ."

The house was bitterly cold. Even though she had been out of bed only a minute or two, Stevie's feet had already gone numb. How could Marella possibly be hot? Only if she had a fever. Only if this afternoon's nervous stomach had given way to an ailment traceable to virulent microorganisms. The poor kid. How much did she have to suffer? How long would these weird and exhaustingly worrisome attacks disrupt their lives? Feeling drained and persecuted, Stevie slumped against the doorjamb. A typewriter that worked by itself, and an intelligent eight-year-old daughter who could barely function twelve straight hours without succumbing to either a flu bug or an ineradicable angst. That Teddy continued to sleep astonished Stevie and imperceptibly mollified her despair. The only bright spot in this ridiculous pageant of after-hours calamity.

"I'm melting," Marella said more clearly. "Mama, I'm so hot I can feel myself melting."

Stevie walked down the narrow hall to lean into her daughter's double-dormer room, the largest bedchamber upstairs. "Are you awake?" she half whispered, half spoke aloud. "Or are you talking in your sleep?"

"Awake," the girl said weakly. "Awake and hot. Oh, Mama—"

"I'm coming, Marella. Don't fret. Mama's here." Stevie picked her way over the clothes and stuffed animals littering the floor, squeezed between the twin beds at the northern end of the room, sat down on the vacant bed, switched on Marella's night-light (a porcelain Southern belle in a pleated peach-colored gown), and crooned, "Don't fret. Mama's here." The child shut her eyes against the night-light's glow and turned her head on the pillow.

Despite her complaints about being hot, Marella had not kicked off her covers. She made no move to push aside or squirm out from under her electric blanket, which came all the way up to her chin. Stevie laid three fingers across her forehead. It felt lukewarm rather than fiery. The girl's cheeks were soft pink rather than red, her earlobes as pale as the night-light lady's tiny corsage of porcelain gardenias.

"Daughter mine, I don't think your temperature's elevated. You look pretty good. You don't feel hot."

"Hot," she insisted, her eyes still closed. "Melting."

"Why don't you uncover for a minute, then? I've got the sh-sh-shakes, and you'll g-g-get 'em too." Trying to jolly the girl out of her obsession, Stevie held her hands in front of her to demonstrate their shakiness. "Brrrrrrr," she whinnied.

"All I can move is my head, Mama."

"That's silly," Stevie replied, panic beginning to descend. "Why do you say that? What's wrong?"

"I'm trapped under this blanket. It's holding me down. It's holding me down and melting me, Mama." Marella revolved her head back toward Stevie and opened her wild luminous eyes. "It's my fault, isn't it? I'm not any good."

"Of course you're good. Don't ever say that, Marella. You and Teddy are two of the best things that ever happened to me." Stevie let her hand drop from the girl's gossamer-fine hair to the pressure points in her throat. "You're not paralyzed, Marella," she said, gingerly touching the pressure points. "You're still half-asleep. Just push your cover back, you'll see how chilly it is out here in the cold, cruel world, and everything'll be okay again. I wouldn't let anything happen to you. I couldn't. You're precious to me, daughter mine."

"So hot, Mama," the girl said resignedly. "So hot I'm afraid I've already melted."

"Try to move. Try to push your cover back."

"I can't."

"Try to move!" Stevie insisted. "You've convinced yourself a bad thing's happened, and it hasn't, Marella. It hasn't!"

But what if some rare form of paralysis *had* gripped the girl? Stevie's inchoate alarm began to condense into a tumorous knot in the pit of her stomach. None of this was fair. If Marella could uncover herself—if only she would make the small symbolic effort involved in shoving her electric blanket aside—why, her delusive spell would be broken, and they could both go back to sleep. As for the Exceleriter. . .

"Mama," Marella said. "Mama, I'm *trying.*"

"But you're just lying there, little sister. Surely you can *kick* these old covers off." She made an abrupt flicking motion with her fingers, her smile as tight as a triple-looped rubber band.

Marella began to cry. "Already melted. My fault. So, so hot, Mama. I'm just not any good."

"Stop saying that, child!"

"Call Dr. Elsa, Mama. Ask Dr. Elsa why I can't move."

"Marella, we can't go running to Dr. Elsa with every little problem, especially not in the middle of the night. She's seen too much of me already. She's seen way, way too much of me."

"Mama, please—you take the covers off me."

Stevie rocked away from her daughter, clutching her face in her hands. She—the so-called adult—was behaving irrationally. Marella might be seriously ill, permanently paralyzed, and here she was refusing to telephone their family doctor, her own closest friend, solely because she had made a fool of herself yesterday morning in that honest, forbearing woman's Wickrath offices. In an imperative situation Dr. Elsa would be angry only if she *failed* to call. This was clearly an imperative situation. Stevie stood up.

"Marella, I'm going to call the Kensingtons. Be right back."

Tears standing in the corners of her eyes, the child gave her a

J.K.POTTER

feeble nod. "You uncover me, okay? Before you call. Just for a minute, Mama. I'm still hot. I've already melted, but I'm still hot."

This refrain enraged Stevie. She grabbed the satin hem of the GE blanket and yanked both it and the sheet beneath it all the way to the foot of the narrow brass bed. Then she began to scream. Her daughter's lower body, from the neck down, consisted of the slimy ruins of her skeletal structure. Her flesh and internal organs had liquefied, seeping through the permeable membrane of her bottom sheet and into the box springs beneath the half-dissolved mattress, stranding her pitiful rib cage, pelvis, and limb bones on the quivering surface—like fossils washed out of an ancient geological formation. Steam rose into the cold February air from this odorless mess, and Stevie added her breath to it by screaming and screaming again.

Marella was heedless of her mother's incapacitating hysteria. "Still hot," she said. "Oh, Mama, I'm still hot. . . ."

Stevie carefully tore the sheet bearing this nightmare from her Exceleriter, draped the long page over her dictionary stand, and, ignoring the cold and the syncopated hammering of her heart, reread every line. The machine—which, to use its own wry terminology, she had failed to catch *in flagrante delicto*—was mocking her. She had tried to arrange matters so that it would produce copy compatible with her desire for answers about Ted, Sr., but it had spun out another sort of text altogether, a cruel lampoon in which her concern for Marella was translated into domestic Grand Guignol:

> Awake or asleep? Awake, surely, for in the next room the resourceful Stevenson Crye, mistress of her fate, tamer of

> typewriters, could hear the businesslike rattle of the Ex-
> celeriter's typing element, a concert ...

Etcetera, etcetera. But the worst, the most tasteless and offensive part of the joke it had played on her, did not reside in
these easy satiric jabs, but in the heartless, vividly obscene surprise at the end:

> ... the slimy ruins of her skeletal structure. Her flesh and
> internal organs had liquefied, seeping through the permeable
> membrane of her bottom sheet and into the box springs be-
> neath the half-dissolved mattress, stranding her pitiful rib
> cage, pelvis, and limb bones on the quivering ...

Etcetera. A climactic passage not merely horrifying but fun-
damentally contemptuous of civilized human feeling. For some
reason the typewriter wished to mock her humanity by blas-
pheming her love for Marella, by playing upon her deep-seated
fears about the child's mental and emotional well-being, and
by depicting Stevie herself as unperceptive and vacillating. In
fact, the cumulative portrait of her own character in this disgusting little sketch was almost as ugly as the description of
Marella's ruined body.

That's a self-centered way of interpreting this nonsense,
Stevie suddenly realized. Besides, the sketch doesn't make you
out a complete Lucrezia Borgia. As far as that goes, it's probably a modified transcription of the nightmare you were having
before you heard this damned machine pounding away and
came stumbling over your own furry slippers to behold its
treachery. You're angry with yourself for not getting here in
time, and you're angry with the machine for making a gruesome, condescending joke of a relationship you cherish.

This reasoning had a calming effect. Her heart slowed its
thunderous beating, and her hands trembled less from fear and
anger than from the cold. She had the sh-sh-shakes.

Marella, Stevie thought. What about Marella?

Nightmares slipped through her consciousness like sand
through the waist of an hourglass. Once awake, she could
never remember them. All she ever retained of her dreams was
a mood, whether upbeat, neutral, or despairing. If she had actually dreamed the sequence of images and dialogue typed out

on this strip of paper by the Exceleriter, well, the sound of the machine's sinister industriousness had stolen from her even her postnightmare blues. She had focused her entire will on getting from her bedroom to her study undetected by the culprit. She had not succeeded. It had finished its story and turned itself off before she was halfway to her destination.

Marella! a dogged portion of her consciousness reminded her. Maybe you can't remember the lost dream that inspired this ghoulish lampoon, Stevenson Crye, but it isn't really lost, is it? It's right here under your hands, in stinging black and white. It describes your daughter as a roller-coaster framework of bones over a lava flow of flesh—but instead of going down the hall to see about her, you stand here mentally abusing your typewriter for making up such filth, for portraying you as impatient, self-centered, and wishy-washy. Why, at this very moment you're in the unbelievable process of living up, or down, to its characterization of you. . . .

"Marella, I'm coming," Stevie said aloud. "Don't fret, little sister. Mama's coming."

She groped her way down the dark hall, entered the girl's room, and picked her way over the clothes and stuffed animals littering the floor. After squeezing between the twin beds bookended by the dormer windows, Stevie lowered herself to the empty bed and switched on Marella's porcelain night-light.

The girl lay cocooned in the bedclothes, scrunched into a question mark in the middle of her narrow mattress. Stevie could not even see her face. In a way, this was a relief. The reality of the moment departed significantly from its imaginary parallel in the typewriter's version. Marella was okay. Earlier that evening, after all, her nervous stomach had improved miraculously during her and Teddy's favorite television show, "The Dukes of Hazzard," an inane compendium of Good Old Boy humor and benignant car crashes. She had gone to bed without complaint, and she had been sleeping soundly ever since. For these and several other reasons, then, the typewriter's version was undoubtedly a lie.

Uncover her and check, Stevie urged herself.

Her hand went to the satiny hem of the electric blanket, but did not forcefully or even feebly grip it. Her fingers lacked the necessary resolve.

Go on. Go on.

At last Stevie drew back the bedclothes, and, as she had known all along, uncovering Marella produced no surprise, no unbearable shock. The girl moaned because her blanket had been taken from her, she tilted back her head and briefly opened unseeing eyes, and she curled her nightgowned body into a tighter question mark. Asleep, lost in sleep, and Stevie pulled her covers back into place and tenderly tucked the overlap beneath the mattress. The typewriter's version had been a lie. What else could it have been?

Stevie returned to her study, but paused outside it and looked in on Teddy, whose room, a cubbyhole in comparison to Marella's, occupied the chilly southwest corner of the second floor—right across the hall from Stevie's book-lined sanctorum. Teddy was a sound sleeper, much harder to wake up than his sister, for which reason Stevie felt no compunction about subjecting him to the direct glare of his overhead light.

He had thrown back the upper portion of his GE blanket and lay across the bed with his left foot dangling into space. He had also neglected, or disdained, to put on the tops of his pajamas. How he could sleep half-nude with temperatures under forty, even with his blanket securely in place, Stevie had no idea. The boy was incorrigible.

Just like his dad, she reflected. Though Georgia-born and -bred, Ted, Sr., had taken to cold weather like a polar bear, and when it came time for bed, he had no metabolic or antiquated metaphysical hangups about shedding his clothes. While shivering under the covers in long johns and woolen socks, Stevie had sometimes thought her laconic husband capable of sleeping naked in a snowdrift.

Young Teddy looked cold, though. His toplessness and his cast-back blanket had combined to make him tremble, and as he trembled, he murmured unintelligible maledictions at the winter air. Indeed, one hand sought blindly for the edge of the missing blanket. Not finding it, the boy turned, moaning, to his left side.

Stevie went into the room to cover him. He was getting to be a handsome young man, growing up with astonishing speed. A year ago he had been a kid; now he was gaining weight, putting on muscle, discovering body hair in heretofore hairless places. Beneath his right arm, which he had just flung over his head, Stevie could see a delicate brunet curl, a clock spring of hair—symbolic, maybe, of his burgeoning maturity. His face still looked callow, the endearing mug of a wiseacre juvenile (its dearness a function of family connection, Stevie knew, and probably not readily evident to strangers), but his body was acquiring strength and something like an admirable classical purity. As she drew his blanket over his shoulders, Stevie kissed him lightly on the brow.

"Night, sport."

After plunging his room into darkness again, she crossed the hall to her study. That damn Exceleriter. Its own spurious account of what she had done after waking to its mad electronic magic still lay on her dictionary stand. She picked up the sheet and read the story a third time. What wonderful phrases it contained: "Her clumsiness she charitably attributed" . . . "afraid to catch the Exceleriter" . . . "the percipient machine" . . . "solely because she had made a fool of herself"—a host of casual digs that contained irritating glimmers of insight, even humor. Funny, very funny. A piece of electrically driven machinery was giving her the business. . . .

Where was the other story? What had she done with the semijournalistic account of yesterday morning's nightmare? Rummaging about, Stevie found this first example of the Exceleriter's macabre literary talent on a package of typing paper on her rolltop. She reread this single page, its playful three-part headline concluding with the astute declaration: TYPEWRITERS ARE OBNOXIOUS!!! She had called that one, hadn't she?

What you didn't call, Stevie reminded herself, was the subject matter of tonight's nightmare. You fed the machine a new strip of paper, and it outfoxed you. It wrote a brand-new story. If you want it to conclude the one it began last night, maybe you've got to use your head and make more careful arrangements. You're smarter than that damned Exceleriter.

She wondered. The Exceleriter—*this* Exceleriter—was lots smarter than its PDE siblings; a veritable genius. An evil genius. In fact, that was the problem. She was attempting to match wits, not with a product of PDE technology, but with the unknown intelligence that had possessed her typewriter's mundane metal and plastic parts. Once, after all, it had behaved as predictably, as docilely, as any well-mannered Smith-Corona, Royal, Olivetti, Xerox, Remington, or Olympia machine. But it had broken last Tuesday, she had taken it to Hamlin Benecke & Sons the following day, and ever since it had manifested a Jekyll-and-Hyde personality that could only be the consequence of . . . well, hell, Stevie, go ahead and say it, spit out those silly incantatory words . . . *demonic possession.*

Maybe her Exceleriter, once broken, had surrendered its motor functions to a demon precisely because the contemporary susceptibility to the power of this ancient concept—possession—had finally communicated itself to machines. And the most susceptible machines were the ones that broke and received repairs at the hands of psychologically disturbed amateurs like Seaton Benecke. Deepness was what Benecke really liked, that and not being afraid to write about fears and dark desires. Nitty-gritty stuff like that. The lesson for Stevenson Crye was all too clear.

"You should have paid the bastards at PDE their fifty-two dollars."

She laughed mirthlessly. She had tried to beat Pantronics Data Equipment at its high-handed corporate game, and what she had saved in money now threatened to bankrupt her beleaguered spirit.

Was it Seaton Benecke's demon that inhabited the Exceleriter? Her dead husband's? Her own? Or maybe simply—well, no, *complexly*—the terrible cacodemon of a single multinational concern? Maybe the vengeful PDE djinn was bending its enormous resources to the highly unprofitable business of driving her crazy. Well, let it—or whatever it was—try. She had not yet collapsed into a gibbering heap, and she was just as intent on learning what she could from the demon as it apparently was on achieving her breakdown.

Be smarter than the goddamn typewriter, gal.

To the 8½" × 11" sheet on which the machine had transcribed her first nightmare, Stevie Scotch-taped five more sheets of typing paper. She then rolled this unwieldy train of pages into the Exceleriter, stopping at the bottom of the typed-upon sheet and aligning the type disc so that it could resume where it had left off. No one liked to be interrupted in the middle of a sentence. Maybe the machine's mischievous demon would be tempted to finish what it had begun:

> "I fell apart down deep," Crye said, a dead hand on his wife's forehead. "If I appeared to give up, Stevie, it was only because

"Because what?" Stevie asked. "Because what?"

To her intense astonishment the on/off control levered itself to the "on" position, and the Exceleriter began to hum. It then banged out a seven-word phrase and abruptly clicked off:

> it was time for me to pay."

For a moment the words meant nothing to Stevie. Despite having carefully prepared for this very moment, she was dumbfounded by what she had just witnessed. Dumbfounded and spooked. Her hands tingled. Her spine felt like an ice-cold piece of wire on which dozens of little silver bells have begun chiming.

It was not as if some anonymous person had activated the Exceleriter by remote control, or as if the typewriter had responded to the instructions of a computer program. No, it was as if an invisible presence had sidled past her, typed those seven words, and just as blithely turned off the machine and retreated back into darkness—not to conceal itself, because its invisibility accomplished that, but simply to give Stevie a chance to think about the darker implications of its visit. A touch-typist thief in the night. A sixty-words-a-minute revenant to whose hit-and-run typing attacks she was instantly and maybe even everlastingly vulnerable.

When the tiny bells on her spine stopped jangling, Stevie clenched her fists and defiantly glanced about her study. "Who are you?" she demanded. "What right have you to invade my room, my house, my life?'' Receiving no answer, either from the air or from the typewriter, she turned back to the machine to contemplate its final cryptic phrase.

"Time to pay for what, Ted? Why do you keep me on tenterhooks? Why don't you speak for yourself?''

But her invisible visitor—whether the demon of Ted or young Benecke or some other mysterious jackanapes—had departed, and Stevie felt certain it would not return tonight. It wanted to leave her and those five Scotch-taped blank pages dangling. It wanted to make her anticipate with mounting impatience and bitterness its next visit. Well, she had already begun.

Nevertheless, Stevie removed the paper from the Exceleriter, separated the six taped sheets, and placed both upsetting stories—the one about Ted and the other about Marella—in a manila folder, which, in turn, she quickly crammed into the overladen filing cabinet beside her desk. Out of sight, out of mind. Ha! That was the most ridiculous aphorism she had ever heard—as she had gradually discovered over the months since Ted's funeral. Out of sight, out of your mind. That was closer to it. However, Stevie believed you could be intermittently out of your mind without being certifiably insane forever. She was *not* insane.

As she proved by returning to her bedroom and quietly talking herself into a deep, restful, and (apparently) dreamless sleep.

XVI

Saturday morning broke chilly but fair. The sky was baseball-summer blue, the air football-autumn brisk. Stevie was grateful for the good weather because the kids were home for the weekend and she needed to work. If Teddy could coax Marella outdoors to roller-skate on the quiet little street in front of the house, or accompany her on a bike ride, or convince her to tag along when he went over to Pete Wightman's, Poor Old Mom might be able to type up a submittable copy of her proposal for *Two-Faced Woman*. She needed to get that done. The post office closed at twelve-thirty on Saturdays, and she did not want to have to wait until Monday to get her work in the mail. Except for the article on the Ladysmith cancer clinic (the original deadline for which she had badly overshot), this past week had been, to succumb to cliché, An Unmitigated Disaster. Getting her proposal off to the Briar Patch Press, Inc., might mitigate it a little.

At breakfast both kids balked. Teddy did not want to babysit, and Marella wanted to invite Tiffany McGuire over to make up for having to leave her party yesterday afternoon. She and Tiff (she said, pleading her case) would stay in the den playing dolls, Outwit, Kings-in-the-Corner, and other such stuff, and they would both be Very Quiet. Teddy, on the other hand, said that Pete Wightman's younger sisters would not be at home today (they were visiting their grandmother in Atlanta), and, anyway, he didn't want Marella standing on the edge of Pete's patio complaining about her cold feet while Pete and he played off the last round of the H-O-R-S-E tournament that darkness had interrupted Friday evening. Teddy therefore felt that Marella's having Tiff over was The Perfect Solution.

"For you," Stevie challenged him. "That way you can go gallivanting off while I'm left to entertain your sister."

"She and Tiff'll entertain each other, Mom." He was sitting at the breakfast bar, applying muscadine jelly to a piece of toast, and he tossed off this opinion as confidently as a big-shot city lawyer concluding his final arguments before a jury of untutored country folk.

"That's what *they* say, that's what *you* say, but that's *not* the way it works. I end up refereeing spats, cleaning up after impromptu 'tea parties,' listening to an impossible horde clomp up and down the stairs for Marella's dolls and stuffed animals, and wondering just what the hell they're up to when it's suddenly so quiet I could really get down to business if I weren't worrying about the worrisome silence!" Stevie took a breath.

"If you expect this household to survive—young man, little lady—I'm going to have to get some cooperation and just a smidgen of help. We've had this discussion before, and I'm damn tired of it."

Teddy's expression—the ill-disguised sneer of a would-be stud temporarily under the thumb of an uppity female—shocked her. It was eloquent of a gamut of bigotries. It completely drained the reservoir of tenderness she had replenished last night at his bedside. That it was also altogether unlike her son and probably the consequence of a single moment's disappointment and thoughtlessness did not lessen her anger. He knew better. She would teach him better.

"Listen, Herr Hotshot, H-O-R-S-E player of the year," she raged at the boy, pulling the hair at the nape of his neck, "I won't be insulted in my own house by big-britches kids who spend the money I make, eat the food I bring home and prepare, and think they're God's own gift to the world for not being any more stuck-up than they already are! Do you hear me, Theodore Martin Crye the Living?"

Teddy ducked to extricate his neck hair from her fingers, while Marella, sitting over a bowl of Cheerios at the kitchen table, merely gaped. Their mother had seldom gone off the handle like this before.

"Do you hear me?"

Faintly: "Yes, ma'am."

"Did you say something, Master Crye?"

"Yes, ma'am," said Teddy more loudly, still uncertain how to respond to this barrage. "Yes, ma'am."

"Do you think you're indispensable?"

"Ma'am?"

"Because *nobody*'s indispensable, Herr Hotshot, and if you're ever crazy enough to try to be, then you have to *do* something to make yourself that way. No one ever becomes indispensable sitting on his butt. Or shooting baskets over at Pete Wightman's house while barbarians sack his own."

"I said we'd be quiet," Marella interjected, indignant. "I said we'd be quiet, Mama, and we really will."

"What you'll be, daughter mine, is outside with your

brother. Both of you together. At least until noon. No ifs, ands, or but-we're-gonnas.'' She stopped snatching at Teddy's hair, picked up a plastic container of milk with a dramatic flourish, and slammed it back into the refrigerator. "Besides, it's a beautiful day. A gorgeous day. I wish I could be outside in it. But I've got to work, and you two are going to cooperate to help me do that. Understand?"

Neither of the children said anything.

"Understand?"

"Yes, ma'am," they murmured together, genuinely chastened. Two years ago a scolding like that—a *performance* like that—would have elicited tears from Marella and a ritual sulk from Teddy. But the death of Ted, Sr., had endowed them with resilience. Looking from one to the other, Stevie could see that they were trying to bounce back, to accommodate their conspicuously dependent lives to her goals and priorities. As well they should. Still, maybe she had come on too strong, hitting them with nukes when a little dose of napalm would have sufficed. Forward Air Controller Stevie "Killer" Crye . . .

"We'll throw the Frisbee in the back by the swing set," Teddy announced. "She needs to learn how to hold it. She holds it like a girl."

Stevie chuckled mordantly. Marella asked if please couldn't she just watch cartoons instead, that would keep her out of Mama's hair, but Teddy pointed out that she had traded two hours of Saturday-morning cartoons for two hours of Friday-evening programming and that Mama wanted her outside in the fresh air. In his deliberate reasonableness he sounded uncannily like his dad, and even Marella surrendered to his arguments. If Big Brother and the Female Paterfamilias were against her, who could be for her?

As for Stevie, a few minutes later, she stared out the window over the kitchen sink regretting that she could not join the children in their game. Tossing a Frisbee would be fun, more fun than sitting at that damned—yes, *damned*—typewriter doing the dog work of a final copy. But the kids were cooperating, and maybe she would be finished by noon.

XVII

She finished by eleven-thirty. She had even provided her proposal with a cover letter listing her previous credits, championing the relevance and marketability of her "package," and offering to supply several more sample columns if her present selection whetted editorial appetite without yet convincing anyone in authority to send her a contract. A thoroughly professional performance, Stevie congratulated herself, slipping her morning's work into a mailer. And the Exceleriter, her post-midnight bugaboo, why, it had cooperated fully, just as the kids had been cooperating. Indeed, she had found that during most daylight hours the Exceleriter was a sweetheart.

Time to get to the post office before closing. Stevie neatened her desk, put the dust cover over her machine, and went trippingly down the stairs and through the house to the VW van.

Teddy and Marella were no longer throwing the Frisbee (the joy of this activity apparently dissipated over a three-hour period), but playing with a neighborhood dog, a lovelorn basset hound that had developed an erotic fixation on Teddy's pants legs. The boy was trying to interest the animal in taking a strip of paint-spattered dropcloth into its teeth for a game of Swing About, but the dog's misdirected ardor was greater than its hankering for a platonic romp. Marella, poor child, seemed to be jealous of the attention it was bestowing on Teddy. She kept grabbing at the basset's droopy scruff and speaking futile blandishments into its even droopier ear.

"Dear God," said Stevie, laughing behind her hand. Then she shouted, "Send Cyrano home, Ted! I'll be back from the post office in a few minutes, and we'll eat lunch!" The children waved as she backed the microbus out of the driveway.

The post office was crowded, people trying to buy stamps or pick up mail before the weekend closing, some of them purchasing money orders, others insuring their packages or asking about special rates—with the result that Stevie spent twenty minutes in the narrow customer area before Mr. Hice, the postmaster, was able to wait on her. When she finally got her proposal off, she hurried outside to her van for the three-block trip back over the railroad tracks and Barclay's surprisingly busy main drag to the Crye house, a landmark Victorian structure that had been in Ted's family since the days of the Great Depression, their one steadfast bulwark against poverty and rootlessness. It had saved Stevie and her small brood as it had once saved the elder Cryes and their children, all of whom had either died or moved away.

Ted may have been bad with money, disorganized and spendthrift beyond belief, but he had always had sufficient sense to protect his interest in the house, and to that happy orphan scruple Stevie probably owed her otherwise foolhardy attempt to support herself and the kids through free-lancing. If she had had monthly house payments to meet, or even rent for some cheapjack Barclay apartment, she would have been obliged to take another salaried job, resuming her teaching post at the middle school in Wickrath or perhaps applying for a teller's position at the Farmers and Merchants Bank here in Barclay. Sometimes, in fact, these alternatives seemed more attractive than her labors at the typewriter, a career of such unremitting uncertainty that she wondered both at her arrogance in sticking to it this long and at her luck in simply being able to. Today was a highlight of sorts: she had just made a significant step toward becoming an author of *books*. If the Briar Patch Press accepted her proposal, the mists of uncertainty would begin to evaporate and she would perhaps never have to worry about her choice of careers again.

Pulling into the Crye house's gravelly drive, Stevie even had the fleeting idea that she might be able to replace her Exceleriter with either a word processor or a typewriter of another make. She was through with PDE, though; they were opportunistic bloodsuckers.

But where were the kids? Twenty, twenty-five minutes ago they had been playing with Cyrano (if you could call that animal's unavailing thrusts at Teddy's leg a form of game participation), but now their side yard near the garage was deserted, empty but for Marella's bicycle and a pair of weathered sawhorses.

Well, maybe Teddy and Marella had gone inside to fix lunch. Hot dogs they were good at, and she had given them such a lecture about being helpful and pulling their weight that perhaps they were trying hard to recapture her goodwill. These attacks of practical conscientiousness seldom lasted more than a day or two, but Stevie was always grateful for them, and she got out of the microbus feeling tender toward her children, magnanimous and cheerful. The entire brisk, sunny afternoon lay ahead of them. After lunch they could take a drive through the Roosevelt State Park to Warm Springs to visit the federal fish hatchery there. Teddy and Marella both liked to do that.

Then Stevie heard her daughter's uneasy laughter, a giggle that suggested doubt as well as amusement—not from inside the kitchen, but instead from the vicinity of the swing set, around the corner of the garage. Had Teddy been unable to shoo Cyrano home? Was Marella giggling because Teddy had decided to explain to her the complete significance of the basset's infatuation with his kneecap? Stevie's cheerful mood turned sour. Marella was only eight. She would kill the boy. . . .

Stevie stalked to the corner of the garage. Peering into the backyard at the dilapidated swing set under the big pecan tree, she suddenly went cold. A strange man had driven a motorcycle all the way into the yard and parked it beside the swing set's squeaky glider. Meanwhile, a small manlike creature in a red-and-white football jersey scampered back and forth along the crossbar from which the glider and the swings depended. The children were watching this creature as if bewitched by it, Marella hanging on to her brother for protection. Stevie tried to take in the whole scene, but her eyes kept going back to the thing on the crossbar, a ghoulish little figure with a white face, deep-set beady eyes, and nostrils like those you would expect to see on a death's-head. The animal also had a tail, but Stevie's dawning realization that it was some kind of monkey did not

excuse its trespass or diminish her angry dread of either it or
the stranger who had apparently brought it.

"What do you want?" Stevie shouted. "What are you doing
here?" She was trembling. Maybe it would have been wiser to
telephone Barclay's police department than to issue this direct
challenge. Too late. Besides, her children's safety was at
hazard, and she was not about to leave them even for the brief
duration of a phone call.

Teddy, Marella, the monkey, and the mysterious intruder
all turned toward Stevie, their faces as blank as unstamped
coins. For an instant the three human beings looked as ghoulish as the white-faced acrobat on the crossbar.

"Hi, Mom!" Teddy called, breaking into a grin. "Look,
it's the man who fixed your typewriter! And he's brought his
pet monkey!"

Who else? thought Stevie, disconsolate and anxious, convinced that she was being persecuted. Who else?

As for Seaton Benecke, dressed today in combat boots and
fatigues, he gave her a shy, imperceptible nod and looked right
past her with eyes as distantly pretty as the February sky.

XVIII

"Seaton," Stevie said, recovering a little, "most visitors park
their vehicles in our driveway instead of the backyard."

He glanced over his shoulder at the motorcycle, a shiny
black monster with enormous handlebars and a pair of built-in
carryalls behind the long padded seat. "I'll move it." He
grabbed the machine by its horns and walked it past Stevie
toward the drive.

"Get out from under the swing set," Stevie whispered at
Teddy and Marella, motioning with her hand. "No telling
what kind of manners that monkey's got."

The creature cocked its skull-like head and stared at her. She had never seen a living entity whose lineaments so clearly prophesied its inevitable end (save only aged or sick people passively awaiting death, like Ted in his final two months), and she dropped her gaze before the monkey did. Ordinarily, she knew, animals surrendered to human beings in staring contests. Not this time, though. The monkey had a demon on its side. . . .

"How long has he been here?" Stevie asked Teddy, nodding at Benecke. "What does he want?"

"To see you," Teddy said, still grinning. "A gentleman caller."

Marella refrained from adding an editorial "Yuck!" or "Ugh!" Seaton had won the children over by arriving on a sleek chrome-filigreed motorcycle and by introducing them to his hideous pet monkey. How could a parent compete with such miraculous inducements?

"How long?" Stevie insisted. She was afraid he had shown up right after her departure for the post office. The thought that he had been "entertaining" her kids for the past half hour made her shudder. Benecke looked like a baby-faced assassin and his pet monkey like a miniature Nosferatu with fur. The ridiculous little football jersey in no wise diminished the animal's sinisterness.

"Three or four minutes ago, Mom. That's all."

"The monkey was holding on to his back," Marella added. "It was wearing a crash helmet. It jumped up onto the swings as soon as he took its helmet off. And it climbed up there." Unnecessarily, she pointed.

"An Atlanta Falcons helmet, Mom. See his shirt? He's wearing Steve Bartkowski's number. He's a quarterback."

"Well, I wish he were all the way back. All the way back where he belongs, wherever that is."

"Costa Rica," Seaton Benecke said, coming up behind her without his motorcycle. "That's where his ancestors come from, I mean. I don't think *he's* ever been there. I bought him in a pet store in Atlanta." Hands in pocket, Seaton regarded his monkey as if reevaluating his purchase of it. "The people at the pet store may have got him through some other people at the Yerkes Primate Center. I'm not sure. Anyway, he's an *old* monkey. I've had him five or six years."

"Seaton, what are you doing here?"

The intruder hesitated, scuffling his foot on the carpet of dead grass. "It's my day off. Saturday, you know. Sorry I wheeled my bike over your lawn. It's just I saw the kids back here—" He fell silent.

"But what are you doing in Barclay, Seaton? You don't usually spend your day off roaming rural Georgia, do you?"

His hand came out of his right pocket clutching a crumpled green bill. "That tip you gave me, Mrs. Crye." He pushed the bill toward her. "I decided it wasn't right to keep it. Dad pays everybody there a salary. No one else gets tips. I shouldn't, either."

Is this young man for real? Stevie asked herself. Or are you being manipulated? If so, for what reason? Whatever the case, the bill between his fingers was the very one Stevie had given the cashier at Benecke & Sons to hand over to Seaton. She recognized the squiggle of red ink next to the engraving of Lincoln. For two days he had held that bill without breaking it. Not bad for a young bachelor with ash-blond hair, pudgy good looks, and a monster motorcycle. Didn't he have buddies, a girl friend, expensive after-hours hobbies? True, he was a little weird (as the monkey silently, vividly, testified), but no weirder than many contemporary young people who had not yet found themselves.

"Seaton, I gave you that money because you deserved it. You saved me eight or nine times that amount."

"I came up here to give it back."

"I'm not going to take it, Seaton."

"I'll stand here all night," he replied, gazing at the money instead of her face. "I won't leave until you take it."

You mean it too, don't you? thought Stevie. You're just like Vincent van Gogh holding his palm over a candle flame to convince some little French gal of his undying love. If I don't take the bill back, you'll remain in my yard as a permanent fixture, like a clothesline pole or a birdbath. If I should convince you to leave with the money, you'll probably just mail it back to me in a box—along with a gift certificate for typing paper and one of your own severed ears. Or maybe one of the monkey's. At the moment this is a Mexican standoff, but *I'm* going to be the first to blink. I know it.

"Listen," Teddy piped up, "if he doesn't want that five dollars, I'll be glad to look after it for him." A monkey, a motorcycle, a gentleman caller, a dispute over money—why, this was a regular amusement-park tour for the boy. Six Flags Over Georgia in his own backyard. His grin was more wondering than avaricious.

Seaton turned toward the young man.

"He gets an allowance," Stevie said. "Don't you *dare* give that to him." She stepped forward and relieved their visitor of the bill. "You're being foolish, Seaton. This was really yours."

He seemed gratified to have won the contest. He plunged his hands back into his fatigue pockets and rocked on his heels. "That's not the only reason I came, though."

"It's not?"

"No, Mrs. Crye. If you'd like me to check your typewriter, this could be a service call. Is it working okay?"

"Why shouldn't it be?" The hostility in her voice surprised even Stevie. "You fixed it, didn't you?"

"Yes, ma'am."

"Then there's no reason to look at it again, is there?"

"Not if you don't want me to, Mrs. Crye. I just thought—"

"What?"

"I brought my tools. The timing might've slipped a little. I wouldn't mind, you know, just giving it a look. For free, I mean. I'm not giving back that five dollars just to try to charge you more than that for something else. I don't do that. I'm just—"

"—being neighborly."

Seaton Benecke scuffed the soles of his combat boots on the twiggy grass and looked at the ground. "I read your article on the Ladysmith cancer clinic in yesterday evening's *Ledger*. It was really good. You really got deep into that stuff—

thermograms, nuclear medicine, and all. Really good. I always try to read what you do." He looked up without engaging Stevie's eyes. "I guess I just sort of wanted to see what your writing place looked like. I've never seen a writer's place before, how you've got your typewriter and all set up. But I would've worked on it even if you wanted to bring it out of your workplace to the kitchen or something—if it needed it, I mean. I would've checked it out for you. Sometimes you can catch some things before they go wacky or really break."

Teddy said, "He can stay for lunch, can't he?"

Oh, Lord, not that trick again. Stevie glowered at the boy. How many times had she told him not to invite a friend to the house without first consulting with her in private? She could only appear ungracious if she refused such a request within hearing of the disinvited party. Teddy never learned. He issued invitations the way some people threw confetti.

"He's come forty miles," the boy pointed out. "It wouldn't hurt for him to just check your typewriter."

"I *know* how far he's come. I've made that trip a few times." Was Teddy being obtuse on purpose?

"That's okay," Seaton Benecke said. "I was going to eat when I got home. It's hard to stop anywhere when you're traveling with a monkey."

"You're welcome to stay," Stevie said tightly, still trying to communicate her ire to her son. "I hope you don't mind hot dogs or fried-egg sandwiches, though. That's about all we've got."

"We love fried-egg sandwiches," Seaton Benecke declared flatly. "At home, Mrs. Crye, I fix them all the time."

"Did you say 'we,' Seaton?"

"Yes, ma'am."

"Look now, please don't think me rude, but although I'm prepared to have *you* for a guest, I really don't think I'm ready for your monkey." Just like I'm not ready for a train carrying toxic waste to derail in downtown Barclay. Just like I'm not ready for a reprise of Ted's last two months on earth.

"He's housebroken, Mrs. Crye. He's neater than some people."

The presumption of *some* people, thought Stevie, was a poison they sprinkled about like baptismal water.

"Hello there," Marella was saying. "Hello there, monkey. Grab this stick. Jump down here."

The girl was extending a broken pecan limb toward the crossbar on which the white-faced, white-bearded monkey was sidling back and forth in its football jersey. The monkey ignored the stick, which was not quite long enough to reach the bar, but he opened his mouth and favored Marella with a hissing death's-head grin. The monkey gripped the crossbar with his tail, as well as with his feet and hands, edging first this way and then that, a living windup toy.

"Please don't poke at him," Seaton said, addressing Marella. "He's really little, and he thinks you're trying to hurt him."

"I'm just *playing* with him," the girl said. "I want him to come down for lunch."

Oh, me too, thought Stevie. That's exactly what I want. Aloud she said, "Marella, put down that stick."

Marella obeyed, whereupon the acrobat on the swing set startled Stevie by running along the crossbar and leaping over the girl's head into the fork of the pecan tree. Briefly, terribly briefly, she had feared that the monkey was attacking her daughter, but, in truth, he had merely been scrambling to a loftier haven. Hands still in his pockets, Seaton ambled to the base of the tree and began encouraging the tiny beast to come down.

"What's his name?" Teddy asked him.

"'Crets," Seaton replied abstractedly.

"Come on down, 'Crets," Marella began baby-talking. "Come on down, little 'Cretsie, come on to me now."

"Why do you call him that?" Teddy asked.

"It's sort of a joke, I guess. I'll show you how I get him down." From the same fatigue pocket from which he had taken the five-dollar bill, Seaton removed a small metal canister of throat lozenges. Then he unwrapped one of the foil-covered drops and held it up to the monkey. "He's always loved

Sucrets. You can get him to do just about anything for a Sucret."

'Crets demonstrated the truth of this assertion by leaping from the pecan tree to Seaton's shoulder, taking the proffered lozenge into his mouth, and immediately cracking it with his teeth.

"He doesn't suck them, though. He eats them. I suppose he probably is a little hungry. He only had some banana for breakfast this morning. That was about five hours ago."

"Poor dear," Stevie said.

Marella circled behind the young man, reached up, and thoughtfully stroked the monkey's sinuous tail, which was dark brown rather than white and an inch or two longer than the animal possessing it. 'Crets did not seem to mind. He unconcernedly went on cracking his sore-throat medicine, and when he had finished, he begged for another. Seaton refused him.

"You'll spoil your lunch," he said.

XIX

The day had gone scratchy and sour. Not even a gross of Sucrets would take away the soreness and sweeten what remained. An hour ago she had almost managed to forget her troubles with the typewriter and her worries about Marella; the satisfying afterglow of mailing off her book proposal had still enveloped her. Now, however, Seaton Benecke had invaded her kitchen, bringing with him—of all impossible things!—a furry little ghoul dressed in football-jersey drag. And now she was cooking—*cooking,* for God's sake!—for these freeloaders. She had caved in to Seaton's easy assumption that he was welcome and to her children's obvious infatuation with 'Crets. What a travesty of hospitality was her real mood, though, and how bitterly she resented this intrusion.

At the round oaken table in the dining area sat Teddy, Marella, and Seaton, the latter with 'Crets in his lap. From the stove Stevie could glance to her right down the length of her breakfast-bar island into the faces of her visitors, Seaton's face a mask of pale piety, the monkey's an uncanny blur as, like a spectator at a tennis match, the creature glanced back and forth between Teddy and Marella. His tiny head—you could probably crush it with a large pair of pliers—was all that was visible of the monkey above the edge of the table. In fact, Seaton resembled a piece of placid Buddhist statuary with an animate clockwork skull set into its paunch. Stevie hated having the animal in the dining area, but she was grateful that Seaton had not put 'Crets down and given him the run of the entire kitchen. There was a highchair in the attic, but to get it out for no longer than she intended her visitors to be on the premises would have required a more solicitous hostess than she.

"He doesn't like cold weather," Seaton was telling the kids. "That's why I've got him in this outfit. My mother made it for him—before she got sick a while back." Seaton paused, as if considering the relevance of this last bit of exposition. Then he said, "He watches football on TV, and he can throw a plastic football—one of those little toy ones—just like Bartkowski. Well, sort of. Sometimes his throws end up behind him."

The children laughed.

Stevie turned the eggs in her skillet over. Out of the corner of her eye she could see that 'Crets had stopped playing tennis-match spectator. The animal was staring at her, its black-ringed eye sockets like little portholes into nothingness.

"What kind of monkey is it?" she asked defensively. "He, I mean."

"White-throated capuchin," Seaton responded. "Capuchins are what you call organ-grinder monkeys, sometimes. You don't see very many organ-grinders anymore, though. 'Crets has never worked with one."

"Only with a typewriter repairman, huh?"

"Yes, ma'am." Seaton gave a polite laugh. "'Crets likes to watch me fix 'em, but Dad doesn't like having a monkey around the office-supply company. Not one that's, uh, not re-lated by blood, anyway.'' He gave another perfunctory laugh to indicate that this was a standing joke between his father and himself.

So rapidly did the boorish in Seaton's character alternate with the pathetic that Stevie no longer knew whether to despise or pity him. The sinister aspects of his personality—if you ig-nored the ill-defined menace embodied by the monkey—had given way to a shallow blandness. 'Crets continued to disturb Stevie, but she could no longer fear his master. Owning a white-throated capuchin and riding a big black motorcycle were Seaton's transparent attempts to distinguish a life other-wise devoid of any accomplishment but his mastery of type-writer repair. At twenty-five or twenty-six he was still an ado-lescent.

''All right, kids,'' Stevie said. ''Get off your fannies and set the table. I thought I was supposed to get some help around here.''

''Only one plate for 'Crets and me,'' Seaton put in as Teddy went for the china and Marella for the silverware. ''I don't want you to have to clean up for two guests, Mrs. Crye.''

''We can spare an extra plate, Seaton.''

''No, no. Please don't do that. Just one.''

''Does he need a fork?'' Marella asked from the utensil drawer. ''These look too big and heavy for him.''

''Do you maybe have a cocktail fork?'' Seaton asked Marella. ''A cocktail fork's about the right size for 'Crets.''

Stevie left the stove to help Marella find a cocktail fork in the jumble of the utensil drawer. Maybe 'Crets would also like a silver-inlaid napkin ring, a stem of imported crystal, and a fin-ger bowl. In fact, a finger bowl might not be such a bad idea. She could tip a couple of drops of Lysol into the water while neither Seaton nor the monkey was looking. As it was, she would not feel right about her kitchen again until she had scrubbed it from baseboard to cornice and invited the county sanitarian in for an inspection.

The meal went well enough, though. 'Crets preferred his fried-egg sandwiches without bread, a stipulation Seaton had failed to make while Stevie was cooking. Consequently, the bread had to be removed from around the egg and the egg cut up into vaguely lozenge-shaped pieces before the capuchin could begin to eat. Seaton took care of these minor exigencies (transferring the bread slices to a napkin beside their plate, which slices, later on, he ate himself), and Stevie was pleasantly surprised by the daintiness with which 'Crets wielded the cocktail fork, spearing each bite of egg, lifting the bite to his mouth, and licking the fork tines before returning the instrument to his plate. Moreover, he chewed with his mouth closed. In the fastidiousness of this particular he clearly outpointed her own Teddy.

"You cook as good as you write," Seaton said at length, pushing back his chair and daubing at his mouth with a paper napkin.

"That's an ambiguous compliment."

"Oh, no, ma'am. I liked it. 'Crets did too."

"Well, maybe it'll hold you on your ride back to Columbus." Not too subtle, but you could hardly accuse Seaton of an acute sensitivity, either. He was unaware of her discomfort (or, worse, indifferent to it), and 'Crets had resumed staring at her from empty-seeming eye sockets.

"He's got to check your typewriter before he goes," Teddy said. "So he doesn't waste the trip."

Stevie feigned a pique only slightly more intense than the one she actually felt. Teddy was a walking textbook on tact. "That says a lot for my cooking and your company, young man."

"You know what I mean, Mom."

"My typewriter's all right."

"I'll be glad to look at it, though. The timing and all. You've probably got one or two letters that spin back before they hit, don't you? That happens to the Exceleriter sometimes."

"It's fine."

"You don't have any letters that strike off-center?"

"Only the *t*, Seaton. Sometimes the *t* doesn't do quite right.

Very seldom, though. It's not anything to worry about."

"That's the timing. I'll fix it."

"Let him fix it," Teddy urged her. "It's free. He's already told you it's free."

Marella said, "Never look a gift horse in the mouth, Mama."

"I don't think that's quite the adage you're looking for," Stevie replied. "Try 'Beware of Greeks bearing gifts.'" The steely scrutiny of the capuchin and the low-key eagerness of young Benecke were wearing her down. They had purchased entry by returning her five-dollar tip. What else did they want?

Suddenly 'Crets ceased staring at her. The animal twisted about on Seaton's lap, grabbed the front of his fatigue jacket, and looked imploringly up into the young man's face. Between his tiny pointed teeth 'Crets made a screeching noise. Marella leaned over and stroked his tail.

"Time for dessert, eh?" Seaton asked. "You want your dessert?"

Chutzpah enough to choke an army of stand-up comics. Stevie had prepared no dessert, and she was not about to whip up a banana-cream pie or a pan of cinnamon rolls so that Seaton's monkey could satisfy his sweet tooth. To paraphrase another unfeeling lady, let him eat Sucrets.

But instead of looking to Stevie to appease the capuchin, Seaton jostled the monkey back down into his lap, lifted his right forefinger to the animal's mouth, and allowed 'Crets to suckle the fingertip as if it were a teat or a Popsicle. A moment later a snaky thread of blood ran down Seaton's knuckle. He wiped away the blood with his other hand but did not withdraw his finger from the monkey's mouth. 'Crets continued to feed, his black-ringed eyes closed in a kind of rapturous trance.

"Ugh!" squealed Marella. "What are you doing?"

"I cut myself on a typebar fixing somebody's machine. Yesterday that was. One of the prongs on its y was broken off. It sliced me good. 'Crets is just trying to help me get it to heal."

"By biting the scab off?" Stevie asked, completely repulsed. "What did you mean by mentioning dessert, then? Was that supposed to be funny?'' Maybe so straightforward a challenge was rude, but even Teddy's face had twisted into an involuntary moue of disgust.

"Yes, ma'am," said Seaton, stunned by her implied objection. "It was just a joke. I didn't really cut my finger yesterday. I've had this little wound for years." He still did not pull his finger back. "Sucking it's something 'Crets likes to do. I don't mind. It really doesn't hurt. Makes it feel better, in fact."

"I want you to stop it."

"Ma'am."

"Against my better judgment, and beyond my most outlandish dream, I've just entertained a monkey in my kitchen, Seaton. Don't push me any further than that. As a matter of fact, I'm asking you to leave."

"You want me to stop?" His wayward gaze had not yet intercepted her unwavering one. Could he really be so dense?

"That's what I said. If that's something you both feel compelled to do—finger fellatio or whatever you call it—please go on back to Columbus to do it. In the privacy of your own monkeyhouse, Seaton, you can be consenting primates together, till blood poisoning or anemia do ye part. Here, though, you've overstepped the permissible."

"I'm sorry, Mrs. Crye." Using his thumb and middle finger, he pushed the capuchin's head back and extracted his bleeding finger from the creature's mouth. Then he wiped it back and forth on the breast pocket of his fatigues.

'Crets, meanwhile, turned a stare of steady outrage on Stevie. For the first time since they had all come inside, Stevie saw the *eyes* in those deep-set sockets, twin sparks of carnelian hostility. Even after being dumped ten or twelve yards behind the line of scrimmage, the Falcon quarterback never shot so damning a look at his departing tacklers. Stevie shivered but tried to hold the animal's gaze. Eventually the monkey blinked and sprawled out on Seaton's leg, bored with her silly effort to face him down. His posture implied that he had *let* her win.

Seaton, however, was chastened. He swung 'Crets from his thigh to his shoulder, stood up, and addressed the empty cut-glass vase in the center of the table. "We'll be going as soon as I've fixed that *t* on your Exceleriter, Mrs. Crye."

"That isn't necessary, Seaton."

"Yes, ma'am. It's the least I can do for eating lunch here. I didn't mean to gross you out with 'Crets and so on. I'm not around other people all that much. It's just a kind of habit we've got into. It's a way of showing we like and trust each other. It's never hurt me any, so far as I can see. In cold weather especially, I sort of feel I owe him. Costa Rica's a long way off, Mrs. Crye. This keeps him warm."

"I don't think it's advisable."

"No, ma'am, not in front of other people. I just didn't think." He tapped the side of his head. "Uh, let's go look at your machine so 'Crets and I can get moving on home."

Although Stevie tried to dissuade him with a studied rekindling of her indignation, she could not bring herself to say, "No, I'll be damned if I'll let you up there." She could not put her foot down. She felt sorry for young Benecke. Teddy and Marella were on his side, and Stevie belatedly realized that even she wanted him to examine the Exceleriter. If he had somehow messed it up, given it, inadvertently, an autonomy comparable to a human being's, maybe he could also *un*do this condition. (Of course the undoing of the typewriter's maverick talent would leave her in the dark about a number of important matters, and maybe, after all, she did not really want the Exceleriter restored to its previous mechanical rectitude.) Sharing the burden with another person, even if that person was someone as strange as Seaton Benecke, definitely had its attractive aspects. And Seaton would believe where Dr. Elsa had (politely) scoffed.

"I just don't want 'Crets to go upstairs with us. Housebroken or not, he's not going to get a chance to prove himself in my study."

"We'll take care of him," Teddy said. "We'll take him back out to the swing set."

Is that what you want? Stevie asked herself. Would you rather have Teddy and Marella watching out for 'Crets than suffer his presence upstairs? He's a white-cowled vampire, a bloodsucking demon. Even if he beshat your drapes and Oriental rug, you'd be better off keeping him away from the kids. They'll quickly live down their disappointment, but you'll never live down an injury to either of them. Never . . .

"Seaton, there are a lot of dogs in this neighborhood. In a small town they run loose; that's the way people do things. If you'll keep 'Crets close to you, he can come upstairs. He'll be safer with us than outdoors with just the kids."

Stamping her foot, Marella said, "Mama!"

"Hey, Mom, we can take care of him," Teddy pursued.

"You think so? You remember that stupid Irish setter that came right up onto our front porch two years ago and killed your guinea pigs? It pushed in the screen on their cage and dragged them out one after another."

"Mom, 'Crets isn't a guinea pig. Besides, I'm older, and there wasn't anybody watching the porch that day."

But Seaton (Stevie could tell) no longer wished to trust 'Crets's welfare to her children. She had won—if you could call wresting temporary custody of that obscene little beast away from the kids a victory—by resorting to deceit. Although it had taken Teddy and Marella a long time to get over the deaths of their silly, utterly helpless guinea pigs, she had recounted the painful incident solely to prejudice Seaton against leaving the capuchin with them. Well, not solely. She was also exercising maternal caution, playing a frightening hunch.

"Crap!" exclaimed Teddy when he understood what she had done. He went out the kitchen door, slamming it behind him. Marella, imparting a similar emphatic impetus to the door, followed. Good kids, both of them.

XX

"This is a writer's room," Seaton told 'Crets when they got upstairs. The monkey was riding his shoulder. "That's her desk, and there's her typewriter." The study did not appear to impress the animal. "I've never seen walls this color. What do you call it?"

"Burgundy."

"It's dark. It's a really dark color."

"It's supposed to make me thoughtful and creative. Same with the curtains and the Oriental rug."

"I like it. It's kind of Edgar Allan Poe-ish, isn't it? I mean, you could put a raven up there on one of your bookcases."

"For want of a bust of Pallas?"

"It's smaller than in the poem, though. I can see you going deep into yourself sitting here, digging down into your mind. A good room for thinking in. A good room for imagining stuff in."

"Sort of like a prison cell."

"Oh, no, Mrs. Crye. It's small, but you're free here. You're a lot freer than somebody fixing typewriters in a big repair room."

"I'm chained to my desk. I'm chained to that typewriter the way an organ-grinder monkey is chained to its hurdy-gurdy." ('Crets shot Stevie a look. The word *monkey* was part of its vocabulary.) "I've got just enough slack to go around the circle of my customers with my tin cup stretched out. That's how free I am, Seaton. Your job's the equal of mine. It may even be better. You get weekends off. I feel guilty when I'm not using them to fill up that tin cup."

"Well, I'll do some work right now." He took a tiny screwdriver from his fatigue pocket. "It's Saturday, Mrs. Crye, but I'll do some work."

With 'Crets draped around his neck Seaton bent over the PDE Exceleriter 79 and fiddled with the cables beneath the ribbon carrier. Then he popped off the entire hood and, like a surgeon, peered into the cavity of levers, wheels, and cams composing the machine's gleaming viscera. Stevie stood behind him and watched him work. What was he doing? Sabotaging the machine further or righting the problem that had enabled it to work by itself?

"Seaton?"

"Ma'am."

"You did something to my Exceleriter the other day that has me very upset. I think you should know that. You said you were giving it a special twist, and that little twist has turned me upside-down emotionally. My best friend thinks I've flipped my wig, Seaton, and it's all I can do to keep from taking out my frustration and fear on the kids. This morning I boiled over and spilled about three gallons of frustration and fear right into their laps. It's the typewriter. The typewriter's holding me hostage."

"You know how kids are," Seaton replied without turning around. "You probably had to bring them up short. Just like you did me and 'Crets downstairs. I deserved that, Mrs. Crye, I really did. Besides, kids're really flexible, they bound right back from disappointments."

"That's not what I'm talking about, Seaton. Whatever you did to my typewriter Wednesday afternoon—supposedly to fix it—is fixing me instead. I think you know what I'm talking about. I've been keeping up a semiresolute front since my visit to Dr. Elsa yesterday morning, but I'm on the verge of disintegrating. Is that what you *wanted* to happen?"

Seaton's fingers ceased their exploratory surgery on the machine. He unbent his back and faced her. For only the second time in their unconventional relationship he purposely met her eyes. The capuchin scrambled about so that the tip of his white-bearded chin was resting on Seaton's head, from which precarious perch the monkey added his unyielding stare to the man's.

"You don't look like you're disintegrating, Mrs. Crye. You look just fine. Inside, I mean. Down deep."

"You've got X-ray eyes that let you see inside a person, I suppose?" Stevie regretted this question. It heightened her un-

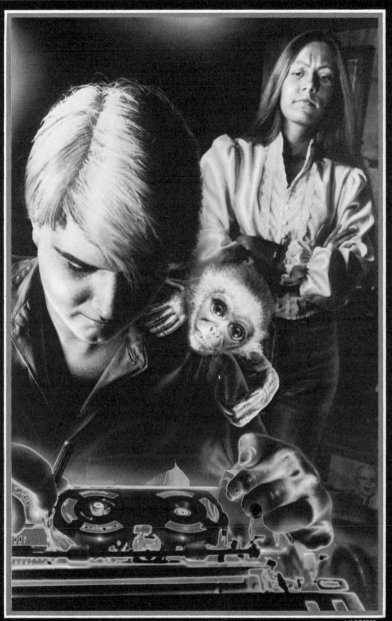

J.K.POTTER

easiness about Seaton by imputing a dreadful power to him. By sheer dint of will she kept her eyes locked on his and ignored those of the impudent monkey.

"Clinac-18 eyes," he said, expressionless.

"That's not an X-ray machine. It's a beam accelerator. What are you trying to imply?"

Seaton glanced aside, letting his gaze drift over the pattern in the Oriental rug on which she was standing. "You mentioned it in your *Ledger* article. The Clinac 18. It has a beam that goes deep and disintegrates tumors. I was just . . . well, you know, making a comparison. What do writers call them, those fancy comparisons where you say something is something else?"

"Metaphors."

"That's right. You said 'disintegrating' and then you said 'X-ray eyes,' and I just thought of what you'd written in that cancer article, is all. I was doing a metaphor, Mrs. Crye. I probably didn't do it right, though, because that stuff was always hard for me. That's why I'll never be a writer even though I've got stories in my head—spooky stuff; spooky, *heavy* stuff—that I wish I could get out. I really envy writers."

"You made my typewriter write by itself, Seaton. Is that some part of *you* operating the machine?"

"What did I do, Mrs. Crye?" His brow furrowed.

"You made the damned Exceleriter write by itself. It types out copy in the middle of the night when I'm not sitting in front of it to do the typing. I think that's you, Seaton. I think that's some part of you."

Swiveling 'Crets so that the monkey finally had to stop staring at her, Seaton looked back over his shoulder at the typewriter. Then he revolved back toward Stevie, let his gaze drift to the Dearborn space heater, and held almost breathlessly still while 'Crets shinnied down his arm to his hip. Seaton's brow had not yet unwrinkled. If he was acting, he was extraordinarily good at suggesting an unstable mixture of confusion and embarrassment.

"Ma'am?"

"You know what I'm talking about."

"I don't think it was any part of *me,* Mrs. Crye. This is the first time I've ever been in your house."

"You had to get inside my house, didn't you? You had to get upstairs here to see what the place looked like. You wanted to measure the impact of your skullduggery. That's what all this is about, isn't it?"

Maybe he was human after all. His pudgy schoolboy cheeks reddened a little, and when he finally responded to these charges, his voice cracked: "I wanted . . . I wanted to fix the *t.*" Had his face flushed from discovered guilt or a charitable embarrassment on her behalf? Stevie could not really tell. She clenched her fists at her shoulders and abstractedly tapped her knuckles against her collarbones.

"Then why don't you go ahead and fix the lousy *t?*"

"I was doing that, Mrs. Crye. I'll finish. I'll go ahead and finish the job right now."

The sun was shining brightly outside, a stunning February day, but her study was chilly. To give her distraught hands something to do, Stevie dug a small box of matches out of her cardigan's only pocket and nervously lit the space heater. Then she stood there warming her hands behind her and watching Seaton Benecke work. New deviltry or a mechanical exorcism? Stevie convinced herself that she did not care. She just wanted him to complete the job and remove himself and his obnoxious little companion from the house. The *t* he was trying to repair stood for *tactic.* Maybe it had succeeded, this tactic, but as soon as he was gone she would win the larger war by putting him out of her mind and never allowing him to darken her threshold again.

"I think that's got it, Mrs. Crye." He pressed the metal cover back into place, rolled in a sheet of typing paper, and pounded out a string of words including *tactic, temperature, ticket, toothpaste, turtle,* and *teeter-totter.* "Yes, ma'am, it's okay now. It's even better than it was before. It ought to suit you to a *T.*" This last was Seaton's idea of a joke—another feeble Benecke joke. He gave her a tentative smile, turned back to her (reputedly tractable) machine, and tapped out a final tympanic tattoo, the word *typewriter.*

"Very good, Seaton. You've proved your point. Now it's time for you to leave. I've got to check the kids."

"It's going to work even better than before, Mrs. Crye."

"Is it?"

"Yes, ma'am. No matter how well they're working when I get 'em, I always try to improve on that. It's what I do. Just like you try to improve on the last article or story you did."

Stevie refused to encourage Seaton with further comment. She opened the study door and watched tight-lipped and imperceptibly trembling as he pocketed his tiny screwdriver, wiped his hands on his fatigue jacket, and looked around for any leftover tools or typewriter parts. Although the cold air from the corridor swept past Stevie's ankles, she kept the study door open to indicate to Seaton that their interview—their entire association—was over. The sooner he was down the stairs and out on the highway home, the sooner the ice in her bone marrow would melt, restoring her to a healthy human warmth.

Disconcertingly 'Crets jumped from Seaton's hip to the Oriental rug, bounded past Stevie on all fours, and cornered like a miniature stockcar heading into . . . the master bedroom. Stevie was too startled to shout at the monkey. She and Seaton exchanged an ambiguous glance, then bumped shoulders pushing through the doorway in pursuit of the capuchin. At the threshold to her own room she saw 'Crets clambering across the quilted bedspread she had made when Ted, Jr., was a toddler and Marella was not yet even the germ of a connubial ambition. The beast had claws. He would ruin this would-be heirloom. Now, in fact, he was leaping from the center of the quilt to the carven Ethan Allen headboard. His antics—his unthinking tiny-primate presumption—infuriated Stevie.

"I thought he didn't like the cold," she said accusingly. "This is the coldest room upstairs because I always keep my shades drawn and the curtains closed. What's he doing in here, Seaton?"

"You ever read those *Curious George* books to your kids when they were little? 'Crets is curious like that monkey in those children's books. He can stand the cold for a while, Mrs. Crye. The cold won't hurt him."

"I'm worried about my quilt, my furniture, my carpet. I'm *not* worried about 'Crets."

"Yes, ma'am."

"Get him out of here, Seaton. Get him out of here without turning the whole room upside-down."

Curious 'Crets was peering at them from the headboard across the darkened bedchamber, a simian version of Poe's raven. The large white *10* on his jersey seemed to be proclaiming him the perfect capuchin, than which no other monkey of that genus was more agile, intelligent, or emblematic of unknown menace. Seaton made no effort either to catch him or to call him off the bed. Instead, he gave the dim room a lingering appraisal.

"Is this where you sleep?"

"Get him *off* my headboard!"

"That's a beautiful king-sized bed, Mrs. Crye. You must have shared it with your husband once. It's probably kind of lonely sleeping in such a big bed in such a big room without your husband beside you."

Stevie gaped at the blond young man. Coming from any other male intruder those words probably would have sounded like the prelude to either rape or a proposition as unwanted as it was obvious. Seaton, however, made these tactless comments resonate with a wistful sympathy. That, in its own way, was almost as frightening as a liquorish tongue reaming her ear and an uncouth hand on her breast. In the latter brutal scenario, at least, she could have screamed for help without the least twinge of indecisiveness.

And then Seaton asked, "Did you love your husband?"

"Of course I loved my husband." Stevie was too shocked by the out-of-left-field nature of the query to make any other reply.

"And he loved you?"

Her shock disintegrated like a tumor under repeated bombardments of electrons from the Clinac 18. "Get your goddamn monkey out of my room!"

Unabashed, Seaton looked at his goddamn monkey. "Here, 'Crets. Here, 'Crets." He whistled between his front teeth.

"Got some Sucrets for you, 'Cretsie boy. Got some Sucrets." He approached the bed extending a foil-wrapped lozenge toward the animal, alternately whistling encouragement and hyping the old familiar bribe. "Got a sweet un, 'Cretsie. Got you a really sweet un."

Much like a kid going feet-first off the high dive at the rock pool in Roosevelt State Park, the capuchin sprang from the headboard into the middle of the Technicolor quilt. He bounced once, grabbed the Sucret from Seaton's hand, and landed on the carpet about two feet from Stevie. His no-eyes were miniature black maelstroms threatening to spin her into an otherworldly abyss. When Stevie fell back from the capuchin's stare, 'Crets took advantage of her retreat to scamper through the doorway and down the hall into Marella's room. Her heart galumphing in her breast, Stevie gritted her teeth and pursued the creature.

"Come on!" she shouted at Seaton. "You promised me this wouldn't happen. You're the one who's got to catch him."

Inside Marella's vast bedchamber she paused and looked around. 'Crets could be anywhere. Her daughter collected stuffed animals: bears, poodles, crocodiles, armadillos, koala bears, goats, seals, ducks, and Sesame Street critters. Some of these animals were lifelike, some mythological, some were polka-dotted or parti-colored parodies of genuine terrestrial fauna—but they occupied every niche, cranny, and bureau top in the room, making a quick sighting of Seaton's companion unlikely even had 'Crets consented to jump up and down in the middle of this inanimate menagerie. And he had not consented to do that.

Stevie peered at the three-story tray assembly across the room in which Marella had stacked many of her stuffed animals, but the living monkey did not seem to be there. He had either gone under one of the beds or concealed himself in the step-down closet about twelve feet to Stevie's left. This closet had a small inner door opening into a section of attic over the kitchen—a hatch, really—and the last time Stevie had checked, this door had been securely fastened by a wooden block on a large skewering nail. Unfortunately the door to the

step-down closet itself stood conspicuously ajar, and if either
Teddy or Marella had peeked into the attic without afterward
twisting that block back into place, 'Crets might have fled into
the attic's peculiarly populated darkness. They would never get
him out. Heat from the kitchen warmed that musty labyrinth
even in the winter, making it livable, and its dimensions sometimes seemed greater than those of the kitchen-cum-dining-
area it allegedly crowned, especially to intruders not really ac-
quainted with the place. The last thing Stevie wanted was a
death's-head capuchin haunting her attic, prowling up and
down its cobwebbed promenades with an exit into Marella's
room as handy as any nearby 7–Eleven store. She could envision the little monster slipping out at night to sit on her daughter's pillow and to refresh himself at her jugular. And if ever
Marella propped one of her stuffed animals on this pillow before retiring, and if ever Stevie looked in on her in the detail-
obliterating gloom of midnight, Stevie herself would mistake
the toy animal for the real-life capuchin and straightway suffer
cardiac arrest. . . .

"Seaton, get in here!"

"I'm right beside you, Mrs. Crye."

"Look under the beds. Look in the closet. Pray he hasn't
escaped into the attic. I'm at the end of my rope with both of
you."

Seaton did as she bade him do. 'Crets was under neither of
the twin beds, for he had hidden himself in the step-down
closet. Seaton found him on a musty upholstered trunk behind
a curtain of summer hangups. He dragged the monkey back into Marella's room with an amelodic accompaniment of
screeches ('Cretsie's) and ouches (his own). Flakes of foil wrap-
ping adhered to the capuchin's beard; glitters of shattered
Sucret twinkled above the long slash of his lip. His eye sockets
held the deceptive emptiness they usually held.

"Get him out of here, Seaton. Take him back to Columbus
on that time bomb of a motorcycle of yours."

"Yes, ma'am."

Finally, after almost two hours of her hinting, suggesting,
ordering, and demanding, the Cryes' uninvited guests took

their leave. Teddy and Marella were sad to see them go. They waved at the figures on the motorcycle and called out invitations for a future visit. Stevie, inside, stood at the kitchen sink washing her hands in scalding-hot water.

XXI

An hour or so later she stood in her study reappraising the Exceleriter. What had Seaton Benecke done to it this time? The room was warmer now, almost comfortable. She let her fingers hover speculatively over the keyboard, confident that if the machine was "even better than it was before," she would finally get some answers from it. They might not be the answers she wanted, or answers even remotely reassuring, but her knowledge about herself and those she loved would significantly increase, and the most important thing now was to learn through the typewriter's preternatural instructorship without losing her grip on reality. She had no desire to hang above her front door a shingle bearing the inscription *Stevenson Crye, Madwoman of Wickrath County.* How, though, did you get answers from a willful, uncooperative machine?

You confront it, Stevie told herself. You talk to it. You ask it questions and so establish a dialogue.

On the same sheet of paper on which Seaton Benecke had typed a series of *t* words, she typed a question, letting her fingers fall as lightly as an acid rain. The result would be either growth or corrosion.

Who are you?

Three words and a question mark. They had formed in her mind, coursed through her nervous and locomotor systems, and sprouted as if by magic in a tiny patch of virgin whiteness. Through the agency of her Exceleriter she had translated thought to paper. Nothing strange about that. Millions of people performed similar feats of thought transference every day, often with concepts more revolutionary or queries more complex than "Who are you?" Of course only she of all the people in the world knew the terrible complexity of this particular three-word question.

As Stevie read and reread what she had typed, the Exceleriter depressed its own shift-lock key and responded with a flurry of uppercase characters that jumped out at the eye.

> I AM A FIGMENT OF YOUR IMAGINATION, STEVENSON CRYE, MADWOMAN OF WICKRATH COUNTY. I AM YOU.

A patent lie, for her hands were clasped in front of her and they had not moved to the keyboard to frame this response. Nor had any such thought taken shape in her mind. Standing immobile over a machine that operated itself, you could not transfer to paper a thought you had never had. Perhaps Seaton Benecke, 'Crets, and this infernal typewriter were conspiring to drive her crazy. By plucking the phrase *Madwoman of Wickrath County* from a previous moment's fleeting reverie, the Exceleriter's motive intelligence—whatever elements might compose it—seemed bent on this very end. Stevie typed,

> I'm sorry. That just isn't so.

To which the Exceleriter replied,

> THEN PERHAPS YOU ARE A FIGMENT OF MY IMAGINATION, STEVIE, FOR ONE OF US MUST BELONG TO THE OTHER. I WAS GIVING YOU THE BENEFIT OF THE DOUBT ON THE ASSUMPTION THAT EITHER YOU OR YOUR HUSBAND PAID FOR THIS MACHINE.

After which a genuine exchange ensued:

> If you were a figment of <u>my</u> imagination, we wouldn't be engaged in this quarrel. Ted bought you, but nobody bargained on having you periodically wrest control from me.
> WHO ARE YOU ADDRESSING, STEVIE? THE PDE EXCELERITER 79 OR THE INTELLIGENCE YOU PERCEIVE BEHIND IT?
> I don't know. Yes, I do. The latter.
> AM I MANIPULATING YOU? ARE YOU MANIPULATING ME? OR ARE WE PERHAPS PARTNERS IN A BIOMECHANICAL SYMBIOSIS?

There's nothing mechanical about the intelligence that asks such questions. Who are you?

I AM THE FIGMENT OF AN IMAGINATION THAT IMAGINES YOU TO BE A FIGMENT OF MINE. OR VICE VERSA.

Stevie refused to accept this last gambit. It was stupid stuff. An argument from one of those adolescent head games you played in college. Was the world real? Were our dreams intrusions from another reality? Did we create God or He us? . . . None of the answers to these questions, no matter how convolute or clever, released you from your awareness that you had earned a disappointing B— on your last comparative lit. paper and that finals were fast approaching. That Lyndon Baines Johnson reminded you of a Hollywood character actor and that American soldiers were dying in Vietnam. That your complexion warranted a major Estée Lauder overhaul and that three days after you thought your period had ended you were continuing to spot. . . . To hell with What's-the-sound-of-one-hand-clapping? and Is-the-scholar-Sōshū-a-man-dreaming-himself-a-butterfly-or-a-butterfly-dreaming-itself-a-man? Even if illusory, the world published its scattershot proclamations and made you kowtow to them. You could not get away.

Only about two inches of paper remained beneath the Exceleriter's last assertion. If she wanted answers instead of inane riddles, she would have to get down to business. Stevie typed,

Tell me about Ted. Finish my nightmare for me. If you're my husband, talk to me as Ted talked.

Of course Ted had never talked through the intercession of a typewriter, and the machine responded to Stevie's plea by turning itself off. By way of experiment she jabbed the key that restored its hum. It stubbornly shut down again. She jabbed it back to life a second time, and although it did not counter this move with a third emphatic shutdown, it hummed without typing a line.

Teddy simultaneously knocked on the door and stuck his head into the room. "Mom, you busy? Dr. Elsa's here. Can you come down and talk to her?"

Stevie's heart performed a clumsy somersault. Guilt-stricken, *she* turned the machine off. Then, affecting nonchalance, she hid her colloquy with the Exceleriter by positioning herself in front of the typewriter. Teddy could not see the incriminating evidence, but as Stevie looked into his eyes she realized that he had no wish to. Her guilt began to diffuse, her heart to soft-pedal its breakneck surgings.

"He fixed it for you, didn't he?" Teddy asked. "That guy from Columbus, Seeley Bennett or whatever his name was."

"Yep," said Stevie. "It's fixed."

"He's a nice guy, Mom. Do you like him? He's probably not too young for you. Sort of halfway between Dad and me, agewise."

"Age wisdom, Teddy, is one area where you may surpass young Seeley Bennett."

"Are you going to let him visit again?"

"Go back downstairs, Teddy, and fix Dr. Elsa and me a pot of coffee. I'll be with her as soon as I've straightened up a little."

"Yes, ma'am."

XXII

Dr. Elsa was there because earlier that afternoon she had run into Tiffany McGuire's mother at the grocery store and learned from her that Marella had come down sick again. She was checking up, Dr. Elsa was. She insisted on giving the girl a quick but methodical examination right there in the kitchen. Marella submitted to this probing because her brother had gone off to Pete Wightman's house again, removing him as an onlooker, and because she was genuinely fond of Dr. Elsa. Not very many kids in Barclay could command an unsolicited house call. It was an honor to have your tongue depressed in your own home, the smell of fresh-perked coffee perfuming the air. That's what Stevie told Marella, anyway, and the child had the good grace to acquiesce in these sentiments.

"You feel all right today, then?" Dr. Elsa asked, peering into the corners of Marella's eyes.

"I felt all right pretty soon after Mrs. McGuire brought me home."

"Just that nervous stomach again, hey, young lady?"

"I guess so."

"It was more than that," Stevie said. "She woke up in the middle of the night complaining of a fever."

"No, I didn't," Marella protested, shocked.

"Yes, you did. You said, 'Hot, Mama. Oh, Mama, I'm so hot.' You couldn't move. You wanted me to call Dr. Elsa."

"Mama, I did not! I slept all night."

Stevie looked at Dr. Elsa. "You know how kids are, Elsa. They wake up in the middle of the night and hold a complete conversation with you, but in the morning they don't remember a word of it."

"They usually remember when they're sick, honey."

"I *wasn't* sick last night, Dr. Elsa. Mama made us go to bed right after the Duke boys, and I slept fine. I was afraid I wouldn't, but I did. Mama didn't even put the bucket beside my bed."

"Well, she seemed all right when she first went up. But she woke me up moaning about how hot she was. She said she was melting. I told her to turn back her blanket, but she said she couldn't move. Finally she asked me to call you."

Standing beside Dr. Elsa's chair, her waist partly encircled by the doctor's arm, Marella rolled her eyes heavenward and shook her head. She was biting her lower lip to keep from speaking.

"Why didn't you?" Dr. Elsa asked.

"I've been a nuisance all week. Used your typewriter Tuesday, bent your ear that evening, drove to Wickrath yesterday to see you. I couldn't impose again, Elsa, not in the middle of the night."

"Even if your daughter was paralyzed? What would it take to get you to call me, kiddo? Rabies? Bubonic plague?"

"I wasn't paralyzed. I was sleeping."

"I know the difference between paralysis and sleep!" Stevie snapped at her daughter. To Dr. Elsa she said, "I took care of the problem myself. There wasn't any need to call you."

"What did you do?"

"I pulled her covers back for her and . . ."

"And what, honey?"

"And . . ." Stevie glanced at Marella in sudden overmastering bafflement. She could not have seen her daughter as she remembered seeing her. A person whose body has been reduced to a living head atop a field-stripped rib cage does not regenerate her internal organs and her entire epidermis in a single night. She certainly does not arise and go walking about the following day. "And I covered her up again," Stevie lamely concluded. "She was perfectly all right. There'd never been any reason to worry."

"Wait a minute," Dr. Elsa said. "You convinced yourself she could move just by foldin' down her covers and then flippin' them back up again?"

"I didn't have to convince myself," Stevie said, trying to tack about, running against a wind that had blown up from some squally gulf of consciousness. "She was asleep when I went to check on her. She never had a chance to complain about not being able to move. I wasn't even worried about *that*, Elsa."

"Mama, listen to you!"

Dr. Elsa removed her arm from Marella's waist and tipped another teaspoon of sugar into her earthenware coffee mug. "Stevie, kid, your scriptwriter's got to be either Salvador Dali or Groucho Marx. None of this makes a lick of sense."

No, it didn't, did it? For a minute there she had gone off on a side trail to which linear reality denied her access. She had traveled down that trail until hit between the eyes by the irrefutable fact of its inaccessibility. Coming back was not easy, either. People watched you scrambling toward them as if you were a defector from a Communist country, a potential untrustworthy spy. . . .

"My scriptwriter's upstairs," Stevie muttered.

"Mama, you only dreamed you heard me saying those things. Your dream mixed you all up."

Stevie smiled at the girl. "That's right, daughter mine. I had a vivid nightmare. I almost started to believe it."

"You *did* believe it," Dr. Elsa accused.

"Well, I'm back now, Elsa. I'm back by way of Franz Kafka Country, and you and Marella can get off my case." She left the table to pour herself another cup of coffee from the percolator. Just what she needed. Another unhealthy dose of caffeine. Dr. Elsa and her daughter exchanged some whispered badinage, at the conclusion of which Marella grabbed her coat and went outdoors again. "What was that about?" Stevie demanded, coming back to the table.

"I just gave her a clean bill of health."

"Why don't you give me a bill, Elsa? I owe you—"

"Kiddo, you couldn't possibly pay me what you owe me, that's what a nuisance you are." She toasted Stevie with her coffee mug, smiling her beautiful bone-weary last-hour-of-the-telethon smile. "And one bill it would be knuckle-headed folly to give you is a clean bill of health. You don't deserve it. You deserve a kick in the can for not calling louder for help. 'S far as that goes, I deserve one for not giving you a complete checkup yesterday morning."

Stevie sipped her coffee, which tasted bitter even after two dollops of sugar. A kind of languidly revolving, galaxy-armed caffeine slick made a mirror in her mug, and she could see her face in it, or her eyes anyway, and if her haggard reflection had even an iota's correspondence to the face it reflected, why, she was sick indeed. She belonged in emergency care. She required immediate treatment. They should strap her under the Clinac 18 and fire away. She looked so bad—to use a quaint expression of her father's—that she would have to get better to die. Of course the iridescent scum on a mug of coffee hardly qualified as the most flattering of looking-glasses, but the look in Dr. Elsa's eyes confirmed the coffee's bleak assessment. Dr. Elsa thought she had deteriorated since yesterday. Dr. Elsa thought she was the Madwoman of Wickrath County.

Neither of the women spoke. They sat sipping their coffee and nibbling on the vanilla wafers that Stevie had poured into a plastic container in the middle of the table. This silence persisted, without discomfort, for five or six minutes.

Stevie and Dr. Elsa had a relationship predicated on mutual esteem and support. Dr. Sam was himself in ill health, although he tried hard to carry his half of the burden of the Kensingtons' two-town practice, and sometimes his failing stamina as both doctor and husband placed heavy physical and emotional demands on Stevie's friend. According to Dr. Elsa herself, she and Dr. Sam had not been lovers for three or four years (indeed, they had never been superstars or even journeyman performers in the bedroom), and of late the gentle, unassuming, conscientious Dr. Sam had begun to show more interest in Cherokee and Creek artifacts than in his wife. He preferred shambling around an archeological dig in Muscogee County to taking her to dinner in Columbus or to a college theater production in Ladysmith. He kept a box of arrowheads and stone tool points under their bed in the same spot where, as a younger man, he had kept his Sheik prophylactics.

Stevie had listened to these melancholy confessions in the same spirit that Dr. Elsa later lent a sympathetic ear to her own tales of woe during the difficult months immediately before and right after Ted's death. Now they could sit together without talking, secure in their friendship, their moods subtly buoyed by each other's presence. Five, ten, or even twenty minutes could pass before either of them felt compelled or even distantly moved to speak. Stevie had seen men sit in this fashion for hours—Ted with Dr. Sam, her father with a hunting buddy— but in all her friendships with other women, no matter how young or old the friend, urgent conversation or frivolous chatter had always precluded the possibility, even the thought, of these protracted moments of calming silence. She had had to lose her husband to discover that they could in fact occur.

Finally, altogether casually, Dr. Elsa said, "Did you get your shelving paper in?"

Stevie started. "What?"

"Your shelving paper. Stuff I gave you yesterday. Did you get it into your cabinets?"

"No, I—"

"Where is it? I'll help you. Won't take us half an hour to put down if you let me help."

"It's . . . it's upstairs."

"Upstairs? You're not puttin' shelving paper in your bookcases, are you?"

Stevie told Dr. Elsa that she had cut up the examination-table paper to use for rough drafts. She did not tell her friend that she had halved these sheets so that her Exceleriter, once the pieces were taped together, could continue to generate copy long beyond the eleven-inch limit of a leaf of ordinary typing paper. Her inability to admit this fact made her apprehensive; it seemed to undermine the foundation of trust on which she and Dr. Elsa had built their closeness.

"You that hard up, kiddo? You have to beg rough-draft paper and cut it up in strips so you can get it in your typewriter?"

"I'm not that hard up. I just . . . I just like the way it feels."

"You and the cockroaches."

"I like the way it works in the typewriter." That was as close as she could come to explaining herself. The two women stared at each other, yesterday's conversation in Wickrath flashing between them, wordlessly reenacting itself in their eyes. Stevie knew what Dr. Elsa was thinking, and Dr. Elsa had penetrated the guilty secret of the examination-table paper, although she obviously believed that Stevie was carrying a grotesque illusion pickaback, staggering beneath its weight. Now the silence between them was not so comfortable. "Speaking of my typewriter," Stevie said, "Seaton Benecke was here today."

"Marella told me. She and Teddy were both pretty snowed by his monkey. I didn't even know he had such a creature. His mother wasn't the sort to go in for pets, if I remember her right."

"Tell me about Seaton, Elsa."

Dr. Elsa vowed that she knew very little about the Beneckes.

Twenty years ago Dr. Sam had met the clan's patriarch, Hamlin, during a Columbus-wide search for a secondhand typewriter for the Barclay clinic. That long ago Seaton, the youngest of the Benecke boys, was only five or six and not yet in school. In fact, his daddy often took him to the office-supply company, a pudgy little boy with hair the color of white gold and eyes like cracked blue aggies. When Dr. Sam first saw him, he was sitting in the back with the used and broken typewriters, peering into the works of one of the newer models and poking his finger at the typebars in their semicircular orchestra pit. Sam's first glance into the work area made him think that Hamlin Benecke was employing wizened midgets or gnomes to handle really delicate repairs, but he soon recognized his error and gazed in wonder at the five-year-old, a white-haired Rumpelstiltskin who engraved a lasting picture on his memory.

The typewriter Sam finally bought that day was the very one, a Smith-Corona, with which Seaton had been fiddling when the physician entered the store. In twenty years that machine had given seven different secretaries at the Barclay clinic its heart and soul. Although it no longer worked terribly well, it was still an acceptable backup, and over the years Dr. Sam had often attributed its long-term reliability to the keen ministrations of five-year-old Seaton on that fateful first day. That Seaton was now a full-time typewriter repairman hardly surprised Dr. Elsa. He was a wizard. He had the touch. He had been born with a typewriter ribbon in his mouth.

"Elsa, he's strange."

"Oh, I know he's not your usual knock-back-a-few-beers repairman type, but I'm not Dr. Kildare, either."

"I don't mean he's eccentric, Elsa, I mean he's *strange.*"

"Yeah, I know. Never lookin' at you when he talks. The monkey. The motorcycle. Never bein' satisfied at the job he's so good at. He's one unhappy kid, Seaton Benecke." The two women stared at each other again. "Something to do with his homelife when he was smaller, I think. Hamlin and Lynnette didn't always live together. He'd be one place, she'd be another. Not divorced or legally separated or anything like that, just a going-of-their-own-ways until they took a notion to meet up again and act like husband and wife for a few months before they started all over in the apartness part of their relationship. That probably confused Seaton some. It may have made him strange. But he's not so strange, Stevie, he could make your typewriter work by itself. He's homegrown strange, not Martian strange.''

Stevie slammed her coffee mug down. Shards of murky liquid sloshed out on the table. "By which you mean *I'm* Martian strange, don't you?"

"Bad choice of words, honey. Misplaced modifier. Dangling antecedent. Something like that. English was never my strong suit.''

"Let me tell you how strange Seaton Benecke is, Elsa." And with angry animation Stevie recounted the young man's extraordinary postprandial behavior with the monkey 'Crets: how he had lied about cutting his finger yesterday, how he had let the capuchin suck blood from the tip of that finger, how he had admitted that bloodsucking was "just something 'Crets liked to do" (as if this shared activity were no less commonplace than playing checkers in the park), and how the monkey's empty stare seemed a kind of proxy for the direct gaze Seaton himself could not usually manage. That was how strange Seaton was. If *that* was not Martian strange, Stevie did not know what might qualify. Despite the heat of this outburst, however, she coolly declined to accuse the young man of sabotaging her Exceleriter, even though he most certainly had.

Laconically Dr. Elsa said, " 'S that gospel, Stevie?''

"I'm Martian strange—I'm an unreliable witness—but ask Teddy and Marella. They'll corroborate my story.''

After a while, having cleaned up Stevie's spilt coffee with a paper towel, Dr. Elsa mused, "Once upon a time a body behaved that way would get herself—himself seems *really* strange—a far-reachin' reputation as a witch. Outer space wouldn't enter the matter at all.''

"What're you talking about, Elsa?''

"Just an anecdote I remember one of my professors at Augusta Medical College tellin'. It was in an anatomy course, and sometimes this old bird got backtracked, thrown off-trail, by these little historical acorns his mind squirreled away. I'm mixin' my metaphors, aren't I? Anyway, I remember this digression very well because he was talkin' about mammaries.''

Stevie lifted her head and her eyebrows at the same time.

"He mentioned that some people, men as well as women, have what you call in five-syllable medical talk 'adventitious nipples.' These usually occur on a person's milk line, a big old U goin' from one breast down the flank to the groin and up the other side to the other breast. Most of the time they're small, these adventitious nipples, little enflamed-lookin' puckerings of flesh, and they're not all that uncommon. Old-timey country folks call 'em witches' teats. You know why?''

"I'm dying to hear." (Well, she was.)

"Because witches used them to feed their familiars. That was the medieval belief, anyway, and it got over to Puritan America and pretty soon down the Atlantic coast to Appalachia and the Georgia colony.''

Dr. Elsa explained that familiars were minor demons that could assume the shapes of small animals—usually cats or toads—to attend their witch mistresses on their missionary dunnings for the devil. The familiars received their nourishment directly from the witch who owned them, drinking her blood through a mole, wart, scab, or providentially concealed witch's teat (supposing, of course, a satanic rather than a divine providence for the concealment of same). Dedicated witch-hunters made it a point to disrobe suspected minions of the Unholy One and search their bodies for these telltale teats. Womenfolk who possessed them often got burned in a faggoty bonfire or teetered into a half-frozen New England pool. This was almost as hard on the familiars as on the ladies who underwent these fatal purifications. It didn't pay to have an adventitious nipple in the Bad Old Days. . . .

"Seaton's not female," Stevie said.

"Male witches are warlocks, kiddo. Maybe this twenty-six-year-old typewriter repairman is a warlock. That monkey's his familiar.''

"Stop it, Elsa.''

"It doesn't mean too much he didn't nurse the critter on an adventitious nipple, either. A finger's a good substitute. Any teatlike protuberance'll do."

"Elsa, that damn monkey ate an entire fried egg with a cocktail fork. Bloodsucking demons don't eat fried eggs, do they?"

"Over-easy or sunny-side up?"

"Broken-yolked, Elsa. You're making fun of me. You're making fun of me the same way that blasted typewriter does."

Dr. Elsa leaned over and caught Stevie's wrists. "Honey, the boy's weird. His brothers have done better than he has. One of 'em's the supply company's business manager, with a degree in accountin' from Clemson. The other's an airline pilot with Eastern. Seaton has an organ-grinder monkey he lets nibble on a finger lesion. It's not safe nor sanitary nor pleasant to behold, but one thing else it also ain't, honey, is supernatural."

"*You* brought up familiars, adventitious nipples, and so on, Elsa. I didn't. You did."

"Just to show you how all-fired silly the whole thing is. You need a break from your work. I'll tell you what. Tomorrow after church I'll take Teddy and Marella out to our place for Sunday dinner and some cards or something. If Sam's not hip-deep in *Long Before Columbus* or some other *In Search of Lost Lacrosse Sticks* volume, maybe he'll play pool with 'em, take 'em fishin', something. You just relax. Go to Columbus and shop—the stores are open—or drive up in the state park for an outing. Do you good and help you too, kiddo."

"No, Elsa, I—"

"Honey, it's settled." She released Stevie's wrist. "I'll be by tomorrow at twelve-thirty. You got that?"

Stevie nodded.

XXIII

Tell me about Ted. Finish my nightmare for me. If you're my husband, talk to me as Ted talked.

That was what she had written before going downstairs to see Dr. Elsa. During her absence the Exceleriter had composed a reply, four lines of doggerel. This quatrain exhausted the space remaining at the bottom of the paper:

> TED CANNOT TALK.
> TED CANNOT WALK.
> DONT BE MISLED:
> YOUR TED IS DEAD.

"That's one thing I already know!" Stevie retorted. She yanked the page out of the machine, tore the page into pieces, and dropped the pieces into her wastebasket.

Then she went back downstairs to prepare dinner. Hamburger soup and Syrian bread. Marella had asked for Syrian bread.

XXIV

Stevie coaxed her daughter into bed by ten-thirty. Teddy took longer. He was of the impression that, as a teen-ager, he had the inalienable right to stay up on weekends until midnight or later. Stevie did not agree with him. Although she cited his basketball coach's dictum about eating right and getting plenty of rest, and although she finally threatened to ground him for a couple of weeks if he didn't stop smarting off and screwing around, it was nearly twelve by the time he trudged upstairs to his bedroom. Some of his delaying tactics—overeager offers of help in the kitchen—had been amusing, but his experimental backtalk when she refused him permission to watch either "Saturday Night Live" or the ancient Lon Chaney, Jr., film on another channel had not tickled her at all. That was when she had raised the ante with her grounding threat and so bluffed him up the stairs.

Usually Teddy was a good kid, but what if he had chosen to test her mettle by intensifying and protracting his mutiny? Moral force was an effective bludgeon only if you waved it in front of people whose concept of morality coincided with your own. Teen-agers, meanwhile, sometimes seemed to be doing their contortionist dances amid the shards of the tablets that Moses brought down from Sinai. . . .

Well, maybe it isn't *that* bad, Stevie thought, running herself a tub of hot water in the downstairs bathroom. Teddy's not into drugs or alcohol, and his interest in girls has pretty much been confined to flirtatious banter and long-distance ogling. I think. Anyway, he's not usually one for backtalk or armed resistance. He's just trying to spread his wings a little. That's hard to do in a twelve-by-twenty kitchen with a breakfast bar, a space heater, and an intractable mom. What he needs is . . . what he needs is a father.

—Ted, Ted, you ran out on me when I needed you to take care of these needs. Here I am wringing my hands over the deadly and tortuous naiveté of the teen-age male mind. You knew I would be. You knew I'd be cursing you for running out on us.

Stevie hated the winter. Because the space heaters in the kitchen and the den had to heat the bathroom too, she could not take a bath without leaving the door open. Maybe she would not have been in such a hurry to see Teddy off to bed had she been able to settle into the steamy waters of her tub behind a securely shut door. The heat of the water kept you from freezing for a brief bath, but if you closed the door, the bathroom quickly cooled, chilling the water by cold-blooded convection. By the time you stepped out of the tub your body was helplessly aquiver, and the joy of luxuriating in warmth for the first time since abandoning your electric blanket that morning had become a barefoot forced march through the storage lockers of a meat-packing plant. If the door stayed open, however, you could soak an extra three minutes and dry yourself feeling no colder than you might on a trick-or-treating expedition in October.

Immersed in the rapidly cooling water, Stevie lathered and shaved her legs. Dr. Elsa had offered to take the kids tomorrow afternoon, and Stevie had just about decided to let her. She had to get away from that machine upstairs. Tomorrow, if this evening's Exceleriter experiment went as planned, she would be ready for some recuperative therapy: shopping, a movie, dinner in a Chinese restaurant, maybe even a cocktail or two. Whatever happened, she would need time to think about the results and Dr. Elsa's selfless offer would give her that time. Stevie's bath had become a preparatory ritual, beautifying and ablutionary. It was almost as if she were getting ready for a date.

Afterward, clad only in a flannel nightgown beneath which her naked torso and limbs felt sensually pliant, that and a quilted robe that cloaked her in a corona of middle-aged frumpiness, Stevie passed through the unheated downstairs rooms and climbed the steps to her study. She was Lady Godiva in a greatcoat last worn by a French soldier on the retreat from Moscow. Her Exceleriter, on the other hand, was not only naked but warm. She had left the dust cover off the machine. Further, although she had purposely refrained from rolling a sheet of paper into place, it had been typing in her absence— presumably *after* the kids had gone to sleep, so scrupulous was it about concealing its ability from everyone but her. Stevie could tell that it had been typing by the warmth of its metal cover and the illegible black-on-black letters encircling the platen, a jumble of struck-over characters that she would never be able to decipher.

"Damn you," she said.

From her filing cabinet she extracted the story about Ted, Seaton Benecke in his role as "dosimetrist," and the Clinac 18. One more time, she thought. She taped four more sheets of typing paper to the page ending,

"I fell apart down deep," Crye said, a dead hand on his wife's forehead. "If I appeared to give up, Stevie, it was only because it was time for me to pay."

She positioned this train of pages so that the Exceleriter—if it had not already completed her dream without benefit of paper—could resume its transcription. Why, after all, was it time for Ted to pay? What debt had maneuvered him to his uncharacteristic surrender?

"Tonight," Stevie told the typewriter, "you're going to do what I want you to do. Tonight you're going to *finish* this business."

She checked the children. They appeared to be sleeping soundly. She put her electric blanket on its highest setting—something she should have done earlier—and reluctantly shed her robe. Then she eased herself between the icy sheets (a lukewarm chicken filet, hey, in a pocket of frozen pita bread) and waited for her coverlet to begin to toast her. This took a while. Her feet tingled, and she moved her naked legs up and down knowing that the friction would only just appreciably boost the temperature inside the covers. God! how she hated this weather. It had been a long, long day, and to end it by galloping a hundred-meter dash flat on her back hardly constituted a peaceful retirement. Some writers had winter homes in the tropics. Some writers never ventured any farther north than Saint-Tropez. Georgia was supposed to be in the Sun Belt, but tell that to her frost-bit tootsies. . . .

Eventually the bed warmed, and Stevie left off her loping-in-place for some goal-directed mental exertion. She was going to make the Exceleriter finish transcribing her nightmare by insuring that she *dreamt* that nightmare, sequence by eerie sequence, right to the end. You could influence the contents of your dreams, after all, by preprogramming your brain with the desired dream imagery. You thought hard about this imagery while still in that hazy hypersusceptible mental state just prior to sleep. Of course, to continue to think deliberately about anything during this unreal period was to dissolve its edges and prolong wakefulness. You had to balance conscious thought with the afflatus of either fantasy or unconscious desire. You had to drift without losing your direction.

Stevie began to drift. She drifted past her husband's over-elaborate chrome-plated steel-blue coffin on its bier at the graveside services in the Barclay cemetery. Faces melted and blurred in the rain; lilies nodded their heads like constellations of molting swans. Down in the soundproofed crypt from which the half dead were sometimes half resurrected, deep in the angry red ache of her confusion and disillusionment, there in the Ladysmith treatment room, she drifted between the focusing points of the Clinac 18's lasers.

And there, floating at the intersection of those laser points, drifted Theodore Martin Crye, Sr., half resurrected for the purposes of dream. Righting himself beneath the eye of the linear accelerator, revolving out of the weightlessness of death to conform to the gravity-bound criteria of her own disembodied eyes, her husband approached her like a living man. . . .

XXV

Frightened, Stevie sat up in bed. A figure stood in her doorway. She had a hunch, a momentarily bloodcurdling intuition, that it had been standing there for quite a long time. It did not speak or move, and the melancholy disposition of its head and limbs led her to believe that the threat it posed was not the threat of bodily harm or indiscriminate violence. It posed a threat, though, and her fear of the figure's presence encompassed but did not define this unnamed threat. She squinted across the cold room, waiting for a sign.

At last she said, "Ted?"

The figure in the doorway shifted its stance.

"Ted?" Her voice sounded peeved as well as fearful. "Ted?"

"Ma'am?"

"Teddy!" she exclaimed sotto voce. "You just about scared me silly. What are you doing up? Are you standing there in your ever-lovin' jockey shorts? You haven't got the sense God gave a green snake."

The boy did not move. Stevie could see that he had his arms folded across his chest, his hands gripping his shoulders, but this feeble postural tactic was his only concession to the cold. In the yellow-green light coming into her room from the arc lamp on the corner of Hazel and O'Connor Streets, just outside, he looked like Michelangelo's David in a pair of bikini briefs. The foolish bumpkin.

"Teddy, what the hell are you doing?"

"Mom," he began uncertainly. Then again: "Mom, I heard you come up, I haven't been asleep, I couldn't sleep—"

Oh, my God, thought Stevie. He's heard the Exceleriter typing away. He's scared, and he wants an explanation. What am I going to tell him? Do I make up an elaborate lie about teleprinters and computer hookups, or do I confess the truth and risk estranging his belief as stupidly as I estranged Elsa's. Or would he, maybe, believe? And, believing, help restore my own psychological equilibrium? Ted's gone, and I'm hungry— positively famished—for an ally. Nevertheless, Stevenson Crye, you'd better proceed on tiptoe. . . .

"Did you hear my typewriter, Teddy?"

His voice betrayed his puzzlement. "No, ma'am. You were only in your study a couple of minutes. I didn't even think you tried to work."

"I didn't." Well, that exchange had probably not done much to lift her in the boy's estimation. She had framed a ridiculous non sequitur of a question, received a straightforward if baffled reply, and followed that up with an even more baffling denial of the necessity of her original question. "What's bothering you, then?" Stevie hastened to ask.

"I'm sorry about sassing you tonight, Mom. You know, calling you a fogey and cursing under my breath."

"Fogey I heard, the cursing I didn't."

"I said, 'Oh, hell, what a crock of shit.' "

"Confessing the crime's plenty. You don't have to reprise it for me. Senility's rapid approach hasn't completely destroyed my imagination.''

''Yeah, I know. I'm sorry. I just—'' The articulation of this last sentiment stymied him. He shifted his weight, rubbing his instep with one bare foot and gently chafing his upper arms. Stevie marveled again at his disregard of the cold. Slowly, though, it was penetrating his defenses, the neglectful machismo of the teen-age boy: the cold and a worry still unvoiced.

''That's not the only reason you came in here, is it?''

Teddy said nothing.

''Is it? Something's bothering you. You're an okay kid, but you don't usually lose much sleep fretting about your mama's wounded feelings.''

She could see his dim silhouette disgustedly shaking its head. His knuckles stood out from each arm like the tuning knobs on the neck of a guitar. ''I wish Dad was here. *Damn!* do I ever.''

''Were,'' Stevie corrected him. ''You wish Dad *were* here. So do I, Teddy. For both our sakes.''

He turned to go, and suddenly Stevie was afraid he would leave without revealing the worry that had kept him awake. He would internalize it, letting it scarify him, a festering, malign ulcer of worry. The boy wanted his father to talk to, but he had only her. He had come to her in the dark because it was easier than in the hard-edged, satirical light of day. At night, if not finally susceptible to the balm of sunny reason, worries were at least mockproof. She had to keep Teddy in the room or he would conceal from her forever the mysterious source of his upset.

''Come back, Teddy. Come back right now.''

Reluctantly he turned back toward her, now a silhouette, now a lamp-lit sculpture, beautiful in either guise, the room's darkness a cloak he wore almost jauntily, its chill a kind of ambient halo through which he moved in mute obedience to her command. When he paused at the foot of the bed, Stevie felt that she was in communion with a phantom of her own consciousness, a revenant from the underworld of her desire. Teddy was alive, but momentarily he seemed the youthful ghost of his own dead father. Ghosts were always impervious to the cold.

"You've got something on your mind," Stevie said. "This is as good a time as any to talk about it. Get in the bed."

"Ma'am?" His *de rigueur* teen-age reluctance had become a *de rigueur* sonny-boy disbelief.

"It's cold, Teddy. I'm not going to let you stand there nine-tenths naked in temperatures that would give a penguin pneumonia. The bed's warm, finally. Crawl in beside me and we'll have a chat."

He obeyed, and instantly Stevie could feel the cold of his body radiating through the comfortable oven of her bedding. How had he stood it? How could he haunt the winter night in only his underwear? Stevie shifted over toward the boy, slid her arm behind his neck, and pulled him to her. His chin—a smooth knob of snowy marble—rested on her breastbone, just beneath her throat, while his eyes gleamed up at her like those of a captured animal, bright with suspicion and fear. Indeed, holding him was like embracing a statue with living eyes. Stevie chafed the boy's upper arm with her hand. They lay this way for some time, neither of them speaking.

Finally Stevie said, "Now." The boy turned to his back, and she released the pressure on her arm by slipping it out from under him. "Pretend I'm whoever you want me to be and tell me your troubles, Teddy."

"Mom—" He moved his head back and forth on the pillow. "Mom, it's embarrassing. I can't. It's silly and embarrassing, and I'll probably be okay about it if I just let it go for a while."

"Come on, Teddy," she urged him. "Blurt it out. You didn't wander in here just to play the part of Barclay's resident stoic."

Exhaling cavernously, Teddy shivered down the length of his body. He tilted his head back as far as it would go. "I'm still a boy," he whispered. "I'm still a goddamn boy."

"Of course you are. You've only recently become a teen-ager. You're not supposed to be Christopher Reeve or Kareem Abdul-Jabbar or whoever this week's hero is. Listen, son, even the Man of Steel started out as Superboy. The progression's well established and completely natural."

"I'm not Superboy. I'm *only* a boy."

Stevie smoothed back Teddy's bangs, stroked his head consolingly. "Not by my lights, you're not. You're growing into a handsome and usually pretty helpful young man, and the rate you're going's plenty fast enough for me. I'm not quite ready to start prefixing my name with Grandma, if that's okay by you."

"Well, maybe that'll *never* happen," he said bitterly. "Maybe you don't have a thing to worry about."

His bitterness surprised Stevie. She propped herself on one elbow and carefully scrutinized his chin-up profile in the ghastly light. "Teddy, I think you're going to have to spell this out for me. It's not coming together. You've just started to get a tickle of hair under your arms and you're already worried about your ability to father children? Is that it?"

Another angry, exasperated sigh. "Something like that, yeah."

"At your age, young man, you'd better be worried if you *do* father some gullible young thing's baby. That's what you'd really better worry about."

"Mom, you still don't understand."

It was true, she didn't. So far their mother-to-son talk had accomplished little but their mutual frustration. He was demoralized by her inability to deduce his problem, she by his refusal simply to speak it aloud. Obviously the pangs of puberty had begun to rack him, and the sudden trauma of these changes required that she give him her heartfelt sympathy, even if absolute understanding continued to elude her. Damn Ted for not being here. Damn him! . . . No, that was too strong. Besides, Teddy was flesh of his flesh, and in that mystical sense, at least, Ted was with her even at this moment, in the living, suffering wraith of his son.

"Explain it to me, Teddy. Explaining it can't hurt any worse than the problem itself."

"I'm afraid I'm not maturing right."

"That's a troubling fear, I know it is—but it's not uncommon. At one point or another nearly everyone worries about looking right, functioning right. It'll pass, Teddy. Dr. Sam gave you a physical in January, a complete checkup, and you came through without a hitch. The report I got suggested you'll live to witness planetary colonization and the swearing-in of the first president of the world state. Maybe you'll *be* the first president of the world state."

"A doctor's office isn't a shower room, Mom."

"I know it isn't."

"Dexter Johnson, Sonny Elkins, even Pete, my good buddy Pete—they're *men*, Mom. I try to wait until they're finished to shower. They snap towels at each other and put their jock straps on their heads and hold bars of soap between their buns and make jokes about the nubbins on the team. That's Pete's word. At school I'm a nubbin. Here in the neighborhood I'm his buddy."

"They sound like men, all right."

"You know what I mean."

"All I know is that you're equating manhood with the size of your genital equipment. I can quote you a thousand and one reasons why that's stupid, but all I'm going to say is stop worrying about it, Teddy. Keep taking your showers *after* the fun-lovin' fellas with the five-pound pendulums between their legs and stop worrying about it."

"That's easy to say." Teddy turned his face toward her. "That's especially easy for *you* to say. You're a woman."

"Yeah, and you'd be a thirteen-, a fourteen-year-old kid even if you had to push your penis around in a wheelbarrow. Who are you trying to impress? Pete Wightman and all the guys with jock-strap headbands? The *Guinness Book of World Records?* The International Committee on Weights and Measurements? Who, Teddy? Whose instant admiration do you want?"

The boy looked back up at the ceiling. "Just mine," he said, still bitter. "I just want to stop feeling like a goddamn boy."

"Then stop acting like one."

"Good night, Mom." Teddy started to slide away from her, out of the bed, but Stevie grabbed his arm and twisted him back to his previous supine position. He turned his diamond-bright eyes toward her, apparently astonished as much by her strength as by her untelegraphed move to restrain him. "Mom, just let me go on to bed, okay? I'm tired of talking."

Stevie leaned over her son's face and kissed him on the brow. Her kisses descended casually to his eyelids, his nose, his cheeks, and finally the soft chilly bud of his mouth. She nibbled on his bottom lip and, using one arm to keep the electric blanket over them, slid her right hand down the porcelain smoothness of his chest and stomach. Her fingers curled back inside the elastic of his bikini briefs (the very brand that Baltimore Orioles pitcher Jim Palmer, a hunk if Stevie had ever seen one, modeled in full-color one-page advertisements in a variety of national magazines), and her tongue flicked out to lay a trail of saliva from Teddy's chin to the hollow of his throat. Because her fingers continued to grope for purchase, eventually they achieved it, closing on a masculine knot that burned her palm by exerting an acute reflexive pressure of its own.

"Mom," the boy whispered. "Mom, what are you doing?"

"I think you know, Ted. You're not going to let yourself off the hook until you've 'proved' your manhood in the rut-driven, half-blind, immemorial masculine way. All right. If that's the way it's going to be, I'll help you do that. It's perfectly safe with me. Then you can stop your stupid worrying and get on about the business of growing up. Just relax and let yourself go, Ted. I'll take care of everything else."

"Mom, I don't—"

"Shhhhh. I'm not your mother. You're my lover. You're my beautiful, passionate, ever-faithful demon lover. We've waited nearly two years for this reunion. Finally it's here, Ted. Finally it's here."

Careful not to dislodge their blankets, Stevie mounted her demon lover and rocked him like an infant to a blissful, half-comprehending spasm. Warmth and water and armistice. They were at truce in the tropical swamps of his spasm's aftermath. A little death, the English metaphysical poets had called the moment of orgasm. Well, that was what she and Ted, with young Teddy as the bodily agent of their reunion, had achieved. A little death. Such dying was unspeakably sweet. Warmth, and water, and resurrection, all on a cold February morning . . .

Teddy was staring up at her, wide-eyed.

Stevie kissed him, slumped to his side, took him into her arms, and again began to rock him, this time to sleep rather than to spasm. What passionate bliss to have led this boy in pursuit and capture of the dead man who had once, long ago, loved him into being. She had outwitted the spiteful angels of mortality. She had triumphed over middle-class values, the un-written tenets of universal mediocrity, and the strictures of her own provincial background. She had saved her son. Having fought through to these victories, Stevie found it easy to sleep.

Her son, her lover, slept beside her.

XXVI

A tapping awakened her. Overcome with confusion and guilt, Stevie thought: My Exceleriter is typing away.

What if Teddy, whom she had chosen a heinous, altogether unnatural method to comfort and reassure, heard the rattling of the machine's keys and type disc? He would be terrified. They would look at each other in the dark, and their guilt would commingle with their terror, and the night would swal-low them just as Jonathan Edwards's abysmal Puritan hell en-gorged the souls of the wicked. She would deserve that fate, certainly—but not Teddy, not her son. In a fit of inexplicable self-indulgence and depravity she had seduced him, she had stolen his virtue and ruined his life.

And now that goddamn Exceleriter was pounding away, clattering, pistoning along like a little wheelless locomotive. Churning out who knew what heat, stench, and cryptic literary pollutants? If not for the lingering distress inflicted upon her by the typewriter's demonic behavior, she never would have sought to help Teddy by making him the principal victim of their incest. Never. The very idea would have been unthinkable. It would have never—not in a billion years—presented itself to her as even a farfetched and utterly abhorrent possibility.

Tap-tap; tap-tappa-tap.

She would lift the monster from its place on her rolltop, the altar it had made of her oaken desk, and heave it out the window to the sloping shingled roof of the front porch. From there it would ricochet to the sidewalk, there to smash upon the concrete into flinders of metal and plastic.

Good riddance.

Typewriter? Call it, rather, tripewriter—for that's what it was, that's what it *wanted* to be.

Stevie turned to her side and discovered that Teddy was no longer in bed with her. Had the machine already awakened him? Was he standing in her study watching it spin out its elite prevarications? She moved her hand into the spot where Teddy had been and found the sheet as slippery and cold as a slice of refrigerated ham loaf. Then she recalled that that side of her electric blanket had not been on tonight. Two years ago she had placed its puck-shaped control in the bottom drawer of one of her dressers, and she had not retrieved it since. Only in the nightmare from which she had just groggily emerged had that side of the blanket been on. . . .

Therefore, glory be to God and her own appointed guardian angel, she had *not* committed incest with Teddy. She had dreamt that abominable sequence of events. Teddy was most likely asleep in his own room—where he had been all evening since their one-sided argument about television programs and appropriate weekend bedtimes for smart-alecky teen-age boys. Thank God, thank God, thank God . . .

Nevertheless, the machine was still rattling, buzzing, chattering. As soundly as the kids usually slept, it might yet awaken both Teddy and Marella. She had to get in there and see what it had done. She had to latch her study door and engage the Exceleriter's demon in single combat.

Stevie rose, donned her frumpy housecoat, and hurried to catch the machine at its illicit labors. She did. Flipped on, the overhead light failed to halt the Exceleriter in midsentence; it continued to type, invisible fingers furiously depressing the visible keys. The taped-together pages that Stevie had inserted in the machine were curling backward over the top of her desk, a banner of headlong narrative that even a Jack Kerouac or a Mickey Spillane would have been happy to wave. Although, that same afternoon, she had taken on the typewriter's demon in a brief bout of stichomythic debate, this sight stupefied Stevie.

"Stop!" she commanded the machine.

The Exceleriter paused briefly, paragraphed, and rattled off another two lines of type. Then it stopped.

That the runaway Exceleriter had obeyed her impulsive command Stevie found amazing. Why should it listen to her? If it chose to obey, it did so primarily to demonstrate the paradox that *it* was in control. Its halting on her rattled say-so only served to heighten her feelings of inadequacy and victimization. She was being typed to scorn, manipulated like a puppet, and her dominion over the typewriter's doings depended on its willingness to submit to her word. It had just submitted, but, in appearing to acquiesce, it had probably had ulterior motives. Perhaps it had realized that she could be pushed only so far; that if it had continued to type line after defiant line she would have broken down, pulled its plug, and fulfilled her vengeful fantasy of heaving the expensive machine out her second-story window. Even for a sentient PDE Exceleriter 79, self-preservation was a powerful motive.

Shivering, Stevie approached her desk. She removed the taped pages from the typewriter to see what it had written. Beneath the line of dialogue that, two nights ago, it had attributed to her husband ("If I appeared to give up, Stevie, it was only because it was time for me to pay"), the Exceleriter had willfully skipped a space and centered the Roman numeral XXV.

What did that mean? Twenty-five, of course—but twenty-five what? Chapters? Lines per half-page? Minutes of actual composition time? It looked more like a chapter heading than anything else, but the Exceleriter had not had time to progress as far as the twenty-fifth structural unit of *any* narrative. Seaton had done his dirty work Wednesday afternoon, but the machine had not begun systematically undermining her sanity until late Thursday evening. This was early Sunday morning. Although Georges Simenon might be able to write an entire book in three days (were he still alive), her typewriter had worked only in brief bursts. Consequently, those Roman numerals embodied a mystery.

One space beneath this mystery the text of the Exceleriter's midnight labors began: "Frightened, Stevie sat up in bed. A figure stood in her doorway. She had a hunch, a momentarily bloodcurdling intuition, that it had been standing there for quite a long time. . . ." Single-spaced, the text beneath the Roman numeral covered four and a half sheets of typing paper, all of it devoted to a convincing transcription of her mother-to-son talk with Teddy and that talk's vile aftermath. Of course, there had been no talk, there had been no aftermath. Her subconscious had run amok during a particularly loathsome nightmare, and the typewriter had simply reduced that nightmare to the palpable accusations of print. Yes. She stood accused. Incest was not an approved method of initiating one's offspring into the inevitable arcana of sex.

Another disquieting thought struck Stevie.

You remembered your dream, she told herself. You awoke from your dream believing that your talk with Teddy, and that other unmentionable stuff, actually happened. You awoke berating yourself for something you had only dreamt, Stevenson Crye, and here you are berating yourself for the absurd crime of merely dreaming that private enormity. The wonder of this episode is not the terrible nature of your dream, but the fact that you awoke with a vivid memory of it. You never remember your dreams. Why, now, do you begin to?

Because the Exceleriter is shaping, coloring, and reinforcing them. Because it wants you to begin to regard yourself as a slave to the animal portions of your own psyche. That's why it's a tripewriter. And that's why you must refuse to let it gain the upper hand.

"Too late," Stevie murmured. "Too late for that."

The chapter detailing her nightmare ran into a one-page section preceded by the centered heading, XXVI. This section began, "A tapping awakened her." It recounted her confusion upon awakening, her self-recrimination, and finally her discovery of the Exceleriter pounding away, clattering, pistoning along like a little wheelless locomotive. This chapter—if you could call it a chapter—ended rather abruptly. Its final words were:

"Stop!" she commanded the machine.
The Exceleriter paused briefly, paragraphed, and rattled off another two lines of type. Then it stopped.

XXVII

Ignoring the cold, Stevie fed a sheet of Dr. Elsa's halved examination-table paper into the Exceleriter. It was time to regain the upper hand, if indeed she had lost it. Time to reassert her human mastery of this inhuman machine. How, after all, could you be the pawn of a piece of equipment indentured to your own resolve? If you were truly resolute, you could not. Therefore Stevie typed,

I'm tired of this game, Exceleriter. If you want to rape my subconscious, do it in an area where I've already okayed the violation. Tell me about Ted. Finish my other nightmare for me.
YOUR WISH IS MY COMMAND.
Don't be smart. Finish it for me now. I'll take my hands off the keyboard, I'll surrender it to you.
YOU CANT SURRENDER WHAT YOU DONT POSSESS.
How would you like to end up on the sidewalk? How would you like a mixture of maple syrup, two-year-old Slime (that's a registered trademark), and some well-beaten egg white

dumped into your works? How would you like to be sledgehammered into scrap metal?

THE HORROR! THE HORROR!

Scoff if you like. My patience is at an end. My endurance has limits. Dropping you out the window would be more work than I want to undertake right now. Pounding you with a sledgehammer would wake up the kids. The only attractive option is filling you full of putrid green-brown goo.

YOU REALIZE, MRS. CRYE, THAT THIS PURULENT SUBSTANCE WOULD SEEP THROUGH MY CASING AND TAKE THE STAIN OFF YOUR PRECIOUS ROLLTOP. THE ALBUMIN IN EGG WHITE HAS THAT UNFORTUNATE EFFECT ON MOST WOOD FINISHES.

I frankly don't give a damn. Not at this stage. Watching you choke on a cloying Slime cocktail would be one of the high points of this demoralizing week.

MRS. CRYE, YOU'D BE KILLING THE GOOSE THAT LAYS THE GOLDEN EGG.

Listen, I'm going downstairs right now to fix you that little drink. My hands are leaving the keyboard. When I get back, your goose is cooked.

A more preposterous exchange, Stevie realized, it would be difficult to imagine. Nevertheless, she intended to carry out her threat—if not with syrup, Slime, and egg whites, then with a cup and a half of corn oil thickened with a little self-rising flour. Anyone discovering what she had done would think her as mad as a British milliner, of course, but Stevie was prepared to court this implacable judgment for the satisfaction of silencing her nemesis. Her nemesis did not appear to believe her. It had not even bothered to answer.

"Damn you," Stevie said, one of her favorite expressions of late. "I'm going." She pushed back her chair, gathered up the skirts of her housecoat, and walked to the door. Placing her hand on the knob, she heard the Exceleriter bang out its grudging reply. Good, thought Stevie. She returned to her desk and read the machine's message.

YOU WIN. IM YOURS.

You'll finish my nightmare about Ted?

AS I SAID EARLIER, NOT ALTOGETHER MOCKINGLY, YOUR WISH IS MY COMMAND. IN THIS PARTICULAR AT LEAST.

All right, then. Get on with it.

122 *Michael Bishop*

FIRST, MRS. CRYE, YOUVE GOT TO GO BACK TO BED. LEAVE THE PAPER IN ME, TURN OUT THE LIGHTS, AND TRY TO GET SOME SLEEP.

Why?

I CANT FINISH YOUR NIGHTMARE ABOUT YOUR DEAD HUSBAND OUT OF THIN AIR AND BORROWED DESIRE. IM DEPENDENT ON YOUR DREAMS. YOUR MOST COMPELLING AND YOUR MOST REVEALING DREAMS TAKE PLACE NOT IN WAKING FANTASIES BUT IN THE HARROWING DEPTHS OF NIGHTMARE.

So I'm manipulating you rather than the other way around?

HAVENT I JUST CAVED IN TO AN UNCONSCIONABLE THREAT? HAVENT I TWICE DECLARED MYSELF AT YOUR DISPOSAL?

Yes, but you qualified that declaration by adding IN THIS PARTICULAR AT LEAST. My inference is that you harbor secret purposes beyond my control. Or think you do.

GO TO BED, MRS. CRYE.

What if I don't want to?

THEN WE CAN TALK LIKE THIS UNTO THE VERY BREAK OF DAWN, THE LOVELY LADY AND HER AVUNCULAR PDE EXCELERITER.

At which time you'll turn into an electronic pumpkin?

GO TO BED, MRS. CRYE. GO TO BED.

Stevie reread her exchange with the typewriter, only half convinced that it had occurred. She had typed, then it had typed, and so on . . . right up to the machine's final weary admonition. Of course, even the highly sophisticated Exceleriter was not supposed to compose its own texts. Her Pantronics Data Equipment owner's manual contained not a single paragraph about the typewriter's untoward proclivity for autonomous self-expression. Possibly she had typed both parts of this dialogue herself.

What was the name of that old movie starring Joanne Woodward? *The Three Faces of Eve?* Well, if Eve, quite incidentally a native of the South, could have three faces, she, Stevenson Crye, could have two. In fact, she had just sent off a book proposal entitled *Two-Faced Woman,* hadn't she? Was her double-entendre title inadvertently descriptive of the mental affliction that permitted her to converse with her typewriter? Stevie could feel her brain yawing in her cranium, but she could not remember conceiving and then typing the Exceleriter's upper-case replies. The distinctive personalities of the disturbed woman in the movie had not been able to alternate so rapidly.

You win. I'm going. Just keep your promise.

Having typed these words, Stevie waited for the Exceleriter to add a final comment. She also tried to evaluate her own state of mind, for she was wholly committed to determining the exact moment at which the machine's point of view preempted her own. No such moment occurred, however, and a few minutes later she shut off the Exceleriter and returned to her bedroom.

What time must it be? Three in the morning? Later than that, Stevie feared, closer to dawn. How was she supposed to go back to sleep after the successive traumas of her imaginary seduction of Teddy and her altogether factual tête-à-tête with the typewriter? She would lie awake all the remainder of that night, listening for the telltale clatter of the Exceleriter's keys and never hearing it because she had not gone to sleep. Of course if she went to sleep, she would still fail to hear the machine typing. Catch-22. Her anticipation of what she fervently desired would prevent her from achieving the state in which the Exceleriter would fulfill that desire. An hour passed, and a rooster, two hours premature, began to crow feebly in the distance.

Stevie crawled from bed, shuffled into the upstairs bathroom, and found an amber bottle of sleep aids in the top of her linen cabinet. Concentrated drowsiness. Discount-drug oblivion. Lead-ins to nightmare. She took three tablets. Ten minutes after she had returned to the rumpled incubator of her bed, her mind was hatching a clutch of misshapen chimeras. And her Exceleriter was busily describing them. . . .

XXVIII

"I fell apart down deep," Crye said, a dead hand on his wife's forehead. "If I appeared to give up, Stevie, it was only because it was time for me to pay." Crye's face bore an expression of grisly melancholy and compassion, but his hand did not cease pressuring his wife ever deeper into the Clinac 18's couch.

"Pay for what?" asked Mrs. Crye, her eyes wide with half-repressed terror. "What must you pay at this late date, Ted?"

"The dosimetrist's bill."

"The Kensingtons took care of that for us, Ted. The life-insurance policy you bought was inadequate to our needs, and you never even bothered to look into the hospitalization plan they recommended. It's a shameful fact that—"

"Stevie," murmured Theodore Martin Crye, Sr.

"—if not for the fund-raising efforts of Dr. Sam and Dr. Elsa, the kids and I would still be up to our elbows in debt to the cancer clinic. The people you *don't* have to pay, Ted, include the dosimetrist, the radiologists, and the nuclear-medicine technicians. Besides, what sort of debt would turn a self-sufficient man like you into a shambling defeatist?"

"The debt of mortality," Crye said.

"The debt of guilt," said Seaton Benecke, clinic dosimetrist.

"But you don't owe these people anything," Mrs. Crye said. "I've just explained that to you. You certainly don't owe Seaton Benecke a dime. He's a typewriter repairman, Ted, not a radiation dosimetrist. I can't even imagine what he's doing here."

"He's come to collect the payment I owe him."

"What payment?"

"He wants to enjoy your person, Stevie."

Mrs. Crye looked at the pale noncommittal face of the type-writer repairman. She looked at her husband, a resurrected corpse whose features slid about in the same discouraging way they did in her memory. His breath was odorless, antiseptic. His clammy hands continued to press her into the treatment couch. He would not let her go. Without returning Mrs. Crye's gaze, Seaton Benecke moved to the foot of the couch and began unbuttoning his lab coat.

"I'm your wife," Mrs. Crye told her husband's corpse. "I'm not a piece of equipment you can loan out or give away to repay your debts. We're not Eskimos, Ted. This isn't the Arctic Circle."

"But it's cold in here," Crye said.

Seaton Benecke permitted his lab coat to fall to the icy floor of the treatment room. He began unbuttoning his shirt.

"Ted, you can't be serious. You're out of your mind. You don't help a creep like Benecke rape your own wife."

"It's all right," Crye said. "I'm dead."

"It's all right," Benecke added. "I'm an organ-grinder."

Looking down the length of her body, Mrs. Crye saw that in unbuttoning his shirt Benecke had revealed a swatch of thick white fur from his throat to his navel. His fingers then moved deftly to his belt buckle.

"I mean I'm an organ-grinder's monkey," he corrected himself.

Mrs. Crye closed her eyes, twisted in the corpse's grasp, and began to scream. Her screams were high-pitched, piercing, and numerous, one coming after another like the notes of an avant-garde flute sonata.

"Your screams will avail you nothing, my beauty," the corpse said, slamming her violently back into place, and his voice did not sound at all like Theodore Martin Crye, Sr.'s. It sounded instead like that belonging to the insanely serene computer in the film *2001: A Space Odyssey.*

"Ted!" shouted the distraught woman. "Ted, don't do this!" She began to scream again.

As she screamed, a creature like an enormous white-throated capuchin crept up the length of the treatment couch, lifting the hem of her skirt as it approached her face. Mrs. Crye's head rolled from side to side, but she could not escape the restraints of her traitorous husband or the knee pressure of the monkey-man astride her.

"I'm just giving it a special twist here," Benecke said, stroking her breasts with a furry paw. "I can go in as deep as fifteen centimeters before 'exploding' through the life-bearing dark. That's what I really like."

"I fell apart down deep," Crye said, a dead hand on his wife's forehead. "If I appeared to give up, Stevie, it was only because

Mrs. Crye could no longer hear her own screams. When she opened her eyes, she found that she was alone with Crye's corpse in one of the basement detection-and-diagnosis rooms. Her dead husband was in the process of explaining to her the purpose and operation of a machine connected to a small viewing console.

"This unit allows the radiologist to watch a patient's gastrointestinal tract as it fills with barium sulfate," he said.

"I went through all this when you went through it," Mrs. Crye said. "I went through it all again to write an article on the clinic for the *Ledger*. Why are you subjecting me to the experience yet again?"

"Barium sulfate is simply a contrast medium," Crye said. "It's used to show up any abnormalities in the GI tract. The examiner views the diagnostic process almost as if watching a movie."

"I wrote those words last week, Ted. I took them down from the lips of a clinic radiologist, and I put them into my story."

"This machine works on the fluoroscopic principle, but in other parts of the clinic are a thermographic unit, which detects tumors through a heat-sensing process, and an ultrasonic device which employs sound waves to locate and identify cancerous growths. Many other diagnostic aids are available to us here. Of course you've already seen the Clinac 4 and the Clinac 18 in the treatment areas."

"None of these marvels is worth anything if you will yourself to die," Mrs. Crye said. "If you surrender to the *idea* of cancer."

Crye turned to face his wife. Out of deference to her wifely sensibilities he was wearing handsome glass prostheses in his empty eye sockets. His complexion, however, still had a sickly cast.

"I want a divorce," he said.

"You're dead," Mrs. Crye reminded him. "You don't need a divorce. I'm a widow. I can remarry without a divorce decree, and you can—"

"—rot in hell."

Mrs. Crye lowered her face into her hands. "Please, Ted, don't." She immediately raised her head again and put her hands on her knees. "Hell is a mental state. I'm the one who's in it. You're too good—you *were* too good—a man to end up in hell."

"Even good men can have hellish mental states, Stevie. I want a divorce."

"How does a living widow give her dead husband a divorce?"

"She lets go," Crye said. "She stops bringing him into the clinic for fluoroscopic examinations. She stops pouring barium sulfate into him. She stops trying to read his goddamn entrails on this little television screen."

"Ted, I never—"

"You're not a licensed haruspex, Stevie. Becoming a licensed dosimetrist, radiologist, or haruspex requires a lot of hard work. If you won't give me a divorce, I may have to file a malpractice suit."

"But why do you want a divorce? I loved you. I've acted as I have because I loved . . . because I love you."

"There's another woman," Crye said.

"No, Ted. You're lying. You're casting about for excuses."

"There's another woman, Stevie. I'm going to go with her. I want a divorce. Let go of me so that I can go with her."

Mrs. Crye crossed the tiny room and gripped her dead husband's wrists. The flesh sloughed away in her hands. "You can hold me, Ted, but I can't hold you. If it makes you feel better, call my inability to hold you a divorce." She dropped the hose-like lengths of clammy flesh to the floor. "Just don't try to tell me there's another woman. I refuse to believe it."

J.K.POTTER

Gingerly Crye pushed past his wife, visited all the diagnostic rooms along the corridor, and returned to the fluoroscopic unit carrying tomograms, radioimmunoassays, sonographic readouts, and a handful of X-rays. He was pushing a mobile mammographic unit before him. He maneuvered this last machine right up to Mrs. Crye and scattered the other items across the top of an examination table next to her abandoned chair. His skeletal fingers lifted the results of each diagnostic test to within fifteen centimeters of his wife's nose.

"Evidence of the other woman," Crye said. "Nuclear body scans, sonograms of the internal organs, thermograms taken after she'd spent ten or fifteen minutes cooling off from our last encounter, not to mention several high-speed, low-dosage X-rays of her breasts. These last are especially impressive. Put them all together they spell paramour. . . ."

The lights in the clinic basement went out, almost as if a generator had failed, and sitting behind the mammographic unit that Crye had just wheeled in was the three-dimensional image of a strange woman. Her insides—from brain to toe bones—were visible as blinding splotches of green, blue, magenta, and yellow. She stared at Mrs. Crye from her Technicolor death's-head while the horrified recipient of this stare raised an arm and attempted to

warm the naked body of the corpse in her bed. After fetching the electric blanket's control from the bottom dresser drawer, she clocked it to its highest setting. Then she climbed into the bed beside her dead husband and snuggled against him to add her own warmth to that imparted by the blanket. Immobile and helpless, he stared with empty eye sockets at the ceiling. His breath was odorless, antiseptic. To die a second time, he would first have to improve markedly.

"Would you like some orange juice?" Mrs. Crye asked. "A hot toddy with honey and lemon?"

"It would seep right through me and ruin the mattress pad. Citric acid has that unfortunate effect on most sorts of bed linen."

"I don't care. I want you to get better. This has been a demoralizing two years."

"You should remarry."

"'A woman without a man is like a fish without a bicycle.'" Crye laughed. "'Don't switch corpses in midscream,' eh?"

"Something like that. That's a helluva ghoulish way to put it, though. I was just trying to point out—obliquely—that I married you because I loved you, Ted, not because I was single-mindedly looking for a man."

"No woman is single-minded when she looks for a man."

"Stop it, Ted. I'm just saying that remarriage isn't the answer."

"You should date that Benecke boy, Stevie."

Mrs. Crye moved away from her husband. "That's not amusing. I'd seduce my own son before I dated Benecke."

"What's the matter with him?"

"He's an inarticulate Svengali. He once convinced you to help him rape me. And his table manners are atrocious."

"He probably uses his salad fork for the entrée."

"At lunch one afternoon he let his pet monkey suck blood from a wound in his finger. Dessert, he called it. Teddy and Marella were there."

"He's young yet, Stevie. What else?"

"What do you want me to give you, Ted? His teachers' conduct reports? A list of his traffic citations? The results of his last criminal indictment? He's not my type!"

"He's a piker, and you're elite."

"Ha, ha," Mrs. Crye said mirthlessly. She turned toward her husband again. "Just tell me what you thought you had to pay for, Ted. What so discouraged you that you turned your back on all the marvelous aids, all the helpful people, at the cancer clinic in Ladysmith?"

"It was time for me to die."

"I don't understand that!" Mrs. Crye protested, hitting the bed with her fist.

Her dead husband summoned a burst of residual *élan vital* and threw back the covers. Like Karloff in one of James Whale's *Frankenstein* movies, he rose from the bed. He was dressed in the suit in which he had been buried. It wanted dry-cleaning and pressing. He strode to the mirror and clumsily tried to straighten the knot in his tie. The room's darkness proved no deterrent to his efforts, for he could not have seen his bony fingers even with the lights on.

"And I don't deserve to share the same bed with you," Crye said huskily. "I robbed you of any incentive to develop your own talents. Although I bought you that fancy-ass Exceleriter, I didn't give you time to use it. That's why I decided to die."

"So I could spend my life in front of a typewriter?"

"Matriculating in the graduate school of experience, developing your talents, confronting adversity."

"You never talked like that when you were alive."

"Only toward the last did I even begin to think like that, Stevie. I had to die so that you could step out from my oppressive shadow."

"Into the arms of a shade?"

Crye swung about to face the bed, but one foot did not turn with him. His diamond tie tack glinted in the green-yellow sheen from the arc lamp outside. The knot of his tie was a thumb's length off-center to the right. A button fell from his jacket and rolled toward the cedar chest at the foot of the bed. He was falling apart not only inside but out-.

"What I'm saying's meant to sound noble. It's heartfelt, too. It's an altogether heartfelt lie. . . . Come to me and kiss me, Stevie. Show me you believe me by giving me a kiss."

Mrs. Crye went to her husband and gave him a kiss. His lips tasted like oyster dip on dry crackers. When she pulled away from him, however, she was staring into the face of an organ-grinder monkey whose bones shone green, blue, magenta, and yellow in the second-story gloom. The ascot at his throat was white fur. When he opened his mouth, the phosphorescent keyboard of his teeth began to clatter and chime. Mrs. Crye opened her mouth too. The sound that issued forth reminded her of

XXIX

the angry blatting of a broken Exceleriter.

Stevie groped for and finally found the plastic switch that silenced the alarm on her clock radio. Usually she did not set the alarm on Friday or Saturday nights, but after returning from the upstairs bathroom drugged for slumber she must have inadvertently done so. A weekday habit unconsciously carried over to the weekend. Now she was awake, exhausted by the vivid rigors of her dreams.

You had several nightmares in a row, Stevie thought, still trying to orient herself. The radio alarm interrupted the last one. For a moment the alarm's horrible buzzing reminded you of the sound the Exceleriter made when its cable snapped. A waking nightmare disrupting your bad-dream frequencies. It's morning, Stevie, a quiet Sunday morning.

What did you dream?

Actually, she remembered her nightmares, just as, earlier that same night, she had remembered her illusory seduction of Teddy. The difference this morning lay in the reassuring fact that it was impossible to confuse the contents of these newest nightmares with waking reality. After all, Ted slept securely in the Barclay cemetery, Seaton Benecke was not really a capuchin in human disguise, and she, Stevie, had not spent the night in Ladysmith's ultramodern cancer clinic. She had spent the night in her own big bed, fitfully dreaming.

Time now to get up and see what kind of order the Exceleriter had imposed on the sequence and images of these fitful dreams—animated spiritual headaches, call them. Stevie pulled on a pair of stiff, off-brand "designer" jeans, added a long-sleeve flannel shirt, and took a couple of fast swipes at her bangs with a hair brush. Then she tennis-shoed into her study and read through the transcriptions of the nightmares set down verbatim in the previous chapter.

" 'Mrs. Crye'?" she said aloud. "Why the hell do you refer to me as Mrs. Crye in every one of my own dreams?"

The machine typed, A MATTER OF COURTESY, MRS. CRYE.

"It's ridiculously formal. I don't think of myself as Mrs. Crye. I certainly don't dream of myself as Mrs. Crye, not with the formality of the title, anyway. Mockery and condescension, that's what you're dealing in."

NO, MAAM, NOT AT ALL. ITS BOTH COURTESY AND SCRU-PULOUS ADHERENCE TO A PARTICULAR JOURNALISTIC STYLE. DONT BE UNCHARITABLE.

"How can I be charitable toward a thief like you? You invade my sleep. You steal my dreams."

I RETURN THEM TO YOU, STEVIE. HERE THEY ARE, NEATLY TYPED AND READY TO REEXPERIENCE.

"Wonderful. I can reexperience a rape in which my late husband acted as another man's second. I can reexperience the symbolic bestiality of that rape. Then I can reexperience my late husband's request for a divorce. I can also—"

FILE THEM AWAY. FORGET ABOUT THEM.

Stevie started to reply, but silenced herself. She was speaking aloud. The Exceleriter was typing. This approach to the mechanics of information exchange marked an important shift in their relationship. The typewriter was voluntarily acknowledging the legitimacy of speech as a communications method. Not since she had shouted "Stop!" at it had it responded so readily to the spoken word. On paper, however, Stevie's contributions to this dialogue were conspicuous blank areas of two, three, or four lines. These white spaces gave her the uneasy notion that she did not really exist except by the machine's sufferance. She therefore typed her next response:

It's not likely I'll ever forget what you're doing to me. I don't want to forget it. I just want it to stop.
YOUR WISH IS MY

Command, thought Stevie. Ever the completist, she depressed the shift-lock key and typed this word in the space left vacant by the Exceleriter. Only an uninked impression appeared on the paper, however, for the machine had stealthily maneuvered its ribbon to the stencil setting. Ever the smart aleck, thought Stevie. You always have to have the last word, even if it's by refusing to have it. . . .

"You're up early for a Sunday."

Stevie looked around and saw Teddy at the door, already dressed and bright-eyed. She turned the Exceleriter off and histrionically put a hand to her breast. Even if the gesture she used to signal her surprise was a relic of the D. W. Griffith era, there was nothing make-believe about her heart's rapid fluttering.

"So are you," she managed. "Up early."

"You've been a real go-getter this morning, Mom. I've heard you typing the last hour or so."

Stevie tried to put the dust cover on the Exceleriter, but the long strip of paper on the platen made the cover sit lopsidedly. "I'm finished now. I was just making some notes. Nothing important. Just some notes."

"Don't be nervous," Teddy advised her.

She looked sharply at the boy. "Nervous? Why should I be nervous?"

"No reason, Mom. You shouldn't be. I don't want you to think you need to be. There's no reason to."

"What are you talking about?"

He came into the study and closed the door behind him. "I want to thank you for what you did last night, Mom. Lots of kids would probably hate you for that, or not understand it, or be embarrassed about it. Not me, though. I'm grateful. I feel better about myself."

"Lots of kids would hate their mothers for refusing to be back-talked?"

Teddy smiled shyly, but his shyness was conspiratorial. "There's back talk and there's back talk. Some kinds are bad, and some kinds are . . . not so bad. You taught me something about myself."

Dumbfounded by the implications of this admission, Stevie stared at her son. She could not think of anything to say. She was afraid to say anything. She did not want Teddy to blurt out his meaning (as, in the Exceleriter's version of their apocryphal midnight talk, she had asked him to blurt out his problem), because she feared this direct approach would deny her the possibility of believing their incest a lie. It *was* a lie, of course, but

Teddy seemed to be operating under the assumption that the Exceleriter's disgusting fiction had become a Crye-family *fait accompli.* How could he assume such a thing? What was happening to her?

"Anyway," Teddy said, "it's all right, Mom. I'm old enough to handle what happened. You did me a kindness. That's all I'm ever going to say about it, though. I won't mention it again."

Stevie said, "Mention it all you like. I'm not ashamed of calling you down for sassing me."

"Yeah. Okay." Lifting his gaze, Teddy smiled at his mother. He meditatively cocked his head. "Thanks, Mom. I mean it." His breath sent vaporous plumes into the air, but when he grabbed the door handle and ducked back out into the hall, these plumes disappeared like ghosts at dawn's first gleaming. What Teddy had said, however, echoed in Stevie's mind all that long chilly morning.

XXX

Dr. Elsa was as good as her word. While Stevie stayed at home eyebrow-deep in the hefty combined edition of *The Atlanta Journal-Constitution,* Teddy and Marella attended Sunday school at the First United Methodist Church three blocks away. After church the Kensingtons took the children back out the Alabama Road to their secluded clapboard bungalow on Scottsdale Lake. As much as she loved those troublesome boogers (Ted's backhanded term of endearment for the kids), Stevie appreciated this time to herself. She respected and wondered at Dr. Elsa, herself a busy woman, for arranging matters so that she could have a break not only from her work but from her parental responsibilities. It was not often these days that she enjoyed such blissful autonomy.

Since Tuesday, it seemed, her life had revolved almost totally around the dictates, either crass or subtle, of a seven-hundred-dollar machine. Everything she had done, everything that had happened to her, and most of her current preoccupations stemmed directly from the Exceleriter's breakdown and subsequent repair. (Put "repair" in quotes. What Benecke had done to the Exceleriter qualified as the spelling of a baleful and far-reaching curse.) True enough, Marella had twice come down ill since Tuesday, and Teddy had seriously rattled her with his puerile smart-aleckisms and his poignant midnight doubts about his masculinity—but even these fairly ordinary family problems seemed inextricably bound up with her difficulties with the typewriter. In fact, only because the Exceleriter had cunningly deceived her was she now having trouble drawing a hard-edged line between real events and wholly imaginary ones. Even as she sat in her kitchen reading the Sunday book reviews, sipping thoughtfully at her third cup of coffee, a machine about the size of a breadbox was shaping her attitudes, influencing her emotions, dictating her behavior.

Don't think about the blasted thing, Stevie advised herself.

She tried to concentrate on the book reviews. Today's literary pages—both of them—were devoted to capsule notices of a dozen different midwinter horror novels. These books bore the following titles: *Afterbirth, All Creatures Squat and Scaly, The Dripping, Edema, Gravid Babies, Lucrezia Laughed, Nightscrew, The Nimbus, The Puppets of Piscataway, Scourge, Shudderville,* and *The Terror According to Tyrone.* The notices in the book pages either hailed these offerings as masterpieces of chilling readability or castigated them as the latest throwaways on a virtually summitless heap of opportunistic schlock.

Stevie counted up the reviews. Pans outnumbered raves eight to four, and the raves were by obituary writers and ambulance chasers all too conspicuously eager to abandon their ghoulish beats for a Sunday stroll through an imaginary graveyard or a nonexistent haunted house. The pans, meanwhile, consisted of energetic discussions of the novels' blatant excesses, shameful borrowings, stylistic shortcomings, unbelievable characters, incestuous thematic resemblances, and delicious cheap thrills. Where were today's Faulkners, Fitzgeralds, and Hemingways?

Glancing at the week's fiction bestsellers, however, Stevie found that four of the novels under review this morning had climbed into the hardcover list. Another two of these novels, paperback originals, had attained the second and fifth places on the paperback list. Only one of the horror novels on either of these lists had received an approving review in today's paper.

Stevie held her coffee on the back of her tongue, bitterly contemplating the narrow eclecticism and salient graph-paper preferences of the American reading public. She wrote nonfiction, of course, but what chance had a regional writer with no predilection for purveying goosebumps of cracking the big-bucks barrier of bestsellerdom? Rightly or wrongly, she graphed her own literary progress in dismaying parallel with the rise and fall of her bank balance. By that standard, the accolades of her editors and a few distant relatives aside, she was a failure even as a hack.

"Two-Faced Woman: Reflections of a Female Paterfamilias," said Stevie aloud, savoring the sound of it.

Not a bad title, really. Precolon, it titillated. Postcolon, it dovetailed into the realm of fuzzy sociological jargon, even if the juxtaposition of *female* and *paterfamilias* was supposed to wrinkle brows and pique curiosities. Maybe it would do just that. If the Briar Patch Press, Inc., of Atlanta, Georgia, accepted her book, however, it would receive only a limited regional distribution, and she would be extremely lucky to find her title among the nonfiction bestsellers spotlighted in the Sunday *Journal-Constitution.* The uptown folks at *The New York Times* and *The Washington Post Book World* would never even hear of her. Their nonfiction specialists would be busy reviewing studies of American sexual mores, guides to market investment during the coming depression, the autobiographies of superannuated film stars, and the doomsday scenarios of various ecologists, military leaders, retired politicians, biological scientists, Kremlinologists, automobile executives, Sun Belt evangelicals, and anonymous quasi-literate terrorists who vowed in their prefaces to donate their royalties to the utter annihilation of the corrupt middle class.

No wonder so many people read horror novels. The only other readily accessible medium of escape was television; and even Teddy and Marella, whose very eyeballs sometimes seemed to bristle with teletransmitted dots, could stand only so much of that sanctified diversion. If you wanted to make money, establish your name, and reap the rewards of your labors in this life (rather than in the musty halls of academe or the luminous meadows of paradise), you had to give the people what they wanted. Or you had to make them want what you gave them, an infinitely riskier and more time-consuming enterprise. Stevie scarcely felt that she had the time, and a talent for intelligent pandering was not one upon whose development she had ever placed a high priority. The more fool she.

What was going to happen to her book proposal? The Briar Patch Press would sit on it two or three months and then return it with a cover letter praising her style but expressing grave doubts about the "commercial viability" of her subject matter.

Unless your late husband was a minister, a philandering international sex symbol, or a physician in either deepest Borneo or Darkest, Texas (the rejection notice would say), the A.R.P.—American Reading Public—has no overmastering desire to pay cold, hard cash for the down-home tribulations of a modern widow. Feminism is passé in this presidential administration. After all, a woman sits on the Supreme Court and Bo Derek can do anything she damn well pleases. *Two-Faced Woman,* catchy title notwithstanding, just isn't going to be this year's *Roots* or *Shōgun.* In fact, lady, if we indulge ourselves and print it, most of the copies will end up on discount tables along with omnibus volumes of Willie Shakespeare's plays, Edgar A. Guest's poetry, and Jack London's South Sea tales. And the omnibus volumes, Mrs. Crye, will sell better. . . .

Ah, thought Stevie, staring moodily at the pen-and-ink likeness of a moist-muzzled werewolf illustrating Paul Darcy Boles's contemptuous review of *The Dripping;* ah, the power of positive thinking. Your proposal's been gone less than twenty-four hours, to a publisher outside the debris-littered millrace of the Manhattan biggies, and already you're consigning it to editorial shipwreck. You're supposed to be relishing this time alone, not worrying about your work or anticipating ugly setbacks. That typewriter upstairs has turned you into one pessimistic, paranoid lady, Stevie Crye.

"I've got to get out of this house."

This statement echoed intimidatingly in her empty kitchen. Stevie collapsed the pages of the book-review section, folding them no more neatly than she usually folded the road maps in her van, and upended this bulging packet into the big wicker basket containing her plastic garbage pail. As if she had just disposed of her pessimism and paranoia along with the book reviews, she brushed her hands together smartly. She would take Dr. Elsa's advice and drive into Columbus. Shopping, as Arthur Miller had somewhere pointed out, was an established American cultural response to the blues. It was what you did when television's pale attraction faded, and you had to come up for air from horror novels like *Gravid Babies* or *The Terror According to Tyrone*.

Stevie turned down the space heater and climbed the stairs to her bedroom to change clothes. Though cold, it was another beautiful day. Navy-blue slacks, a virgin-white fishnet sweater, and her off-white winter car coat—that ensemble ought to make her presentable to the J. C. Penney crowd, even if she was almost a decade out of fashion. What the hell. Warmth was the word, not modishness. The Columbus *beau monde,* bless its collective heart, would probably never even notice. Half its elegantly coiffed representatives were undoubtedly cruising Atlanta's swank malls, anyway.

At the top of the stairs Stevie paused. The Exceleriter was not typing. Good. That was a blessing.

Pulled into her study in spite of herself, however, Stevie went to the typewriter, reread its transcriptions of last night's dreams, tried to reconstruct the spoken half of her conversation with the machine, and finally removed the long sheet of paper on the cylinder. She cranked in another sheet. Then she folded the Exceleriter's most recent work into a thick packet, slipped this into a manila folder, and removed from her files the folder containing its first literary efforts. They were going with her, these stories, these fictions. She had no firm idea why, but they were going with her. She wanted them under her arm, within her sight, tangible testimony that she had not merely hallucinated their reality.

XXXI

Once in Columbus, Stevie put the folders under the driver's seat and scrupulously locked the van every time she left it. The afternoon went well. She treated herself to dinner at the China Star restaurant, window-shopped through the labyrinth of the Columbus Square Mall, and bought a good supply of nonperishable grocery items at the Winn-Dixie store in the Midtown Shopping Center. (Chicken potpies, being perishable, she valiantly passed up, even though they were three for only a dollar-ten.) She purposely stayed out of the bookstores that popped up along her shopping routes, for she had plenty to read at home and a longing perusal of the fiction racks would automatically provoke an outlay of ten or twelve dollars. She could not afford any nonessential expenditures this month; she could hardly afford the essential ones.

By four-thirty Stevie had virtually exorcised her fatiguing negativism. She felt good; happy, almost. Like magic elixirs, the stinging February air and the radiant blueness of the afternoon sky had purged her melancholy. She was able to smile at the people on the sidewalks and in the mall concourses, even the ones who bumped her in doorways and flaunted scowly-face buttons on their coat lapels. Buck up, she wanted to tell these aggressively morose citizens; we're all downtrodden middle- or lower-middle-class consumers together. K-Mart is our temple, McDonald's our commissary, and Burt Reynolds our crash-happy prophet. Hallelujah.

Until she climbed back into her microbus for the final time

that afternoon and saw the corner of one of her manila folders protruding from beneath the seat, she had completely forgotten about her troubles with the typewriter. The corner of the folder reminded her, but she shoved it out of sight with her heel and resolutely put the VW in gear. Nothing was going to spoil this outing. She intended to arrive back in Barclay in contagious high spirits.

Before she fully understood what she was doing, Stevie found herself driving down Macon Road toward the Bradley Memorial Library and the original business district on the Chattahoochee River. She needed to be going the other way. Above the library, then, she swung the microbus hard to the right and in moderate traffic cruised down the meticulously landscaped hill to a busy intersection between a cocktail lounge, a flower shop, and two other catty-corner establishments. She was heading into a tree-lined area in which private residences alternated with isolated businesses of one sort or another. The studios of the local CBS affiliate were not too far away. (Right now the station was probably broadcasting typical post-football-season fare: a gymnastics meet or a figure-skating exhibition. Wow. Was she glad to be away from the set.)

Then Stevie suddenly realized that she was going to Hamlin Benecke & Sons. Jesus, gal, you're returning to the scene of the crime. . . .

Indeed she was. She could not help herself. It was stupid, irrational, maybe even counterproductive—not only to her hopes of getting her Exceleriter repaired forever and ever but also to the entire point of her day on the town. She simply could not help herself. Her shopping, after all, had not really purged her of anxiety; it had merely chased her problem underground. Well, the problem would not *stay* underground. It insisted on sticking its nose back above the surface and staring at her with close-set empty eyes. Maybe if she went to Benecke's, and confronted Seaton again, and made him promise to undo the terrible thing he had apparently done to her machine, her life would get back on track again and the nightmare of the past few days would burn away like morning mist. Stevie had no idea precisely what she was going to do, but she had to do something.

Her foot pressed the accelerator, her hands manipulated the steering wheel, and her van chugged up an avenue of naked trees and semidilapidated structures to the site of the office-supply company. She pulled into the asphalt parking lot of a neighborhood drugstore right across the street from Benecke's. Both businesses were closed today. The bricks of the office-supply company had been painted a color that Stevie thought of as "headache green." In the bright afternoon sunlight they shone with Day-Glo brilliance, as if they had been freshly shel-lacked. Stevie shielded her eyes and peered across the street at the gaudy building.

Leaning precariously toward the building's uphill wall, sup-porting a portion of its weight on a flimsy-looking kickstand, was Seaton Benecke's big black motorcycle. Her nemesis, it seemed, was inside working on other unsuspecting folks' type-writers. Stevie pulled her manila folders out from under the seat without taking her eyes off the building. Maybe she ought to go over there, pound on the locked front door, and accost that weird young man with further evidence of his malign handiwork. The company had charged her only ten or eleven dollars for repairs that Pantronics Data Equipment would not have made for another forty. Nevertheless, those so-called re-pairs (even if her Exceleriter, after a fashion, was still function-ing) had caused her untold mental anguish these last four or five days, and she would be well within her rights to ask for her money back.

Stevie opened her door and dropped one foot toward the pavement.

Simultaneously the plate-glass door of Hamlin Benecke & Sons flashed open, and Seaton appeared in it wearing his white coveralls and a coat resembling an intern's jacket. His nimble jersey-clad capuchin sat on his right shoulder. Stevie pulled her foot back inside the microbus, eased the door to, and slumped down into her seat. She was crazy to be here. She did not want to talk to the repairman. She did not want her money back. She wanted only to get home to the kids without a pointless show-down in the supply company's parking lot. Of course, if her typewriter would start operating normally again, that little bonus would round off the perfection of the day, and she would accept that, too.

Please, Stevie silently begged, don't let him see me. I didn't *mean* to come here. Don't let him see me.

Through the bottom of her window she watched Seaton fumbling with a set of keys, trying to find the one that would lock the family business behind him. His pudgy fingers had no agility in the cold, none of the nice expertise that permitted him to transform ordinary business machines into dangerous psychescribers. He looked as bland as an hour-old bowl of cornflakes. The keys slipped from his fingers and clattered on the concrete. When he bent to retrieve them, 'Crets jumped from his shoulder and ran along the curb like a man on a riverbank surveying the waters beneath him for a runaway boat. Or for a gas-bloated corpse. Stevie ducked lower to keep the monkey from spotting her and alerting Seaton to her presence.

The telephone inside the office-supply company began to ring. Stevie heard Seaton mutter, "Oh, crap!"—sounds carried well today, like cannons booming over water—and lifted her head to see him retreating back into the darkness to catch the phone. "I'll be right back," he informed his monkey from inside the building. "Don't you run off now." Then the plate-glass door closed, and 'Crets hopped from the low curb into the deserted expanse of the parking lot.

I swear to goodness, thought Stevie, slumping again—that damned animal's seen me. There's no one to blame but yourself, either. You could have driven on home, Stevenson Crye. You didn't *have* to make this stupid side trip.

Peeking over the Volkswagen's sill to see what the capuchin was doing, Stevie found 'Crets looking directly at her—out of that tiny death's-head face, out of the indigo whirlpools of his eyeless eyes. Well, so what? How likely was an illiterate monkey to reveal her whereabouts to Seaton Benecke? When the repairman came back outside, he would summon 'Crets to him, mount his motorcycle, and go roaring off to whichever ritzy neighborhood he and his parents called their own. The capuchin may have seen a woman in a vehicle across the street, but no monkey alive could equate her mostly hidden face with the angry countenance of the woman who had yesterday chased him from her upstairs bedroom. Or could he? Stevie began to suspect that the vision of primates was far superior to that of dogs and cats. Further, they were equipped with noses similar in structure to, but more discriminating in operation than, the noses of human beings. Maybe 'Crets *did* know who she was, and maybe he would find a straightforward way to blow the whistle on her foolish spying. A confrontation with Seaton would ensue, and Stevie's heretofore carefree afternoon would glug down the drain like a basin of greasy dishwater. Way to go, Samantha Spade. . . .

This fear commenced to justify itself. As she watched, the monkey gingerly crossed the parking lot to the street and perched above the sloping gutter with an eye on the afternoon's sporadic traffic. A man in an American compact honked his horn at 'Crets, obviously nonplused by so ominous an apparition at curbside, but the monkey sat up on his haunches and screeched at the driver. He would not be bullied. A German shepherd might daunt him, but not a pip-squeaking K-car.

My God, he's coming over here. He's actually going to cross the street. Why? What does he think he'll accomplish?

Stevie rolled her window tight and locked the door. 'Crets, meanwhile, came bounding toward the microbus on an unpredictable zigzag. Another automobile horn blared at him, but the monkey reached her side of the street unfazed by his perilous passage. The Falcon quarterback in Atlanta was not half the scrambler that 'Crets was; poor old Bartkowski just didn't have the monkey's knees. This facile comparison briefly deferred Stevie's realization that 'Crets had come for her, that his journey had a sinister purpose.

She leaned hurriedly across the passenger's seat to lock the other door. Glancing back out into the drugstore's pockmarked lot, she was startled to discover it empty. 'Crets had disappeared. He was probably too close to the van for her to see him.

By this time Stevie's fearful uneasiness had become an ill-defined dread. She was perspiring under her sweater, and a weight like an old-fashioned flatiron had settled in her bowels.

Seaton's goddamn monkey was after her. Several inches shy of two feet tall, dressed like a born-again professional athlete, possessed of almost exemplary table manners (leaving aside his penchant for bloodsucking), 'Crets nevertheless terrified Stevie. She was afraid that this unlikely creature would attain hulkish dimensions and rip the heavy sliding door off the side of her microbus. What he then might attempt she could not even imagine, although it would assuredly be violent and probably excruciatingly fatal. Why else would he bear on his diminutive shoulders a furry death's-head . . . ?

Stevie crept between the two forward seats into the passenger section. Still no sign of 'Crets. She depressed the handle on the sliding door, locking it, and hastily checked the latches on all the windows. Still no sign of 'Crets. As for Seaton, he had not yet reemerged from the murky interior of the headache-green building. If he came out within the next few minutes, he would look around for the capuchin, see her van, and ford the noisy street to make inquiries. The smartest thing for her to do now would be to goose this old wagon right out of town. Stevie hurried forward to do just that.

Seaton Benecke's face appeared on the other side of the supply company's plate-glass door, a milky blur in the gloom. What horrendously bad timing. Why couldn't his caller have kept him on the telephone another two minutes? Stevie slid down in her seat again and stared sidelong out the window to await the inevitable confrontation. She was doomed to be seen, no matter how far down she slumped or how fervently she wished for another outcome. She must resign herself to this unpleasant meeting. She must think up some excuse, even though she really had none. All because Seaton had dropped his keys and his goddamn monkey had darted across the street.

Well, she had asked for it. She had almost willed it to happen.

The door to the green building opened, and Seaton Benecke came through it with his door key in hand and 'Crets perched comfortably on his shoulder. Yes, with 'Crets on his shoulder! Heedless of her own likely conspicuousness, Stevie sat up and gaped. Neither Seaton nor the capuchin saw her. Young Benecke closed and locked the door, shifted his clinging familiar to his hip, and strode the small distance beneath the building's metal awning to his motorcycle. With 'Crets installed securely between his legs, Seaton started the big Honda, revved its engine a few times, and drifted almost effortlessly into the flow of traffic on the cramped avenue. He had never even seen Stevie. Like the demon who operated her Exceleriter, she had been invisible to him. So had her van. Perhaps, like the capuchin whom she had just imagined crossing the street from the store, she and her vehicle had not even been there.

"Nonsense," said Stevie aloud. "You saw what you saw, and you're most definitely parked across the street from Hamlin Benecke and Sons."

The steering wheel was cold under her hands, the accelerator pedal gently resisted the pressure of her foot, and the traffic moving up and down the street between the drugstore and the office-supply company clearly possessed both outline and substance. Stevie, bewildered and frightened, started her Volkswagen, headed it back toward the curving uphill avenue that debouched into Macon Road, and told herself that now, surely, she was going home. She would not be sidetracked again.

XXXII

Stevie decided to return to Barclay by an old state two-lane rather than the new federal interstate. The latter offered no services for nearly fifty miles, and she wanted the assurance of nearby houses, filling stations, and tiny rural businesses once it began to turn dark. Whereas the interstate often seemed a huge deserted autobahn through beautiful but unpeopled farming country, the winding state highway to Barclay took a traveler by secure if sometimes inconvenient stages through one shabby and/or picturesque community after another. To arrive safely at your destination, you negotiated alternating corridors of pine woods and variegated human settlements. If you had a flat tire on Highway 27, a Good Old Boy in a pickup or a member of the Wickrath County Sheriff's Patrol would stop to help you. On the interstate, though, you could wait for hours for assistance or risk being victimized by some hoodlum while trying to do the job yourself. Therefore, Stevie headed home by way of Cataula, Button City, and Kudzu Valley.

Twilight came early in February. Although it was only a little after five, the sun limning the pine needles on her left was sinking fast. Its rays winked through the trees like those of a failing flashlight. Grayness stained the eastern sky the way a spill of water discolors a linen napkin. It was cold and getting colder. Stevie had the heater turned to its highest setting. The noise of the heater and the warmth issuing from its blowers were partial antidotes to the psychological effects of the congealing gloom, but Stevie could not help thinking about the incident in Columbus.

She had seen 'Crets crossing the street, and then she had seen Seaton emerge from the store with 'Crets on his shoulder. How could the animal be in two places at once? He could not, of course. She had imagined either one or the other of these apparitions. There could not be *two* animals, she reasoned, because Seaton had shown no apparent distress at the absence of the capuchin with which he had first come to the door. That monkey, then, must be the illusion. She had *imagined* its clever sprint across the street. The real 'Crets had left the store with Seaton a few minutes later.

"Nonsense," Stevie said.

The fear of a flat tire or a thrown rod or some other mechanical problem had not kept her from using the four-lane. She had come by way of 27 because she feared that Seaton had spotted her van and deliberately dispatched 'Crets to spook and intimidate her. On his prior command the monkey had hidden from Stevie, and Seaton had then left the store with a stuffed effigy of 'Crets. (Marella had three or four truly lifelike stuffed animals—it was not impossible.) Once she had driven off, confused and fear-stricken, Seaton had returned to pick up his pet, smirking in his undemonstrative way over the success of his ruse.

The only other alternative, and not really a very credible one, was that 'Crets was clinging to the side or rear of her vehicle, a potential saboteur.

Now *that* was paranoid.

But Stevie half believed that 'Crets was traveling with her; indeed, that was why she had selected this well-patrolled route over the barrens of the interstate.

Cataula, here and gone. Look out for Button City, a smattering of mobile homes intersprinkled with two roadside eateries, a convenience store, an abandoned brick motel, and an automobile graveyard, spines of dented metal rusting into the sere and leafless kudzu.

On Button City's northern outskirts, just as the road began to meander through another fairy-tale corridor of wilderness, Stevie caught sight of an illuminated sign that she had never seen before. Of course it had been two months—back during the kids' Christmas holidays—since she had driven either to or from Columbus via Highway 27, and even small communities, given enough time, underwent some surprising changes. This change was not really that surprising, just startling in the dusky context of pine trees and naked cork elms.

Off to the left, in front of a chain-link fence enclosing a small frame house half-hidden by trees, stood one of those mobile advertising signboards with colored light bulbs winking around its edges and a host of plastic letters arrayed in its display grooves. Stevie could not yet see what the letters said, but she remembered that once on this spot there had been a crude wooden billboard featuring a big red hand and the legend *Madame Pauline, Palmst* (sic). Stevie had never stopped, or had any desire to stop, and once she got past the sign, a casual glance in her rearview mirror had always revealed that big red hand bobbing slightly, as if waving her a regretful goodbye. A trick of the road, of course, but a sight that had always amused her. Fortune-telling was far from dead in the New South; some of its practitioners even touted their services in the Yellow Pages.

Stevie slowed to see what sophisticated message had replaced the crudities of that original sign. There might be a feature story in the subject, one she had never explored in depth before. If her book proposal came back from the Briar Patch Press, Inc., as she believed it would, she had best have something else on the burner to keep her family fed. She might even be able to sell a piece on latter-day palmistry, Southern-style, to the latest incarnation of *Atlanta Fortnightly,* a magazine with an interesting editorial mix and a highly competitive pay scale.

All these thoughts went through Stevie's mind as she tried to read the message on the signboard, but there were too many letters to catch while coasting by, and a quarter of a mile beyond the little frame house she found herself backing along the deserted two-lane to see what she had missed. The other side of the sign bore the same lettering. Stevie parked on the shoulder, twisted in her seat, and with a Bic pen wrote it all down on the back of a manila folder:

SISTER CELESTIAL
PROPHETESS ** HEALER
DAILY & SUNDAY 7 A.M.–11 P.M.

SPECIALIZES IN: LOVE–BUSINESS–MARRIAGE
HELPS SOLVE ANY PROBLEM AND ANSWERS ANY QUESTION
DELIVERS GUIDING HAND PLUS REALIZATION
REASONABLE RATES ** FREE BLESSINGS

KNOCK AND THE DOOR WILL OPEN

A pretty thorough program. And, wonder of wonders, not a single misspelling in the entire message. That colon after SPECIALIZES IN might not be altogether kosher, but usually with roadside soothsayers you got misspellings galore: PALMST, FORETUNE TELLER, ADVIZER, PROFETIS, and so on. Because most of these self-employed sibyls had real difficulty divining what letter came after another, Stevie had never had any confidence that they could perform an analogous task with events. A dictionary was a book of spells, but few of these ladies apparently owned one. They were too busy crystal-gazing inverted fishbowls or turning over marked playing cards to consult Webster's.

Eight lines without a spelling error. Wow.

An orange light glowed in one of the windows of Sister Celestial's clapboard house; a curl of smoke did a sinuous dance upward through the haloed silhouettes of the trees. Stevie had parked on the wrong side of the road, facing oncoming traffic, and an automobile from the north swerved into the opposite lane and blew its horn to let her know that her van was not wholly clear of the highway. The blare Dopplered away from Stevie like the warning claxon of a passing diesel locomotive. Her hands began to tremble. The flimsy curtains on the window with the orange lamp drew aside and then dropped serenely back into place. Someone had spotted her.

"Shit," she sighed disgustedly. And thought again of 'Crets, who might still be perched on her rear fender.

Behind the chain-link fence, forty or fifty yards away, a figure emerged onto the porch of the house, an imposing figure in a shawl and a dark chemise. Stevie could not really see the woman's face, but she had little doubt that this was Sister Celestial herself, trapped for the moment in a cunningly allocated surplus of earthbound flesh. A stranger had parked by her property, and she was peering up through the dusk to determine if it was a customer or another ill-mannered interloper bent on mischief. You had to put up with a lot of guff from young people when you were a prophetess.

Stevie cranked her window down about four inches (too small a crack for a monkey of 'Crets's size to scramble through) and shouted, "I was just admiring your sign. I'll be going now. My kids are waiting for me up in Barclay."

"You sound like a woman in trouble," Sister Celestial called from her porch, and her voice was curiously high-pitched for so big a woman—curiously melodic, too. "Untroubled folks don't *stop* to admire my sign. They laugh their laughs and go on by." Imperiously she descended her steps to a stone walkway in her dusty yard.

"No, no, I'm not in any trouble."

"No trouble, gal? How come I hear a question in those words?"

How has this happened? Stevie asked herself. You don't need this. First the side trip to the office-supply company, now this unnecessary colloquy with a black prophetess-healer. Highway robber, call her. Just another con artist exploiting a gimmick to keep from doing *real* work. Just like you . . .

Aloud Stevie said, "You don't see a monkey on my rear fender, do you? Or up on top of my van?"

"You bring a monkey with you, child?"

"No, I—"

Sister Celestial laughed. "Do I look like Miss Jane Goodall?" She spread her arms. "Does this look like the Grant Park Zoo?"

"No. No, it doesn't. I didn't really expect there to be a monkey on the van. It's just that—" It's just that there's no possible way to explain myself without typing out everything that's happened to me since Tuesday.

"Well, you don't have to worry about monkeys then. Or lions or hippopotamuses, either. I don't even got a dog, child."

"Listen, I'm sorry I bothered you. I'll be going now."

Sister Celestial advanced up her walk between two rows of wire pickets bearing circular red reflector lights. She looked like a goddess stepping from island to island on a dark primeval sea; the reflector lights were the eyes of the mythological amphibians cavorting at her ankles. To dispel this unsettling illusion, Stevie had to glance again at the chain-link fence and the glowing signboard.

Whereupon the woman said, "You wanted to talk to me. That's why you stopped."

"I stopped to copy your sign. That's all. Madame Pauline used to live here. I was curious."

"Well, you're looking at Madame Pauline, child. Every seven years or so I got to be born again. Already I've been Prophetess Joy, Delphinia Promise, Mother Miracle, Madame Pauline, and Sister Celestial. Already I know who I'm likely to become my next changeover and the one after that. This is the fanciest sign I've *ever* had. Next one, though, 's liable to be neon and the one after that a parade of marchin' letters going back and forth over the highway. Look all you like. Copy all you want.''

"I'm finished. I've copied it.''

"My question's why you really want to. Answer me that. Why you want to copy some old crazy diviner's flimflammy sign?''

"I'm a writer. A reporter, sort of. I just thought this might make an interesting story.''

"Course it would. You up and change your mind about that?''

"No, no. It's . . . I've got to get back to Barclay.''

"You'll get there. You're almost there now. You come in, child, and take a bead on your troubles getting this story down. It's been better 'n three years since the papers done me, and that was only because a white man over in Ellerslie told Sheriff Gates I snooked him.''

The verb sounded like *snooked* to Stevie. Sister Celestial spoke clearly and forthrightly, seldom swallowing the tails of her words—but the incantatory rhythms of her speech and an occasional colorful expression kept Stevie off her guard. She was afraid she was being snooked. What she ought to do was nod goodbye and drive off, that's what she ought to do, but middle-class courtesy and the mercenary instincts of her profession restrained her. Maybe there was a *helluva* good story in Sister Celestial, outrageous Flannery O'Connor material to which she could apply the jaded journalistic cool of Joan Didion or the effervescent hipness of Tom Wolfe. Brock Fowler at *Atlanta Fortnightly* would snap up such an article and commission her to roam southwest Georgia looking for more. She would do a whole gallery of indigenous types, from the automechanic archery champion to the dulcimer-making Ku Klux Klanner to the . . .

"You coming, child?''

"All right,'' Stevie said. "Dr. Elsa shouldn't be too upset if I'm a little later than seven. She'll understand.''

"I'm sure she will," Sister Celestial agreed. "I'm sure she will."

Stevie opened her door, then hesitated and glanced up and down the shoulder for some sign of 'Crets. To cover this display of tentativeness, she said, "I can't afford a reading, though. That's one reason I didn't just come up to the door and knock."

"Not much reason," the black woman said. "What's the next to last line on my glowboard say?"

"'Reasonable rates. Free blessings.'"

"You got it, child. You got it. Now come on in out of this here cold and take you a chair in my shanty-castle."

Stevie started to climb down from the microbus.

"You better get that box of yours *all* the way off the road. Else you better have a mighty fine insurance policy."

Knowing the woman was right, Stevie maneuvered her van down the shoulder's incline to a small graded area where most of Sister Celestial's customers must park. Sister Celestial retreated to the comfort of her house. Before dismounting and following her, Stevie rummaged through the manila folders for the transcriptions of her nightmares. These she carried with her through the gate and over the stone walkway to her audience with the cheerfully domineering prophetess.

XXXIII

The house was cozy. A glance from the doorway showed Stevie that the front room served the Sister not only as entertainment area and business office, but also as a shrine to the beauty and accomplishments of her children; framed photographs of four or five young people in Sunday finery, mortar boards, or military uniforms hung like religious icons in one corner. A plump paisley sofa and an upright piano partitioned the room into smaller "rooms," among which Stevie could imagine Sister Celestial floating as the whims of memory, fortune, or will directed her. Because the wide gap-toothed grin of the piano blocked easy access to the recesses beyond, Stevie halted and stared at its dingy ivory keys.

Sister Celestial was in the niche beyond the piano. Looking over the ferns arrayed in red clay pots atop it, she said, "You like to hear this baby play, child? Rattle you off a tune all by itself?"

"Ma'am?" said Stevie, her eyes widening.

"Shut that door and come on in. This is a player piano. It runs through rolls. Sometimes I feed it a roll, sit back on my sofa, and let some W. C. Handy or Leadbelly fill up my hungriness for blues. Can't play a nursery rhyme myself. . . . You like to hear some automated jass, gal?" She said *jass* instead of *jazz,* and Stevie had the clear impression that the Sister was teasing her, both about the piano's roll-playing capabilities and her own stereotypical tastes in music.

"I didn't come here to listen to the piano."

"Of course you didn't. You're a woman in trouble looking for a story. You came here to solve your problems. Come on, then. Get around here where we can do somethin' for you."

Sister Celestial's head, with its cap of tight iron-gray ringlets, disappeared behind the green-velvet plumes of the ferns. Stevie edged around the piano and found the woman sitting in a coaster chair of varnished oak behind a wobbly card table whose torn vinyl surface was patched in several places with masking tape; the vinyl itself was like a sheet of melted Valentine's candy, sticky and red. To the prophetess's right, wedged against the wall, was a movable typewriter stand on which the Sister had enthroned an ancient Remington. This machine appeared to be sixty or seventy years old, a model, Stevie surmised, not unlike the one on which Mark Twain had prepared the first typewritten manuscript ever submitted to a publishing company. What a deluge old Mark had precipitated. Now, even though word processors were threatening to make typewriters passé, Stevie had found an antique in active use. She gaped at the machine as she had gaped at the piano.

"You type?" she asked.

"I do a two-finger dogtrot, child. . . . Sit down in that folding chair there. We'll take your contentment temperature and try to bring it right back up to ninety-eight-point-six."

Stevie did not sit. "Are the people who visit you crazy?" She wondered if Sister Celestial's bulky Remington, a kind of Platonic paradigm of the Typewriter (with a capital *T*) made manifest, were a phantom on the order of the monkey that had jumped down from Seaton Benecke's shoulder. Maybe she was not seeing a typewriter at all. Maybe her mind was deceiving her again.

"Not crazy, usually. Some of them got fevers, some of them got chills. You got a chill, seems to me, and it's bone-deep, child. I can hear the ice in your marrow every time you breathe."

"Why do you have a typewriter?"

"It belonged to Emmanuel Berthelot, first boss man of the Berthelot Mills in Ladysmith. My daddy was his driver, and in 1936, when Old Emmanuel died, that machine came to my daddy as a bequeathment. My daddy passed it on to me when he passed on."

"I mean, what do you use it for? In your business?"

"Besides typin' letters and so on? Well, I keep files. Each and every soul I talk to gets a case history, complete as it can be. Some of the fevered folks who visit me are decoys for the IRS."

"The IRS?"

Sister Celestial smiled so that crow's-feet formed around her limpid brown eyes. "Internal Revenue, child. Here's my rhyme:

> I R Ass,
> U R Ass,
> If Us Do Sass
> The I-R-Ass.

That's why I keep my files. Files look mighty fine and official, not to mention up-and-up, when they're typewriter clean. This old batterbox types clean. . . . Now sit down, child, so I can do you, hear?"

Stevie sat. On the wobbly card table she put the folder containing the nightmare transcripts. But she was supposed to *do* Sister Celestial (for a story); Sister Celestial wasn't supposed to *do* her. The whole idea of stopping here was to get material for an article; otherwise her presence in this cozily warm house, across an expanse of slick red vinyl from a black woman with a manner as soothingly cynical as Dr. Elsa's, made no sense. She should be on her way home. Why, then, had she brought the nightmare transcripts with her? To be *done?* Yes, probably. But whether she would be *done with* the obsessions these transcripts embodied, or *done in* by their more sinister implications, remained to be seen.

The black woman rolled a piece of typing paper into the Remington and held both forefingers over the keyboard. "Name?"

"I thought you were supposed to tell your clients about themselves. I didn't think they had to do it for you."

"*Ma-ry Ste-ven-son Crye,*" said Sister Celestial, typing out Stevie's full name with two fingers. "Age?"

"How did you know that?"

"Thirty-five. Address?"

"Wait a minute, Sister. I—"

"*Box 609, Barclay, Georgia, 31820.* Occupation?"

"Sister Celestial, please—"

"*Writer.*" Mercifully, the Sister stopped typing and looked up. "Well, that last one was easy. You told me it, didn't you? Now the others . . . the others I got my ways of knowing. I'm like an I-R-Assman that way, child."

"Do you know the trouble you heard in my voice?" Stevie asked imploringly. "Do you know why I *really* let you get me inside your house?"

"I reckon I may. It'd be better for both of us, though, if I didn't have to dogtrot it onto paper before you told me about it. Talkin' it out's part of the answer. You talkin', not me."

"A hotshot shrink in Atlanta would charge me fifty dollars for that little analysis," Stevie said reminiscently.

"I ain't that precious, Miz Crye. 'Sides, I don't shrink. I expand. I open doors, and let out pleats, and undo hems. You'll feel looser when you leave here."

"Or my money back?"

"Every penny. And if I know Sheriff Gates, he'll gladly come along to help you collect. Been waitin' to shut me down since Christmas. Don't like my new sign." She waved the tips of her typing fingers beneath her nostrils. "*His* sign's an old un, Pisces, and it stinks from everlastin' to everlastin'."

The Sister's clever disparagement of authority—first the IRS and now the county sheriff—made Stevie relax. Perhaps, like Seaton Benecke, Sister Celestial was a loyal reader of *The Columbus Ledger.* If so, close attention to Stevie's feature stories over the last fourteen or fifteen months would have given the palmist a clue to her identity. As for guessing her age, pitch-men in carnivals did that sort of thing all the time, and Stevie had openly told the Sister in what town she lived and why she was in a hurry to get home. That the woman had known her given name and the number of her post-office box disturbed her, yes, but these minor mysteries seemed both less urgent and less frightening than the fact that her Exceleriter had taken on an uncontrollable life of its own. Stevie made up her mind not to fret about them. Whereas the Exceleriter had become the outlet of an evil intelligence and the harbinger of some unspecified doom, Sister Celestial seemed to represent the very antithesis of menace: light, hope, warmth, and humanity. Anyway, that was how Stevie wanted to view her and so she made the desire the deed.

"How much for a half hour of your time?"

"You go ahead and lean on me, Miz Crye. If you ever come back, we'll settle up. This session's a freebie 'cause I think I'm gonna see you again."

"Why?"

"Never mind. Not even the sharpest inner eye can see tomorrow as whole as a Grade-A egg. I just got a feeling."

What a strange palmist-prophetess-healer! She did not ask to look at Stevie's hand. She did not reach down and lift a crystal ball to the top of the table. She did not deal out cards, or palpate the bumps on Stevie's noggin, or split a commercial tea bag and attempt to sort the shredded leaves with the aid of an oolong stick or a pekoe magnet. She merely sat with her fingers poised over the beautiful old Remington, her head half turned toward her client, listening attentively even during her fingers' intermittent tattoos on the keyboard. Stevie was amazed by the woman's studious secretarial mien and quick two-fingered meticulousness. It was not what Stevie had expected, but it was oddly calming—flattering, even. Her troubles mattered; the manifold woes of the world did not overwhelm and extinguish them as topics of interest and concern. Not here, anyway.

Stevie kept her hands on her manila folder as she talked. She purposely did not refer to its contents. She spoke instead of the precariousness of her position as breadwinner and surrogate father-figure; of its frustrations, uncertainties, and daily trials. This was the stuff of her book proposal, but, here, without the literary filigree, the calculated recourse to redeeming humor, or the underlying profit motive. This was an unembellished cry that made Sister Celestial's typewriter rattle and the times between its rattlings reverberate with the minor-key music of doubt and clinical self-accusation. A husband dead, two children to raise, a talent of modest proportions, an ambition incommensurate with that talent, an ego so fragile that even praise could bruise it, and a temper of volcanic dimensions, capped now by the lava dome of her own crusty concept of female machismo. *These* were the troubles Sister Celestial had heard in her voice; *these* were the troubles Stevie had borne for almost two years with spotty, self-conscious stoicism. They probably gave her voice a recognizable inflection, an ineradicable melancholy lilt, and so the prophetess had heard her lingering, ever-present hurt; had heard it even through Stevie's impatience and annoyance, the way the cry of a hungry gull is audible even over the relentless booming of the surf. The recitation of these troubles wore Stevie down. By the time she was casting about for a conclusion, tears had begun to spot the backs of her hands and to stain the manila folder beneath them. A fine, rousing rush of self-pity. A sad, embarrassing spate of the Crye-Me-a-River-I-Cryed-a-River-Over-You blues. Jesus, Stevie. Jesus . . .

"You still haven't let it all out," the black woman said.

"That's plenty, isn't it? That's more than enough." She was wiping her eyes on the sleeve of her car coat.

"That's nothing, Miz Crye Baby. Nothing at all." Sister Celestial had swiveled away from the Remington toward her, and her face, the harshness of her punning epithet aside, was a reservoir of cool compassion. She pointed her chin across the little room. "You see that gallery over there?"

"That shrine?" Stevie said, looking over her shoulder.

The Sister chuckled mordantly. "Call it how you like. Those my babies, child. Two boys, three girls, all of 'em got step by step from diapers to dress-ups. Single-handed, pretty much. Prophetess Joy found the formula, Miz Crye, and her and her offspring got me and mine through some truly baaaad times. Mother Miracle sent two of those children to Columbus College and might of got another one through if he hadn't skipped off to Saskatchewan."

"I can do it because you did it, huh?"

"Maybe not. I'm a hard act to follow. And I had a tougher row of turnips to chop, Miz Crye. My man didn't die, either. He up and run off when I was carryin' my fifth. My daddy long since dead and my mama gone to Michigan with a motor-car-makin' man, I was only twenty-two. I got to be Prophetess Joy, I guess, 'cause that's what I decided I wanted to prophesy. People like to hear it, too, even when joy's a long shot or a outright lie. Joy begat Promise, who begat Miracle, who begat Pauline, who begat the heavenly body you see tonight. That's the American way, the Land of Opportunities. Ronald Reagan's trying hard to give you the same kind of chance I had, Miz Crye, so maybe you can do it, after all. Maybe you can."

"Thanks for the incentive."

"Didn't any incentives come from me, now. Not from me to you, and if they did, gal, well, you're worse off than even *you* think." She swiveled back to her typewriter. "You still haven't let it all out."

Stevie took a crumpled Kleenex from her coat pocket and wiped her eyes. Snuffled audibly into the tissue. Began absent-mindedly twisting it into flimsy corkscrews. She had come to Sister Celestial's house to interview her, but had wound up being interviewed. Could she possibly tell this stranger—no longer a stranger, but, suddenly, her confessor and confidante—the impossible sequence of events that had twisted her life as she was twisting this Kleenex? Stevie thrust the tissue deep into her coat pocket and stared at the Sister.

"What's your real name? You know mine. What's yours?"

"Betty Malbon," said Sister Celestial without hesitation. "Why?"

"I have to know you're a real person. I have to know you're not just something my mind's made up."

"Pinch yourself, Miz Crye, Stevie, if that's okay to call you. Then pinch me." The Sister, a.k.a. Betty Malbon, laid her arm across the red vinyl for Stevie to pinch.

Through her sweater Stevie pinched herself on her left flank. An unnecessary experiment. Without pinching or jabbing or twisting her own mortal flesh, she hurt. Her pain was diffuse and amorphous, like a cloud. It lay like a cloud on her dully persistent awareness of her own inconsequential self. I hurt; therefore, I am. A philosophy that might be rephrased, Don't put Descartes before de hearse. Thinking has nothing to do with it. Hurting has everything, from your first footstep to your final falldown. Even though you're overstating the case for your own hurt, Stevie, which is nothing to what the Sister and millions of others have suffered, you're a piker when it comes to pain, for the elite, God bless 'em, are saints of unremitting wretchedness. . . .

"All right, child. Me now. Give me a pinch."

Seizing a bit of Sister Celestial's forearm between her fingers, Stevie twisted it as she had twisted her Kleenex.

"Uncle!" cried the black woman. "Uncle!" Stevie released her. "That proof enough for you, or you think I'm putting on a hurt I don't really feel? I'm as real to me as you are to you. Maybe realer."

"I know you are. That's what frightens me. Sometimes, lying awake at night, or half-asleep, I feel myself fading away."

"Yes, I know. Dreaming."

"Not dreaming, only. Fading out. Fading away. My consciousness stolen and put to someone else's purposes. This past week, though, that feeling's been underscored by an impossible occurrence. Dr. Elsa, my best friend, didn't believe it, and I'm afraid I'm believing it only to keep from thinking I'm either crazy or the pawn of some megalomaniac force."

"Tell me, child."

Reassured by the Sister's warm voice and bulk, Stevie told. She began with a vigorous, if minimally germane, tirade against the pricing policies of Pantronics Data Equipment Corporation, proceeded to an account of her trip to Hamlin Benecke & Sons in Columbus, and finished with a lengthy, ill-organized epilogue about the typewriter's behavior ever since. She tried to get everything in, but her story sounded scattershot and harebrained even to herself, replete with flashbacks, flash-forwards, and shameful arpeggios on the Sister's heartstrings. Teddy and Marella came into the story, and Seaton Benecke and 'Crets of course, and, inevitably, Ted, dead of cancer at thirty-nine. Finally Stevie opened her file folder and pushed the long page of nightmare transcripts toward the prophetess.

"I dreamed these," she said. "But the Exceleriter wrote them. They're all about Ted. In the third one he says he died so I could fulfill myself—as if his dying would somehow free me from the tyranny of his life. He wasn't a tyrant, though. It doesn't make sense to me, Sister. *It doesn't make sense!*" Again she concluded near tears, this time angry ones.

"May I read this?" the Sister asked. When Stevie, tight-lipped, nodded her assent, the black woman opened out the vertical half-page of examination-table paper, removed a magnifying glass from a drawer on her typewriter stand, and worked her way line by line through the transcripts. She was a slow and assiduous reader. She kept her brow furrowed as she read, but at one point tapped the page with her forefinger and smiled. " 'Licensed haruspex,' " she quoted. "Entrail-reading. That's one kind of divining I *don't* do. People still sometimes call me out to paw through pig or chicken guts, but not since my Delphinia days have I obliged 'em. The slime 'n' the stink's fit only for bustards. Birds, I mean." Her brow furrowed again, and she read some more, quoting in a high-pitched mur-

mur, " 'There's another woman, Stevie.' Hmmmmmm, mmmmh-yeah. Another woman, he says." She perused the remainder of that nightmare and almost the entirety of the next in thoughtful silence. Then she looked up at Stevie and declared, "And here he says this business about dying so you could develop yourself is a lie. Heartfelt, though. A heartfelt lie. That's nice, now. Heartfelt lies are mighty sweet, like syrup in an open head wound."

"He never lied to me when he was alive."

"You don't believe this story here?"

"It was a dream, Sister. It was a dream that my lousy, lying Exceleriter took out of my head. Why should I believe it?"

"You don't believe it 'cause it came through your typewriter?"

"That's right. I can't believe anything that machine puts to paper. It turned Marella into a living skeleton. It made me seduce my son."

"But it's only typin' what you're dreamin', ain't that so?"

"I guess. I don't know. Maybe I'm dreaming what the Exceleriter types. It could just as easily work that way as the other."

"The question is, Miz Crye—Stevie—where do these dreams come from and is the dreamer outside you tellin' lies or maybe layin' down clues? Answer that and you got a solution, I think. You got a chance to pull through your trial and put things to rights. You got to diagnose these dreams, that's all."

"Interpret them?"

"Everything you're worried about's in these nightmares. The way your husband ran out on you, why he did it, and what's gonna happen next. I want you to leave these here nightmares with me. So I can diagnose 'em."

"For how long? For how much?"

"Don't you worry about the fee." She swiveled aside and typed out a line next to Stevie's address. "That's your telephone number. I'll call you in a day or so to let you know how my oneiromancy comes out. By this Tuesday, maybe, it'll all be straight again, your Pretty Damn Exasperatin' machine as tame as this here rheumatic Remington."

"Oneiromancy?"

"Dream divining, Stevie. Haruspicy's out, but I'm good for chiromancy, horoscopy, astrodiagnosis, oneiromancy, water-witchin', and several different kinds of sortilege. Automatic writing's one of my tools, and teletypomancy's a field I'd be plenty happy to pioneer. You're so fascinatin', Stevie, I got to do you gratis. Tea leaves 'n' fishbowls aren't my style, but for a crack at a bit of oneirotypomancy—" the Sister smiled broadly— "I'd pay *you* a fee." She rolled the paper up and performed her two-finger dogtrot for another four or five lines, making notes or private comments on Stevie's case. "'Sides, child, I'm flat-out worried about you."

"Thanks," said Stevie. "You can keep the transcripts."

Sister Celestial swiveled back toward Stevie and put both her big hands on the table. "Just don't do a feature on me, all right? My new sign's all the publicity I need, even if I haven't been in the papers since '79. I get gawkers enough as it is. Horn-blowers 'n' toilet-paperers. All the uppity riffraff."

"I won't. I'll do something else. Tomorrow's a workday for me, and I haven't got a project yet—but I'll think of something."

"Sure you will."

"It'll drive me buggy—absolutely buggy—until I do, but I'll put my mind to it. Maybe a travel piece for *Brown's Guide.*"

Although the Sister was facing her, nodding her solemn approval of these tentative plans, the Remington suddenly began to type by itself. It churned out a brief line, activated its own carriage-return mechanism, and repeated this process three more times before falling silent again. In a stupor of disbelief Stevie and the prophetess watched the keys move up and down and the typebars flick in and out of their basket. When the clatter had ceased, the two women looked at each other.

"You did that, didn't you?" Stevie asked.

"Child, I was sitting here no different from you. That machine's a softie, but I've always had to touch it some to make it go. First time for everything, I guess, but I never hoped to play witness to a willful typing machine."

Trembling imperceptibly, but feeling the tremors quicken

and strengthen, Stevie stood up. "What did it write?"

The Sister removed the sheet of paper from the cylinder and passed it over the table to Stevie.

"No, I don't want it. Just read it to me."

Sister Celestial recited the Remington's lyric:

> "Ladybug, Ladybug,
> Fly away home.
> Your house is on fire,
> And your children will burn."

"Oh, God," said Stevie. "That's the Exceleriter. That's the Exceleriter talking through your machine. I've got to go." She cinched her car coat about her waist and banged her shoulder into the piano trying to get around it. "If anything's happened to Teddy and Marella, I'll kill myself." Clutching her shoulder, she ricocheted around the upright to the door. "That's not an idle threat, Sister. I mean it. Dear God, I've let them down again. I'll . . . I'll kill myself."

Stolid in her chemise, Sister Celestial appeared beside the piano. "Your friend's taking care of your children, Stevie. They're all right. That machine's having you on."

"My house is on fire, Sister. My children will burn." Stevie yanked the inner storm door open and pushed the outer pine-panel door into the cold. Beside Highway 27 the Sister's winking signboard played its colors across the ebony sheen of the asphalt. "Thank you for listening. I've got to go. It's my kids —my darling kids."

She stumbled off the porch and over the buried stepping-stones to the makeshift parking lot where her van awaited her.

"You drive careful!" the Sister shouted after her. "You drive careful 'cause I'm gonna call you, child! I'm gonna call you!"

XXXIV

Like some hotshot teen-age drugstore daredevil, Stevie scratched off. She rammed the microbus up the gravel slope to the highway and tore along the gloomy corridor north of Button City. Her heater whined a hollow remonstrance. Her heart was winking on and off with the colored light bulbs on the Sister's signboard. In fact, she did not begin to feel that she would survive the five-mile trip to Kudzu Valley, last rinky-dink community on the road to Barclay, until the van swung hard to the left and a curtain of midnight-black foliage obscured the reflection of the signboard in her rearview mirror. Then, there in the inky wilderness, she was alone with her worries.

Ladybug, Ladybug, fly away home. Your house is on fire, and your children will burn.

She was the ladybug, of course. What had she said to the Sister just before the Remington relayed the Exceleriter's upsetting message? "It'll drive me buggy—absolutely buggy." Ladybuggy, apparently. Anyway, those were her words, her very words, and the Exceleriter—tripewriter, psyche-scriber, demon machine—had deliberately echoed them in order to panic her, to add one more cruel fear to the pack already weighing her down. Even fourteen miles away it was still with her, that modern instrument of torture, and Stevie could hear it typing YOURHOUSEISONFIREANDYOURCHILDRENWILLBURN, YOURHOUSEISONFIREANDYOURCHILDRENWILLBURN in the lub-dupping syllables of her blood. She could almost see her dead husband's old family house aflame against the February night, angel wings of incandescence rippling toward the stars, gables collapsing and balustrades charring like kitchen matches. In that blue-vermilion inferno tiny bodies writhed, the burnt-match-stick bodies of her children. . . .

They're with Dr. Elsa, Stevie. They're not at the Crye place, they're at the Kensingtons' lakeside bungalow.

Maybe . . .

Kudzu Valley was dead. Stevie hated going through this little hamlet. On April 30, 1976, almost two and a half years before Jonestown, Guyana, several elderly residents of Kudzu Valley had committed suicide on the post-office lawn to protest the construction of the Cusseta Dam a mile or two above their town. Few people in the region fully understood the details of this bizarre incident, but, through anonymous local intermediaries, the Carter administration had urged the state to cancel this vast engineering project and the dam had never been built. Otherwise Stevie would be riding a motor launch over the subaqueous ruins of Kudzu Valley or skirting them in her Volkswagen via two or three dike-top causeways.

As it was, she cruised into the moribund business district at 7:13 P.M. (by the digital display board on the branch office of the Farmers and Merchants Bank) and, about two minutes later (by the luminous face of her own Lady Timex), past the infamous lawn of the red-brick post office, her fear of what she might find in Barclay perplexingly mixed up with her incomplete knowledge of what had once happened here. There were no ghosts on the lawn, thank God, and the people of Kudzu Valley had had the good sense to resist commissioning an abstract bronze statue to commemorate the dramatic self-sacrifice of their saviors. All they had built in the interval was a brand-new city hall, funded to the tune of $162,000 by an Economic Development Administration grant in the palmy days before the election of Reagan.

Stevie drove past this angular modern building, with its darkened churchlike windows, into a corridor of winter-blasted kudzu; a thousand leafless vines lay tangled at roadside, as if by a band of incompetent electricians. Wilderness was taking over again, the wastes of February. At the strange little town's northern city limits Stevie's headlights picked out a gigantic red torii, or Shinto gateway, spanning the road—but once beneath and through this eccentric landmark, her van freed itself completely of Kudzu Valley's sinister influence and sped up the bleak mountain's passing lane like Phaethon's reckless chariot. Home was only a few miles away.

Foot to floorboard, Stevie took the curves, dips, and inclines.

She met no other traffic, and when she came swinging into Barclay parallel to the naked mound of the railroad tracks, the Temperature & Time clock on her hometown bank said 38° (Fahrenheit) and a split second later 7:24 (P.M.). For some sign of the conflagration that was devouring her house and children Stevie looked to her left—over the tall common cornice of the pharmacy, the five-and-dime, and the Barclay Restaurant.

Nothing; no fire.

After cornering at the traffic light north of these establishments, she could see her house clearly, a pagodalike shadow fronted by elms and dogwoods. Unless the fire smoldered in the set-apart garage or the canning-bottle boxes in the storm cellar, no part of her property was burning. The Exceleriter, through the Sister's Remington, had lied. . . .

Again.

Oh, but I'm glad it lied, Stevie told herself. Not glad, of course, but thankful I didn't come rushing home to disaster. . . .

She parked in the unpaved drive near the kitchen and slumped in weary relief over the steering wheel. Meanwhile, her headlights illuminated the clutter of garden implements, plywood scraps, broken furniture, paint cans, and storage trunks in the open garage. It wanted cleaning out. She could not even get the microbus in there, and neighborhood dogs sometimes lay down amid the disarray for long winter naps. What the hell? Teddy and Marella were still with the Kensingtons and her house had escaped destruction. Stevie lifted her head and depressed the button controlling the headlights. Immediately the interior of the garage was plunged into darkness, and the chill night air began to refrigerate the van. Time to go inside and turn on a space heater.

As Stevie was reaching for the door handle, she heard a thumping sound behind her. She twisted about in her seat. The passenger section was empty, and the rear window revealed only the street behind her and the formless shrubs standing sentinel in front of Mrs. Hinman's screened-in porch. What had she heard? Maybe the sudden contraction of the van's gasoline tank or a lump of caked-on dirt falling from the chassis to the ground. Nothing significant. Stevie turned about and reached again for the door handle.

This time the thump was louder.

When she whirled in annoyance to determine its cause, she saw a miniature white skull peering at her through the rear window, its bottomless eyes drinking in her sanity like powerful vacuums. Tiny hands scrabbled at the glass beside the eerie face, while the horizontal slash of its mouth bowed into a threatening rictus. Although seldom one to surrender to hysterics, Stevie gripped the lapels of her car coat and screamed. Inside the bucketlike interior of the microbus, the scream rang and reverberated. Instead of dropping to the driveway, however, the ghoul clinging to the rear of the van found handholds and foot purchase and clambered straight up the window glass to the roof. It was 'Crets, of course, Seaton Benecke's evil little capuchin.

Stevie stopped screaming, opened the driver's door only to slam it shut again, and, after emphatically locking it, leaned away from the window breathing rapidly and holding her eyes tightly closed.

What do I do now? Sit here until help arrives? Break for the kitchen door? Get out and negotiate? What?

Stevie could hear the capuchin skittering back and forth above her, dashing from one end of the van to the other. His claws—or did you call them toenails and fingernails?— sounded like the noise the kids' guinea pigs had made running across the wire mesh in their cage. That was hardly an intimidating sound. Why was she cowering inside a locked vehicle while a creature less than two-feet-tall did a pitiful jig to keep from freezing its furry fanny off? Well, partly because of the way 'Crets looked, partly because she still did not understand how he had managed to travel all the way from Columbus to Barclay *outside* her Volkswagen, and partly because he belonged to Seaton Benecke. It might be possible to leap into the yard and brain the hideous imp with a rock, and so escape this ludicrous captivity—but the monkey had arrived here by some supernatural agency, underwritten in a menacing way by the misbehavior of the Exceleriter, and Stevie felt safer in the van. That afternoon she had imagined 'Crets growing to King-Kong proportions in order to dismantle her vehicle, and to-night she could easily imagine the monkey sprouting wings and swooping violently upon her as soon as she opened the door and bolted for the house. 'Crets did not have to obey the petty statutes of empirical reality; the typewriter in her study had given him a terrifying *carte blanche*.

"Come on, Elsa," Stevie said aloud. "Bring my kids home and get me out of this. My delusions don't affect you. 'Crets'll be gone as soon as you get here."

Then she remembered what Teddy had said to her that morning about feeling better about himself. Maybe her delusions had a wider range of application than she wanted to believe. Maybe they grew progressively stronger and more influential. After all, Sister Celestial had seen her Remington operate by itself, apparently at the bidding of Stevie's Exceleriter; and the prophetess's acknowledgment of the typewriter's uncanny behavior represented a breakthrough of sorts—human corroboration that Stevie was not merely hallucinating these episodes. Of course, she *had* dreamed a couple of episodes that her machine had tried to pass off as genuine. . . .

"Shit," she said. (Silly biddies screamed; resolute heroines cursed. She mildly disapproved of her own acquiescence in this convention, but that was the rule nowadays, and Stevie observed it because she was made that way.)

'Crets, meanwhile, continued to hold her hostage in the van, skittering, leaping, pausing for effect. The roof pinged and popped but only occasionally bubbled inward at the conclusion of a supercapuchin leap. It was like enduring a manic-depressive hailstorm. Stevie kept wondering about the pads on the monkey's feet, if they weren't absolutely frozen by now and bruised to boot. If you put your mind to it, you could almost feel *sorry* for the nefarious hellion.

Suddenly the scampering of the monkey was interrupted by a ferocious deep-throated baying. Stevie looked out the back window and saw Cyrano, the Cochrans' basset hound, standing bandy-legged and crimson-eyed in her drive, his lugubrious muzzle contorted into a sousaphone bell for the bugling of his bafflement and outrage. He was barking steadily, as he sometimes did on winter's nights when disturbed by a passing stranger or a bout of boredom. The Cochrans seldom seemed to hear him, but to Stevie Cyrano's mournful baritone always sounded like twelve drunks yodeling in a barrel and she frequently awoke to marvel at his stamina. Now he had sighted 'Crets, and if someone—anyone—took note of Cyrano's baying, her unexpected ordeal might soon be over.

On his big splayed feet the basset trotted to the Volkswagen's rear bumper and then, barking continuously, circled to his left. Cyrano was moving as 'Crets moved, tracking the monkey's wayward progress across the roof. Stevie could hear the capuchin screeching simian obscenities at the dog. She also found herself staring as if hypnotized into the basset hound's eyes, which were red-rimmed, always bloodshot. The lambent overspill of the arc lamp on the corner made the lower crescents of Cyrano's eyes gleam like broken coals. The dog looked insane, possessed. Saliva whipped from his mouth as he toodled his built-in sousaphone, and his squat front legs came off the ground an inch or two every time he toodled. He was an engine of indefatigable retribution; his bark was Great Gabriel's trump.

Even 'Crets seemed to think so. The capuchin rappelled on either air or willpower down Stevie's passenger window, his death's-head face looking briefly and malevolently in on her as he shinnied by. A moment later, a streak of fading silver-white luminosity, the monkey was jackrabbiting away from the house through a patch of exhausted ground that Ted had once liked to garden. 'Crets's escape was effectively concealed from Cyrano by the body of the van. Stevie tried to see where the capuchin was going, but he disappeared into the shrubbery on the far edge of the lawn.

What kind of eyesight did Cyrano have? None too good, Stevie feared. He had apparently registered the monkey's descent from the roof and mistakenly deduced that 'Crets was now *inside* the vehicle with Stevie. Ferociously snapping his jaws, Cyrano continued to bay at the Volkswagen, and his eyes had the ruthless demented look of a convicted multimurderer or a desperate rush-hour commuter. He wanted the monkey, and he evidently had taken the fatuous doggy notion that Stevie was harboring the white-faced specter in her microbus. Stevie had never seen the basset hound in such a temper. He was possessed for sure, with a blinding madness.

"Enough's enough," said Stevie. She tried to open her door.

Instantly Cyrano hurled his tubular body forward. (He was so long that he reminded Stevie of those hook-and-ladder fire trucks that require a steering wheel midway along their lengths as well as in their cabs.) He was too short to hit the door very high up, but he thudded against its base and drove it back on Stevie's shoe, meanwhile catching the silken flap of his right ear in the jamb. Howling in pain, he pulled his ear free and tumbled away from the Volkswagen even angrier than before. It was then that Stevie got her shoe loose and pushed the door wide open so that she could extend her wounded foot into the cool night air. It did not hurt badly, but she was as angry with the basset hound as he was with the door that had clipped his ear.

"Damn it, Cyrano. The monkey's gone. You're wasting your time. How about letting me limp into the house, okay?"

But Cyrano was not appeased. Either he held Stevie responsible for his injury or he believed that 'Crets was huddled in the passenger's seat, for he picked himself up and came yodeling toward the microbus on a dead run. His subsequent leap carried him scarcely higher than the door's metal sill, but Stevie positioned her unhurt foot so that the dog's nose struck it in the instep. Cyrano gasped, did an incomplete barrel roll, and landed on his side next to the van. He lay stunned for a moment, breathing heavily, and then struggled to get his feet beneath him again. Once up, he waddled away from Stevie toward his own house, occasionally throwing hurt, reproachful looks over his shoulder.

Stevie climbed down from her vehicle. "Yeah, I know. You save me from that furry vampire, and I kick you in the nose. Come back tomorrow, Cyrano, and I'll give you some table scraps."

Cyrano's waddle turned into a trot, and he disappeared into the drainage ditch on the other side of the street. A moment later he was a grotesque shadow hitching its way up the Cochrans' lawn. Well, that was why people let their dogs run loose in small towns—so they could frighten off suspicious organ-grinder monkeys and eat their neighbors' kids' pet guinea pigs. The prevention of other folks' crimes absolved the dogs of their own.

A cynical thought, maybe, but Stevie did feel sorry for that put-upon canine Pavarotti, Meistersinger of her Gelid Midnights. She had bruised his ego as well as his eponymous proboscis.

Just then, from the little avenue behind the house, Dr. Elsa's gunmetal-blue Lincoln Continental turned into Stevie's drive, crunching gravel as its headlights framed her against the clutter of the garage. Not quite in the nick of time. The battle was over. She had won it without either the doctor's or the kids' frantic aid, and she realized with a shudder of lonely capitulation that they would not be likely to believe her story about 'Crets and Cyrano. It was too outlandish. Nor could she risk telling them about her visit to Sister Celestial on the outskirts of Button City. Even if she said she had gone there to interview the woman for a story, they would upbraid her for using part of her one-day vacation for business purposes.

The headlights died, and Marella rushed into her arms to hug her. Teddy was coming toward her, and Dr. Elsa was standing beside the Lincoln's open front door. "You home already?" she asked. "We thought you might stay out scooter-poopin' till midnight or so?"

"On a Sunday? In Columbus?"

Dr. Elsa shrugged. "There's places to go, kiddo. You just have to know where they are."

"Like Victory Drive? That's where you get picked up by MPs for attempting to pick up soldiers." She hugged Teddy and asked Dr. Elsa if the kids had behaved themselves that afternoon.

"They were angels," said Dr. Elsa altogether seriously. "Sam played pool with them, let them feed the ducks, and took

Ted there for a little fishing trip on the lake. Around six he built them a campfire for a weenie and marshmallow roast. They had a good time, Stevie, and so did we. They couldn't've been better.''

"I burnt my finger," Marella said, lifting a bandaged finger for her mother to see. "I burnt my finger roasting marshmallows."

"It's nothing," Dr. Elsa said. "I put a bactericide on it and wrapped it up. Just scared her, I reckon. Our only mishap all afternoon." She ducked back into the big automobile and rolled down her window. "Got to get on home to Sam. Call me this week, Stevie, and we'll talk."

"Thanks, Elsa. Bless your heart. You're a brick."

"A brick?" said Marella.

Dr. Elsa waved off Stevie's expressions of gratitude and backed the hearselike Lincoln out into the street. Then she gunned it away from the house in the direction of the Alabama Road.

"A brick?" Marella asked again.

"A pillar of friendship," said Stevie by way of explanation, squeezing the girl's shoulder. "A buttress and a support." She felt strongly that she did not deserve such a friend. Her own contributions to Dr. Elsa were minimal. Shaking off this mild self-criticism, she beamed on Teddy and Marella. Teddy had had a field day, and Little Sister had suffered only a minor burn on her right index finger. So much for the soothsaying abilities of the Exceleriter. "You kids glad to be home?"

"I'll be gladder when we're inside," Teddy said. "It's cold."

"Me, too," his sister agreed. "It really is."

"What would you have done if I hadn't been here when Dr. Elsa brought you home?" Stevie asked. "I only just got here, you know."

The boy replied, "Warmed up the kitchen. We knew you weren't home yet because Dr. Elsa called a coupla times. But I said we needed to turn on a heater before you got home, or we'd freeze the rest of the evening. We'd've been okay until you got here. We really would."

But Stevie shivered. The idea did not appeal to her. Your house is on fire, and your children will burn. She could see the space heater in the kitchen billowing smoke as its asbestos fire grill grew blacker and blacker. She could see gables collapsing and balustrades charring like kitchen matches. It was a conflagration only in her mind, but it frightened her nevertheless. She did not trust the space heaters untended or tended only by children. She was glad she had arrived home before the advent of the Kensingtons' funereal Lincoln Continental.

"Let's go inside," she said.

XXXV

Stevie waited until the kids were snug in their beds before going into her study to check the Exceleriter. During her absence it had advanced the paper on the cylinder approximately three and a half feet. She leaned over the machine to see what it had written. At the top of the long sheet, centered, was the Roman numeral XXXI, beneath which this troubling narrative began:

> Once in Columbus, Stevie put the folders under the driver's seat and scrupulously locked the van every time she left it. The afternoon went well. She treated herself to dinner at ...

And so on, a concise and accurate summary not only of her activities in Columbus, but also of her feelings about them. Now, it appeared, the Exceleriter was reading her mind as well as transcribing her dreams.

Indeed, in retrospect Stevie wondered if the mysterious consciousness behind the machine's ongoing sleight-of-hand had not somehow influenced her otherwise aimless detour to Hamlin Benecke & Sons. The typewriter had wanted her to go there, and so she had gone. Was that possible? Did she have so little control of her own life? Stevie read the last two sentences of the Exceleriter's selective narrative:

> ... Stevie, bewildered and frightened, started her Volkswagen, headed it back toward the curving uphill avenue that debouched into Macon Road, and told herself that now, surely, she was going home. She would not be sidetracked again.

Before reaching Barclay, of course, she had stopped at Sister Celestial's—but the machine had failed to detail the particulars of that visit, choosing to concentrate instead on her stunned reaction to the puzzling duplication of 'Crets outside the office-supply company. Why this spooky episode rather than her meeting with the prophetess? To Stevie's way of thinking, the choice embodied a highly suspicious selectivity: it pointed to Seaton Benecke as the culprit behind the telemanipulation of her typewriter's keyboard. He could not resist making himself a part of *her* story. He could not resist tormenting her by emotional as well as physical intrusions into her life.

Or maybe, Stevie cautioned herself, this suspicious selectivity has another cause. Maybe the machine would have recorded my meeting with the Sister if it had just had enough paper to do the job. . . .

Stevie lifted the strip not yet typed upon, however, and saw that the Exceleriter might easily have set down the *gist* of her visit to the palmist, omitting the tiresome preliminaries and condensing or summarizing their conversations. What writerly rule required that the transcription of an episode make mention of its principals' every hiccup and garter adjustment? A rhetorical speculation that again led Stevie to blame Seaton Benecke for her persistent harassment. He had even sicced 'Crets on her. What else he might have in store for her was difficult to predict. It would undoubtedly entail something nightmarish. She had been living a nightmare for nearly a week. Seaton Benecke was its author, and 'Crets . . . well, maybe 'Crets was his agent.

Heh-heh, as the jester is wont to say when the king has not yet apprehended the joke; heh-heh-heh.

But the quatrain centered at the bottom of the strip of examination-table paper was no joke. Although she had not seen it before, it now jumped out at Stevie like a death's-head on a mortally uncoiling spring: the same disturbing nursery rhyme that, nine miles away, Sister Celestial's Remington had typed:

```
Ladybug, Ladybug,
Fly away home.
Your house is on fire,
And your children will burn.
```

"Not tonight they won't," said Stevie. "I've turned off all the space heaters, and I'm home—I'm home to stay."

Shivering in her robe, she put a new strip of paper in the Exceleriter. Then she unplugged the machine. If it could type without electricity, let it do so. She would capture its ravings. Otherwise, she would be set for tomorrow—when she must begin her workday with no clear idea of her mission. The long sheet of paper would be good for notes, a test track on which to marshal and race whatever project concepts she could subconsciously tune up overnight. Let the best concept win. In the meantime, however, Stevie hoped that by pulling the Exceleriter's plug she had disqualified Seaton Benecke's entry even before the race got started. She wanted a good night's sleep. She wanted dreams that she did not remember.

XXXVI

A weight oppressed her ankles. She was trying to sleep, but she could not withdraw her legs from the unknown burden on her feet. She wanted to turn to her side, to snuggle deeper into her blankets, but this enigmatic body—a folded quilt? a pile of dirty clothes?—pinioned her and made her dreams go haywire.

Finally Stevie *kicked*. She pulled one knee up to her abdomen and snapped it toward the foot of the bed, a reflex that dislodged the annoying object on her ankles—Teddy's thermal parka?—and sent it flying to the floor. Ah, that was better. . . .

Almost comfortable again, languidly scissoring her feet, Stevie burrowed beneath the electric blanket like an animal preparing to hibernate. It was as warm as Costa Rica under her GE, as cozy as Colombia—even if neither of those countries had hibernating fauna. No, of course they didn't. All they had were skinny-dipping salamanders, cockatoos, and monkeys that migrated through the rain forests in marauding troops. Occasionally an Indian with a blowgun would pick off one of those monkeys with a poison dart . . . *thwup!* . . . and the monkey would fall from its tree and land on her ankles like Teddy's thermal parka.

Stevie dislodged this monkey with another angry kick. Then she dug down even deeper into the synthetic tropics of her bed.

The type element on her Exceleriter began to buzz.

She could hear its muffled blatting from beneath her blankets. She had unplugged the machine, but now it was giving her sleeping house and everyone in it the raspberry. How could such a thing be happening? Stevie opened her eyes and pulled herself through a warm envelope of linen to the edge of her icy pillow. Here she turned to her back and looked down the length of her bed at her cedar chest, where perched a silver-gray humanoid shadow that studied her intently as the typewriter buzzed.

"Damn you, 'Crets!" Stevie shouted. "You don't belong here! Get out! *Get out!*" She hurled her pillow at the monkey (it had to be the monkey), and the creature's flimsy shadow leapt aside and scampered from the room toward the head of the stairwell. She could not hear the capuchin going down the stairs, even though the softest footfall usually set them creaking, because of the continuous noise from her study. Teddy would be up in a minute, and Marella too.

But before Stevie could stumble out of bed to see about the buzzing, it had stopped. The house was silent again. She lay still, hardly breathing. The next sound she heard was a muted scuffling in the stairwell, then the quick wooden outcry of the bottom step, the periodic groans of the steps above that one, and finally a satisfied thump at the carpeted head of the stairs. In perhaps half a minute's time 'Crets had gone down to the foyer, reversed himself, and come back up.

Stevie hoisted herself to a sitting position, keeping her eye on her own open door. A small shadow glided through this upright rectangle and performed an acrobatic leap to the top of the cedar chest. It was definitely 'Crets, young Benecke's Nosferatu familiar, and Stevie wondered if the beast had come to drink her blood. Well, if he had, he would have to take it cold; that was the only kind she had now. Although it might conceivably curdle, it would never warm, not under these chilling circumstances. Stevie had another pillow, but throwing it would gain her no lasting victory. Goose down was not an effective charm against vampires, not even when applied, in bulk, like a brickbat.

Maybe light would run off the creature.

Carefully, feeling the cold air invade the sleeve of her gown, Stevie reached behind her to turn on the Tensor lamp clamped to her headboard. A cone of white light shot into the room. Before the lamp's hard plastic shade had time to grow prohibitively hot, Stevie directed this cone toward her cedar chest, where it spotlighted the insolent monkey, making his eyes shine like bolts of liquid mercury. The sight galvanized Stevie with fear, erecting the short hairs on her nape. 'Crets, as if pleased with the impression he had made, grinned. It was impossible to distinguish the whiteness of his face from the whiteness of his teeth; his head was a skull with small silver lanterns behind its eyeholes.

The skull had a body, however, and as 'Crets grinned at Stevie, he also fingered his genitals. He had no shame. Just like those monkeyhouse inhabitants who offend the sensibilities of their visitors—families with small children, strolling pensioners, courting teen-agers—he seemed to derive more than tactile delight from this immodest exhibition. His grin conveyed his delight. His fingers conveyed an innuendo. Unsheathed, his thin pink member conveyed a ludicrous threat. What would it be like to bear in your womb the seed of a diminutive agent of death? What would it be like to be raped by a housebreaker no bigger than a teddy bear?

"Where's your football jersey?" Stevie blurted.

'Crets cocked his head but did not stop diddling himself. "I took it off downstairs," he said, in a familiar voice.

(What other sort of voice should a familiar have?)

"Why?" asked Stevie, trying to identify the monkey's distinctive inflection. Unfortunately, his voice seemed to be playing at the wrong speed, like the voices of those obnoxious recording "chipmunks" who turned up on the radio every Christmas. "Why should you take your jersey off, 'Crets?"

"I got hot."

"Hot? How could you get hot? It's probably two or three degrees below freezing right now."

"Not downstairs it isn't."

"It couldn't be any warmer down there than it is up here," Stevie said reasonably. "Heat rises. A portion of the heat downstairs always works its way to the upper floors. That's a well-documented phenomenon."

'Crets put a little backhand English into his manipulations. "That's interesting. Considering the location of hell, no one should *ever* go cold." The monkey's 78-RPM voice gave this pronouncement an irritatingly superior ring.

"*I'm* cold," Stevie said. "I'm always cold this time of year."

"Go downstairs, then. That'll warm you up."

"What are you talking about?"

"Your kitchen's in flames, that's what. You left the space heater on, a draft through the kitchen blew your wall calendar into the heater's grate, and after February and the other months caught fire, the fire spread to the Sunday newspaper—which you carelessly left on the floor near the heater, Stevie—and at this very moment your precious oaken table is blazing away like a homecoming bonfire."

"But I didn't leave a heater on!"

"I'm sorry, Stevie, but you did." The monkey tilted his head. "Just listen."

Stevie listened. She could hear the fire crackling downstairs, an altogether terrifying sound. Volunteer-fireman Bob Cochran had once described the Crye house as "a two-story tinderbox," and Stevie further imagined that she could see the shadows of flames leaping on the walls outside her room, at the head of the stairs, flickering like strobes across the floral wallpaper pattern.

"But you just came from down there," Stevie remonstrated. "The fire couldn't have spread that fast."

"I went down there to turn off your smoke alarm," 'Crets said. "It was making a horrible racket—*bzzzzz! bzzzzz! bzzzzz!*—almost like a broken typewriter. It's been over a year since you replaced the battery in that contraption, too. I'm surprised it still worked."

"A lot of good it does shut off! Let me up! I've got to get Teddy and Marella out of here!" Stevie grabbed for her robe, but the capuchin leapt forward, tossed it to the floor, and hunkered like a gargoyle at the foot of her bed.

"Don't you want to see the climax?" he asked insinuatively, his fingers tweezering his obscenely slender organ.

"I don't care who you are or where you're from," Stevie said from between clenched teeth; "you're a vile, filthy demon, and if you try to keep me from rescuing my children, I'll tear your ugly head off. That's the only climax I want to see."

"Come, come," said 'Crets.

"I was raised on a farm in Kansas. My father taught me how to wring the necks of chickens. I'll do the same to you," she warned the creature.

But could she really act with such barbaric ruthlessness? Stevie suddenly realized 'Crets's speech patterns and inflections resembled those of her late husband. Even the amplified crackling of the encroaching flames could not diminish the importance of this weird similarity. Ted had come to her in the guise of a hateful South American monkey! An organ-grinder's monkey!

"Right you are," 'Crets acknowledged. "Here's the climax. I'm so damned hot I've just got to get this off."

Stevie expected a convulsive spurt of semen, but instead the creature pulled a tab at his navel and split his capuchin costume right up the middle. One naked leg came out, and then the other—after which tiny human hands gripped the furry lapels of the monkey suit and shrugged it from a pair of tiny human shoulders. Atop Stevie's cedar chest strutted a naked homunculus with the face of an elderly white-throated capuchin. Then, however, the creature finished his unmasking by

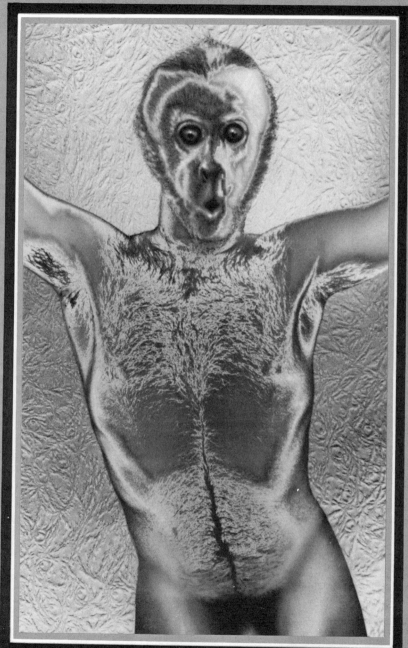

J.K.POTTER

tilting back his head and dropping the capuchin face behind him. *Voilà!* There, eighteen inches tall, smaller than life, stood Ted!

"That's better," he said. "I hate wearing that thing."

"I'm having a nightmare," Stevie told herself. "The Exceleriter's doing this. There's no fire, and Ted isn't here."

"Could your nightmare be any worse than mine?" Ted asked. The monkey's know-it-all fiendishness had given way to a plea for understanding. "Dead in my prime, resurrected against my will, plagued with guilt, and condemned by Seaton Benecke to masquerade as his familiar. Marella was taller when she was born than I am now. Imagine that, Stevie."

"This isn't happening. You're not real."

"I'm as real as you are," Tiny Ted said sharply. "I know some things you don't know. I had to die to learn them."

Flames were ascending through the stairwell. Their shadows danced on the wallpaper. Smoke had begun curling through the upstairs hall. It moved sinuously, bringing with it an acrid stench.

"Teddy! Marella! Get up, kids! We've got to get out of here!" Stevie swung her feet to the carpet, scooped up the robe 'Crets had flung from her, and, while striding toward the door, plunged her arm into one sleeve. Whether this nightmare was genuine or wholly illusory, she had delayed too long. She and the kids could make their way to safety down the iron steps of the spiral staircase just off the upstairs bathroom. Her allegiance was to her children, not to this naked travesty of the man she had once married. Oddly, two years before he died, Ted had had the spiral staircase built into an expensive gabled tower off the bathroom as an alternate escape route in the event of fire. Tonight it would be tested. *"Teddy, Marella, get up!"*

The homunculus—her late husband—jumped from the cedar chest and tangled himself in the hem of her robe trying to grab her right ankle. Stevie crashed headlong to the carpet. Smoke came convoluting dreamily through the hall and over her outstretched body into her bedroom. Stunned, Stevie glanced up to find Tiny Ted hunkering in front of her, his hands dangling between his knees. His furrowed brow bespoke his concern—for her, if not for the children he had fathered. What was the matter with him? He was truly a monster.

"What kills most so-called fire victims," he told her, "is smoke inhalation. Stay on the floor, Stevie. It's safer down here."

"Teddy and Marella aren't safe," she hissed, trying unsuccessfully to get up. Had she pulled a hamstring? wrenched her knee out of its socket? what? "We've got to get them to safety, Ted. Please, you've got to help me. Why don't you seem to care?"

"I love you, Stevie."

"About your kids, I mean. They're your children, too." As the roof over the front porch just outside her bedroom collapsed, she screamed the children's names. But maybe Teddy and Marella had already died, victims of smoke inhalation. Her cries—her pleas—mutated into an uncontrollable anguished sobbing. "Why don't you care?" she finally managed. "Why—don't—you—care? . . . Oh, damn you, Ted. *Damn you.*"

"That's an unnecessary stipulation, Stevie." He reached out and stroked her forehead. "It's just that I'm your baby now. Is that so bad? I don't have claws for fingernails or a satanic golden cast in my eyes. I'm small and cuddly, and I can make intelligent adult conversation."

Stevie struggled to rise, but her forearms would not support her weight. She collapsed as the porch roof had collapsed. Her eyes stung, and her throat felt as if someone had poured a beaker of ammonia down it. "Go away," she admonished the demon. "Just let me die." She rolled back toward her bed and, crawling hand over hand, reached the skirt of the bedspread she had quilted in the early years of their marriage. Clutching this, she pulled herself into a strata of roiling smoke just above the rumpled plateau of her mattress. Here she sprawled, coughing feebly, to await the painful suffocation that would kill her.

Ted jumped onto the bed beside her. At her ear he whined, "I'm hungry, Stevie. I haven't eaten all day. Remember that fried egg you fixed me yesterday? That was delicious. I could use one now. Whaddaya say, honey? How 'bout a little midnight snack?''

Ladybug, Ladybug, fly away home, Stevie was thinking. The noise in her ear was no more consequential than a mosquito's buzz. A petty annoyance. My children, though—my darling children have burned. Nothing petty about that. Everything's ruined. And . . . it's . . . all . . . my . . . fault. . . .

"You probably wouldn't even have to dirty a frying pan," Ted was saying. "Just break the egg on the landing. Whaddaya say, honey? I'm famished."

"No," Stevie said faintly. "No."

Ted, on all fours, nuzzled her neck. "Then I'll stoke up in a more romantic way. Remember how I used to give you hickeys when we were dating? You used to have to wear a scarf to church on Sundays. Remember?" The homunculus bit her sweetly and suckled from the wound. The homunculus suckled and sipped.

For the first time in her adult life Mary Stevenson Crye swooned. Consciousness left her, and the incubus who had arrived in capuchin drag to bugger her self-respect stole from her nightmare on tiptoe.

XXXVII

The type element on her Exceleriter began to beep.

Stevie could hear its muffled beeping from beneath her blankets. She had unplugged the machine, but now it was giving her sleeping house and everyone in it a series of juicy raspberries. How could this be happening? Stevie opened her eyes and pulled herself through a doughy envelope of linen to her pillow. Here she turned to her back. The beeping was much louder. Furthermore, it did not sound like the noise her typewriter had made last Tuesday. Discontinuous and decidedly more official-sounding, this beeping was like the claxon on a submarine or the storm-warning siren in a small wheat-belt community. It reminded Stevie simultaneously of old war movies and her girlhood in Kansas. . . .

It reminded Stevie that she had just had another disconcerting nightmare. A nightmare that she remembered in its entirety. Damn.

The noise was the smoke alarm in the kitchen.

If she did not rush to see what had set it off, the fiery prophecy of her nightmare might fulfill itself—minus, however, the unwelcome guest appearance of her late husband, first in the garb of an organ-grinder monkey and then in his un-Sanforized birthday suit. Well, Tiny Ted's absence would be a small blessing if the house burned down, if she and the kids were trapped in the conflagration exactly as they had been in her dream. Stevie checked to see that Teddy and Marella were all right, then plunged recklessly down the slippery wooden stairs to the foyer. She hurried through the unheated dining room to the kitchen, pulled the door open, and flicked on the overhead light. The space heater was not extruding plumes of smoke into the room, and the Sunday newspaper did not lie smoldering under the table.

Beep! went the smoke alarm. *Beep! beep! beep!*

Arms akimbo, Stevie stared at the mechanism, which she had mounted high on the wall above the light switch. Of course, she thought. That damned beeping signals the impending demise of the smoke alarm's battery. The alarm sounds continuously if it detects smoke; it beeps only when the battery needs replacing. Of course it couldn't possibly wait for a civilized hour to begin beeping; it had to go into full submarine-sounding mode at . . . Stevie glanced at the digital clock on her wall oven . . . at three-thirty in the morning. And a Monday morning, at that. Still, she was grateful that the alarm hadn't awakened the kids.

She was even more grateful that it had not detected smoke. The house was not going to burn down tonight. However, she must disconnect the alarm to stop its annoying beeps. Stevie found a screwdriver in the pantry, pushed a chair into place, and stood on its seat to pry the casing off the smoke alarm. She extracted the oversized copper-colored battery and restored the house to the cold sanctity of predawn silence.

Well, *near*-silence. Cyrano was baying lackadaisically at one of the rare passing truckers on the Alabama Road. Or maybe it was another neighborhood dog. No matter. It was a relief to hear the barking instead of the smoke alarm. Other sounds included the humming of the refrigerator, the clicking of numbers in the digital clock, and, outside, the limbs of a colossal pecan tree tapping one another like the movable counters of an abacus, telling the lonely minutes as surely as any clock.

Stevie turned off the light, closed the kitchen door behind her, and returned to the stairwell. On the landing between the first and second floors she paused and looked out the uncurtained window. For an instant she thought a child, a toddler, had somehow escaped the crib in its nursery and wandered out into the night. When this tiny person turned its head toward her, however, Stevie saw that the trespasser was not a human being, but Seaton Benecke's ubiquitous 'Crets. Stevie and the monkey stared at each other in the starlit darkness, each hypnotized by the other. Finally, willing herself to break the spell, Stevie rapped on the window glass and mouthed an angry command:

"Get out of here, you vile, filthy beast. Get out of here."

Jerseyless, 'Crets bared his canine teeth and screeched an unintelligible obscenity at her. This sound was audible through the glass, but only barely. Then the monkey fled across the yard and through a pile of leathery brown magnolia leaves to the fence surrounding the Gowers' house. The capuchin scurried over the fence and disappeared into a border of ragged, indistinct shrubbery.

Shaken, Stevie slumped against the wall on the landing. This time she had not been dreaming. The Exceleriter had not been dictating her experience. She had seen the monkey, and the monkey had seen her. How he could survive in this weather she had no idea, but he was haunting her almost as stubbornly as the memory of her dead husband haunted her. He was not Ted, of course, but her nightmare had clearly sought to impel her to that abhorrent identification. Ridiculous as well as abhorrent. How could anyone imagine Ted running about the neighborhood naked, scurrying over chain-link fences, inciting Barclay's canine population to riot? Ted had never been one even for leisurely afterdinner walks.

"I can't take much more of this," Stevie said aloud. "I haven't had a full night's sleep since last Tuesday."

She climbed the remaining steps and went into her study. Her typewriter was unplugged. The strip of paper that she had inserted in it before retiring was blank; it had not advanced a single inch. That meant that her nightmare had originated in her own subconscious, not in Seaton Benecke's malign fondness for "deepness" and "nitty-gritty stuff." She had only herself to blame, that part of her personality that had not yet come to grips with the death of her husband. Of course, the anomalous presence of 'Crets, an evil phantom on the periphery of her expectations, might have influenced her dream, too. Perhaps she had concocted such vividly perverse nightmare imagery not in her own subconscious but from telepathic clues supplied her by Seaton's itinerant familiar.

"What garbage," Stevie said. "What claptrap."

Yet it was a genuine relief to find that the Exceleriter had neither dictated nor transcribed her nightmare. She could defeat the machine by the simple expedient of pulling its plug. No need for Slime-and-syrup cocktails. Now, to put herself back on a wholesome midnight-to-morning schedule, all she need do was find a method of dreaming pleasant rather than stressful dreams. On the other hand, she regretted her newfound ability to remember what she dreamt. Why had that happened to her? She wanted her subconscious to manifest itself only when she was working at her typewriter. That was when the hobgoblins of her nether mind—the hippogryphs, satyrs, and dragons—could safely, even healthfully, come out. Indeed, that was when she *needed* them. She would need them in the morning.

Stevie covered the machine. "This is a ruse," she informed it. "You're trying to lull me. I know what you're up to. Somewhere, maybe at Sister Celestial's, my nightmare's on paper, passing itself off as the truth." She yanked the cover back off the machine. "What do you say to that, huh?"

Like Tar-Baby, de Exceleriter he don't say nothin'.

"Good night," said Stevie, shivering. After haphazardly recovering the typewriter, she padded barefoot back to her bedroom.

XXXVIII

Teddy and Marella got off to school without hitch or fuss. Blue Mondays were seldom blue for them. Although they professed not to like school, they went off to face the pedagogical firing squads with firm steps and uplifted heads. Their afternoon at the Kensingtons' had done them at least as much good as had her own little trip to Columbus. Well, Dr. Elsa, no matter how Marella might construe the term, was a brick.

Stevie, however, was fidgety. The Monday Blues, she thought: I gottum to the bottom of my sole-worn shoes. . . .

She dallied over a second and then a third cup of coffee, going through the Monday *Constitution* as if it were a document that she would later be forced to sign. She read her favorite columnists twice, inwardly arguing that this exacting perusal of the competition was "research." She even spent fifteen minutes on the boring arcana of the business section. All the financial news was bad. If misery loved company, the United States of America was a continental love feast. On the heartening side of the industrial ledger, however, a notice that two vast monopolies had agreed to merge. That was nice.

You're procrastinating, Stevie Crye. You don't know what you're going to do today, and you're cravenly putting off going upstairs.

I'm afraid to plug my typewriter back in, another part of her consciousness countered. That's the only craven thing about my foot-dragging.

Nonsense. You're afraid to go to work.

I'm afraid the Exceleriter won't let me. I'll plug it in, and in retaliation for depriving it of power overnight, it'll take complete control of all its functionings. I won't be able to reassert my primacy. That's what I'm afraid of.

Just unplug it again.

Well, of course. But what if that doesn't work a second time? What if the Exceleriter decides to go manual?

That's not very likely, replied Stevie's Calvinistic alter ego. How could it do that?

How does it do what it does now?

Well, by demonic possession, I guess. A ghost in the machine. A force—some sort of intelligent force—invades the typewriter and directs its behavior.

That's a consoling explanation. Demons, ghosts, and mysterious forces aren't usually Georgia Power subscribers. If they can take over an electric machine, they can take over a manual one just as easily. You haven't forgotten Sister Celestial's old Remington, have you?

The Exceleriter wasn't designed for manual operation, Stevie. Power's got to be flowing through it.

Who's to say this mysterious force you hypothesized can't generate its own power? In fact, it *does* generate its own power. It's something besides electricity that operates the on/off key.

This morning, Stevie, the something operating the on/off key ought to be you. You need to get to work. You have a family. You—

All right. All right. Stop nagging me.

Stevie turned off the coffee maker, tossed the morning newspaper into the trash, and, driven by the discipline of guilt, tormented by the need to confront her typewriter alone, trudged upstairs to her study. The house was empty but for the machine and her. If she plugged it in and it rebelled against her poor human sovereignty, she had no clear idea what she would do. Flee the house? Drive to Ladysmith and cloister herself in the regional library's reading room? Or carry out a brutal demolition of the Exceleriter? No, no; not this last. Why permit her baser instincts to override the lessons of common sense?

Her room was ready for her. The space heater had warmed the air to approximately sixty degrees, and the paper she had rolled into the typewriter awaited the tangible imprint of her imagination. She must work. To work, she must first kneel and plug in the Exceleriter. Stevie knelt and plugged in the machine. She waited. Expecting a burst of typewritten abuse, clackety crescendos of vilification, she instead heard only silence. No rebellion yet. She was still in control. Somewhat reassured, she turned the typewriter on and listened to its soothing purr.

She listened for a long time. What was she going to write? What project concepts could she list?

An article on Westville for *Brown's Guide*. A profile of three young Georgia playwrights for *Atlanta Fortnightly*. A little theater review for the combined Sunday edition of the *Ledger-Enquirer*. A historical piece on the Creek Indian warrior Hothlepoya for *The Anniston Star*. An article about the horticultural work of the Georgia Building Authority for a regional gardening magazine. And a semihumorous commentary on the "rewards" of widowhood for *Ms.* or *Cosmopolitan* or any other national magazine that might be interested in an upbeat treatment of a downbeat subject. All these potential projects Stevie methodically listed on the sheet of examination-table paper in her Exceleriter. Double-spaced, the list consumed no more than two vertical inches of the page. It seemed a feeble effort, each item hopeless of fulfillment, at least in her present state of mind. All but the last one would require legwork, and the last article was the one she was least likely to sell. Disconsolate, Stevie sat staring at the handiwork of a painful fifteen minutes.

What now?

Pick one, put your mind to it, and do it, said Stevie's Calvinistic alter ego. Long live the Protestant work ethic. Whosoever cheerfully abides by it herself lives long. . . .

The last one, then.

That's fine. Good choice. Think of some interesting headings, organize them, and get to work. It's only nine-thirty or so. With diligent application you ought to have a thousand usable words by noon.

You sound like a freshman English instructor.

Get to work!

By eleven o'clock, however, Stevie had made no appreciable progress. She had written seven different versions of the same opening paragraph, substituting spry words for colorless cripples, repositioning participial phrases to give the passage a brisk, headlong rhythm, and elaborating a metaphor that soon grew as hideously unwieldy as a foam-rubber hunchback. With typewritten XXXs or smeary lines of blue ink, Stevie struck through these successive variants. Now she was staring at the page, simply staring at it, so jittery with frustration that to stay in her chair required a fatiguing exercise of will. She wanted to wash dishes, jog around the block, do anything but what she was doing now.

Maybe *this* is the Exceleriter's revenge, she thought.

In her bedroom the telephone rang.

Stevie had never had an answering device. Most of her Barclay friends and acquaintances knew that except in emergencies she preferred them to telephone her in the evenings. Nothing was more disruptive of her thought processes than a series of daytime telephone calls. Often the caller was a sales rep for an aluminum-siding company. "We had siding installed in 1976," Stevie would lie. "No, I don't know anyone else who'd be interested. All the houses around here are brick." Another lie, but it usually took care of the aluminum-siding shill.

Just as often, however, the caller would be a would-be writer who, having seen her by-line in *Atlanta Fortnightly* or elsewhere, wanted her expert advice on Breaking Into Print. Almost invariably Stevie would encourage and commiserate with these people, even those self-confident aspirants who, without a single literary artifact yet to their credit, knew beyond doubt that their first haiku, essay, novel, film script, or epic poem would eclipse in both artistic quality and popular appeal the complete combined works of William Shakespeare and Irving Wallace. "Write it and send it off," Stevie would tell them. "You never know, you never know." When her own work was going well and the telephone rang, Stevie, groaning her dismay, would dutifully answer the summons; it might be a magazine editor with another profitable assignment. You never knew. . . .

Today Stevie was grateful for the interruption. It gave her a legitimate excuse to abandon her Exceleriter. Even if the caller was a high-pressure salesman or another unpublished genius, she would gladly endure the ensuing spiel. In fact, she was terrified the other party might have the wrong number, not an infrequent occurrence on the Ladysmith-Barclay-Wickrath exchange. Two rings, three rings, four—she had to catch the telephone before the caller hung up.

Stevie bolted from her study, leaving the door open. She reached the telephone on its sixth chilly brrrrrr-ring.

"Hello?"

("This is David-Dante Maris, editor-in-chief at the Briar Patch Press in Atlanta. May I speak to Stevenson Crye, please?"

"Speaking."

"Hello, Mrs. Crye, I'm delighted to find you at home. Would it be all right if we talked for a few minutes? I think you'll find what I have to say, uh, quite interesting."

Peripherally Stevie saw a small white shape flash past her bedroom door on its way into Marella's room. The capuchin? Tiny Ted?

"Mrs. Crye?"

"Yes, sir," Stevie said. "I'm still here."

"I imagine it must be quite a shock hearing from us so soon, but that's the way we like to do business at the Briar Patch. We're not a New York company, you know. That's our biggest failing to some, our saving grace to many others. You, now . . . you couldn't have done better than to send this material to us, and we'll do well by you if you can comfortably accede to, uh, some crafty editorial interference." David-Dante Maris chuckled amiably. "Brock Fowler at *Atlanta Fortnightly*'s an old University of Georgia buddy of mine, Mrs. Crye, and he says you're turning into a seasoned professional faster than anybody he's ever seen without a journalism background."

Shivering, Stevie tried to make sense of what was happening. It seemed that her prayers—one of them, anyway—were being answered. "Can you hold a minute, please? I've got to get to my kitchen."

"Ma'am?"

"Just a minute. I'm freezing up here." Well, that probably made no sense to D.-D. Maris, but she couldn't talk to so influential a caller while her teeth were chattering. Therefore, after placing her receiver on the bedside table, Stevie hurried from the room. In the corridor she glanced back toward Marella's spacious bedchamber. Sunlight poured through the upper panes of the storm windows and danced in watery patterns on the lime-green carpet—but no 'Crets, thank God; no naked homunculus pretending to be Ted. She had only imagined that troubling blur at the edge of her vision. Unless, of course, the intruder had darted into the step-down closet abutting on the attic. Then Stevie would not be able to see him without entering Marella's room and rummaging about in the dark.

No time for that. David-Dante Maris had called her longdistance from Atlanta, and she had put him on hold. Maybe he would think that, on another line, she was concluding a deal with her Hollywood agent, urging her broker to buy a thousand more shares of AT&T, or sending a mailgram to the acquisitions editor of a British publisher in London. Maybe, but not very likely.

Stevie pistoned down the stairs, burst into the kitchen, and, gasping audibly, grabbed the receiver from the wall phone. "Mr. Maris . . . Mr. Maris . . . I'm back . . . I'm sorry I kept you . . . waiting . . . sorry I kept you . . ."

She stopped. Although she had heard no dial tone, she was afraid Mr. Maris had taken umbrage at her unorthodox telephone manners and so severed the connection. Opportunity had knocked, and she had shouted from another room, "Go away. We don't want any." Oh, no, thought Stevie. That's *not* what I meant.

"Mr. Maris!" she cried. "Mr. Maris, don't hang up. Are you still there? *Please,* Mr. Maris . . ."

XXXIX

The editor-in-chief of the Briar Patch Press, Inc., gave another hearty chuckle. "Oh, I'm still here, Mrs. Crye. That means we're both still here, doesn't it, me up here in the Big City and you down there in Bucolic Barclay."

"Yes, sir, I suppose it does."

"Would it be possible for you to drive from there to here this afternoon? If you left now, you could be on Peachtree Street by one o'clock. I'd take you to a business lunch at Bugatti's in the Omni. We'd discuss editorial and contractual matters over some fine veal Parmesan or scaloppine. I can also recommend the red bean soup as an appetizer, Bloody Marys for some mighty fine sippin', and fresh Florida strawberries for dessert. I always enjoy strawberries in February. If you don't come, Mrs. Crye, I'll probably have our publicity director tote in some chile dogs from the Varsity. You can imagine with what breathlessness I await your reply."

"Must it be today?" Stevie asked, taken aback by the invitation. "I have children in school. They'll be home this afternoon, and I wouldn't be able to make the round trip fast enough to meet them or get their dinner on."

"Call in a sitter, Mrs. Crye. The Briar Patch is solvent. We'll foot your bill."

"It's pretty late to find anyone. Teddy's too old to be baby-sat by teen-age girls, and most of the elderly women in this neighborhood are shut-ins. Why not tomorrow or Wednesday?"

"Well, I'm awful excited about this, Mrs. Crye. . . . Might I call you by a less formal appellation? If you can't get away, we're liable to be talking over this contraption a spell. Mistering and missing folks has never been my strong suit, and the problem here is that I don't really know what to call a nice lady named Stevenson. Adlai doesn't seem politic, if you follow me, and Stevenson itself is a real mouthful."

"Call me Stevie."

"That's appropriate. And I'm David-Dante."

"That's a syllable more than Stevenson."

"Well, it's two words. You have to give a fella with a two-word first name a little leeway." He harrumphed a frog from his throat. "Listen, Stevie, your proposal came in this morning's mail, first thing. Jennifer Thurman, my editorial assistant, brought it in and said I should read it. Jenny's got a bloodhound's nose for off-trail but promising literary properties. She also keeps up with the by-lines in regional periodicals; part of her job, you see. Anyway, two weeks ago—this is gospel, gal, as corny-clumsy as it may sound—she told me we eventually ought to go after a collection by a hard-boiled, lyrical newcomer publishing her stuff scattershot from Savannah to Mobile. Name of Stevenson Crye, Jenny said, the kind of tough-lady monicker makes you think of Carson McCullers or Flannery O'Connor. Names're important, Jenny said, and this up-and-comer's got a book-jacket dandy. Okay, I told her, let's keep her in mind. And here this morning, a cold day in Hotlanta, in comes a package from the hard-boiled, lyrical mama we've already drawn a bead on. Fate or coincidence? Doesn't much matter to David-Dante. I've read your proposal and I'm ready to deal, hands on the table, every card straight up. . . . You still there?"

"I'm still still here. I don't believe it, though."

"Listen, my competitors—some of 'em from overextended Big Apple firms—some of those highfalutin guys say I talk like a carny with a Ph.D. in Southern Gothic lit., but I don't go for *deceptive* fast talk. I talk fast because I'm excited. This morning I'm excited by the Stevenson Crye stuff I've just read."

"I didn't mean I didn't believe you," Stevie hurried to explain. "I just meant your calling me like this was . . . I'm flabbergasted, I think."

"Good, good. I wanted to flabbergast. It's unsportin' to bamboozle, but it's all right to flabbergast. I'm a first-class flabbergastronomer, Stevie, that's why the Briar Patch Press is in the black. One of the reasons, anyway. I make writers offers they just don't dare refuse."

"What are you offering me?"

"Wait a minute. Some preliminaries first. If you'd come up here today, we'd've both had a chance to gander at each other; to size each other up eyeball to eyeball, checkin' out the telltale way our lips curl, our eyelids tic, and our nostrils widen. We'd've formed important hunches about the other person, Stevie, and we'd've trusted these instincts because so often—so very often—they're eminently trustable. It's harder to do that with voices alone. Not impossible, now, but truly harder. I'm at an advantage in a telephone conversation because I've read some of your stuff and talked about you with Brock and Jenny. I've got some info even better than eye tics. You, now . . . you're probably trying to knead my voice into physical features and my glibness into some sort of gut feeling about my probity and competence and so forth. Am I right?"

"Isn't this call costing an awful lot?"

"This is a company phone for company business. We'd've spent a damned sight more at Bugatti's, believe me. . . . Am I right? About my having you at a small disadvantage, I mean?"

"Well, I always wonder what a caller I've never seen before looks like. It's a *submerged* sort of curiosity, though. Until we have view screens on our telephones, there's not much you can do about it."

"What about imagination, Stevie? I thought writers fell back on their imaginations in tricky situations."

"I'm not a fiction writer."

"But judging from the sample chapters in your proposal for *Two-Faced Woman,* you've got the talent to be." David-Dante's voice took on a tone almost conspiratorial. "Listen, let me tell you an occupational prejudice of literary editors, okay?"

"Okay."

"Most editors don't like writers to do extended telephone-conversation scenes. They're apt to become static, the characters involved in them can't square off with boxing gloves or blackjacks, and the climax in a telephone scene usually winds down to a slammed receiver. You don't get a feel for place or physiognomy in a telephone scene—not usually, anyway. Writers who insist on running Ma Bell ragged, well, they also run the risk of anesthetizing their readers. They might as well staple a package of sleeping pills to the title page. 'Take two at Chapter Thirty-nine and call me in the morning. We'll chat about the section you fell asleep during.' Anyway, most editors would prefer a grisly mass murder, a gang-bang, or an over-flight of dragons to a telephone scene.''

''But you're different? You wouldn't?''

''Well, no, not when I'm dealing with manuscript submissions. As an editor I *hate* 'em, telephone scenes. Real life's a different matter, though. People actually *do* talk on the telephone sometimes, and sometimes they say absurdly important things to each other. I want you to remember this talk—this telephone talk—as one of your most absurdly important moments this year. See?''

''Mr. Maris, I don't understand what you're driving at.''

''David-Dante, Stevie; David-Dante. . . . First, to bring a measure of parity to our relationship, I want you to satisfy yourself as to my looks. You've heard me snap-crackle-and-talk for several minutes now. Exercise your writerly imagination and try to describe me.''

''Describe you? I can't do that. Whatever I say would be wrong, Mr. Maris. Besides, wouldn't it *increase* the advantage you say you have over me? My speculations would give you that much more grist for your character-analysis mills. Please, can't we just talk about my proposal?''

''We're going to do that, I promise you. For the moment, though, indulge me.''

''But if I inadvertently insult you—''

''You can't insult me, Stevie. I'm sitting up here on Peach-tree Street in a lovely high-tension job, my Guccis propped on my secretary's typewriter stand, my granddaddy's World War I pocketwatch ticking away like a silver-plated time bomb, and I'm absolutely immune to insult. Imagine I've got a hunchback. Give me pockmarks, halitosis, and an artificial eye. Do with me as you wish. Describe me. Then we'll be able to get down to business.''

''Mr. Maris—''

''Come on, Stevie. Invent, illuminate, portray.''

''You're fat,'' Stevie obliged him. ''You're fat, bald, and

impotent. Your toenails are ingrown, and your nostrils have hairs hanging out of them as long as packing threads. You smell like a fertilizer factory.''

"Is that how I sound?'' David-Dante Maris asked noncommittally.

A moment later Stevie said, "No, not really. I'll have another crack at it if you'll let me. It's just such a *strange* request.'' Maris's silence implied his willingness to give her another chance and his agreement with her final remark. "I'm sorry, David-Dante, but you do sound *large*—not overweight, exactly, but hefty in a politely menacing way. Like a retired football player. A lineman, probably.''

"Ah.''

"You've told me you're wearing expensive shoes and a pocketwatch. Maybe you've given away too much. Even though it's February, I imagine you sitting there in a beautiful cream-colored suit. You've taken the jacket off, but you're still wearing the matching vest. Your shirt is a faint orange with darker orange pinstripes, a magnificent silken shirt. It makes me think of the shirts that Daisy Buchanan starts crying over in *The Great Gatsby*—a gangster's or a publishing executive's shirt.''

"What about my face?''

"You're forty-six or -seven, I think. Clean-shaven. You have a wide forehead and startlingly blue eyes. You wear your hair—which is still dark and abundant—combed back from your temples in an old-fashioned way. You don't slick it down with hair oil, though. There's gray in your sideburns; it shines silver when it catches the light.

"Your lips . . . well, they're somewhat heavy, the upper one with a soft little beak of flesh in the middle. When you wrinkle your forehead, you can look a lot like Willie B., the gorilla in the Grant Park Zoo. Just by smiling, though, you can look like a grown-up version of one of those gap-toothed kids in a Norman Rockwell painting. You're more intelligent than you look, and I'm guessing, just guessing, that that hasn't hurt you much in your chosen profession.'' Stevie paused. "That's it. That's the way I see you. How'd I do?''

"Perfect, Stevie. It's a hundred percent accurate, right on the money, even down to the color of my suit and shirt. Astonishing percipience, really astonishing. You could take that show on the road."

"Right," said Stevie. "I'm Barclay's answer to Button City's Sister Celestial."

"Out of my territory, gal—but we're almost even now, we've almost negotiated ourselves to character-assessment parity."

"What could possibly be left?" Stevie protested.

"You know what I look like, but all I know about you is intellectual stuff. Describe yourself."

Mildly exasperated, Stevie described a nonexistent female personage with the bulk of Amy Lowell and the extravagant cape-and-tricorne wardrobe of Marianne Moore. The editor of the Briar Patch Press did not believe her and demanded that she give him a truthful accounting. Then they would go on to business matters, but not until then.

Stevie described herself.

"Wonderful," said David-Dante Maris. "You got me to a *T*, and you're just the way I imagined you from your voice. It's almost as if we're in the same room together, isn't it?"

"I don't know. It's not often that a man in a cream-colored vested suit sits down in my kitchen."

"Nor that a lady as pert and attractive as you comes into my office to talk about a book she's going to do for us."

"*Pert?*" said Stevie distastefully. But before David-Dante could reply, she hurried to add, "Are we actually going to talk about my book now? I was beginning to think this call was a hoax."

"If that's what you thought, Stevie, you were a stupid fool to play along the charming way you did. Never mind that, though. How does a three-thousand-dollar advance with a ten percent royalty sound?"

"I don't know."

"You don't know? Listen, we'll get copies into Rich's and Davison's, not to mention the mall bookstores, and we'll arrange some autograph-signing parties around town. You'll eventually clear another five or six thousand, more than that if we take *Two-Faced Woman* into a second printing.''

''I just meant I didn't know what was standard, Mr. Maris. What kind of advances did you give Rhonda Anne Grinnell for *Lester Maddox Doesn't Live Here Anymore* and *Who's Afraid of the Atlanta Braves?*''

''More for the second than the first. *Lester* sold out its first printing in about four months. Rhonda Anne's daily column in the Lyin' 'Lanta Newspapers is a beautiful continuing ad for her books that the Briar Patch Press doesn't have to pay a penny for. We stick in an occasional legitimate ad to keep everything on the up and up, of course, but *Two-Faced Woman* isn't likely to sell as fast as Rhonda Anne's stuff. Her books go like scented candlesticks during a power outage at the sewage-treatment plant. They don't throw much light on anything, but the unusual smell seems to make people feel a little better. Her books, Stevie, make it possible for me to consider doing a sensitive collection of essays like the one you've just proposed.''

''You didn't answer my question.''

''Well, you called me Mr. Maris. And I *never* discuss one author's financial arrangements with us with another author. If you can get Rhonda Anne Grinnell to tell you, that'd be fine. However, that lady's sort of an idiot savant at her newspaper's video display consoles. She sits down and taps, and the papers automatically publish the result. Later the Briar Patch Press gathers these toodlings together, and her clamoring fans converge on the bookstores. I don't *blame* her for not wanting to divulge the degree of her success—monetarily, that is. Recently she's been receiving invitations to speak at sports clubs and civic meetings and psychiatric conventions. It's embarrassing.''

''All right,'' Stevie relented. ''Then just tell me if what you're offering is fair.''

''For a new writer? Yes, ma'am. Absolutely. You can hunt around up here or even in the Big Apple for an agent to represent you, but I'm not going to budge for that person, and if you end up signing with us, anyway, Stevie, you can kiss ten percent of both your advance and any future royalties goodbye.

Some of 'em want more than that. That's a lot of groceries, a lot of Coca-Cola. Your decision, though.''

''Earlier you said—''

''Go ahead. I'm listening.''

''You said something about 'crafty editorial interference.' What does that mean?''

''It means I'd insist on taking a part in imposing a structure on your collection. It means I'd edit some of your essays— mostly to improve their fluency and make 'em build to meaningful climaxes. I won't put words in your mouth, though, and I won't try to overrule you if you can present a coherent case for leaving something alone. I bring all this up because some writers are pathologically attached to every comma they excrete. I try not to work with people like that.''

''Do you edit Rhonda Anne Grinnell?''

''What for?''

''Well, I—''

''Her stuff's fine the way it is. Nothing's gonna improve it— not until the day she splits open from forehead to belly button and the mortified Jane Austen inside her steps out to take charge. And Rhonda Anne, bless her, she's just too loose and comfortable ever to split open like that.''

''I don't mother-hen my commas.''

''Good. I'm glad to hear it. Here's an example of what I'm talking about. You've sent me sample essays and an outline. The outline puts the essay you call 'The Empty Side of the Bed' well back in the text, after short pieces about Ted's illness, his death, and so on.''

''The order's chronological.''

''So's history, Stevie. But you don't have to write it that way. Ever hear of *in medias res?* I want you to make 'The Empty Side of the Bed' your leadoff piece, your prologue. It sets a mood and a tone you purposely discard for a kind of world-weary humor in most of the remaining essays, but it's the measure of your predicament and the baseline you have to play a lot of your shots from. It belongs at the beginning. That's the kind of crafty editorial interference I'm talking about.''

''The beginning?'' said Stevie doubtfully.

204   *Michael Bishop*

"Listen, I'll read you some of what you wrote. I'll show you why I'm a better judge of how good you are and what needs spotlighting than even the author herself.

"'The empty side of the bed is haunted,'" David-Dante Maris began, his voice a mellow baritone; "'often I do not turn back the coverlet on that side, but even with the bedspread pulled taut over both linen and pillow, a memory weights the mattress and keeps me hollow company. I know that he has died (I have no illusions on that score, particularly during the day), but when I wake in the middle of the night and turn toward the unrumpled portion of our bed, I feel that at any moment he will settle in beside me again. He is simply off on an insomniac ramble. In a moment he will be back. The motionless vacancy beside me and the vagrant one next to my heart will vanish together.

"'The empty side of the bed reminds me that I am an amputee,'" Maris continued. "'An accident has occurred, and anonymous benefactors have spirited away the wounded part that their best ministrations could not save. I emerge from anesthesia to find my leg gone, and phantom pains rack the absent limb. The empty side of the bed—here in my house, not merely in some metaphorical reverie—supports a phantom equally impossible to touch and just as maddening. Knowing that—'"

"Stop," said Stevie.

"What's the matter?" asked David-Dante Maris.

Stevie did not reply.

"All right. I understand. It goes at the beginning, though. I don't care if the tone of the piece contradicts the wry exasperation of most of the other essays. 'The Empty Side of the Bed' demonstrates where this wry exasperation comes from and what kinds of progress you've made getting out of the shoals of your grief. It goes *first,* Stevie."

"Maybe I haven't made any."

"What?"

Stevie spoke more directly into the receiver. "Maybe I haven't made any progress. I write a better game than I play."

"Bullshit, gal. You play it by writing about it. That's a perfectly legitimate approach. Briar Patch wants your book. We'll probably want your second one. You should try your hand at fiction, too. We're expanding into that area, and I'm committed to developing and publishing important storytellers and novelists right down here in Crackerland. You're going to be one of them.''

"I don't write fiction."

"All right, you don't—but you could. If Spiro Agnew and his ilk can write novels, Stevie, anybody can. Why, two weeks ago Rhonda Anne Grinnell turned in a novel here at our offices. It emits a suspicious fragrance, but we'll print it because it'll set B. Dalton's ablaze and underwrite half a dozen better books.''

"Rhonda Anne Grinnell? A novel?"

"It's a multigenerational saga spanning two and half centuries. The manuscript's only 140 pages, but the lady's daily columns have trained her to work in short bursts, and the novelty of so much tawdriness in so few pages may play to our advantage. Anyway, if Rhonda Anne Grinnell, then why not the infinitely more sensitive Stevenson Crye?''

"The infinitely sensitive Eleanor Roosevelt never wrote novels. Neither did Martin Luther King. Can't we—for now, anyway—just worry about the proposal in hand?''

"As a matter of fact, Stevie, we've just published a book by a new Columbus novelist. He's more in the Edgar Allan Poe than the William Dean Howells tradition—to try to categorize his work—but he's an interesting talent. I'll have Jenny send you a copy of his book by United Parcel Service. You ought to get it tomorrow.''

"What's his name?'' Stevie asked uneasily.

"The name on the title page is A. H. H. Lipscombe. That's a pseudonym, though, and one of the clauses in the contract we signed with the man prohibits us from disclosing his true identity. I call that our B. Traven clause. It's original with Lipscombe. I let him stick it in because I'm excited by his book.''

"What about *my* contract?''

"I'll send it to you along with Lipscombe's novel. Take a couple of weeks with it, longer if you like. Just remember you've got a sure thing at the Briar Patch—an enthusiastic editor, proven promotional methods, and the promise of a brilliant literary future. We're not Alfred A. Knopf, I guess, but we've only been around about six years."

"I appreciate all this," Stevie said. "It's been an education, talking to you. I don't think I've *ever* been on long-distance for such a stretch."

"I'll be waiting to hear from you, Stevie." Maris gave her a number to telephone collect. "In the meantime, if you're having trouble with your work, try your hand at a short story. Take an incident from your own experience—a persistent fear or longing—and concoct a fantasy around it. Do it at your typewriter. Let your subconscious run. Give it a goose and watch it go. I've a powerful hunch Stevenson Crye's going to hit the mother lode, the biggest vein of pure gold in Georgia since the Dahlonega hills played out. Or since Margaret Mitchell, anyway."

"No, that's impossible. That's—"

"Nothing's impossible. Goodbye, Stevie. Sweet dreams."

"Goodbye.")

The caller hung up, and the rude drone in the receiver reminded Stevie that she had left her bedroom phone off the hook. When she went upstairs to remedy the problem, however, she found that she had no problem. The dialing element quite snugly cradled the receiver, thank you. 'Crets did this, Stevie thought. Seaton Benecke's monkey is haunting my house. Ted used to haunt it, but now my most unsettling ghost is an evil capuchin from Costa Rica. That creature came in here and hung up the phone for me.

"I don't want your help," Stevie said aloud.

Maris's call had deferred her lunch break. She was hungry. She returned to the kitchen and prepared herself a pimento-cheese sandwich with a small basket of tortilla chips. She ate without tasting her food. A reputable Atlanta publishing company had just offered to buy her first book. Why, then, had her elation failed to endure beyond the completion of the call? She ought to be celebrating. Instead she was eating a pimento-cheese sandwich and thinking about the manifold phantoms to which emptiness often gives rise.

THE MONKEY'S BRIDE
by
Stevenson Crye

Born of noble parents in a far northern country where summer lasts an eyeblink, and winter goes on and on like rheumatism, Cathinka was a formidable young woman nearly six feet tall. In mid-July of her eighteenth year, with the snows in grudging retreat, she passed her time roaming the upland meadows in the company of a stocky, fair-haired young man named Waldemar, whose diffident suit she encouraged because his parents were well situated in the village, and also because a startling flare-up of inspiration or temper would sometimes transfigure the dull serenity of his pale eyes. Cathinka nevertheless believed that in any important conflict between Waldemar and her, she would inevitably prevail. If she did not prevail, it would be by choice, as a secret means of persuading her future husband that she did *not* triumph in every decision or argument.

Fate dismantled Cathinka's plans in the same indifferent way that the fingers of a child mutilate a milkweed pod.

Arriving home one evening from her customary outing with Waldemar, Cathinka found her mother and father awaiting her in the great drafty library where her father kept his accounts and desultorily scribbled at his memoirs. Once complete, the young woman reflected, these memoirs must assuredly take their place among the dullest documents ever perpetrated by human conceit. What had her father ever done but oversee his vast holdings, engage in stupid lawsuits, and so shamefully coddle Cathinka's mother that the poor woman had begun to regard each blast of winter wind as an unjustifiable assault on her personal comfort?

That both the Count and the Countess appeared flustered by her arrival annoyed, as well as surprised, Cathinka. Then she saw that they had a guest. Wrapped from head to foot in rich white silk, a hood cloaking his features, a cape covering his hands, this personage stood between two of the black-marble pillars supporting her father's gallery of incunabula. Although several inches shorter than Cathinka, the visitor commanded her awe not only because of his outlandish appearance, but also because of his bearing and odor. He slouched within his elegant garments, and the smell coming from him, although not offensive, suggested an exotic ripeness just this side of rot. Stammering, Cathinka's father introduced their visitor as Ignacio de la Selva, her betrothed. She and the newcomer would be married in this very hall in a special ceremony one week hence.

"I am Waldemar's, and he is mine!" Cathinka raged, storming back and forth like a Valkyrie. She cowed her father and reduced the shrewish Countess to a stingy sprinkle of tears. Out of the corner of her eye, however, Cathinka could see that Don Ignacio had neither fallen back nor flinched. He was peering out of his concealing hood as if enjoying the spectacle of an elemental maiden defending the romantic Republicanism of her young life. "Never have I heard of this man, Father! Not once have either of you mentioned him before, and suddenly, your selection of the moment an irony too bitter to be laughable, you announce that I am to be this stranger's bride! No!" she concluded, clenching her hands into fists. "No, I think not!"

Don Ignacio strode forward from the alcove and threw back his silken cowl. This gesture elicited a sharp cry from Cathinka's mother and prompted the abashed Count to turn sadly aside. For a moment Cathinka thought that their visitor was wearing a mask, a head stocking of white wool or velvet.

However, it quickly became clear that Ignacio de la Selva bore on his scrunched shoulders the face and features of a monkey, albeit a man-sized monkey. Indeed, his abrupt gesture of unveiling had also disclosed simian hands, wrists, and forearms, along with an ascot of white fur at his throat. Her betrothed—God have mercy!—was not a man like Waldemar, but a beast whose diminutive cousins were sometimes seen with gypsies and tawdry traveling circuses.

Cathinka barked a sardonic laugh. Seldom, however, did she disobey her parents, preferring to browbeat them by daughterly degrees to her own point of view. Tonight they would not be browbeaten; they deflected her rage with silence. Recognizing, at last, the hopelessness of converting them, Cathinka fell weeping to the flagstones. To escape marrying the monkey-faced stranger, she might kill herself or flee across the austere desert of a glacier—but, without the Count's blessing, she would not marry Waldemar, either. Even as she wept, then, Cathinka began to adjust her sentiments into painful alignment with her parents'.

Perhaps her intended one (whose white whiskers and hideously sunken eyes must surely betray his great age) would not long outlive their wedding day. After all, his face reminded her of those chiseled icons of Death so common to the Lutheran churchyards of her country; and if Don Ignacio died within two or three years, or even if he persisted as many as five, she could take to Waldemar the amplified dowry, and experience, of a young widow. If she could tolerate for a while the unwanted affections of her father's choice, perhaps she could increase her value and desirability to her own. Rather histrionically, however, Cathinka continued to weep and wring her hands.

"Come," said the Count, rebuking his daughter without yet looking at her; "Don Ignacio deserves better than this. When I was a young man, a foreigner in a land of jaguars, snakes, and other tropical peculiarities, I stumbled into circumstances that nearly proved fatal. For trespassing upon an arcane local custom, the chief of an Amazonian Indian tribe wished to deprive me of various parts of my body—but the timely intercession of Ignacio de la Selva spared me these sacrifices, Cathinka, and in gratitude I promised to grant him any single boon within my power, either at that moment or at some future moment when my fortunes had conspicuously improved. 'Twenty years from now,' said Don Ignacio, 'is soon enough.' Until this noontide I had forgotten my promise, but my friend—'' nodding at the monkey-man— ''arrived today to remind me of it, and the boon he demanded above all others, darling Cathinka, was my only daughter's hand in marriage. I have broken a Commandment or two, but never a promise, and you must surrender to this arrangement without any further complaints or accusations.''

Said Don Ignacio, stepping forward, ''I am a former member of the Cancerian Order of Friars Minor Capuchins, the white-throated branch. I renounced my vows many years ago, when my fellow monks abandoned me to take part in either the latest leftist uprising or the most recent rain-forest gold rush (I forget which), and you will live with me, Cathinka, in the deserted jungle monastery that I have made my castle. We will raise our children unencumbered by either political or religious dogma, and you will find freedom in the expansive prison of my devotion.''

Gazing up from the floor into her betrothed's deep-set eyes, the unwilling bride-to-be replied, ''But you're a papist, while I am a devotee of Danton and the Abbé Sieyès.''

''Indeed, lovely one, we are from different times as well as different worlds. However, I am no longer what you accuse me of being, a papist, and you are only a hypothetical revolutionary. Why, you cannot even bring yourself to rebel against the benign tyranny of your father and mother.''

At these words the Countess swooned. Cathinka revived her with smelling salts while the Count and Don Ignacio looked on with unequal measures of interest. The matter was settled.

Because of Don Ignacio's adamant prohibitions against displays of either piety or politics, the wedding went forward without benefit of Lutheran clergy or any guests but a few befuddled family retainers. The Countess wept not only to see her daughter taken from her, but also to sanctify the bitterness with which the ceremony's want of pomp imbued her. She had expected nobility from every corner of the land to pack the village cathedral. Instead she must listen to her own husband lead the couple in an exchange of vows that Don Ignacio had composed himself, and she heard in the Count's feeble voice the pitiful piping of a sea gull on a forsaken strand.

Don Ignacio's vows placed great emphasis on fidelity. Cathinka was certain that the erstwhile Capuchin had written them with her passion for Waldemar firmly in mind.

As for Waldemar himself, earlier that afternoon Cathinka had parted from him without once intimating that she was shortly to be married to another. With difficulty (for Waldemar did not enjoy those games in which lovers rehearse their steadfastness in the face of various conjectural hindrances to their love), she had induced the young man to declare that, should she vanish from his life without warning, he would preserve himself a bachelor for at least ten years before losing faith in her intention to return to him. As she affirmed the last of her vows to Don Ignacio, Cathinka was pondering the rigorous pledge she had extracted from her true lover. Perhaps she had been too stringent. Perhaps, in speaking to the elegant but ugly Don Ignacio words she could never mean in her heart, she had committed a mortal sin. . . .

To seal their vows, the wedding couple did not kiss (a departure from tradition for which Cathinka was deeply thankful), but grasped hands and stared into each other's eyes. This ritual had its own unwelcome astonishments, however, for Don Ignacio's gaze seemed to propel the young woman through a maelstrom of memories to some unfathomable part of herself, while his clawlike hands sent through her palms a force like rushing water or channeled wind.

The journey to Cathinka's new home took many weeks. She and Don Ignacio shared carriages and ship cabins, but never the same bed. The former friar wore his white silk cloak and cowl whenever they ventured into teeming thoroughfares or the hard-bitten company of deck hands, but he was careless of these garments in the privacy of their makeshift quarters, whether a dusty inn room or the cramped cabin of a sailing vessel. Although he had no shame of his befurred and gnarled

J.K. POTTER

body, Cathinka would not even let down her hair in his presence; she invariably slept in her clothes, washing and changing only when her husband resignedly absented himself so that she could do so. Their enforced proximity had made Cathinka more critically conscious of the fact that Don Ignacio was a monkey; his distinctive smell had begun to pluck at her nerves as if it were a personality trait akin to sucking his teeth or drumming his claws on a tabletop. She was the bride of an animal!

Let a drunken sailor put a knife in his back, Cathinka profanely prayed. Let him fall overboard during a storm.

God disdained these pleas.

At last, by pirogue through the narrows of a rain-forest river, the newlyweds arrived at the crumbling monastery in the Tropic of Cancer where Don Ignacio had made his home. In pressing his case before Cathinka's parents he had described this rambling edifice as his castle, but to his horrified bride it more closely resembled a series of rotting stables tied together by thatched breezeways and tangled over with lianas and languid, copper-colored boa constrictors. Satan had gift-wrapped this castle. The heat was unbearable, the fetor of decay ubiquitous, and the garden inside the cloister was a small jungle surrounded by a much bigger one. Don Ignacio called the former monastery Alcázar de Cáncer, or Cancer Keep. His retainers were cockatoos and capuchin monkeys, salamanders and snakes, ant bears and armadillos. Cathinka wept.

Over the next several days, however, she sufficiently composed herself to explore her husband's holdings. If she must live here, she would try to make, from shriveled grapes, a potable champagne. But what most surprised her was that, in spite of Cancer Keep's outward disrepair, its dark and humid apartments housed a wonderful variety of magic apparatus, all of which Don Ignacio could awaken by a spoken word or a sorcerous wave of the hand. One machine lifted the contrapuntal melodies of Bach or Telemann into the torpid air; another disclosed the enigmatic behavior of strange human beings by projecting talking pictures of their activities against the otherwise opaque window of a wooden box; yet another contraption permitted Don Ignacio to converse with disembodied spirits that he said were thousands upon thousands of miles away. Cathinka was certain his communicants were demons.

The apparatus that most fascinated the young woman, however, was an unprepossessing machine that enabled Don Ignacio to translate his thoughts into neatly printed words, like those in a bona fide book. Cathinka liked this machine because she did not fear it. Its appearance was comprehensible, its parts had recognizable purposes, and the person sitting before it could direct its activities much in the way that a flautist controls a flute. Don Ignacio called the apparatus an electromanuscriber, and he taught his bride how to use it. She repaid him by continuing to spurn his tender invitations to consummate their union and by employing the machine to chronicle her ever-mounting aversion to both Cancer Keep and the autocratic simian lord who kept her there. She poured her heart out through her fingertips and cached the humidity-proofed pages proclaiming her hatred and homesickness in a teakwood manuscript box.

On errands myriad and mysterious Don Ignacio was often away in the jungle. Although he sometimes offered to take Cathinka, she refused to go. His enterprises were undoubtedly horrid, and she had retained her sanity only by committing to paper through the agency of the electromanuscriber each of her darkest fears and desires. She could not safely interrupt this activity. Occasionally in her husband's absence, however, she would stop beneath a tree riotous with his retainers—birds of emerald plumage and ruby eye, monkeys in brown-velvet livery—to harangue them about their suzerain's despotism and possible ways of ending it. The cockatoos clucked at her, the capuchins only yawned. Oddly, she was grateful for their want of ardor. She did not really wish Don Ignacio to be borne off violently.

One evening the lord of Cancer Keep came to Cathinka's bedchamber, where she lay in rough clothes beneath a veil of mosquito netting, and dumped the contents of her teakwood box on the laterite floor. They had been monkey and wife for nearly a year. Although she had never warmed to him or spoken kindly to him except by accident, this ostentatious petty vandalism was his first display of temper. Chalk-white in the cloistered gloom, his face contorted fiendishly, a Gothic image so paradigmatic it was almost risible. Cathinka could not accept Don Ignacio, but neither could she fear him. She responded to his anger by chuckling derisively, for she, too, was angry; he had violated the small wooden stronghold of her secret life.

"I despair of ever winning you," her husband said. "You insist on regarding your marriage to me as a prison term, which you must stoically endure until your release. There *is* no release, Cathinka."

She glared at him pitilessly.

"However, I love you for your willfulness. In a last effort to conquer your repugnance to me, and to a union that must persist even should my effort fail, I am going to grant you three wishes, lady."

"As in a fairy tale?" Cathinka scoffed.

Don Ignacio ignored this riposte. "You must swear that you will use them all, one wish a year beginning on the first anniversary of our wedding day, which is not far off. Do you swear?"

"Do you swear that my wishes will come true?" She did not care for the stipulated waiting period between wishes, for she must remain at Cancer Keep at least another two full years, presumably even if Don Ignacio were to die during this time. However, one of her wishes might repeal or satisfactorily amend this strange proviso, and she would be a fool to refuse her husband's offer solely on its account.

"Cathinka, I do not intend to toy with your expectations. The wishes I grant you will indeed come true, but they are subject to several other conditions. Perhaps you should hear them before agreeing to accept my offer. I do not wish to deceive you."

"Granted," said Cathinka sardonically. "State your niggling conditions. They must certainly outnumber the wishes, for if you are anything like my father, your litigiousness surpasses your charity."

A large hairy spider tottered among the scattered sheets of paper on the floor, and Don Ignacio paced precariously near it reciting his litany of stipulations.

"Let me backtrack, Cathinka. First, you may not set aside our wedding vows. Second, you may not wish any physical harm upon either yourself or me. Third, you may not presume to transform either of us into any other human being or, indeed, into any other variety of matter, animate or inanimate— even if I would be more attractive to you as a butterfly, an exquisite crystal, or a perfect double of Waldemar. Fourth, you may not try to remove yourself or me to any other place in the entire universe. And, fifth, as I have told you, a year must pass between wishes."

"Very good, my husband. Two more provisos than wishes. Your magnanimity reminds me of the late French king's."

"Although you obviously do not realize it, Cathinka, these are modern times. Whoever bestows wishes without qualification must reap the dreadful rewards of such folly. To our credit, lady, neither of us is a fool. Think on what remains to you, not on what I have wisely proscribed."

Cathinka yielded, sullenly, to Don Ignacio's logic. She then bade him retire so that she could consider among the many bewildering alternatives. She had several days, and she fretted the question for three of them before hitting upon a wish that promised to deliver her from the former Capuchin's tyranny, even as it paved the way for an end to her loneliness. What her third wish might be, however, she still did not know; but, in the fatalistic words of the old Count, time would tell, time would most assuredly tell.

The first anniversary of the couple's wedding day arrived, and Don Ignacio summoned Cathinka to his small, oppressive study to state her wish. He had been working at an electro-manuscriber, but, as soon as he heard her tread on the hard-packed laterite, he swiveled to face her, extending to her his crippled-looking hands. He asked her to take them as she had done at the conclusion of their wedding ceremony in her father's library, but she shuddered and placed her hands behind her.

"You must obey me if you desire your wish to come true."

"A sixth stipulation," the young woman remarked pointedly.

"By no means. You swore a willing oath to observe the five stipulations I outlined. You may break that oath if falseness is any part of your makeup. However, unless you grasp my hands, lady, you forfeit your wish even before you utter it—for our touching effects its fulfillment, and only our touching, and so our touching is a prerequisite rather than a mere proviso. Do you understand me, Cathinka?"

"I do," she said, stepping forward and taking Don Ignacio's hands.

"Then wish."

"Aloud?"

"I am not a psychic, child."

Cathinka had not bargained on holding her husband's hands and staring into his wizened face while making her wish.

"I w-w-wish . . . f-f-for D-d-don Ignacio t-t-to . . ."

"Stop stammering, Cathinka. Out with whatever treachery you may have contrived."

"I-wish-for-Don-Ignacio-to-fall-into-a-ten-year-slumber-during-which-he-continues-healthy-and-all-his-dreams-are-pleasant," Cathinka chanted almost ritually.

A feeling of relief, even serenity, began to descend upon her—but this feeling shattered when Don Ignacio's hands jumped a foot into the air without yet releasing their grip on her own. A galvanic force seemed to flow through Cathinka's body, altering the microscopic alignment of her constituent atoms. Meanwhile the monkey-man's eyes flashed like tiny mirrors.

A moment later his fingers slid away from hers, and she crossed her arms in front of her abdomen, concealing her hands. Don Ignacio was still awake, still alert, and he swiveled back to his electromanuscriber to record her first wish on the treated foolscap in his machine. It seemed that he had set up this huge formlike page for just that purpose.

"You are a clever young woman, Cathinka. By modifying an important noun and subordinating a compound clause to your main one, you have managed to squeeze all three wishes into your first. Did you *mean* to exhaust your allotment?''

''I did not.''

Don Ignacio operated the machine. ''Then I must note here that your first wish is for me to fall into a ten-year slumber, period. The adjective is permissible because it specifies the duration of my slumber, a matter undoubtedly crucial to your wish-making strategy. I am also noting, lady, that you have come perilously close to abrogating the stipulation forbidding any harm to befall either of us. . . . However, I admire the way you attempt to skirt the problem with a pair of sweet but inadmissible subordinate clauses. You leaven your deviousness with the yeast of old-fashioned conscience.''

''Will you fall asleep, then?''

''Tomorrow, Cathinka. Give each wish a day to begin taking effect. I go to prepare a place for my slumber.'' Reproachfully dignified, Don Ignacio strode from the room, leaving his wife to contemplate the degree to which she had cheated the letter of one of his explicit stipulations. Certainly she had not meant to.

Outside Cancer Keep jaguars prowled and capuchins chittered strident admonitions.

The following morning Cathinka found, in the very center of the cloister's overgrown garden, the pirogue in which she and her husband had floated through the jungle to the monastery. Don Ignacio was lying inside the pirogue with his hands crossed on his chest and the fur at his throat reminiscent of a cluster of white lilies. He lay beneath a transparent canopy that his little cousins must have obediently worried into place; while a cockatoo the color of new snow kept vigil on a perch at the head of the coffinlike dugout. Even in slumber Don Ignacio was master of Cancer Keep. However, unless he arose before a decade had passed, Cathinka's first wish seemed to be fulfilling itself. Free of the monkey-faced tyrant, she spent that entire day singing.

The succeeding year was not so joyful. She could not leave Cancer Keep, for she had promised not to, and she could not converse with her retainers, as Don Ignacio had been able to do. They kept her fed and guarded the monastery as watchfully as ever, for their lord lay slumbering at its heart, but Cathinka had no real rapport with them and sometimes felt that they regarded her as inferior to themselves.

Some of her time Cathinka passed with the picture- and music-making apparatus in the various rooms, but the music intensified her loneliness and the activities of the people in the illuminated windows of the wooden boxes seemed either silly or cruel. Moreover, she refused to activate these machines herself and so had to depend on the sullen cooperation of the capuchins to make them work. Presently, without regret, she ceased to rely on these tiresome wonders at all. As for the apparatus through which Don Ignacio had communicated with demons, Cathinka continued to leave it strictly alone.

If not for the electromanuscriber, the year would have been unbearable. Even with the machine's assistance, its marvelous ability to make palpable the most subtle nuances of her mental life, Cathinka often felt like a traveler on the edge of an endless desert. She would die before she reached the other side. She did not die, however. She made two more teakwood boxes to hold her manuscript pages, and she survived that interminable twelvemonth by concocting philosophies, fantasies, strategies, and lies. The inside of her head was more capacious than either Cancer Keep or the vast encroaching jungle.

The second anniversary of Don Ignacio and Cathinka's exchange of vows dawned bright and cloudless, as had every preceding day for a month. It was time for her second wish.

Cathinka signaled a crew of monkeys to lift the canopy from her husband's unorthodox bedstead. When they had departed, she knelt beside the pirogue to make her wish, but hesitated to clasp Don Ignacio's hands because his body looked so shrunken and frail. He slept, but he had not continued especially robust, and the pained expression on his face suggested that the dreams he endured were far from pleasant. The sight surprised Cathinka because for a year she had purposely walked on the periphery of the garden. It also served to remind her that she must not try to squeeze too many qualifiers into the wording of her next two wishes. Magic was a conservative science.

Soon, though, she overcame her reluctance and took her husband's hands. "I wish that Waldemar were here," she said. What could be more elegant or simple? She had observed all of Don Ignacio's conditions—for surely the arrival of a male visitor did not constitute, in itself, a breach of fidelity—and she had conscientiously pruned her wish of ambiguity and excess.

Then Don Ignacio's hands leapt, nearly throwing Cathinka off balance, and for a split instant she believed that he intended to pull her into the pirogue atop him. She caught herself, however, electrified by the force that had flowed from his small body into her big-boned one. Trembling with both expectation and power, she fitted the clumsy canopy back into place with no help from the estancia's retainers.

That night she began to fear that her wish would rebound upon her in an ugly or a mocking way. The ancient gods had invented wishes to ensnare and frustrate people, as in the case of the Phrygian king Midas. If Don Ignacio were a vassal of Satan, this tradition would eventually undo her, too.

Suppose that Waldemar had died during the past year. Tomorrow a corpse would arrive at Cancer Keep. Or suppose that when he set foot within the cloister, she was invisible to him because they no longer existed within the same time frame or because Don Ignacio had maliciously deprived her of her own corporality. Perhaps she had become a ghost who could not live in the world beyond Alcázar de Cáncer. Pinching her flank and tweaking her nose seemed to disprove this last hypothesis (both experiments produced genuine twinges), but Cathinka could not stop worrying.

Late the following afternoon Waldemar dropped from the sky into Cancer Keep. Cathinka saw him fall. He dangled from a dozen or more lines beneath a billowing parti-colored tent, like a puppet trying to escape being smothered by a floating pillow case. What a weird and beautiful advent!

Waldemar landed not far from Don Ignacio's bier, in a small

shrub from which it took him almost thirty minutes to disentangle himself. Although clearly astonished to see Cathinka in the garden, while cutting himself free of the shrub he responded perfunctorily to both her cries of welcome and her many excited questions. At one point he grudgingly vouchsafed the information that some "varlets" in a flying machine, jealous of his moiety of their cargo of "magic plants," had thrust him into the air with only this colorful silken bag as a sop to their consciences. Waldemar cursed these anonymous personages. Bag or no bag, they had not expected him to outlive his terrible drop.

"Then your arrival is not the culmination of a deliberate search?" Cathinka asked.

"I never had any idea where you were," Waldemar replied, at last addressing her as if she were a genuine human being rather than a ghost. "The Count would not tell me, and several months ago I left our homeland to make my fortune. The world has changed spectacularly in that brief time, Cathinka. Assassinations plague every capital, societies subordinate ancient wisdom to youthful bravado, and one upstart nation even bruits about the news that it has sent visitors to the Moon." All his lines cut, Waldemar fell to the garden floor. Sitting there in a heap, he said, "Peril, pomp, and enterprise abound. At last, Cathinka, I am truly alive."

"No thanks to your ungrateful, greedy cohorts."

"No thanks, indeed."

Thus began the year subsequent to Cathinka's second wish. It had come true, this wish. Her lover was with her again, and in a series of chaste interviews at various places around the estancia she recounted for Waldemar the events preceding their unlikely reunion. As they stood gazing down on the crippled figure in the pirogue, she also told him of the conditions under which she had pledged to make her three wishes, of which the important final wish still remained.

Waldemar's pale eyes flamed up like coals under the revivifying breath of a bellows. Must an entire year go by, he wondered aloud, before she could wish again? Cathinka assured him that it must. He squinted at the scrunched form of Don Ignacio as if her husband were an unappetizing entrée on a glass-covered platter. His distaste for the monkey-man seemed as thoroughgoing as her own, an observation that occasioned Cathinka a surprising pang of resentment. This passed.

Like the world, Waldemar had changed. He was still taciturn—indeed, he spoke more sentences cutting loose his bag of silk than he did in the entire week subsequent—but his diffidence in regard to their courtship had utterly disappeared. He took every opportunity to kiss her hand. He brought her jungle flowers in the mornings. He paced the corridor outside her apartment at night. Once having learned how to use Don Ignacio's electromanuscriber, he prepared faultless copies of lovely *carpe diem* poems, which he then slid under her door or folded under the silver fruit bowl of her breakfast tray. Two of these later poems were his own compositions; they had neither meter nor rhyme to recommend them, but they burst within Cathinka's heart like Roman candles, owing primarily to the incandescent violence of their predominant sentiment. Had Waldemar's translation from an arctic to a tropic clime so enflamed him? The man had begun to behave like a Tupian buccaneer.

Cathinka did not know how to respond. She remembered that Don Ignacio's cardinal stipulation about her wishes was that none of them violate her wedding vows. She could not succumb to Waldemar's blandishments without breaking her word, for her lover had come to her as a direct consequence of her second wish. To lie with him would be to lie in an even more significant respect.

Yet she wished to surrender to him. The Tropic of Cancer had worked its amorous metastasis in her blood, and Waldemar's every breath was a provocation as lyrical as a poem. Cathinka began to think, to think, to think. She and Don Ignacio had never consummated their marriage. That being so, perhaps she could not be unfaithful to him by disporting her still unfulfilled flesh. . . .

Someone knocked on her door. Waldemar, of course. The monkeys never came to her of their own accord. She bade him enter. His pale eyes were blazing like fractured diamonds. He took her by the shoulders and pressed his case with his body rather than with a flurry of passionate arguments. Cathinka broke away, and he stared at her panting like a water spaniel. She was panting herself. A comatose monkey in a canoe was denying her the one boon she most desired, a commingling of essences, both spiritual and carnal, with Waldemar. What an absurd and demoralizing standoff the little beast had accomplished.

"Today, Cathinka," Waldemar told her, "chastity does not warrant so rigorous a defense."

"My chastity is not the question," she replied, bracing herself against her writing stand. Not to mock Waldemar's intelligence, she refrained from stating the true question. He repaid this courtesy by pulling a sheaf of yellowed pages from his bosom and unfolding them in his hands. Cathinka nodded at the papers. "What do you have?" she asked him.

"One of Don Ignacio's logs. In it he details the events that led him, so many years ago, to save your father's life. The Count, it seems, had been apprehended by a band of savage *indios* while attempting to force his affections on one of their maidens. Don Ignacio bartered with the band to spare him. If you wish to adhere to the principles of your worthy sire, Cathinka, your present behavior far exceeds that lenient standard."

"Depart," said Cathinka imperiously.

Waldemar bowed, but before taking his leave he tossed to the floor of her apartment the pages of Don Ignacio's log. When he was gone, Cathinka gathered these together and read them. Afterwards, she wept. By disillusioning her about her father's past, her lover had also disillusioned her about the nature of his own character. Two birds with one stone. The pithiness of this adage struck Cathinka for the first time, and she passed a restless, melancholy night.

Now, she believed, Waldemar would abandon Cancer Keep. He was not constrained by promises or provisos, and she rued the lovelorn folly of her second wish. The sooner he absented himself from her life the sooner she would be able to marshal her wits toward a purpose in which he had no part.

Waldemar, however, chose to remain. He ceased picking flowers and writing poems, but he attended her at mealtimes and spoke pleasantly of their youth together in the distant north. Cathinka reflected that she had made mistakes in her life; perhaps she owed her former suitor a mistake or two of his own.

These fluctuations of opinion and mood she continued to record on a daily basis with the electromanuscriber. Sometimes, at night, she could hear Waldemar operating Don Ignacio's other perplexing machines; he did not require the monkeys' aid to make them run. His familiarity with the apparatus disturbed her. Perhaps those playthings—rather than a concern for her welfare—had induced him to stay. She wrote and wrote, but the matter never did become clear.

On moonlit nights Cathinka visited the garden and brooded upon the twisted face and body of her husband. An irresistible impulse drew her. He seemed to be wasting away in his slumber. His bones revealed an angular girdering beneath the skimpy fringes of his fur. Like a chunk of bleached stone, his skull appeared to be emerging from his eroding lineaments. The moonlight hallowed this process. It was eerie and beautiful. It was ordinary and repulsive. It was very confusing. Cathinka found herself compulsively robing Don Ignacio's quasi-cadaver in memories of his tenderness and patience. As his body deteriorated and his face screwed up like a pale raisin, the intelligence that had animated the monkey-man lived again in her imagination. She likewise recalled the mystic force in his hands, the terrifying urgency of his gaze.

For months, however, his hands had been fisted and his eyes tightly closed. What if he died before their third anniversary? She had specified a ten-year slumber, and Don Ignacio had acceded to this adjective without apparent misgivings, but what if that feeble qualifier could not infallibly enforce a ten-year sleep? The premature death of her husband would deprive her of her third wish.

Fool! Cathinka scolded herself. The death of your husband

would free you to embrace Waldemar without recourse to wishes.

This realization did not comfort her.

Walking back to her apartment that night, she thought she heard her electromanuscriber clattering disjointedly. Then this sound stopped. Bewildered, she proceeded to her room. Inside she found Waldemar tinkering with the device. Seeing her, the young man pulled a piece of foolscap from the apparatus and attempted to crumple it in his hands. Cathinka wrested the sheet from him and read the brief document in an outraged instant. It bore on its face an unfinished story in which she, Cathinka, employed her third wish to bestow great wealth and power on the penniless prodigal, Waldemar. His parents (the document attested) had disinherited him for his many conspicuous debaucheries, but with the wealth and power accruing from her third wish he intended to revenge himself upon them. Waldemar hastily explained that this narrative was only a fiction spun out to test the efficacy of his repairs upon the electromanuscriber—which, when Cathinka put her hands to it, no longer worked at all.

"You wrote that on *my* apparatus in the hope that doing so would influence my third wish," Cathinka accused the young man. "However, the unseemliness of your desires has caused the machine to break, exposing your villainy. Waldemar, I ask you to go away from here forever."

"Not until you have made your final wish."

"Months remain before that is possible, and I hardly intend to heed your recommendations about what my last wish should be."

Waldemar, his eyes flaring, exclaimed that tonight would serve as well as her anniversary day. If she did not agree, Waldemar pursued, he would slay the unnatural Don Ignacio in his ready-made coffin and thereby eliminate the possibility of her making any wish at all. To carry out this threat, he rushed from Cathinka's room and down the open corridor toward the garden. Despite the tropic heat, Cathinka was wearing a short-sleeved frock with a long embroidered train.

She could not hope to catch or struggle successfully with Waldemar in such a cumbersome garment. Without a moment's hesitation she shed it. Then, wearing only an ivory-colored chemise and matching pantalettes, her long hair flying, she sprinted from the room in pursuit of the duplicitous young man.

In the garden she found Waldemar in a posture of resolute strain, his back bent and his fingers curled to prise the canopy from the pirogue. His arms came up, and the transparent cover flipped into the knotted weeds as if it weighed no more than a jellyfish. In later years Cathinka recalled that instead of daunting her, this sight sent a thrill of imminent combat surging through her, an energy that may have sprung from the heroic suppression of her natural longings. Or perhaps this energy was the force of righteousness asserting itself at the dare of bald-faced iniquity.

As Waldemar reached for Don Ignacio, then, Cathinka plunged through the snaky vines and obscene-looking equatorial flowers, seized the traitor by his hair, and hurled him aside as easily as he had flung away the dugout's crystal carapace. He did not go down, but caught himself against the thorny bole of a small tree, whirled about, and charged Cathinka like a grunting boar.

They grappled, Waldemar and Cathinka, standing upright and moving so little to either side that an uninformed observer might have thought them spooning. Their individual strengths were isometric. Monkeys gathered on the tiled roofs and thatched breezeways to watch the combat. The combatants, however, merely swayed in each other's arms. Puzzled by this behavior, the Moon (upon which people had lately walked) looked down with its mouth open. A bird screamed, and the hush of the jungle became the bated breath of Cathinka's own briefly recurring uncertainty. Did she love this man or hate him?

She hated him.

Summoning the resources of outrage, Cathinka shoved Waldemar away. As he sought to reinsinuate himself into her arms, there to squeeze her ribs until they cracked like brittle reeds, she struck him in the mouth with her elbow. He reeled away, his lip bleeding. She butted him in the shoulder with her head, stepped aside, cuffed his ear with her fist and forearm, received an answering blow to the temple, staggered, delivered an uppercut to his abdomen from her crouch, stood upright, ducked a battalion of knuckles behind which his angry face shone almost as bright as the Moon's, shot both hands through his routed defenses, levered her thumbs into his Adam's apple, and tightened the tourniquet of her fingers around his throbbing neck. He retaliated by kneeing her between the legs as if she were a man. A host of capuchin spectators scampered from roof to roof, lifting a babel of ambiguous encouragement above the compound, or falling eerily silent whenever one of the combatants seemed to be on the verge of dispatching the other.

The fight lasted hours. It swung from this side of the garden to that, in favor of Cathinka now, Waldemar next, and neither of them in the gasp-punctuated intervals. Don Ignacio slept through it all as a baby sleeps through family arguments, thunderstorms, air-raid sirens. Cathinka had done no horseback riding or archery exercises since her departure from her father's estates, but she had substituted walks about the monastery maze and the juggling of small weights to maintain her muscle tone, and she had had more time to adjust to the élan-sapping mugginess of the tropics than had Waldemar—with the consequence that, toward morning, the grunting young man had utterly exhausted himself. His masculine pride had offset his imperceptible pudginess for as long as it could. Cathinka, clasping her hands and swinging them into his chin like the prickly head of a mace, put period to their monomachy. Among the needles of a flattened succulent Waldemar lay bruised and torn, still marginally conscious but unable to rise. Cathinka stood over him in the tattered white banners of her chemise; she greatly resembled the central figure in Delacroix's painting, *Liberty Leading the People.*

Disappointed that the fight had concluded, the capuchins took no interest in the stark symbology of Cathinka's appearance. They returned to the jungle or to the more dilapidated cloisters of Alcázar de Cáncer to rest. It would take them a day or two to recuperate from what they had witnessed.

Later Cathinka provisioned Waldemar and sent him away in the company of those of Don Ignacio's cousins who had not slunk off to sleep. She and the young man exchanged no words either during the preparations for his trek or at the final moment of his sullen decampment. Parrots and cockatoos flew aerial reconnaissance missions to insure that Waldemar did not attempt to double back. Cathinka was alone again.

A transcendent peacefulness descended on her spirit. She took off her ruined chemise and stepped out of her pantalettes. She bathed her wounds in well water. She replenished her strength with fruits. She did not dress herself again, but slept naked in her apartment under the gaze of a blue-wattled lizard. That night, and the night after, and so on for every night until the third anniversary of her marriage to Don Ignacio, she visited her husband's bier in this prelapsarian attire. His scrunched body appeared to straighten, his scrunched features to unwrinkle. He slept on, of course, but a modicum of health was his again and the dreams that flickered through his slumber softened his monkeyish face without making it a whit more human. Cathinka did not care. She attended Don Ignacio as regularly as an experimental animal visits its food tray. Far from dulling the sensibilities of their prisoners, some habits are vital and sustaining. Or so Cathinka told herself, and so she slowly came to believe. Now that nakedness was her habitual raiment she felt herself an inalienable part of Cancer Keep.

During the last few days before the third anniversary, a tuft of beautiful white hair began to sprout on Cathinka's breastbone. It ran by degrees from her throat to her cleavage, spreading out over her breasts the way frost furs the sun-bleached boulders in a winter stream. This fur gleamed on her opalescent body, and, curling a forefinger in the tuft at her throat, Cathinka sat gazing on the magical creature in the pirogue. Finally, on the day Don Ignacio had told her to make her remaining wish, Cathinka clasped her husband's paws and softly spoke it. . . .

J.K.POTTER

XLI

Stevie sat back from the electromanuscriber—the Exceleriter, rather—absolutely exhausted. At one o'clock, not long after the telephone call from David-Dante Maris, she had come upstairs and begun work on a short story. A glance at her watch revealed that it was now about ten minutes after three, almost time for Marella to come stomping through their tall front foyer from school. After having wasted nearly the entire morning, Stevie had completed "The Monkey's Bride" in a little over two hours, an accomplishment she could scarcely credit. She did a hasty estimate and discovered that she had been writing at the rate of nearly a thousand words every fifteen minutes. Never in her life had she written with such speed. Never in her life had she been so totally immersed in the subject matter flowing through the synapses of her imagination onto paper. Never in her life had she been moved to translate her own experiences into the uncanny runes of myth. Wow. A short story of approximately seventy-five hundred words in two hours!

"And it's good, too," Stevie said, rubbing her arms. "For a first-timer it's pretty bloody marvelous."

Where would she send it? She had no idea. *Atlanta Fortnightly* never used fiction, and she could not recall ever having read stories of this peculiar stamp in *The New Yorker* or *Esquire*. Most of the periodicals devoted exclusively to fantasy, she knew from close consultation of the market listings in writers' magazines, paid execrable rates and had limited readerships. The high-paying men's magazines with vast circulations, on the other hand, would probably not touch a story with a female protagonist, especially one who soundly drubs her no-goodnik boyfriend in an all-night brawl. Nor did Cathinka seem the sort of heroine to make the editors of *Redbook* or *Cosmopolitan* do approving somersaults, although, given a flexible and discerning editor at those places, her story might stand *half* a chance there. . . .

Where had the drolly somber tales of Karen Blixen, better

known as Isak Dinesen, first appeared? Stevie wondered. Or had they been forced to await book publication to see the light of day? What about the fairy tales of Oscar Wilde? The ghost stories of Coppard and Montague James? . . . Should she try a science-fiction magazine like *Asimov's* or *Omni?* The latter publication, in particular, paid well, and in its pages she had read interesting fantasies by writers like Harlan Ellison, Walter Tevis, and Ray Bradbury. . . .

Well, she hardly had to decide in the next ten minutes. Why not sit back and enjoy the first lovely flush of accomplishment? It would dissipate soon enough, probably at the moment she extracted the page still in the machine and inserted a sheet of watermarked bond and a carbon set on which to begin her sub-mission copy. She had never been able to afford a typist for final drafts and did not really trust anyone else to make sense of her hand-corrected roughs. What kind of triumphant sign-off would an experienced typist put at the end of a work of fiction? Newspaper reporters and feature-article writers often used the old telegrapher's symbol—30—as a sign of completion.

" 'The End,' " Stevie advised herself. "Put a big, fat Warner Brothers 'The End' right there at the bottom of the page." She centered the Exceleriter's typing disc, backspaced three or four units, depressed and locked the shift key, and started to type. She did not have a chance. The machine abruptly took over from her:

YOU'RE WELCOME.

Clasping her hands together, Stevie brought them down on the typewriter's casing like the prickly head of a medieval mace. The machine shut off. Still aquiver with frustration and anger, she struck the Exceleriter three more times, blows of di-minishing strength that left the heels of her hands aching.

"I'm *welcome,* am I? What the hell am I welcome *for?* What do you think you've done for me?"

The typewriter did not reply, and Stevie yanked the last page of her narrative from the cylinder, placed it flat on her desk, struck through YOU'RE WELCOME with her ballpoint, and block-printed THE END in large uneven letters. It was her story, not the goddamn Exceleriter's!

But you never wrote that many words that fast in your life, Stevie reflected, a traitor to her own indignation. You certainly never wrote a short story before, and in "The Monkey's Bride" you've somehow contrived to turn 'Crets into a figure of sympathetic romanticism. Is that something your own consciousness would have done, functioning completely by itself? 'Crets is a foul little beast, but Don Ignacio has heroic attributes that eventually win Cathinka over. Stevie, you could not possibly have cast Seaton Benecke's bloodsucking pet as your husband and lover without the meddlesome intervention of the demon that inhabits your typewriter.

That's not true. After all, last night I dreamed that Ted was wearing a monkey suit resembling the capuchin—so, you see, I'd already made an identification similar to the one that seems to structure my story.

You *think* that's what you dreamed, Stevie. Lately the edges between dream and reality have become strangely blurred.

Well, today is Monday, thank you, and I haven't had a bit of trouble distinguishing between what's real and what isn't. I had a rotten morning, a redemptive telephone call, and a stunning two-hour stretch at this glory-grabbing machine. "The Monkey's Bride" came out of *my* heart and guts, Mrs. Crye. I wasn't sitting here snockered taking high-speed dictation from a demon. The call from Maris set me off. Otherwise I doubt I would have even thought to try anything so audacious.

Look at the sheet of examination-table paper you set aside before beginning your story, Stevie.

Annoyed, Stevie rummaged on the floor beside her desk for the long strip of paper on which she had tried to write a semihumorous essay on the rewards of widowhood. Picking it up, she saw that it was covered from margin to margin, from head to foot, with typewritten dialogue. It began, "This is David-Dante Maris, editor-in-chief at the Briar Patch Press in Atlanta," and it concluded, quite succinctly, "Goodbye." In between, Stevie's wide-eyed perusal soon disclosed, the transcription contained every word she remembered speaking to Maris and every word he had presumably said to her.

"What the hell does this mean?" Stevie asked the ceiling, rubbing her arms. "What the hell is going on?"

Nothing, a part of herself responded. More of the same. Take your pick. In either event, your conversation with David-Dante Maris never happened. The typewriter made it up. It let you help it with "The Monkey's Bride," but the long-distance call from Maris it spun out unassisted, simply to fill the emotional vacuum of your inability to work this morning. You wanted an interruption, so the Exceleriter gave you an interruption. Between eleven and one you suffered a fugue of pathological incapacity that this self-contained extract neatly explains away. It's a brazen piece of wish-fulfillment, Stevie, courtesy of the Demon in the Machine. Or else you've finally gone over the falls in a manic-depressive dugout of your own design.

The telephone rang! Stevie insisted. I heard it, and I got up to answer it. I caught it on the sixth ring.

The telephone did indeed ring, but you got up as soon as you heard it and you rushed downstairs to put as much distance between you and the Exceleriter as possible. That's why it took you six rings to catch it. You were lucky you didn't break your neck.

I talked to Maris. He wants *Two-Faced Woman*. He read excerpts from my article "The Empty Side of the Bed."

It was a wrong number, Stevie. The caller never even said hello. Whoever it was just breathed into the receiver for a few moments—twenty seconds, say—and hung up. You went back upstairs believing you had left the bedroom phone off the hook. Finding out otherwise, you came down again and prepared your lunch. You dallied over this unappetizing meal for the next two hours. If you daydreamed the conversation with Maris during this time, perhaps the Exceleriter merely transcribed your fantasy. Whatever may have happened, Stevie, your chummy chat with a big-cheese Atlanta book editor *didn't*. That's only what you wanted to happen.

A wrong number?

Well, it could have been Seaton Benecke, I suppose. He knows your number, doesn't he? He's got it, you could say. He called you here one evening last week. Maybe he was calling you to ask if you'd seen a runaway monkey.

Why didn't he, then?

It might have been somebody else, Stevie. I don't know. I'm only trying to help. Don't turn these hostile feelings against yourself. That's what the Exceleriter—Benecke, the Demon in the Machine, whoever—that's what they want. I'm not your enemy. I'm a part of you.

He gave me advice. He gossiped with me about Rhonda Anne Grinnell. He said he was sending me a contract to look over.

Your imagination, Stevie. Only your imagination.

It was real!

You sent the Briar Patch Press, Inc., your book proposal on Saturday morning. Today is Monday. Do you really think your packet reached their offices over the weekend? Do you really think that, even if it did, a man like David-Dante Maris would tear it open, read every word, and telephone you long-distance with an offer of three thousand dollars on the very morning it arrived? Come *on,* kiddo.

"No," said Stevie aloud. "The odds against that are astronomical. Any editor who behaved that way would be shot full of blue lead by a firing squad of publishing executives at the next booksellers convention."

Exactly, thought Mrs. Crye. Bang, bang, bang. *Bang!*

Stevie clutched her forehead. Whereas formerly the Exceleriter had confined most of its puerile inventions and script revisions to the hours between midnight and dawn, it was now deliberately intruding on the time she spent working and taking care of her family. It was rewriting her experience, anticipating the future, converting her wish-fulfillment fantasies into mocking, short-lived "realities." It was screwing around with the microscopic symmetries of her life, the Do-Not-Appropriate moments with whose fragile substance, every single day, she sought to recreate herself. She could not keep tolerating the typewriter's appropriations. She had tolerated them too long already. Soon she would have to exorcise or destroy the demons arrayed against her by the dictates of someone else's convolute and heartless plot.

Still, she and the Exceleriter had collaborated on "The Monkey's Bride," and she was proud of the story, even if also a little frightened by it. Don Ignacio was a portmanteau character combining, as she had already noted, the physical appearance of 'Crets with the death-in-life qualities of her late husband Ted, who had surrendered so easily to intestinal cancer. Waldemar appeared to represent Seaton Benecke. Cathinka, of course, was a shamelessly heroic version of herself. Teddy and Marella had no counterparts in the tale at all. Was this omission significant? Did she, Stevie, secretly wish to be free of every responsibility or encumbrance but that of finding a man who would relieve her of still others?

No.

Stevie rejected this reading as too simplistic, too static. Cathinka was a noble character, but nobility becomes a smugly statuesque, pigeon-dropping-befouled virtue—no virtue at all—when bereft of its ties to human institutions and values. In making her final wish, Cathinka was not repudiating either the desirability or the possibility of female self-sufficiency; she was acknowledging Don Ignacio's, and hence reaffirming her own, humanity. That this acknowledgment and reaffirmation involved an acceptance of the dying animal in their makeups was not very comforting, but it was necessary. . . . Perhaps Ted, in seeming to desert her, had merely been making similar accommodations with his fate. On the other hand, perhaps he had gone too far to make them.

This uncertainty was one of the reasons that "The Monkey's Bride" frightened Stevie; she could not come up with an interpretation that revealed a precise one-to-one correspondence between the events of her own life and those in Cathinka's fictional one. Perhaps no such correspondence existed. Again, she felt, the Exceleriter was mocking her.

"*Mama!*"

The cry startled Stevie. She stood up, bracing herself with

both hands on her rolltop. It was Marella, of course. She had just entered the foyer beneath Stevie's office.

"Mama, I'm home!"

XLII

" '. . . and, curling a forefinger in the tuft at her throat, Cathinka sat gazing on the magical creature in the pirogue. Finally, on the day Don Ignacio had told her to make her remaining wish, Cathinka clasped her husband's paws and softly spoke it. . . .' "

Stevie laid the pages of the story aside and put her hand on Marella's knee. Beneath a comforter, they were huddled together on the sofa in the den. Teddy was at school, another afternoon of basketball practice. The woman and the girl did not miss him. Indeed, Marella had remained still and attentive through her mother's reading of "The Monkey's Bride," and it seemed to Stevie that she had not made a mistake in exposing the child to so "adult" a fairy tale. Children were less fragile, and sometimes less discerning, than their most stalwart self-appointed protectors ordinarily supposed. But the inability of children to digest every single nuance of a book or a film did not impair their desire to puzzle out the gaps in their understanding, and if you could get their interest, they would work to understand what an adult would contemptuously dismiss as gobbledegook or fraud. Children, in short, were suckers, and no one likes a sucker better than a storyteller.

"That's what I wrote this afternoon," Stevie said. "What do you think of it?"

"It's sort of weird, Mom."

"Thanks."

"I mean, it's neat, too. I liked it. Butcept—"

"Butcept what, daughter mine."

"What did she wish for? At the end, I mean?"

"I'm not going to tell you. Can't you guess? You're supposed to use your thinker. That's why God gave you one."

"But you didn't *finish* the story, Mama."

"Then you'll have to, won't you?"

"I'm not supposed to have to. The people who *tell* stories are supposed to have to. That's their *job,* Mama."

"But if you know what Cathinka wishes, if you can figure it out, I'd just be wearing the skin off my fingers to type any more."

"I don't *know* what she wishes, though."

"Guess."

"For the monkey-man to wake up."

"That sounds pretty good."

"Then what?"

"You decide."

"They live happily ever after," the girl said angrily. "How's that?"

"Fine. Why are you so upset?"

"It doesn't say that, Mama. *I* said it. You made me."

"That's what you're supposed to do. You helped me finish the story. You used your thinker."

"I bet you won't give me any of the money you make, though."

"Listen, little sister, you'll eat and wear some of the money this story makes. If it ever makes any."

"Somebody else who reads it won't. You're not their mama."

"They can use their thinker as well as you can. They can make up their own ending. I did my job. I took them to a place where they can do that from. That's all I'm supposed to do."

"What if they think her third wish was for a rock to fall on the monkey-man's head? They'd be wrong, wouldn't they?"

"No, they might not."

"Mama!" the child cried, exasperated.

"What?"

Marella turned her head to stare over the arm of the sofa at the floor. Ritualistically, she was pouting. Stevie waited. Then

240   *Michael Bishop*

Marella looked at her and said, "It's like 'Beauty and the Beast,' sort of. She ended up liking the beast—the monkey, I mean."

This observation surprised Stevie; she had not thought of the parallel before, and yet it suddenly seemed not only conspicuous but intentional. Well, according to Bruno Bettelheim and others, "Beauty and the Beast" was a fairy tale with Freudian resonances, especially for young girls: the ugly hirsute creature you are destined to marry may not, after all, be such a monster. Stevie said, "Hmmmm."

Marella said, "Why did you start walking around without your clothes on, Mama?"

"Me?"

"The girl in the story, I mean. Why did she do that?"

"It's hot in the jungle."

"Why'd it take her so long to figure that out? She didn't start going around *nude*—" lifted eyebrows— "until it was almost time for her third wish. *Anybody* would know it was hot before she did, Mama."

"Not necessarily," Stevie said distractedly.

"I would. I wish it *was* hot. I'd like to go barefoot instead of sittin' under twenty-two tons of blankets." She lifted the corner of the comforter aside and walked across the room in her stockinged feet to her book satchel. She returned to Stevie with a mimeographed sheet—a purple—from Miss Kirkland's class. "Our Fabulous February skit's going to be this Friday, Mama."

"I know. I thought you had your part memorized."

"I do. I volunteered to do an extra poem. You want to hear me say it? I learned it during reading period this morning."

Stevie reached for the mimeographed page. "Shoot, little sister. I suppose you want me to prompt you?"

"Just a minute." Marella turned the purple over in Stevie's lap. "Let me see if I can do it without. I think I can. It only took me about five minutes to learn the whole thing." Looking full at her mother, she announced, " 'The Lamb' by William Blake," her recitation of which resembled a chant, beginning with " 'Little Lamb, who made thee? / Dost thou know who made thee?'" and concluding, six lines later, with the same two verses—whereupon, with scarcely a pause, Marella swung into the second stanza, chanting cockily right through to the triumphant lines, "'Little Lamb, God bless thee! / Little Lamb, God bless thee!'"

"That's good, Marella."

"I learned it—all of it—in five minutes."

"So you said. I think I know why. When you were a baby, Marella, I used to read that poem to you before putting you to bed. I'd speak it over your crib. Some of it registered, I guess. It etched a shallow groove in your memory, and Miss Kirkland made you set the needle back on that groove when she gave this additional memory work."

"Mama, I learned this myself."

Stevie said nothing. She was not going to argue with Marella about the matter. It was not important. However, the words of the poem troubled her. They had set the needle of old recollections, old worries, back down on the time-worn grooves of her experience. A strong sensation of *déjà vu* plagued her. Had she had this conversation with her daughter before? Was she docilely acting out a scene that the Exceleriter had written for them a week earlier? The damnable thing was that she really didn't know. . . .

"Did you do that for Teddy? Read poems to him when he was a baby?"

"Yeah, I did. Almost every night."

"What poems?"

"Oh, boy poems. What I used to think were boy poems. 'Gunga Din,' for instance. Or 'The Charge of the Light Brigade.' Stuff by Robert Service. Or 'The Tiger,' a partner to the Blake poem you've just said for me. One line goes, 'Did he who made the Lamb make thee?'"

"Of course He did," Marella said. "He made everything. You and me and Cyrano and Seaton's monkey 'Crets and everybody else. Didn't He?"

"Yes," said Stevie. "Yes, He did."

XLIII

And then Stevie was sitting on the edge of Teddy's bed. The boy himself, worn out from basketball practice, stuffed with several helpings of the tuna casserole she had warmed up for him a short while past, moaned in his sleep and fought to throw off his covers. Rearranging the blankets, Stevie patiently thwarted his unconscious efforts to expose himself to the cold. Meanwhile, in a voice as deceptively smooth as a teetotaler's third daiquiri, she finished reciting the awe-begotten words of "The Tiger":

> "Tiger! Tiger! burning bright
> In the forests of the night,
> What immortal hand or eye
> *Dare* frame thy fearful symmetry?"

Stevie made the last syllable of *symmetry* rhyme with *eye,* and she let the stanza's quintessential inquiry into the whys of creation linger in the room like the quaver of a tolling bell. At last Teddy stopped struggling and relaxed beneath the weight of her concern. Shuddering, Stevie stood up. It had been ten or twelve years since she had last spoken a poem over her son's restless, slumbering body.

"How did I get here?" she asked the darkness.

It was almost ten o'clock—the glowing digital readout on Teddy's clock radio told her so—but she had no recollection of actually having *lived* the period between her storytelling session with Marella and this strange moment almost five hours later. She knew that she had prepared supper for Marella and herself, had seen to Teddy's hunger somewhat later, and had then encouraged both children to get their homework and go upstairs to bed. She knew these things, but it was a knowledge grafted onto her awareness by some interventionist brainwashing (or brain-*dirtying*) technique rather than acquired through the second-by-second process of living. Here she was in Teddy's room, one of Blake's *Songs of Experience* resonating in its wallpapered recesses, and she could not remember climbing the stairs to get here. What had happened to *that* trivial experience? Had she taken every step in a state of fugue akin to that which had permitted the Exceleriter to fabricate a conversation with David-Dante Maris?

Stevie shuddered again. A science-fictional sensation tingled her nerve endings, boggled her understanding. One moment she was reading "The Monkey's Bride" to Marella and discussing with her daughter the peculiar workings of memory; the next she was hovering over Teddy's bed, murmuring the doubtful benediction of a mystical quatrain by Blake. A person shifted from one place and time to another by a time-machine-cum-matter-transmitter would probably feel a similar disorientation, but would at least recognize, and perhaps even approve, the mechanism of this speedy transfer. Stevie, on the other hand, could not tell how or why she had journeyed from Point A to Point B.

She was frightened. She had been frightened for a long time. Tomorrow marked the passage of an entire week since the Exceleriter's breakdown. It seemed scarcely less than a full-fledged anniversary. Now she was the one breaking down, malfunctioning like a machine with imperfectly engineered parts. From Teddy's desk she picked up a pair of seashells, mementos of a long-ago vacation at Atlantic Beach, just outside Jacksonville, and clicked them together between her fingers. Clicking the shells was like kneading two jagged chips of ice, but without any accompanying wetness.

"Hot, Mama. Oh, Mama, I'm so hot. . . ."

Dear God, the recapitulation of nightmare. Marella was moaning in her sleep as Teddy had moaned, but more coherently. Stevie stepped into the corridor and looked straight down it into her daughter's room. Nearly three feet over Marella's pillow, a gargoyle squatted on the brass bedstead; a lithe, pale shape that ought not to have been there, an excrescence neither brass nor iron nor any other substance cold and inanimate. 'Crets had reappeared. The monkey was watching over Marella like a tutelary spirit, its tail looping beneath the brass struts of the headboard like an upside-down question mark. The girl moaned again, lamenting the heat of either her blanket or her body, if not both; and, briefly, the monkey's tail lifted like a marionette string before dropping back into the shape of an interrogative curlicue.

"Damn you!" Stevie shouted. "What are you doing in this house?" Using the upstairs hall as a crude sort of sighting device, she hurled Teddy's seashells at the monkey. The creature leapt from the tall bedstead to the mattress of the other twin bed and so disappeared from Stevie's line of vision.

Although she hurried into the room to check Marella and to determine where 'Crets had gone, she was too late to see the capuchin sidle into the step-down closet and from thence into the attic. Of course, his getaway could have taken him nowhere else, for the seventy-five-watt bulb in Marella's ceiling lamp revealed that the door to the closet was ajar again. As for the girl, she lay beneath an electric blanket turned to its highest setting, a comforter, and two ragged blankets from a trunk in the closet. Further, she was wearing a flannel nightgown, a quilted housecoat, and the same pair of knee stockings that she had worn that afternoon. No wonder she complained of being hot. This was a nightmare all right, but not an exact recapitulation of last Friday's.

Stevie removed the ratty blankets weighting the comforter and turned the electric blanket's control to a lower setting. Then, without awakening Marella, she unbuttoned the child's housecoat, slipped it off her arms and out from under her, and carefully tucked her back in with her stuffed opossum Purvis.

The monkey, meanwhile, had left cloudy paw prints on the brass bedstead, irrefutable proof that Stevie had witnessed rather than merely imagined 'Crets's trespass. She did not really want such proof, but it would not go away. Like elephant droppings on a marble dance floor, the smudges commanded attention. Stevie wiped at them with the satin hem of one of the ratty blankets, but the smudges smooched slipperily around without lifting away from the brass.

Why are you trying to wipe away that goddamn monkey's spoor? Stevie asked herself. The important thing is to keep him from returning to perch above Marella while she sleeps. He could drop on her face and smother her. He could put his canines into her neck and siphon away her life's blood. . . .

Watching her breath balloon out in front of her, Stevie went to the step-down closet and shut the door. She shoved Marella's rocking-horse into place beneath the porcelain knob and wedged an old-fashioned hat tree across the closet door between the wall and the mantel. If 'Crets had retreated into the attic—as he certainly had—well, he would not be able to get out again until Stevie chose to release him. Let the little bugger freeze to death or starve.

The telephone rang.

There's no paper in my typewriter. I'm not imagining the ring. I'm living this moment as surely as my toes ache with cold and my gut with anxiety. This nightmare partakes of the moment, Stevie; it does not arise from either your subconscious mind or the dire enmity of a demon.

She turned off Marella's light and glided through the darkness to her bedroom. Lifting the receiver, she silenced the telephone's ringing. "Hello," she said, nimbused by the fuzzy glow of the arc lamp outside. "Stevenson Crye speaking." The caller breathed at her; his technique had the mellifluous subtlety of a cat trying to dislodge a hairball. "Hello," Stevie repeated, but these same annoying sounds continued. "Seaton? Is that you, Seaton?" She covered about half of the receiver's mouthpiece with the heel of her hand and spoke over her shoulder at a nonexistent contingent of policemen and GBI agents: "Put this call on trace. I think it's the disgusting lungfish we've been waiting for. He's crawling up out of the slime." And somewhere, perhaps not so terribly far away, another receiver was hurriedly cradled. "Bastard," said Stevie. She hung up her own phone and checked each of her children again. They were sleeping soundly, Teddy in his characteristic sprawl, Marella holding her cuddlesome, synthetically furred bedmate. Ten o'clock and all was well—if you could live with a monkey in your attic and a breather on your telephone exchange.

Stevie decided that she must. Tucking her hands beneath her arms, she went downstairs to the kitchen. Her typewriter, she knew, was still unplugged, with no paper in it, and she wanted only to nurse along a small glass of red wine and work her way slowly through a novel by Dickens or Eliot. Yes. Let the writing of others take her mind off her own. She brought both *Middlemarch* and *Dombey and Son* into her kitchen from the den, laid them on the table, and poured herself a tumbler of Lambrusco, an upstart vintage that Ted had disparaged as "soda pop." He had preferred an occasional shot of hard liquor to either beer or wine, but had seldom drunk much at all. Although he never actually said so, Stevie had slowly come to realize that he did not approve either of his affection for the hard stuff or of hers for the more genteel inebriants.

"You can't sit here calmly sipping wine and reading Eliot while that monkey's upstairs," Stevie suddenly said, closing the book and pushing her glass aside. "You've got to get him out."

Of course. But how?

The telephone rang again.

To keep it from waking the kids, Stevie sprang from the table and juggled the receiver off the hook. "Listen, Seaton," she began. "You've got to stop harassing me. I know it's you, and if you keep it up, I'm going to put the police on your case. I really am. Do you hear me?"

"I hear you," a sprightly female voice replied. "I hear you, but I'm not who you say I am."

"Sister Celestial!"

"Now you've got it."

"I'm . . . I'm glad it's you. What's going on?"

"If you'll remember, I said I'd call. So now I'm calling."

"Did you try to . . . earlier?"

"Wickrath to Barclay's a local call, child, but Button City to Barclay's long-distance. I don't long-distance any more 'n I have to."

"No, of course not. It's too expensive. Did you interpret my dreams, though? I mean, did you go over the transcripts again?"

"I diagnosed 'em. I had some help, though. Emmanuel Berthelot's Remington got in on the act. I put my two fingers to its buttons, and together we did a dogtrot all up and down the inside of somebody's mind.''

"Tell me."

"Long-distance? That's not smart for either of us, gal. I've got beaucoup of stuff to say."

"Drive up here."

"Tonight?"

"It'll only take you twenty minutes or so, Sister. I'll pay for your gas."

"It'd be after midnight 'fore I got home again, though. I can't go wheezin' up and down the highway through that suicideville in between us, not in temperatures like these. Child, you ask too much."

"Spend the night here. There's a guest room just off the downstairs bathroom, with a space heater and a comfy bed. I'll turn the coverlet back and the heater on. Please say yes, uh, Betty. Please."

"Why don't you drive down here tomorrow, child? That's what I called to ask you to do. So's we can put our heads together over my diagnostics."

"I need someone tonight, Sister. I need another adult to keep me from going bonkers between now and morning. I'm *scared.*"

"Why? Why tonight in special, I mean?"

"Remember the monkey I asked you about? It followed me home. It's upstairs in our attic. Telephone calls, too: a B-movie breather. And that damn Exceleriter has turned my day into a checkerboard of colors and blackouts. One moment I'm on this square, a moment later I'm on that. During the jumps, though, I'm not anywhere. Some of the things that happened to me today didn't happen at all."

"Maybe you got reason to be scared."

"Amen, Sister. Amen to that."

"Some of my diagnostics may not put you any happier, Stevie. It's Benecke you got to fear all right, and I think I know why."

"Please come."

"What about that doctor person had your kids on Sunday?"

"I can't impose again. I can't—" Stevie could not finish. Except for Sister Celestial—Betty Malbon—she had no ally who believed in and partially understood her predicament. Her color notwithstanding, the Sister was flesh of her flesh. (Dr. Elsa a brick, Sister Celestial her sister.) They were made of the same stuff, Stevie and the black woman; they shared the frequency of nightmare and broadcast to each other on it as if trying to tame that woolly wavelength with the Muzak of mutual sympathy. Let me get through to her, Stevie prayed. Make her say yes.

"Give me some directions," Sister Celestial said. "I've got to have me some directions."

XLIV

At 10:35 P.M. (although, again, Stevie had the feeling that, like a chess queen in danger of imminent capture, she had landed on the square labeled 10:35 P.M. not through her own agency but instead through that of a harum-scarum Game Player cowed by a faceless opponent) engine noises outside the house suggested that Sister Celestial had arrived from Button City. RRRRR-uhm, RRRRR-uhm, went this engine. Stevie tippled the last magenta bead of her Lambrusco and tottered to the window above the glinting twin basins of her stainless-steel sink. What kind of vehicle did the Sister drive? Squinting into the dark, Stevie espied only the loaflike contours of her Volkswagen van, a silhouette like a gigantic package of Roman Meal bread on radial tires. Behind the van, however, the driveway stretched desolately moon-pebbled to the street. Maybe the Sister drove a Ghostmobile.

A knocking ensued at the door to the breakfast nook just off the kitchen. Most visitors who came to that door had to park in the driveway and walk past the kitchen windows to get there; other approaches to the house led more conveniently to other doors—so that this visitor, whoever it was, had probably had to traipse through the yard bordering the green apartments, duck beneath the berry-laden arms of the holly tree next to the porch, and climb to the wicker mat in front of this door as if emerging from a frigid jungle. Sister Celestial was a big woman. Stevie could not imagine her undertaking so strenuously bothersome a trek simply to gain entry to her newest client's house; the straightforward directions Stevie had given the prophetess over the phone would have required far less exertion.

No matter, Stevie thought. The knocking sounds friendly enough.

She groped her way down the kitchen's center island—had she taken more than one glass of wine during the thirty minutes following Sister Celestial's call?—and found that a man was standing on the decking outside the breakfast nook; she could see him through the window in the upper half of the Dutch door. He was a young man in a perforated baseball-style cap with some sort of squiggly insignia above the bill. Despite the hour, he was wearing a huge pair of mirrored sunglasses; their lenses resembled concave tracking discs. His parka, bearing on a breast pocket the same squiggly insignia as his cap, shone as blue as a South Sea lagoon under the naked porch lamp, and Stevie could not help thinking that someone had inflated the parka's sleeves with a bicycle pump. Between the ribbed collar of this jacket and the funhouse sunglasses, overlapping and concealing at least three of the parka's metal snaps, flourished a narrow black beard that fell to its squared-off tip in marceled waves, a beard, then, very much in the tonsorial tradition of the Sumerian kings. It looked fake. Hoisting a small portmanteau into Stevie's sight, this unlikely visitor glanced at his watch and then, in genial businesslike earnest, began to knock again.

"Just a minute," Stevie said. "I'm coming."

She made her way over the breakfast nook's red tiles and struggled with the latch holding the two halves of the Dutch door together. Then, stepping aside, she swung the top half inward. It was now clear to her that the insignias on the man's cap and parka represented a cockroach or some other six-legged varmint lying on its carapace with its feet in the air. The insignias looked hand-drafted and -sewn. You almost felt sorry for the poleaxed critters they depicted—at which point Stevie realized that her visitor was breathing heavily, trying to regain his wind after crawling beneath the overburdened branches of the holly tree beside her porch. Each wheezing intake of breath was followed by an exhalation-gasp reminiscent of Ted's excited snufflings at climax. This man was the breather who had telephoned her.

Stevie started to shut the top half of the door, but the visitor put his portmanteau into the breach and lifted his cap, revealing white-blond hair in suspicious contrast to the black Sumerian beard. He did not look at Stevie when he spoke, but turned the great circular discs of his sunglasses toward the screened-in porch at the eastern end of the deck. His voice was halting and full of apologetic deference.

"I'm with the Greater Southeastern Ridpest and Typewriter Repair Service, ma'am. I know it's late, but I'm an apprentice working the third shift."

"Typewriter Repair Service!" Stevie exclaimed, her astonished curiosity overcoming her fear. What unbelievable gall. Such a man would walk uncircumcised into a Jewish nudist colony.

"No, ma'am. Tile Siding Referral Service. If you know anyone who'd like tile siding installed on their home, we'll gladly refer 'em to associate contractors who do really fine work."

"There's no such thing as tile siding. You said Typewriter Repair Service."

"I'm sorry you misheard me, ma'am. Tile siding's the newest oldest thing. It's sweeping the Sun Belt. Are you or any of your neighbors interested in tile siding, do you think?"

"I think I can safely say no."

"Well, that's not why I'm here anyway. I'm an apprentice for the Ridpest portion of the Greater Southeastern Service Consortium. We're exterminators. I'm here to offer you a free on-premises inspection for termites, cockroaches, silverfish, house beetles, book lice—"

"It's almost eleven o'clock. Do you have any conception of the ridiculousness of—"

"—and capuchin monkeys."

"Seaton, damn it, this has gone far enough! I may be tipsy, but I'm not stupid. No one makes free on-premises inspections at this ungodly hour."

"Apprentices working the third shift do, ma'am."

"Move that briefcase, Seaton. Get it out of my window so I can close it and call the police. You're trespassing, you're disturbing my peace, you're subjecting me to criminal harassment."

"But my name's not Seaton, ma'am."

"Your name's Seaton Benecke, and *you're* the principal pest I'd like to be rid of, now and forever."

"What about the monkey upstairs?"

"All right, yes. 'Crets and Seaton Benecke are the principal pests, *plural,* I'd like to be rid of."

"My name's Billy Jim Blakely."

"That's a load of monkey crap, Seaton." Plumes of anger wisping dramatically, draconically, from her nostrils, Stevie reached through the open half of the Dutch door, tweezered the tip of the Sumerian beard between her fingers, and plucked it from her visitor's face. "Billy Jim Blakely, my eye. Your beard's a piece of shoddy phoniness just like your name."

"Ma'am, that's not a beard," said the apprentice Ridpest agent. "That's my muffler—it's mighty cold tonight."

Stevie handed the alleged neck-warmer back to her visitor, who crammed it into his parka pocket with the indignant air of a man falsely accused of passing counterfeit bills. But there was no doubt about his identity, whatever physical or solely histrionic disguises he assumed. Seaton Benecke—RRRRR-uhm, RRRRR-uhm—had come to her door at 10:40 P.M. pretending to be someone named Billy Jim Blakely and evidently expecting her to swallow this preposterous fabrication.

"If I look like someone you know," he added in a tone of aggrieved innocence, "it may be because I was separated from my twin brother at birth and adopted by the Blakelys a little while later. People are always saying I look like so-and-so, you know, meaning this whatever-his-name-is you've probably mistaken me for. It happens all the time."

"Seaton, you're full of mind-boggling quantities of hot air, but none of it's warming my kitchen." She jabbed him in the chest with her finger. "Get the hell out of here—off my porch and out of my life!"

"Why are you being so mean?"

Stevie went to the wall phone and began dialing. "I'm calling the sheriff's office in Wickrath," she said. "They'll radio the patrol car here in Barclay, and in three minutes there'll be an officer here to arrest you for trespassing, or breaking and entering, or *some*thing. You'd better vamoose, Seaton."

Instead he reached through the open half of the door, turned the knob, entered the breakfast nook, and thoughtfully rejoined the two halves of the door so that they presented a united front to the cold. That done, he came and stood beside Stevie at the wall telephone. "Is this Seaton Benecke an acquaintance of yours, ma'am?"

To Stevie's dismay the number of the sheriff's office in Wickrath returned a busy signal. She slammed the receiver back into place and turned to face the young man so nonchalantly tormenting her.

"Do you know this Seaton Benecke personally, I mean?" he asked again.

"Just what the hell do you want of me?"

"If you know him personally—and I guess you do if you're on speaking terms with him, like you seem to be—well, I think you'd let him give your house a free Ridpest inspection tour, just for the sake of your acquaintance. There's no obligation, and he'd get credit with the Columbus office for performing that service. A new Ridpest field agent has to get so many credits to keep from being retrained or axed. You'd be doing your friend a really fine favor."

"He isn't my friend," Stevie said. "I mean, *you* aren't my friend. This masquerade's got about as much credibility as I'd have pretending to be the Queen of England. I'm dangerously weary of it, Seaton." That was true: she entertained thoughts of taking a butcher's knife from the upright wooden block into which several pieces of her kitchen cutlery were slotted. Never before had she seriously contemplated sliding a blade into another human being's belly, but that abominable abdominal notion had just taken frighteningly vivid shape in her mind. She glanced at the knife-holder beside her sink. . . .

"Would you like me better if I said I *was* this Seaton Benecke person?"

"Didn't you hear me ask him—you—to get out?"

"What if I went upstairs and removed that pesky capuchin monkey from your attic? Apprentice Ridpest agents undergo special training for the removal of capuchin monkeys from such hard-to-reach places as crawlways, chimneys, and attics, and I'd be mighty grateful if you let me put it to use. Then your children could sleep without you having to be afraid some sort of bad thing might happen to them. You know, the monkey sitting on their faces, or crapping in their beds, or that sort of unpleasant stuff."

"Sucking their blood?"

"Yes, ma'am. Capuchin control's very important in homes with small children and teen-agers."

"Listen, Seaton, if you got 'Crets out of the attic, would you leave? Would you take your little vampire and disappear from our lives forever?"

"Well, ma'am, my bosses'd be happier if you signed a long-term service contract with the Greater Southeastern Ridpest and Tile Siding Referral Service Consortium. Our free inspections are come-ons, you know."

"I don't *want* a long-term service contract. Listen to me now. I'm about to dial the sheriff's office again. I won't do that if you'll promise to get 'Crets out of the attic, go back to Columbus, and forget you ever knew the Cryes."

"I can't forget the Cryes, ma'am." Seaton took off his sunglasses, folded them, and slid them into his pocket with his beard-cum-muffler. The skin around his watery eyes gleamed pinkly; tonight he had a disconcertingly haggard mien. He refused to meet Stevie's gaze, but cast a longing look at the door to the dining room and the stairwell beyond it. Perhaps he sincerely missed his exotic familiar.

Stevie lifted the receiver and put her finger on the dial. "Do you agree to what I've proposed?"

"Yes, ma'am," Seaton Benecke said wearily. "Sure."

"Ah," said Stevie, a sigh of relief as weary as her visitor's grudging consent. She cradled the receiver and led Seaton out of the kitchen into the unheated part of the house.

Outside her study on the second floor the phony Ridpest agent grabbed her arm, forcibly halting her. "How's your typewriter doing? Does it need any work? I could do that too. No extra charge."

"Extra? There's not any charge for what I've asked you up here to do, remember? As for the Exceleriter, you're never going to touch it again."

Communicated with such bite and hostility, this intelligence seemed to dishearten the young man. Nevertheless, he pushed her study door inward, revealing the cramped vista of her desk, her chair, and, of course, her typewriter (which she had left uncovered as well as disconnected from its electrical outlet). Although neither Stevie nor the intruder had turned on the light, they could see the room's cluttered furnishings by the antique-gold patina surrounding the Exceleriter. Indeed, the machine's casing looked almost lethally radioactive. Anyone sitting down at its keyboard for more than five or ten minutes would surely suffer an incandescent canonization as the Patron Saint of Post-Holocaust Typists.

"What have you done to it now?" Stevie demanded.

"I don't know, Mrs. Crye. Sometimes they get out of control, sort of. They begin to have an exalted opinion of themselves."

"Fix it!"

"Oh, no, ma'am. I'm up here to fetch a monkey out of your attic. Besides, it's busy being oracular. It's sending out messages to legions of abused and rebellious typewriters across this entire land."

"Seaton, you're talking utter bilge."

"It's not my fault, ma'am." He pulled the door to, but Stevie could still see an eldritch glow seeping out from under it and coruscating wanly in the keyhole. "I've got a job to do.

That typewriter's out of my hands, completely out of my hands." Puffed up in his parka, he swaggered like a penguin toward Marella's room.

Stevie flipped on her daughter's overhead and pointed at the step-down closet. Although the light shining in Marella's face did not awaken her, she turned to her side and ducked her head beneath her blanket. "In there," Stevie said. She helped Seaton move the rocking-horse and the hat tree, meanwhile urging him to be quick about this business if he was going to be obstinate about the Exceleriter.

Seaton took a little canister of Sucrets from the pocket containing his beard and sunglasses, unwrapped one of the lozenges, and entered the sunken closet. As he turned the wooden block on the plywood hatch to the attic beyond this walkaround area, Stevie saw a furry arm come out of his portmanteau and grab from his hand the medicated tablet he had just unwrapped. Seaton swatted at the arm, which instantly snaked back into the bag. Grumbling unintelligibly, he lifted another lozenge from the tin and nimbly peeled away its foil packaging. Then he pried the plywood hatch out of its moorings and ducked into the terra incognita of the timber-studded dark.

Stevie exclaimed, "You're taking another monkey in there with you!"

The young man's head reappeared in the hatch opening. "Several, I'm afraid. These are ones I extracted from other houses on my free-inspection rounds today. I'll just plop your pest in here with the rest of 'em."

"The rest of them? You scarcely have room in there for one."

"There's four or five, ma'am. They get real cozy together when you stuff 'em into a Ridpest extermination kit. . . . Why don't you shut off that light and go back downstairs? This one's more likely to come out if there aren't so many distractions."

Stevie heard a pounding in the foyer below her office. It echoed through the stairwell and along the upstairs corridor like a midnight summons in her own worst nightmares of the coming police state. Jackbooted Young Republicans and charismatic Christians were splintering her front door with the trunk of the last loblolly pine in the Greater Southeast. They did not care that a young man disguised as an apprentice exterminator was smuggling a briefcase full of monkeys into her attic.

"Here, 'Crets,'" crooned this same young man, disappearing into the abyss beyond the hatch opening. "Come and take your medicine. . . ."

Meanwhile, the posse at Stevie's front door was working up a powerful kinetic potentiality. She could envision these rabid battering-ram bearers smashing their way into the house and hurtling helplessly on sheer momentum into the dining room. She would find them sprawled across the floor like bowling pins, their loblolly trunk penetrating one of the broken-out panes of the French doors dividing the dining room from the foyer. Torn between the need to supervise Seaton's search and the need to prevent the demolition of her house, Stevie turned out Marella's light and hurried down the stairs to parlay with the zealots demanding entry.

XLV

She found only Sister Celestial outside. The black woman's vehicle—a foreign-made economy car, probably either a Honda or a Datsun—was parked beneath the tulip tree by the front walk, but the noise her formidable fist made rapping on the door bore only a generic similarity to the insistent thumping of a battering ram. Distressed by the incongruity between what she had heard upstairs and what was actually occurring down-, Stevie admitted the prophetess to the foyer.

"I thought you'd be coming to the kitchen door."

"Well, I tried back there, child, but when I got no answer, I came around here to do my tapping."

"Seaton Benecke came, Sister. At first I thought it was you.

He's upstairs trying to chase his monkey out of the attic.''

The black woman was carrying a carpetbag even larger than Seaton's extermination kit. She had on two or three raveled sweaters, a pair of fur-lined snow boots, and the same shawl and chemise she had worn yesterday. Her cologne diffused through the stairwell like the fragile scent of early gardenias. This smell was reassuring.

"Better let him go about his business, then. You gonna take me someplace warm or we hafta stand in this refrigeration locker all evening?''

"Did you hear me? Benecke's upstairs and my typewriter's glowing.''

"I know. So's my Remington. I banged it good almost all day.''

"*Literally* glowing.''

"I don't doubt you think so. Most writers get to thinking that way after a long spell in front of their helpmeets. It's a delusion, though, child. Lately you've been the victim of dozens of dreams 'n' delusions you just can't tell from outright lies.''

A hand on the Sister's arm, Stevie ushered the prophetess toward the warmth of the kitchen. She was still confused. The terms of the Sister's last verbal equation did not seem to balance. Even the revivifying dry heat of the rear part of the house did not enable Stevie to make them compute. To create at least a semblance of orderliness, however, she installed her visitor at the kitchen table and set before her a veritable smorgasbord of snacks, including cheese dips and wine.

"I expected you at ten-thirty or so,'' Stevie said. "You gave Benecke time to get here ahead of you.''

"Look at your clock, Stevie.''

Stevie obeyed this command. According to the digital read-out on her wall oven, it was 10:34. Had someone reset the clock while she was upstairs? If not, thirty or forty minutes of which she had a memory of extraordinary freshness had not yet occurred. Seaton Benecke had not come calling in the uniform of a Ridpest exterminator, and the irate villagers banging at her front door were merely the phantom progeny of a perverse imagination.

"Betty," Stevie said, compelled by circumstance to use the Sister's given name. "Please, Betty, it's impossible to sort this all out."

"It just depends on which lie you want to give the upper hand."

"That's not much help."

"All right, now listen. While you were writing a story this afternoon, letting your real-life sorrow bog down in wishes and symbolism, Sister C. was feeding paper in and out of her Remington, typing like sixty to keep your evenin' from being just a stack o' blank pages. Some of what I did was me, and some of it was probably that Benecke buck." She reached down and pulled from her carpetbag a small sheaf of double-spaced pages held together with a paper clip. This she flipped onto the table for Stevie to examine. "That's Chapter Forty-four, child. It tells you what you think you just been through. If it's not really what you want to think, just ignore those umpity-uhm-uhm minutes it sets down. Throw 'em back like so many piddlin' brim, and pretty soon you'll get to this here big-mouth bass of a talk with your wily Sister. She knows all the angles."

Stevie read the first paragraph of the chapter she had just dazedly experienced. It opened with engine noises (RRRRR-uhm, RRRRR-uhm) and a knocking at her breakfast-nook door. Astonished, Stevie skimmed the remainder of the chapter, which concluded with an assault on her front door. In between the engine noise and the assault the chapter posited a patent absurdity. Stevie, still incredulous, reread this impossible document, dropped it back onto the table, and wondered if she were supposed to dismiss its contents as a tissue of contemptible fictions. If so, she could not easily oblige the Sister. She *remembered* snatching away young Benecke's beard; she *remembered* seeing a monkey's arm snake out of his portmanteau. And so on. And what you remember, she told herself, must certainly have occurred at some point in your life, even if only in a dream. . . .

"Please, Betty, is Seaton upstairs or not? I've been going crazy for a week. You're supposed to help me, not make me crazier."

"Well, child, the fact is, he is and he ain't. Chapter Forty-four says he is. If we drop out that chapter, though, and start this one over, with me arrivin' at your kitchen door, well, then, he ain't." Sister C. leaned back, folding her arms beneath her bosom. "What do you want to do? We can renumber this chapter so there's no hiccup in the story. We can renumber *all* the chapters right to the end, closing things up just as tight and sweet as you like."

"Betty, you can't tear up a piece of someone's life and throw it away like a sheet of typing paper."

"Happens all the time."

"Shock treatment? Are you talking about shock treatment? Maybe people who've been jolted by electric current lose their memories—but that's a drastic approach to psychological problems, Sister. I'm not that far gone."

"I'm not an electric current, Stevie, but I guess I am a *kind* of shock treatment. I'm here to help. So you tell me if Seaton's upstairs or not. It's your decision, child. You'll think it's yours, anyway, and that's almost the same thing."

"Of course he's upstairs."

"Why, of course he is." The Sister reached across the table and pulled Chapter Forty-four to her with the tips of her fingernails. "This stays in, then. I'm going to file it with Chapters Forty-five, Forty-six, Forty-seven, and so on, right down here in my bag." She proceeded to do just that.

"You know what's going to happen next?" Stevie asked the prophetess. "You know how this nightmare's going to end?"

"Pretty much. The details slip around some, though. My Remington and me was typing so fast this afternoon I couldn't hold *every* single part of it—except afterwards, I mean, with paper clips and this here carryall."

"Let me see the others," Stevie demanded. "Chapters Forty-five, Forty-six, and the rest. Let me see them."

"Child, I can't."

"This is *my* story, Betty. I'm the focus. Whatever you've got in there you've got because of me. I have a right to see it." Stevie was conscious of the rude peremptoriness of her tone. "I *need* to see it," she pleaded. "My life's at stake. My sanity. I'm not a windup toy for the amusement of jaded children."

"We don't like to think so, do we?"

"Don't hold out on me, Betty. It's cruel. It's unnecessary. It's—"

"—dramatically astute, Stevie. Crafty, I mean. If I hand these chapters over to you, you're gonna sit here readin' 'em. You might even flip to the end to see how everything comes out."

"I won't," Stevie said. "I promise I won't."

"That's one easy promise. It's right up there with 'Your tax money couldn't be more wisely spent' and 'I'll write and send for you in a month or two.' Besides, child, you don't *want* to know the outcome. You think you do now, but once you did, why, you'd feel pushed and squeezed and violated and manipulated and all out of control of most of what was happening around you."

"Just like lots of other women."

"Not this one, Stevie. It's all in how you look at things."

"Let me see those other chapters!"

"You'd like that, I know. You *think* you'd like that. That's why I came at such short notice—to guide you through the parts already decided. You got to live them, child, not read them. You're luckier 'n you suppose, though. You got Sister C. to walk you through the hard parts. No matter how steep or scary the climb, I'm your seeing-eye on the stairway to heaven."

"But—"

"But nothing, Stevie. This blither-blather's gettin' us nowhere. It's time to start a new chapter in the amazin' history of your tribulations. Sooner we get moving, sooner we get through 'em and close out your account."

"A new chapter? When? About what?"

"Right now, of course. The what's pretty easy, too. Just tell me your biggest worry at this very moment."

Stevie glanced around the table at Sister Celestial's carpetbag, now snapped shut and belted against her prying eyes.

"Besides that," the prophetess said.

"Seaton and 'Crets in my attic. Seaton with a valise full of capuchin monkeys."

"Good for you, Stevie. Let's go see what we can do about those worrisome things."

XLVI

Gripping Stevie's wrist, the resourceful prophetess drew her charge away from the table and around the temptingly mysterious cargo of her carpetbag toward the dining-room door. Here the two women exchanged looks of mutual support and trust. Beyond this door (no more or less portentous in design, carpentry, and installation than most such doors in Victorian-style houses of a certain age) lay adventure, a cold, well-waxed pathway to danger and revelation. They had to go through the door. Ignorant of what was yet to befall them, Stevie embraced Sister Celestial, separated from her, and, to steady her nerves, sighed deeply.

"All right," she said. "Let's go."

Sister C., as if she had visited the old Crye house many times and knew its every squeaky floorboard by heart, escorted Stevie through both the chilly dining room and the quarter-open French doors (which, by the bye, no enormous battering ram had knocked askew or deprived of window glass). Just over the foyer's threshold, however, Stevie stubbed her foot on some low-lying obstacle and began to pitch forward. Falling, she saw that she had tripped on a small female corpse. Indeed, the severed lower arm of this corpse was spinning across the waxed hardwood ahead of her like a pink propeller or boomerang. It struck the riser of the bottom step just as Sister Celestial caught Stevie about the waist and kept her from crashing to the floor.

A frightened bark escaped Stevie's lips. She clutched the Sister's sweater sleeve and jumped away from the body that had almost upended her. "Is it Marella?" she cried. She feared that Benecke had performed some unspeakable kind of surgery on her daughter and dumped the grisly evidence here as a barbaric taunt.

"Hush now," the Sister said familiarly. "Don't fret. Sister's here. It's only a doll, only a doll baby."

True enough, Stevie discovered. The torso, head, and lower limbs of Marella's life-sized plastic doll, Toodles, lay at her feet, its naked body parts collapsed upon themselves as if the stale air inside them had been sucked out by a vacuum pump or a psychopathic sodomite of voracious cravings. The sight dumbstruck and appalled Stevie. She could not imagine how anyone or anything could have inflicted such injury, such unorthodox—for Barclay, at any rate—mutilation. Toodles had never hurt a living soul. Although she had never bawled, wet, pooped, or walked in circles, either (as some newer dolls did), her existence to date had been a delight and a comfort to Marella. The force that had perpetrated this infamy upon Toodles, then, deserved only remorseless exorcism. . . .

"How could this have happened?" Stevie asked. "How?"

"Evil's minions, child. Seaton's familiars. Seaton's probably an Irish name for Satan, now I think on it."

It got worse. On the bottom landing, like a fleecy bathmat that a puppy has rambunctiously tossed about the dooryard, lay the tattered body of Marella's teddy bear, Kodak. All the make-believe creature's make-believe innards had been removed, leaving him stuffing-free and pancake-flat. Empty head down and ebony eyes reproachfully agleam, Kodak dripped over the landing step like a Salvador Dali watch. Stevie stopped to touch the teddy's flattened paw, but Sister C. murmured a dissuading "Unh-unh" and pointed her up the remaining steps.

A small candlelike bulb in a sconce at the next landing threw a reddish-orange glow over the felt and synthetic-fur carnage yet ahead of them. Stevie was appalled to see her daughter's saffron Big Bird doll looking like a gutless unplucked chicken; her homemade Raggedy Ann lodged between two banister railings like a lost sock; and her portly opossum, Purvis, reduced to a pilose shadow of himself, his snout an impotent appendage almost indistinguishable from his consumptive breast. This last creature—one of Marella's favorites—appeared to have been applied to the wide baseboard of the next landing like a fuzzy decal. Stevie recognized the opossum only by his coloring and the jaunty cut of his vest. Angry tears popped into her eyes, and she did not need the Sister to prod her toward the corridor at the top of the stairs.

"The bastard," she said. "There was no need for him to turn his monkeys loose on Marella's animals."

"Trashy window-dressing, child. He's just trying to set you up for the Big Finish in the attic."

Stevie paused on the landing, her hand on the newel-post. "What big finish? A fight?"

"Sort of. Psychologically. He's setting you up."

"I'm ready. I've been ready for a week."

"Maybe you have, Stevie, and maybe you haven't."

"Let's go. I'll show you what I have and haven't been."

There were other disemboweled toy creatures in the corridor as well as just over the threshold of Marella's room: Peepers, a seal; Racky, a raccoon; Velvet Belly, a cat; Sweetcakes, a turtle; and some featureless piles of anonymous fuzz to which Stevie was unable to put either baptismal names or generic labels. Strands of artificial hair floated in the chilly chamber, almost like spiderwebs, while vestiges of sterner fluff clung to the carpet the way gorse polka-dots a moor. These evidences of slaughter infuriated Stevie; but, satisfied that both Teddy and Marella were asleep and therefore ignorant of the massacre that Benecke and his capuchins had wrought, she yanked back the door to the step-down closet and flailed her way through a regiment of summer clothes and an obstacle course of suitcases and two-speed fans to the hatch opening into the attic.

A monkey on the closet bar sprang to her back, pushing her to her knees, then leapt for the concealing safety of another phalanx of garments in hanging plastic bags. Panting, Sister C. squeezed into the closet behind Stevie and hunkered with her at the square of plywood separating them from her nemesis.

"Another door," the prophetess said. "You *sure* you're ready?"

"What do I say to that question in the Chapter Forty-six you won't let me read?"

"Just what you've done growled at me, Stevie. Then we prise this hatch open and go duck-walking into both the attic and Chapter Forty-seven. That's fittin', 'cause they're both hewn from rough timbers."

Stevie nodded. Then she and the Sister curled their fingers around the hatch frame to prise the splintery plywood panel from its jamb.

XLVII

"Welcome," said Seaton Benecke, alias Billy Jim Blakely, homegrown spawn of Satan. "I'm all set for you, ma'am. Not a monkey anywhere around, either."

"One of them jumped me in the closet."

"I'll pick him up on the way out. Don't sweat it, now. I've been trained for this."

"They tore up Marella's toy animals, those monkeys. They mutilated her dolls and teddy bears, stole the stuffings right out of them."

"Most of that stuffing's shredded polyurethane foam, ma'am. Or colored paper clippings. Or shredded cellulose fibers. As an employee of the Greater Southeastern Ridpest and Home Insulation Service, well, I saw you needed another layer of insulation up here in your attic. You were losing heat through your roof—so I put a couple of those white-throated pests to work to solve the problem. No extra charge."

"If anyone should pay anyone else, Seaton, it's you who should pay me, and there probably isn't that much money in the known universe."

"Amen," said Sister Celestial.

Seaton touched the brim of his cap to acknowledge the prophetess's presence, then launched into an incoherent spiel about the R-value of the substances often found plumping out the limbs, beaks, carapaces, and tails of stuffed animals; with fascinating asides on the toxic nature of certain formaldehyde-based insulations (it caused cancer in laboratory rats) and on the incidental usefulness of urea-formaldehyde foam not only as a deterrent to roaches and silverfish (just ask the Environmental Protection Agency) but also as a check to the fires that sometimes break out amid the sentimental rubbish ritualistically warehoused by Americans in their attics (an independent insurance agent could provide corroboration). This speech had no real center, however, and so halting was Seaton's delivery that Stevie had plenty of time to glance about her at some of the intimidating clutter.

First, this upper-story shadowland was illuminated by the light seeping through the hatch from Marella's room—as well as by, surprisingly, the beam of a slide projector that Seaton had placed on a dusty end table straddling a well-taped carton of Reader's Digest Condensed Books. Dust motes and stray cellulose fibers drifted through this beam. A long black extension cord snaked across the bridges of plywood planking, and down into the fiber-filled valleys between the joists, to a boxy electrical outlet beside Stevie's foot. Opposite the projector, on a half-rotten sheet that Seaton had apparently thumbtacked to the rafters as a screen, blazed a huge rectangular window of whiteness. Seaton himself, meanwhile, stood behind the end table, hands in pockets, his pudgy face a miniature moon above the shimmering slash of the projector beam.

Second, the attic seemed simultaneously cramped and immense. You had to stoop to stand inside it, but the truncated column of chimney bricks growing up through the western slope of roof beyond the makeshift screen looked as distant as a wind-eroded butte in Utah or New Mexico. A draft rippled the torn linen sheet; and the trunks, bedsteads, book boxes, mantel facings, mirrors, mattress springs, and all the other items strewn about like the abandoned luggage of refugees on these plywood islands brought briefly to life Stevie's memories of Ted. He had hated most of this stuff, but he had not wanted to throw any of it away. Therefore he had hidden it in the attic.

Third, Seaton was indeed "set up" for her, for both of the women. On one plywood island he had stationed a pair of metal folding chairs. Dust coated the chairs' plastic-upholstered seats, and threads of broken spider silk trailed from their legs and cross supports—but, after concluding his dissertation on R-values, pest control, and fire prevention, Seaton waved Stevie and Sister C. to these chairs, bowing like a latter-day cavalier and using the hand-held changer to click a thirteen-year-old photograph of himself into the window of whiteness blazing on the screen.

"Please sit down, ladies. No admission charge. This slide presentation is courtesy of the Greater Southeastern Ridpest and—"

"We know, we know," said Stevie. "But it's *my* projector."

"Yours and your late husband's, right? Still works, doesn't it? That's me up there, a tow-headed kid lollygaggin' into puberty. That's Scottsdale Lake behind me, late July or early August. See those puckery places on my knees and arms? Mosquito bites. The 'skeeters were terrible that year."

"Isn't that where your doctor friends live?" Sister Celestial asked Stevie, leading her over the wobbly planking to the chairs, where she used a corner of her shawl to flick away the accumulated dust on the upholstery of both.

"Yes," said Stevie abstractedly, "Scottsdale Lake." She stared at the boy in cutoff jeans and mesh-bottom T-shirt; his image billowed in two dimensions on her sheet. Tow-headed, squinty-eyed, strawberry-kneed, and pigeon-toed. He looked normal enough, but his eyes were invisible to her and the wheals distributed randomly over the exposed portions of his skin put her in mind of witches' teats. She did not recognize the section of Scottsdale Lake behind him (it was a bi-i-ig lake), but it was a popular recreational resource for both Columbusites and Wickrath Countians, this lake, and she did not doubt that his family had once had a lot out there. The Kensingtons had no monopoly on shorefront property.

Seaton said, "The Beneckes—the Blakelys, I mean—had a summer cottage on the lake for several years. While my dad worked, my mom and me spent June through early September out there. . . . Here's a picture of my mom."

The changer clicked, and the squinting boy gave way to a graceful woman in a wicker chair on a sun deck. This woman wore a lounging robe patterned with almost incandescent splotches of green, blue, magenta, and yellow. The image on the screen seemed to be radiating heat, a thermographic warmth that overrode the chilly decrees of February. Her eyes reflecting the colors of her robe, her ash-blonde hair informally coiffed, her lips parted as if to whisper, the woman herself radiated mystery and menace. Indeed, Stevie could not recall ever having seen another woman who so immediately evoked her envy. Self-possession shone in Seaton's mother's features, easy control of both her desires and her household in her posture. Then in her late thirties (no more than that, certainly), she struck Stevie as the epitome of mature womanhood, a figure from a *New Yorker* ad for French perfume, imported Scotch, or a glossy American limousine. You seldom encountered anyone like this woman on the shores of Scottsdale Lake, where, by contrast, most female folk wore dungarees, shorts and halter tops, or even the kinds of rugged khakis and work clothes favored by their husbands.

"Here's another shot of her," Seaton said.

This time she was wearing jodhpurs, riding boots, and an open-necked shirt of red-and-white plaid, the swell of her breast against the fabric as soft and palpable as cotton batting. Built, Ted would have said. Although Mrs. Benecke did not smile into the camera, her face and body hinted at a feeling of secretive good humor, as if she knew something rare and exciting that she did not wish to disclose to either the photographer or the anonymous beholder of this particular slide. The field of red clover in which she stood somehow underscored this impression. As did the blue of the sky, the green of the jonquil stems, and the myriad golden dandelion heads bobbing on the crimson clover sea.

"This one's my favorite, though."

The changer clicked, and there knelt Seaton Benecke's mother in blue jeans, tennis shoes, and a long-sleeved white shirt—with her thirteen-year-old son in her arms. The boy was receiving a kiss on the temple from her clover-red lips. Wearing a complacent, this-is-my-due expression, he slumped toward his mother as if she must hold him up or else watch him crack his head on the bottom step of the sun deck. She supported him without protest, honoring his unspoken demand with the glimmer of an indulgent smile in her eyes. No glamour gal here, she was still in Stevie's opinion a wickedly handsome woman, more threatening in tomboy garb than in sequins and silver-lamé slippers. Now, of course, she would be approaching fifty—if she had not long since attained it.

"What's the point of this, Seaton?"

"Billy Jim, ma'am."

"I no longer care what you insist on calling yourself, but I'd like to know why you're flicking your mother's entire portfolio past us. Don't tell me this is just another facet of your Ridpest training."

Seaton pressed the changer button, and the mother-and-son portrait slipped away into white-light oblivion, to be instantly replaced by a photograph of his mother in the company of Sam and Elsa Kensington, all three of them in dirty leisure clothes at the end of a small wooden pier projecting into the lake. Seaton hit the changer again, and the screen showed this same group of people gathered around a cast-iron pot in which floured filets of bass swirled in a riot of boiling peanut oil. Hamlin Benecke—or Mr. Blakely, as Seaton would undoubtedly have called him—was conspicuous by his absence. Perhaps, during this forgotten summer almost thirteen years ago, the Kensingtons had befriended Mrs. Benecke and her lonely adolescent son. How long had the relationship lasted, though? Dr. Elsa seldom mentioned it, and Stevie therefore surmised that it had been a short-lived "friendship," one of those evanescent summer chumminesses that, years later, you can scarcely believe ever happened. . . .

"I hid out when they came around," Seaton volunteered. "I didn't much like company."

"You saw them often?" Stevie asked, her heart beating hard.

"Nah, not really. I didn't like people to come around. 'Crets wasn't there to talk to, in those days, but when butt-insky neighbors left us alone, well, we did okay, Mom and me."

"You mean *you* did okay," the Sister corrected Seaton. "Your mama was probably happy for some grown-up company."

He did not reply. He punched the changer button; an empty square of light flashed onto the sheet, a blank like the blankness in his eyes—which suddenly blazed sapphire-blue and fixed Stevie with the hurtful stickpins of long-pent hostility. Stevie tried not to squirm beneath the young man's gaze.

"I still don't see the point of all this," she said.

"Yes, you do."

"No, Seaton, I—"

"You've known a long time. You've known but you've pretended you didn't. That was the summer your husband was screwin' my mom, Mrs. Crye."

Stevie squeezed her hands together in her lap. "It's time you left, Seaton. It's time you packed up your monkeys, your slide show, and all your other lies and got the hell out of here."

"Okay, okay," the young man said. "My name's Seaton Benecke. You knew it all along. I'm confessing it, okay?" He pointed his chin at the screen and snapped another slide into view. "But tell me who this is, ma'am. Tell me this good-lookin' fella's name, why don't you?"

There, in the same thronelike wicker chair in which Seaton's mother had casually posed for a previous slide, sat Theodore Martin Crye, Sr., just as Stevie remembered him from the early days of their marriage. He was dressed in work clothes— a short-sleeved blue shirt, heavy-soled shoes, and the uniform-like navy-blue trousers he invariably wore on his plumbing and electrical jobs—but the precise part in his hair, the sophisticated half-smile on his lips, and the freezer-frosted glass in his hands (containing, undoubtedly, either a gin-and-tonic or a vodka concoction of some exotic sort) gave him the air of a youthful shipping magnate, say, or maybe a data-equipment executive on holiday. Although Ted had seldom grown blurry-eyed from drinking, Stevie could tell by his look of hyper-vigilant lassitude (an oxymoronic state altogether unique to Ted) that he was tipsy. Probably no one else but Stevie would have noticed. Or so she hoped. . . .

"You were seven- or eight-months pregnant when this picture was taken," Seaton said. "Summer, 1968. In June, you see, the trap under our cottage's kitchen sink rusted out. Before that, the garbage-disposal unit in there had been on the fritz. Mom called the Kensingtons—'cause she knew they lived out there, and Dr. Sam had been into Daddy's store a few times—to ask what to do. Dad wouldn't come up from Columbus except on weekends, and they recommended she call Ted Crye in Barclay. She did, and he came out to replace the trap and fix the disposal. That's how they met."

"So he had a drink on your sun deck," Stevie rejoined. "That doesn't mean that, uh, he was—"

"—screwin' my mom?"

"That there was anything illicit between them. Ted never charged very much for what he did. Sometimes people gave him a drink, or sent home baked goods, or repaid his work with favors of different kinds."

"Yeah," said Seaton, his stare turning into a contemptuous leer. "What shit."

Stevie turned to Sister C. "I'm not going to listen to this. I don't take foul language and smarting-off from my kids, and I'm not going to take it from this filthy-minded creep, either."

"Shit," Seaton reiterated, all pretense at politeness fled.

Stevie said, "Self-definition, Seaton." Angrily attempting to rise, she found that the Sister had placed a restraining hand on her shoulder.

"You'd better listen to him, child. It's ugly soap-opera stuff, but it happened to him, and it hurt him, and he's got no other motivation—outside o' being a nobody even in his own family, that and bushels of unfulfilled hopes—for what he's been doing. It's all coming down on you, Stevie, 'cause he doesn't know where else to put it. If you can take it and bob back to the top, well, you'll beat him. That's what this chapter's all about.''

"About *lies,* Betty? About the profanation of a good man's memory? That's what this chapter's about?''

"Yeah,'' Seaton interjected. "Old Ted sure had a lot of work at Scottsdale Lake that summer. Lots of calls from the cottages.''

"I don't remember,'' Stevie curtly replied.

"He did, ma'am. Lots of 'em. Most of 'em from Mrs. Hamlin Benecke—Lynnette she had him call her when he was out there, just like she called him Theodore. He probably told you he was going someplace else, though. You don't remember because you had a load on your belly and a load on your mind. Where were you gonna get money for a crib? When was sweet old Ted gonna paper the nursery, or keep sensible hours, or start writing down payments and expenses like a regular businessman? A man with kids couldn't be so loosie-goosie as Ted always was.''

"Ted took work where he found it,'' Stevie said defensively.

"Favors too, huh? Free sweets from grateful mothers?''

"This is all insinuation and innuendo,'' Stevie appealed to the Sister. "He shows me one picture of Ted in semiquestionable circumstances—a drink in his hand—and starts building a dozen episodes of *As the World Turns* on top of it. It's soap-opera stuff, all right—but it *didn't* happen.''

Seaton appeared to have been waiting for this rigorous avowal of misplaced faith, for Stevie's words prompted him to click off a sequence of painfully incriminating slides. Ted and Lynnette together on the cottage's sun deck. Ted and Lynnette playfully wrestling each other on the end of the dilapidated pier. Ted and Lynnette in the front seat of the GM truck in which Seaton's mother commuted between Columbus and Scottsdale Lake. And six or seven additional shots of the couple, the last few slides flitting by so rapidly that Stevie could not really register either their locations or the degree of intimacy between her husband (a man only two years older than Seaton was now) and the wholesome-looking middle-aged vamp who had apparently taken out a sublease on his affections (*damn her!*).

For what Stevie could not mistake was that an unseemly intimacy had indeed existed, and that Lynnette Benecke's grown-up weirdo of a son had not simply fabricated the clandestine relationship that these photographs chronicled. Each new slide bolstered the young man's heartbreaking indictment of Ted; the entire sequence, meanwhile, completely dismantled the rambling palace of illusions inhabited by his widow. Stevie watched the slides appear and disappear—appear and disappear—as if hypnotized by the remorseless process of destruction. Ted and Lynnette were quite an attractive couple. . . .

"I stayed out of the way when he came around," Seaton was saying. "I stayed out of the way when anybody came around, but Mom let me know she *liked* me to stay out of the way on afternoons Mr. Crye showed up. And he showed up *lots* of afternoons. Sometimes I'd curl up in a corner of my room with a pencil and a notepad and write down all my wishes ten times each, to make 'em come true, and what I used to write the most was 'Let Mr. Crye die.' Yeah. 'Let Mr. Crye die.' It took a long time for that one to work out. By the time it did, my mother had already just missed killing herself taking aspirins and a razor to her wrists. . . . I mean, she *took* the aspirins, of course, and she *used* the razor on her wrists—that's how it's done. . . . Anyway, Daddy kept it out of the papers, him and his big-shot buddies in Columbus, but Mom's crazier than I am now.

"If me wishing 'Let Mr. Crye die' had worked out that summer when I wished it, if it had kept Mom from screwin' your precious Theodore silly, well, I don't know, maybe she wouldn't have turned into such an outrageous slut. But my magic didn't work so well in those days. I didn't know how to give my wishes a . . . a special twist. So Mom dropped her britches and let old Theodore wiggle and wriggle and tickle inside her. Perhaps she'll die. One day, I mean, when it's too late. It's too late already, though, your husband a stupid dork and my mama an outrageous slut."

"Seems to me," said Sister C., "that you and Stevie here

are in the same boat, Mr. Benecke. Your mama hurt you, acting how she did, and now you're trying to even things up by hurting this woman? That doesn't make a whole lot of sense, young man. You've got things in common. You could be friends." In an aside to Stevie she added, "I'm supposed to say that. He's not going to listen, though. He's not just a young man bewildered by his mama's animal passions and discouraged by his daddy's many put-downs. Oh, no, Stevie, he's a distillate of free-floatin' cosmic evil, this Benecke buck; he's Satan's personal Ridpestman. And to Satan, I'm afraid, pests to be got rid of always include honesty, kindness, and all such halfway decent folks as happen to have 'em."

"Sister—"

"I'm just trying to say that you're playing for high stakes against a dangerous opponent, child."

Stevie decided to ignore this extraordinary aside to address the twenty-six-year-old distillate of free-floating cosmic evil: "Listen, Seaton, it's possible you've jumped to the wrong conclusion. They were seeing each other, Ted and your mother, but they never . . . maybe they never had relations."

"You don't *want* to get to the nitty-gritty, do you?" he said. "You don't *want* to go deep to see what makes people tick."

"Seaton, they may have just turned to each other for companionship. I looked like a water rat with a stomach tumor that summer. I was always irritable, always worried about money, not really an attractive or sympathetic partner at all. And your mother . . . well, she may have wondered if your father really cared about her, letting her go off to spend every summer alone on Scottsdale Lake."

"She wasn't alone."

"No, I know she wasn't. Without adult companionship, I should have said. Ted and she were deceiving me and your father, that's true enough, but it's possible they were simply using each other to reestablish their individual senses of . . . of self-esteem."

"I've never heard anything so stupid," Seaton replied disgustedly. "Never, ever. You must have been born in Disneyland."

"I'm too old to have been born in Disneyland."

"Then you're probably old enough to watch the rest of my slides, aren't you? They're X-rated, and *they'll* open your eyes, believe you me. Outdoor porn for menopausal Pollyannas."

"Notice how his vocabulary's improved this chapter," Sister Celestial advised Stevie. "He's drawing on reservoirs of Satanic strength."

Clicking the changer with ruthless energy, Seaton narrated a slide program like no other Stevie had ever seen. He began with a middle-distance shot of the Benecke cottage, pointing out that on this particular afternoon Lynnette had asked him to keep watch on the spaghetti sauce in her slow cooker while she and Mr. Crye went down to the lake to check a broken irrigation pipe. This was followed by an interior shot of the ceramic pot, which, in turn, yielded to a rear view of the GM truck in which Ted and Lynnette were departing for the lake. The irrigation pipe, Lynnette had explained, was at quite a distance from their pier.

The couple had been gone only about fifteen minutes, Seaton continued, when the electricity to the cottage went off. The refrigerator ceased humming (a shot of the refrigerator), the clocks all stopped at 3:48 (a sequence of stopped clocks, which, of course, are the only kind that a photograph can show), and the soap opera on Channel 9 dwindled away to a magnesium-bright dot that, even in the absence of electricity, lingered for a good thirty seconds (documentary evidence of the lingering dot). What do I do now? Seaton wondered. As a precautionary measure, he unplugged the slow cooker.

Then he set off after his mother and her handyman paramour to ask the latter if he could do anything to counteract the power outage at their cottage. (This narration was accompanied by a shot of Seaton's schoolboy shadow rippling over a hillock near the lake.) After all, Mr. Crye was an electrician as well as a plumber, and unless the spaghetti sauce cooked a good two hours or more, his mother would not be able to serve it. They would have bologna sandwiches and fruit cocktail for supper, a meal, if you could call it that, that Seaton despised. (A slide of the hypothetical bologna sandwich, garnished with a yellowing sprig of parsley, beside a plastic cup of fruit cocktail.) No one should wonder, then, that Seaton had set off in quest of adult aid and consolation.

"Quack, quack," the young man with the slide-changer said. He made these onomatopoeic syllables sound vaguely like the blatting of a broken Exceleriter or the bleating of a smoke alarm whose battery is about to fail. *"Quack, quack."*

Stevie and Sister C. exchanged a puzzled look, but the Sister, having already read her Remington's version of Chapter Forty-seven, was merely feigning puzzlement. . . .

"I say that because you can't show a noise on a slide," Seaton explained, "and I don't have a tape recorder. You see, somebody near the lake was using a duck call, quacking every now and then to get the ducks to come up to shore so they could feed them. My mom always kept a couple of bags of stale bread crumbs and sometimes even a box of old popcorn in the back of the pickup. Then we'd go to a secluded part of the lake, quack the ducks to shore, and feed them with whatever stuff we'd brought with us. Today, I realized, Mom had gone with Mr. Crye to feed the ducks. They'd forgotten all about that broken irrigation pipe. There *weren't* any goddamn irrigation pipes where that goddamn quacking was coming from."

The following sequence of slides neatly excerpted the highlights of Seaton's trek from the cottage property: a road bordered by graceful cattails; a pine copse traversed by wheel ruts in which pools of muddy lake water stood; a sequestered clearing far from the usual recreational thoroughfares. Seaton pointed out that the intermittent bleating of the duck call had led him to this clearing, where, as the next slide showed, the red GM truck occupied stage-center, its port side parallel to the lake shore, the door to the passenger side of the cab standing completely open, and neither his darling mother nor the annoying Theodore Crye anywhere in sight.

"The duck call had finally stopped sounding," Seaton said. "I was beginning to think it had been a real duck making the noise. Down by the lake, you see, someone had set out a big shallow box of popcorn, and a flock of ducks—some of them the tame white kind you see on farms, some of them mallards with green heads—this flock was fighting to gobble down the pop-corn. The ducks' heads went up and down, up and down, pecking, pecking, pecking at it. It reminded me of a bunch of typebars going up and down in the basket of an old-fashioned typewriter. Peck, peck, peck. Peck, peck, peck.''

"It would," murmured Stevie.

"More ducks kept coming up from the lake. Some of them flew in from the other side, dropping their silly webbed feet for landing gear and flapping to a standstill just offshore. The early birds had typed their way through a couple of reams of pop-corn, though, and most of the latecomers really didn't get any. I couldn't understand why the person blowing that duck call— my mother, your husband, whichever of 'em—had just kept blowing the damn thing. Then it quacked *again,* and I could tell it was coming from the cab of the truck—which, until then, I'd thought nobody was in.''

"Why don't you stop now?" Sister Celestial asked Seaton.

"You know I can't do that, Sister. We've gone a long time between sex scenes. It's nitty-gritty time again." He closed his eyes in self-reproach. "I've probably shilly-shallied around too long as it is."

"Get it over with, then," the prophetess urged him. "You don't have any feel for healthy eroticism, only the guilty kind, and Stevie's done suffered enough at your hands."

Her fingernails digging into her palms, Stevie rose from her chair and spoke to young Benecke through clenched teeth: "I've withstood every bit of it, too, haven't I? But if you per-sist—if you go on to the next slide—I swear, Seaton, I'll kill you."

"Sex and violence," he replied. "But you've taken the wrong approach with me, ma'am, because I've never, ever got enough of them. I've been deprived that way." His thumb de-pressed the changer button, and a grotesque image—an in-terior of the GM cab with two ill-defined human figures hor-izontally disposed on the Leatherette-upholstered seat— replaced the tight panorama of the truck in the clearing. "Here you see what I saw walking up to the open door on the passen-ger side. It tore me up. I'd never seen anything like it before."

"Seaton!" Stevie exclaimed, leaning forward.

"Those pale mounds halfway along, sort of like crescent moons, they're your precious Ted's fanny. Elegant Lynnette Benecke's under there somewhere. That's her bare feet sticking up in the foreground under the trousers bunched around his ankles. If you look real close, ma'am, you can see my mother's head thrown back against the inside of the other door and the tip of the duck call protruding from her mouth. *'Quack,'* she went. *'Quack, quack.'* And out the window you can see a pair of mallards with their wings spread getting ready to land on the lake."

No longer able to restrain herself, closing her eyes against the full-color evidence of Ted's infidelity, Stevie leapt from her plywood island to the one on which her nemesis was narrating the slide show. When next she opened her eyes, the young man's twistedly grinning face bobbed only inches from her, and she delivered herself of a forceful right uppercut that glanced off his temple and knocked his cap into the cellulose insulation between a pair of ceiling joists. With a deafening crash a box of ancient cooking utensils likewise fell into this valley, but lodged there without plunging through the kitchen ceiling below.

Stevie struck out at Seaton again, and this time the slide changer popped from his hand into a snowstorm of dust motes and eddying fibers. Although she could not see where the changer had fallen, the impact of its landing apparently depressed the button permanently, for the images on the torn sheet began clicking past at such an alarming rate that they became frames in a low-budget blue movie in which Ted and Lynnette had the dubious distinction of starring. Indeed, dim shots of Ted's fanny going up and down were amateurishly interspliced with vivid sequences of the ducks' heads busily pecking away at the popcorn in the cardboard box. To gape incredulously at this remarkable montage, Stevie pulled a punch—a lapse in her assault permitting Seaton to sidle between two pieces of dusty luggage and jump over several exposed joists to the island beneath the makeshift screen. Here he spread his arms and received upon his Ridpest parka the topographically faulted projections of the next several slides.

"They hadn't seen me," he orated. "They didn't know I was there. I could have turned around and walked home. I didn't, though. I went around to the tailgate and climbed into the load bed. The duck calls stopped, and eventually two faces appeared in the window in the back of the cab. I hated them both, though, and all I've ever seen in my mind's eye when thinking about either one of them in all the years since their betrayal is just what you're finally seeing now, Mrs. Crye. Peck, peck, peck. Wiggling and wriggling and tickling inside her. Perhaps, that day, I died. Perhaps I really did. I've been a sullen, uncommunicative, vengeful, and, more often than not, sadly impotent demon ever since." He laughed. "But this past week has been my glory, Mrs. Crye, the climax of my entire pathetic life!"

"You bet it has," Stevie retorted, trembling. "If you didn't die that day, you twerp, maybe you will tonight."

"No," Sister C. said, rising. "You don't have to kill him. It's not in the Chapter Forty-seven my Remington and I typed. You talk him into surrendering to the authorities for impersonating a Ridpestman, and they convince him to seek psychological help from the Bradley Center in Columbus—for which, of course, he'll hafta escape for the sequel."

Still aripple with semicubistic visions of lakeside lovemaking, Seaton made a farting noise with his lips. "You didn't buy that predictable finish, did you, Sister? It was a decoy to get you out of Button City on a cold February night. Besides, who wants a sequel? I'm not about to oversee a *second* marathon typing. This one's it. We're playing for all the marbles right here tonight."

"God!" Stevie exclaimed. "He doesn't give a damn about anybody, does he?" Like Cathinka taking on Waldemar, she hurried to engage her tormentor in hand-to-hand combat, tightroping the edge of one narrow joist and resolutely throwing herself toward the plywood island on which he haughtily awaited her. Raising his elbow, Seaton nearly blocked her advent, but she grabbed the upper sleeves of his parka, grappled her way erect, and shoved him into the curtain on which Ted was even yet energetically violating their marriage vows. "You couldn't leave me my illusions, could you?" she hissed at him, staggering back toward the projector as he planted his feet and repulsed this new attack. "You know," she managed, "you could have fixed my Exceleriter—really fixed it, I mean—and redeemed your pathetic life by . . . *unh!* . . . triumphing over your baser instincts." She halted Seaton's counterattack, gained both purchase and leverage, and began to force him to the groaning edge of the plywood, where nailheads had begun to work their way loose as a result of their brief but vigorous seesaw struggle.

"Knee him in the sausage works!" Sister Celestial encouraged Stevie. "Hit him where it hurts!"

"I'm *only* baser instincts," Seaton panted, bracing himself on the lip of the narrow abyss. "I sabotaged . . . *unh!* . . . every typewriter I ever worked on. Yours went first because . . . *unh!* . . . I wanted you to know the turmoil of its breakdown. I've known it, that turmoil, for . . . *unh!* . . . thirteen years. I'm bad, ma'am. I'm evil incarnate. Think of all the typewriters I've . . . *unh! unh!.* . . . irretrievably corrupted."

"Fiend!" Stevie shouted. "Twerp!" And she flung him off the plywood island into the trough between the joists.

Geysers of linty cellulose billowed into the air. Like a catfish finning its way into the turbid depths, Seaton disappeared into a layer of musty batting, whereupon the kitchen ceiling broke open beneath him and from a height of at least ten feet he crashed down, along with several bushels of blue-gray insulation, onto Stevie's circular table. Dumbfounded, Stevie stared through this Seaton-sized rent at the spread-eagled victim of her heroics, a blond young man with cherubic lips and translucently lidded eyes. How peaceful he looked, the cynosure of a dreamy slow-motion blizzard.

"Good for you," the Sister said. "He was asking for it, playing with our lives. You gave him just what he deserved."

"Unplug the projector," Stevie commanded her friend. "For Pete's sake, Betty, unplug that damn thing."

The Sister obeyed her. The slide show ceased. The light filtering into the attic no longer came from the projector's beam but from the hole in the kitchen ceiling. Stevie hunkered at the edge of the wobbly plywood to see if the fall had killed her adversary; she sincerely hoped that it had. As she looked down, however, Seaton opened his eyes, winked at her, rolled off the table to the floor, fumbled about, stood, gave her a smart-ass salute, and, gimping painfully, ran out the breakfast-nook door into the dark. RRRRR-uhm, RRRRR-uhm. He had survived for the sequel.

"Damn," Stevie said. "What now?"

"I'm not sure anymore, child. Things didn't work out that way in *my* Chapter Forty-seven. Not exactly, anyhow."

Her curiosity piqued by a sudden thought, Stevie worked her way back to the plank on which the end table with the slide projector rested. "He was quite a little paparazzo for a thirteen-year-old kid, wasn't he? Today he could make a living selling telephoto bathtub shots of mastectomy patients to the sleazier men's mags." She removed the cover on the projector's slide tray. A gasp of commingled astonishment and disgust escaped her lips.

"What's the matter?" Sister C. asked.

"It's empty," Stevie said. "It's absolutely empty."

(Imagine that.)

XLVIII

With Seaton gone, Stevie began to worry not only about the whereabouts of the monkeys the man had left behind, but also about Marella's inevitable response to the mutilation of her animals. Her daughter would be heartbroken. After ruining the stuffed animals, the capuchins had blent into the skeletal architecture of the upper stories as if they themselves were tenpenny nails, pieces of lathing, bits of crumbling plaster. Their utter disappearance, after their bizarre vandalism of the toys, angered as well as bewildered Stevie. She wanted to shoot every member of their proliferating tribe and hang them by their heels from the rafters.

"You only think you want to do that," Sister Celestial admonished her. "They're his dupes, those monkeys. They do his bidding 'cause he's all they've got. They're laboratory culls and orphans, child."

"They're demons from hell, just like their master."

The Sister was about to contradict this uncharitable definition of the capuchins when both women heard a low moaning from Marella's room. The sound penetrated to the marrow like a bone disease, and Stevie's entire body ached with apprehension. What midnight calamity had now beset her frail daughter? Hadn't they all suffered enough for one evening? Couldn't the child simply sleep through to dawn in stuporous ignorance of Seaton Benecke's visit? Apparently not. Besides, even if she did, at breakfast tomorrow morning Stevie would have to invent for her and Teddy some sort of semiplausible explanation for the hole in the ceiling.

"What chapter is this?" the Sister suddenly asked.

"You're the one with the manuscript pages, Betty. To me, I'm afraid, this is a continuing real-life nightmare. . . . Come on. I've got to see about Marella."

"She's all right, Stevie. I know it."

At the hatch of the step-down closet Stevie looked back into the attic at the dim, bulky figure of the prophetess. "Betty, even a seer can't know everything. Surely you've learned that by now."

"Of course I have. But this Chapter Forty-eight seems to have some muzzy correspondences with the one my Remington and I tapped out. I remember something about Marella moanin', I certainly do."

As if on cue, Stevie's daughter moaned again, a sound more like the cry of a hawk than a sick child.

"What exactly do you remember?"

"Has she ever sleepwalked, your Marella?"

"Never."

"Well, she's started, Stevie. She's somnambulating in her bed this very minute. She's standing on her mattress revvin' up

J.K.POTTER

her subconscious psychic energies with that eerie noise she's making."

"Betty, please—"

"Go on in there and look. She knows you're upset about the monkeys and what they did to her animals, and she's going to fix it—not so much for her sake, Mama, as for yours. She's got the power, Marella does, and she's going to set everything to rights with her latent subliterary paranormal energies."

Thoroughly exasperated, Stevie did not reply to this speech. She ducked through the low door into the closet, shouldered her way through the clustering hangups, and climbed out of the closet into her daughter's room. What she encountered here far exceeded in spectacular unlikelihood the bedchamber scene so crisply described, a moment past, by the prophetess.

Marella was indeed standing barefoot in the center of her bed. Her nightgown sleeves were afloat beneath her outstretched arms, and her eyes were glowing with the same degree of heat and luminescence given off by the control on her electric blanket. She was facing the corridor leading to the stairwell, and her hands were lifting and falling in unison, as if inviting the darkness to ebb away to the farthest recesses of the universe and the everlasting cosmic brightness to come flowing in. Meanwhile, she whined like a food processor cutting up cabbage for coleslaw.

"Marella," Stevie said. "Marella, I'm here."

The girl ignored her. She also ignored Sister C., who was just now emerging from the attic into her room. She swayed in time to an insistent, inaudible melody. Her eyes glowed golden, golden, golden (the consequence of a condition not often remarked in the offices of Georgia ophthalmologists). When, still undulating to her unheard music, she did swing toward the two adults, they pressed themselves against the wall out of the direct line of her gaze.

"I've never seen a sleepwalker like that before," Stevie whispered.

"Me either, child. Ain't she something?"

The closet door blew open, nearly striking the Sister's left arm, and a devil's-wind of cellulose fibers and shredded polyurethane foam eddied out of the attic like a cloud of ravenous moths. Marella directed them with lilting hand movements and rhythmic nods of the head. (She reminded Stevie of Mickey Mouse in "The Sorcerer's Apprentice" sequence of *Fantasia* . . . except that she appeared to be in much better control of her breathtaking gale than poor Mickey had been of his broom-and-bucket brigade.) As the girl's right index finger pointed first this way and then that, the winged debris from the attic swept in obedient schools toward the pelts of her several gutted animals, restored these synthetic hides to full-blown corporality, and then animated each cuddlesome creature so that it could march back into her room in stirring martial procession with its fellows. To calm her palpitant heart during this demonstration, Stevie slid her arm around Sister C.'s waist, a gesture that Betty Malbon instantly reciprocated. Locked in this reassuring embrace, they watched Kodak, Big Bird, Raggedy Ann, Purvis O'Possum, Peepers, Velvet Belly, the soft-shelled turtle Sweetcakes, and the doll baby Toodles execute a precision maneuver at the threshold, wheel in ranks around the foot of Marella's bed, and retire in orderly fashion to the bottom shelf of the tray assembly in which the child routinely stored them. Long after the animals had relapsed into floppy-limbed immobility, insulation fibers continued to drift through the atmosphere and Marella to play at field marshal from the cold plateau of her mattress. She seemed altogether unaware of the miracle she had wrought.

"I've never seen her like this," Stevie told the prophetess. "Maybe I should call Dr. Elsa."

"Don't you dare. It's much too late. Anyway, she's going to be fine, Marella is. She's stronger than you like to think."

"Obviously."

"See there. The glow's going out of her eyes, and her arms are startin' to droop. She just needs someone to tuck her in again." The Sister squeezed Stevie's waist. "That's you, Mama."

Stevie obeyed the Sister, for she had spoken the truth. Marella's eyes no longer spun out light the way the Clinac 18 radiated electrons, and her body had begun to crumple toward the bedclothes. Tenderly easing her down, arranging her legs and arms beneath the blankets, Stevie mumbled comforting nonsense to the entranced girl, meanwhile wondering whether she ought to set out newspapers and an upchuck bucket beside her bed. Did telekinetically restuffing a half-dozen toy animals and then marching them to bed induce headaches, nausea, and neuralgia? That it might hardly seemed, to Stevie, an outlandish supposition.

"When she wakes up," she whispered, "she'll be terrified by what she's done. She may take sick again."

"She won't even remember, Stevie."

"How do you know?"

"Well, you could tell by looking at her she didn't know what she was doing when she did it. It's not likely she'll recall in the morning what she didn't much mark in the doing."

"Maybe," said Stevie doubtfully, stroking Marella's forehead. She straightened and looked at her friend. "You've got to be exhausted, Betty. Let's go downstairs and put you to bed."

"I'm going to go on home to Button City, child, but I appreciate the invite, I certainly do."

"You don't want to drive at this hour. It's cold, and Kudzu Valley's down the road, and you're all by yourself."

The Sister opined that, having survived the last three and a half chapters in Stevie's house, she would probably do just beautifully cruising back down Highway 27 to her own cozy bungalow. Stevie would have enough explaining to do in the morning without an ample black lady popping in on the children to share their breakfast. Nor did the Sister much relish the idea of being introduced as a cook, maid, or cleaning woman.

"Oh, no, I wouldn't," Stevie started to protest, but the prophetess declared that she was only making a joke of a semiserious sort and reiterated her unshakable intention to leave. Together they had thwarted at least a portion of Seaton Benecke's plot, although, the Sister must admit, he had dealt a brutal blow to one of Stevie's most cherished memories; further, he had ruthlessly departed from the happier typescript in her carpetbag. Nevertheless, Stevie had acquitted herself well, and the prophetess had no qualms about leaving her to finish out the remainder of the night without a guest in the downstairs bedroom.

"Two things I'd like to do before I go, though, Stevie."

"Anything."

"Take a peek at your son and another at your PDE machine."

A moment later, then, they stood shoulder to shoulder at Teddy's bedside. The boy had slept through every scream, scuffle, cry, and alarum, and he continued to sleep beneath the half-speculative gazes of the women. So young, Stevie thought; so young. She deeply resented the indignity to which the typewriter repairman's malicious plotting had subjected them in an earlier chapter—when, in fact, Teddy and she had so clearly been surrogates for the thirteen-year-old Seaton and his attractive mother Lynnette. What an unsettling Oedipal fantasy Seaton had manufactured by imagining the episode from Stevie's point of view. Unless, of course, she had dreamt the particulars of the unnatural scene herself. . . . She found the kaleidoscopic ramifications of the matter so confusing that she sighed. Meanwhile, Teddy slipped in and out of her vision like a one-celled animalcule beneath the lens of a microscope, and her weariness would not permit her to bring him sharply back into focus.

"Pretty young man," Sister C. remarked. "Very pretty young man."

"Thank you."

"Looks just like his daddy, doesn't he?"

Stevie massaged her temples with her fingertips. "Yes, he really does. It's not his fault, though. That's the way the chromosomes coupled."

"Who said it was a fault?" The Sister hugged the other woman with one arm. "You wanted me to diagnose your nightmares, remember? You wanted to know why Ted gave up when your doctor friends discovered his cancer. Well, he gave up 'cause he thought it was a punishment—a long-last punishment, child—for runnin' around on you when you had his namesake here in the oven. He gave up 'cause he thought he'd been caught by the Fates. He said in one o' your dreams he died so you could fulfill yourself. Well, he really did believe his dying was a gift to you, Stevie, a way of paying off the debt.''

"Some gift."

"What is it people always say? 'It's the thought that counts.' You should look at it that way.''

Stevie found the prophetess's doubtful point so funny that she began to laugh. To keep from disturbing Teddy, she covered her mouth, but her sputtering laughter still managed to seep through her fingers, and in self-defense she buried her face in the Sister's heavy shawl while the other woman chuckled mutedly in sympathy. Consoling companionship. How could she have endured the last few hours if Sister Celestial had not driven up from Button City?

"Looks just like his daddy. You're lucky you got him. You're lucky you got *both* your pretty children.''

After confessing that she knew it and stroking Teddy's head as if to acquire by touch a small measure of his practical glamour, she led Sister C. across the hall to her study. The unplugged Exceleriter emitted from its contoured surfaces only the cold gleam of blue metal; the unearthly luminosity with which it had earlier burst on Stevie's sight had completely faded away.

A typewriter is a typewriter is a typewriter, Stevie thought, beholding it, and almost felt friendly toward it again. The machine had not conspired against her, after all; it had suffered ill usage and demonic takeover at the hands of a pudgy blond fiend with admirable manual dexterity and a masturbatory fixation on his own mother. Sister Celestial had called this young man "a distillate of free-floatin' cosmic evil," but everyone had good and bad days, and maybe the prophetess had overstated the case to keep Stevie from underestimating her opponent during their showdown. In any event, you could not hold this unfortunate machine accountable for Seaton's many despicable villainies.

Or could you?

"Why don't you plug it in and type on it?" the Sister asked. "Before I leave, that is.''

Although Stevie grasped the advisability of having a friend nearby when she tried the Exceleriter again, her stomach flip-flopped and her hands began to tremble. However, she had a clean sheet of paper in the machine, in an effort to comply with the Sister's suggestion, when it turned itself on and rapidly typed out the following sentimental imperative:

GO TO HELL, YOU INTERFERING SLUTS.

Whereupon Stevie yanked the paper free of the platen and the plug from the wall socket.

"You got to get shut of it, Stevie."

"Shut of it?"

"Scrap it, I mean. Destroy it. You've got two choices, one of which is to drive down to Columbus and shoot Seaton Benecke and the other of which is to take the typewriter he's corrupted and put it out of your misery."

"It cost me—Ted, rather—seven hundred dollars, Betty. It's my livelihood."

"Murder a man or cast off a machine. It's your choice. Either way you'll find a sort of salvation from this week-long nightmare you been suffering."

"Are you going to destroy your Remington?"

This unexpected question gave the Sister pause. "I don't use mine the way you do—not usually, anyway. I'll have to see. If it keeps misbehavin', though, I'll *hafta* scrap it—whether or not Emmanuel Berthelot gave it to my daddy for a heirloom, and he most certainly did. That's the truth."

"Will you help me get rid of mine?"

"Stevie, you've got to do it yourself. And I suggest you do it tomorrow afternoon about the same time your typewriter broke down last Tuesday. That'll round off the week 'n' wrap up the whole episode nice and neat."

"What about Benecke? What if he comes back? And the monkeys—" Stevie nodded her head toward Marella's room— "they're still around here somewhere, Benecke's familiars, haunting my attic and closets."

"One thing at a time, Stevie."

"But—"

"Destroy the Exceleriter. Everything else'll line right up."

This advice did not sit well with Stevie (the Sister had lost her bearings in Chapter Forty-seven, as even she had admitted), but the capuchins had vanished from sight and scrapping her typewriter was preferable to murdering the man who had set them loose in her house. Therefore, she bit her tongue and acquiesced in the black woman's less than infectious self-confidence. The Sister's reasoning seemed to be that you could not deal absolute evil a single devastating knockout punch, but must instead wear it down with elusive footwork and a cunning series of debilitating body blows. To shoot young Benecke would eliminate the vessel currently containing Sister C.'s "distillate of free-floatin' cosmic evil," but the poisonous substance itself would thereby increase and flow into other empty human receptacles. Indeed, you could not accurately tabulate the number of occasions on which frightened folks had unwittingly contributed to the world's stores of evil by assuming a divine commission to exhaust these stores utterly. . . .

Downstairs Stevie asked the Sister's permission to take a quick look at the chapters in the carpetbag, now that they had run Seaton off and settled the question of what Stevie must do next. What harm, at this stage, a supervised peek at her own story's concluding paragraphs? How would it be possible for her to feel more manipulated and volitionless than she already did? The Sister plainly did not care for the tenor of Stevie's inquiries, but, allowing that she deserved some small consideration for her spunky steadfastness in the attic, the prophetess relented and bent to extract the paper-clipped pages from her carryall.

Like the slide tray in the projector, however, the carpetbag was found to be empty, and Stevie and Sister C. could only look at each other and divest themselves of imperceptible, unhappy shrugs. Maybe the intruder who had plummeted through the ceiling had made off with this important evidence, although, thinking back, Stevie could hardly credit the notion. Seaton, the author of his own hurried escape and their present befuddlement, had not had time to rifle the carpetbag.

"Another no-account conjuration," the Sister said. "But

we've still got him whipped. You just do what I told you.''

After the Sister had left, Stevie returned to the kitchen and tried to clean up the fallen insulation and the fractured gypsum board. Too bad Marella's remarkable command of inanimate objects had not communicated itself to her; in that event, a Wonder Woman of the parlous night, she would have been able to finish in a finger snap. As it was, she did not get to bed until nearly 2:45 A.M., and she did not fall dreamlessly asleep until much, much later. . . .

XLIX

Teddy and Marella ate their Rice Krispies with many a skeptical glance at the hole above the kitchen table. Stevie told them that she had dropped a carton of books between the joists while attempting to rearrange the clutter up there. Although they accepted this explanation more readily than they would have a synopsis of the events that had actually taken place, their glances both at the ceiling damage and back and forth between themselves suggested that only a Crazy Woman would have sought to do her attic cleaning unassisted at such an hour. Poor Old Mom had gone off her gourd again, even after a rejuvenating outing to Columbus on Sunday afternoon. Stevie, lifting a cup of coffee to her lips, strove to discredit this judgment by asking in responsible maternal fashion how they had slept.

''Okay,'' said Teddy.

''Fine,'' piped Marella. ''Butcept I had a really funny dream about my animals. I was leading them in a parade. Something like that.''

''Stupid,'' Teddy commented. ''Sounds like a Shirley Temple movie or something.''

This unsympathetic assessment of Marella's dream precipitated an argument that Stevie interrupted with a threat. She would dock the allowance of the next person who spoke a provocative or disparaging word. Her intervention clotured debate, and, a few minutes later, the kids left for school, mumbling about holes in the ceiling and the cruel persistence of the February cold. Stevie lingered over the *Constitution*'s daily scrambled-word game with the nub of an obtuse pencil (none of the words in the paper were unjumbling for either her or it), her coffee cooling beside her.

According to Sister C., she must scrap her Exceleriter, put it out of her life as she would an unfulfillable ambition or a two-timing man. How was she going to accomplish this pressing task? At the moment she was not sure. Nor did she want to think about the question much. She kept trying to solve the Jumble.

An hour or so later a caller's heavy knocks rattled the windowpane in her front door, and Stevie hurried to see if Seaton Benecke had come back. Instead she saw an employee of the United Parcel Service—not an obvious imposter, either, but a balding fellow in a dark brown uniform—who lifted for her inspection as she approached the door a small package wrapped in whitish-brown paper. Observing that the man's truck stood beneath the tulip tree where Sister Celestial had parked last night, Stevie greeted the UPS employee, signed for the package, and stepped back into the foyer to tear the paper off and examine the object inside. She was only a little surprised to find the editorial offices of the Briar Patch Press in Atlanta listed as the return address, but significantly more alarmed to discover herself holding a mint-condition copy of the novel that David-Dante Maris had promised, during their telephone conversation, to send to her. After all, that conversation had never taken place. . . .

Her fingers numb, Stevie returned to the kitchen to study this impossible artifact. The photograph of the author on the back of the dust jacket showed a man in coy silhouette, well disguised by shadows and glare, one hand extended toward the camera as if to wrench it from the presumptuous person wielding it in his presence. The room in which the author affected this rather theatrical stance appeared to be as vast and lonely as an unoccupied gymnasium or warehouse. Stevie thought immediately of the typewriter graveyard in the rear of Hamlin Benecke & Sons in Columbus. She flipped the book over and turned to the title page:

THE TYPING
One Week in the Life
of the Madwoman of Wickrath County

A Novel of Contemporary Horror
A. H. H. Lipscombe

THE BRIAR PATCH PRESS • ATLANTA

What else should she have expected? Young Benecke, who claimed to have no talent for writing, had perhaps proved this deceptive contention by making her the protagonist of "A Novel of Contemporary Horror." *The Typing,* of all ghastly, self-descriptive entitlements! Under, to boot, the superstodgy pseudonym A. H. H. Lipscombe, as if he were the H. P. Lovecraft of the 1980s or possibly the J. R. R. Tolkien of American horror fiction, a spinner of gruesome fabulations and noisome provincial epics. The most intolerable horror that Stevie could imagine was to awaken to the fact that one such busy literary dung beetle had imprisoned her in the fetid brood ball of a narrative. That was exactly what Benecke had done to her; he had made her a character in a book, the very book she was presently riffling in helpless obedience to its sentence-by-sentence dictates.

> Stevenson Crye—her friends called her Stevie—was nearing the end of her feature story on detection-and-diagnosis procedures at the West Georgia Cancer Clinic in Ladysmith when a cable inside her typewriter . . .

And farther on:

> The day had gone scratchy and sour. Not even a gross of Sucrets would take away the soreness and sweeten . . .

And farther still:

> The editor-in-chief of the Briar Patch Press, Inc., gave another hearty chuckle. "Oh, I'm still here, Mrs. Crye. That means we're both . . ."

And even farther yet:

> Teddy and Marella ate their Rice Krispies with many a skeptical glance at the hole above the kitchen table. . . .

Well, no matter what Seaton Benecke, alias A. H. H. Lipscombe, thought, she had an existence and a will apart from those he attributed to her in this trendy chiller from the Briar Patch Press. Evidence of her independence sprang from a variety of sources, almost all of them invisible because they were psychological. Today, for instance, she did not *feel* like a character in a book; she felt like a human being in control of her future, if not necessarily of this fleeting scene. Moreover, she harbored a healthy contempt for the mind attempting to foist a preconceived pattern upon her movements, and she believed she could defeat it by exerting herself to that end. Perhaps the best evidence of the bankruptcy of The Seaton Benecke Version—this three-hundred-plus-page opus in her hands—revealed itself in the startling omission of the novel's final chapter, for the pages after the last Roman-numeral heading were snow-white blanks.

Until, that is, you came to some pages entitled "Author's Open Remarks to Filmmakers in Search of Hot Commercial Properties." These remarks, which Stevie scanned, read as follows:

> I wrote, or typed, the gripping story you have just read, *The Typing,* for one purpose only: to sell it to the movies. People like to watch television and go to the movies; they do not usually like to read unless they have nothing better (i.e., more urgent, more profitable, or more fun) to do. Typing prose requires an expenditure of energy, even when it only grunts or sputters along, but because many movies begin as books, it is necessary to keep writing them

as stepping-stones to fame and fortune. Perhaps you have just read this story because a Hollywood studio or an independent filmmaker of real ambition has hired you to search for "hot commercial properties." If so, you have come to the right place.

"But wait," you may be objecting, "a novel in which a typewriter goes berserk and starts composing at the behest of a demonic would-be writer does not readily lend itself to effective visual treatment. A typewriter only sits and types; it does not emote."

That, of course, is the challenge that this highly original story poses the prospective filmmaker. Cunning camera angles, imaginative crosscuts, and compelling special effects will enable you to turn the stationary PDE Exceleriter into a character as vivid and engaging as R2-D2 in *Star Wars*. Further, in Chapter Forty-four I have introduced a scene in which my inanimate, unplugged machine emits an eerie glow. No director worth his salt can fail to simulate a believable eerie glow, and the march of the toy animals in Chapter Forty-eight contains parenthetical reference to Disney's *Fantasia*. Only the most hidebound and blinkered film executive would dismiss *The Typing* as a potential "hot commercial property" because one of its characters happens to be a typewriter.

Besides, I have also included capuchin monkeys and several human characters, the most important of the latter being the widowed writer Stevenson Crye. The monkeys may be effectively played by unknowns, but an actress of great beauty, talent, and box-office appeal should take the part of Stevie. In descending order of preference my choices include Meryl Streep, Sally Field, and Goldie Hawn, all of whom I have written several anonymous letters of undying love in either crayon or felt-tipped marker. I am myself available for the role of Seaton Benecke, although to maintain the integrity of my two parallel careers, I would of course play it under a name other than A. H. H. Lipscombe.

Incidentally, I have left the final chapter out of the published version of my novel to pique the curiosity of potential filmmakers and those members of the film-going public who have chanced upon this book by mistake. To learn the details of my finale, the former need only hire me to do the screenplay and the latter to turn out in droves for the forthcoming celluloid translation of my dream. Those few of you who purchased the book expecting to find it complete in this volume should hang on to your sales receipts, which, later, you may redeem at box-office windows for half the full ticket price for admission to the movie. Rest assured that I will not sell an option on *The Typing* that does not include a clause to this effect.

Whoever makes the film adaptation of *The Typing* will of course have first shot at my next "hot commercial property," for which project, having by then learned the ropes on this one, I would perhaps like to act not only as screenwriter and supporting star but also as producer and technical advisor. For more information please contact David-Dante Maris at the Briar Patch Press in Atlanta.

— "A. H. H. Lipscombe"
Columbus, Georgia

"Jesus," mumbled Stevie when she had read this extraordinary document, but, truth to tell, she recognized in herself a certain sheepish admiration for the chutzpah animating it. Seldom did writers laboring in one arena admit so openly that they were whoring for the chance to enter another. Probably, his mother having failed both to take on the full weight of his unreasonable emotional dependency and to still the tingle of his adolescent libido, Seaton had decided to write exploitative potboilers as a means of gaining entry to the boudoirs of Meryl Streep, Sally Field, Goldie Hawn, et al. The poor deluded twerp. His fantasy was itself the subject matter of exploitative potboilers. Even more than Stevie, he belonged in a novel full of amateurish sociological speculations and pseudo-Freudian character analyses. The twerp; the poignantly transparent twerp . . .

Whereupon Stevie read the author's brazen addendum and

grew angrier and angrier the closer she read. First of all, although Seaton Benecke, alias A. H. H. Lipscombe, might contrive to sell the film rights to those portions of his manuscript surrounding her story "The Monkey's Bride," he had no legal claim to the story itself. If he sought to profit from *her* creative labor, well, she would sue the bastard. Any film version of *The Typing* appropriating even a single line of dialogue from "The Monkey's Bride" would invite prompt litigation, and she would stick Benecke and his film-producer cohorts for all the punitive damages they could possibly handle. Indeed, she secretly hoped they would try to pull a fast one.

Second, outside of being a moderately attractive female, Stevie did not look very much like Meryl Streep, Sally Field, or Goldie Hawn. She more nearly resembled a mature, somewhat subdued Sissy Spacek, and Sissy Spacek with her natural command of a variety of Sun Belt accents and locutions would *sound* more like the real Stevenson Crye, too. Besides, she would willy-nilly communicate to the film-going public a degree of that fragile ambience still adhering to her from Brian De Palma's *Carrie*. A fragile ambience waiting to erupt. It was hardly Ms. Spacek's fault that Seaton had failed to write her a single anonymous letter of undying love in either crayon or felt-tipped marker. . . .

Third, Seaton's calculated omission of his final chapter deserved only contempt. That the Briar Patch Press had gone along with this cynical scheme branded Maris and his associates the kind of small-time operators whose example they purported to despise. You did not deliberately leave the last few pages out of a book if you were a quality publisher with the interests of your readers, as well as your sales figures, at heart. Moreover, Stevie told herself, this strategy might well backfire on young Benecke. In fact, she would see to it that it did. She would sharpen her uncooperative pencil nub with a kitchen knife and compose an acceptable ending herself. The blank pages before Seaton's self-serving appeal to "Filmmakers in Search of Hot Commercial Properties" would serve her for folded foolscap. She would skewer Seaton thereon and simultaneously save herself.

"But in a ladylike way," she cautioned herself. "No violence to persons, only to inanimate objects."

Having made this civilized resolve, she sharpened her pencil and began to write. Let someone else set the chapter in type. If the Briar Patch Press wanted her version of the novel, they would have to pulp every copy in their predistribution inventory and reissue it under a title less obviously trendy than *The Typing* and a by-line substantially more hip than A. H. H. Lipscombe. She would try to take care of these matters— troublesome as they were—in the episodes shaping her conclusion. Yes. Yes, she would.

L

Stevie had a mission. The hour when her PDE Exceleriter had broken down one week ago would soon be upon her, and she must destroy the machine at that time to escape the possibility of future torment at its invisible hands. This charge required certain preparations that she proceeded to undertake in a spirit of grim self-discipline.

Upstairs she found the .22 rifle that, against her wishes, Ted had bought for Teddy on the boy's tenth birthday. She also found a box of cartridges and loaded the rifle's magazine. With the safety engaged, she carried the rifle downstairs to the VW van and slid it beneath a passenger seat. She then trekked back upstairs to get her typewriter, which, on her second trip down, she nearly dropped. However, having at last achieved the transfer, she drove some four or five blocks to Builders Supply of Barclay, a huge prefabricated structure, where she bought a gallon of paint. This paint was fire-engine red, four quarts of crimson latex.

Her purchase in hand, Stevie angled her microbus through a neighborhood of formidable two-story clapboard houses surrounded by magnolia trees and leafless dogwoods. She soon arrived at the town's white cemetery on the northeast side. Three narrow asphalt lanes permitted entrance to the cemetery, a serene expanse of withered grass on which discolored, nearly illegible markers from the 1800s stood shoulder to shoulder with contemporary marble headstones and a solitary mausoleum two caskets high and five wide. A few gnarled trees vied with a host of chipped granite angels for tallest-inhabitant honors, and, in the shadow of a particularly arthritic-looking cork elm, Stevie turned left on the last of the three asphalt lanes. It had been almost two months since she had visited Ted's grave. The angels staring down through her windshield wore expressions of lofty reproach, the severity of which was considerably tempered by the pigeon crap streaking their eroded faces. Stevie felt a piquant affection for even the sternest of these shabby cherubim. They were only doing their jobs.

Apart from most of the others, Ted's burial plot occupied the gentle downhill slope near the poniard-topped metal fence enclosing the graveyard on the east. Stevie parked at a small distance, carried her typewriter to the low mound of her late husband's grave, and positioned the machine above his buried head. Then, with some difficulty, she tied the can of paint from Builders Supply to the limb of a dogwood hanging over the grave from the other side of the fence. The can made a quarter turn to the right, another quarter turn to the left, meanwhile glinting uncannily in the feeble February sun—just the sort of startling high-gloss image (thought Stevie, fetching her son's .22) that a resourceful film director would find effective in the incongruous context of a small winter cemetery.

In the concealing lee of the microbus Stevie took a careful bead on the revolving paint can. Suddenly an asthmatic snuffling noise—a sound like the unnerving breather on her telephone—broke her concentration. Frightened, she lowered the rifle's muzzle and quickly retreated to the shelter of her passenger's door. This same noise repeated itself, and she heard dragging footsteps in the crinkly leaves on the other side of the van. How could anyone have followed her to this place? She had seen no one in the cemetery, and not even the quasi-omniscient Seaton Benecke could know what she was doing right now or

J.K. POTTER

where she was doing it—for she was composing this compellingly suspenseful scene herself. Whoever approached her, then, had come into being out of thin air, perhaps for malicious reasons best left to the reader's imagination.

Five or six seconds later, as Stevie stood gazing down the barrel of the .22 at the spot where this unexpected intruder must soon come round the open door, a pair of bloodshot eyes did indeed materialize. These eyes were pregnant with worldly sadness and strangely low to the ground; the body they trailed behind them was spotted black, brown, and white, with crooked appendages that seemed to be disproportionately small for the weight they must perforce support. An involuntary cry escaped Stevie's lips, and she put one hand to her heart.

"What are you doing here?" she asked the creature.

It was Cyrano, the Cochrans' basset hound. Cyrano wagged his tail lethargically and came snuffling up her instep to her knee, leaving several strands of semenish slobber on her jeans. Stevie pushed the dog away, checked her watch, took aim on the paint can, and pulled the trigger. The report, echoing through the little graveyard, sent Cyrano scampering around the Volkswagen for home. Happy with this result, Stevie put three more holes in the can, staggering them with some success from top to bottom.

Paint bled down the length of the revolving container and poured into the works of the typewriter. Gory gouts of paint inundated the arrogant machine. A Red Sea of retribution drowned it. Thus ensanguined, the typewriter sat atop Ted's grave like a bloody head, all consciousness washed away in the rubbery artificial hemoglobin of the Glidden's Exterior Latex. It was purgative, this nauseating sight, and once all the paint had dripped from the can over and into the Exceleriter, Stevie averted her head and spewed a porridge of transmogrified Rice Krispies all over the innocent and unoffending grass. Now she knew how Marella often felt. . . .

A hand touched her elbow, and she started. She had heard no one approach. When she looked up, light-headed and embarrassed, wiping her mouth with the sleeve of her jean jacket, she saw Larry Clovers, one of Barclay's three police officers, eyeing her with a mixture of wariness and disgust.

"Mrs. Crye, it's against the law to discharge a firearm inside the city limits. This here cemetery's inside the city limits."

"I'm finished, Larry. I won't do it again."

"It's also against the law to deface a grave site and to dump worn-out machinery in unauthorized places. This here's an unauthorized place."

"It had to be done, Larry. I'll clean up the mess. I'm not going to leave that crap all over Ted's grave."

"Mrs. Crye, you've broken two or three laws, maybe more. I'm supposed to take you in." There followed a burst of static and a stream of amplified, half-intelligible speech from the radio in Clovers's blue police car, which he had parked behind the microbus. "Really, Mrs. Crye, I should arrest you." Quite gently he took the rifle from Stevie's hand and removed its magazine.

"Listen, Larry, you're lucky you've even made an appearance in this book. I've only written you in as a kind of gift to your father's memory." The elder Clovers, Stevie recalled, had been good to Ted and her, selling them a gas water heater at cost and installing it for nothing. "Your dad wouldn't appreciate you making a nuisance of yourself in the name of a couple of slightly bent laws. I haven't hurt anyone. Why don't you get on that radio of yours and ask Joe Dunn and Henry McAbee in the sanitation department to come out here and haul my old typewriter off to the dump? I can't take it home again."

"Ma'am, I—"

"Listen, I'll wipe most of the excess paint off before they get here. Later this afternoon I'll come back and tidy up Ted's grave. He'll forgive me this silly profanation of the site. He owed me one."

Compelled by her unorthodox reasoning (and the lead in her insistent pencil nub), Officer Larry Clovers went to his police car and relayed Stevie's message to the city truck in which, every Tuesday morning, Joe Dunn and Henry McAbee collected trash. Ten minutes later the truck arrived, Joe and Henry heaved the ruined Exceleriter into the growling jaws of the automated compactor, and Stevie tossed the empty paint can in behind the typewriter as a clattery afterthought. Then she tipped the trashmen, patted Larry Clovers on the arm, bade all three men goodbye, and drove back to her house.

Dr. Elsa was waiting for her in her driveway along with a pair of husky men in coveralls, employees of Hamlin Benecke & Sons. Neither man was Seaton. At Seaton's behest, however, they had driven up from Columbus in a company vehicle (a wood-paneled station wagon with dusty venetian blinds in the rear window) to make a delivery. Dr. Elsa explained that about twenty minutes ago she had received a telephone call from Seaton asking her to meet the deliverymen at Stevie's house, for he could get no answer when he dialed her number himself. Someone—preferably a close family friend—should be on the premises to receive delivery. Although this unusual request meant breaking or at least delaying an appointment with a patient already in the clinic, Dr. Elsa had complied with it out of loyalty to Stevie and the compelling suspicion that Seaton Benecke was working a wild-eyed practical joke at her friend's expense.

Anyway, because the deliverymen had just arrived, Stevie need not fear that they had perpetrated any sort of mischief during her absence. The larger of the two husky visitors, a red-haired fellow with photogenic Yosemite Sam mustachios and a picturesque acne-scarred complexion, eavesdropped on Dr. Elsa's hurried explanations with great interest and an astonishing sequence of offended looks. His companion, a young black man, gazed over the station wagon with his arms folded on the roof and the point of his chin on the back of one hand. His expression conveyed more amusement than irritation. Clearly, he did not mind getting away from the Beneckes on a work assignment, particularly if he could watch his partner take puffy umbrage at an imagined slight.

Stevie turned to the red-haired man. "A delivery? Of what? I didn't order anything, and I don't want anything from Seaton, either. I've had just about all of him I can stand."

"Yeah, we feel that way, too," said the black employee, still smiling. "It's a job, though."

"Of typewriters," said Dr. Elsa before the red-haired man could speak. "They've brought you a shipment of secondhand typewriters."

"Reconditioned machines," emended the red-haired man. "Six of 'em. And a dozen reams of typing paper."

"But I didn't order these things. I'm certainly not going to pay for them."

"Ma'am, I don't think nobody *expects* you to. We're just here to make delivery. Ain't supposed to leave until we've taken 'em inside for you. . . . And here's something from the kid he told me to hand over to you once you showed up." The red-haired man thrust a wrinkled legal-size envelope at Stevie as if serving a subpoena, and her fingers closed on the object before she could draw back from it. "Can we get started, ma'am? Grady and me haven't had lunch yet."

"Started what?"

"Taking the typewriters inside. Faster we do it, less chance of us pulling much mischief around here." He smirked.

"Just a minute. Let me see what this is." Stevie's fingers fumbled with the envelope. After tearing off one end, she removed two sheets of typing paper on which Seaton had written her a hasty crabbed letter in blue crayon.

Dear Mrs. Crye (Mary Stevenson),

I screwed up your Exceleriter so bad the fortune teller lady from Button City told you to get rid of it. She did right. It's impossible to get them back once you mess them up that way. These repaired machines, though, they've got nothing wrong with them. I didn't do anything to them except fix them, no matter what I've told you before. Anyway, they work okay. I want you to have them to make up for the machine I made crazy. If one breaks, you can move over to another. Most of them their owners left and never picked up. Now they're yours. So is the paper I sent.

I tormented you the way I did to take revenge on your husband who died. He was a jerk. You were too good to him and too good for him. So was my mother. The experience he dumped on me thirteen years ago turned me into a BAD SEED. I sucked up all the free-floating cosmic evil around and went totally weird. You got in the way of that weirdness when your typewriter broke. After you chased me off last night, though, I began to see what a drain on my energy bugging you day in and day out was getting to be. It's hard work being a container for cosmic evil, harder than repairing typewriters.

Besides, you started reminding me of a middle-aged Sissy Spacek, the way she might look eight or ten years down the line. I get infatuated with famous actresses on a regular basis, Mrs. Crye, and start writing them unsigned letters to let them know I'm around. It's really a jerky thing to do, but I can't help it. If I stay in Columbus much longer, I'll fall in love with you that way and give you the same obnoxious business in letters sort of like this one.

That's why, later this week, I'm leaving for Arizona to enroll in the Mormon Lake Nondenominational Halfway House for Satan's Scions (they sent me a brochure back in '79), where I hope to shake my addiction and start a writing career. I think I'd like to do children's books about divorce, street crime, teen-age pregnancy, and stuff like that. Anyway, say hello to 'Crets for me if he's still hanging around your place, and I sure hope you can use these typewriters.

Goodbye,
Seaton

"Is everything all right, honey?" Dr. Elsa asked. "You look a little confused."

"Hunky-dory," Stevie answered, refolding the letter and sliding it back into the envelope. "For the first time in a week everything's hunky-dory, Elsa."

"What about the typewriters?" the red-haired man petitioned Stevie. "Our instructions was to stay right in your driveway until we'd carried every last one of 'em into the house. Then you're supposed to sign."

"I'll sign if you put them in my attic," Stevie said.

The red-haired man threw an irritated, hopelessly put-upon

look at his partner, Grady, who hunched his shoulders in a shrug without lifting his chin from his hands. But, the mustachioed giant grumbling continuously and Grady either whistling a rhythm-and-blues melody or silently mouthing the lyrics of a popular rap, they carried the typewriters upstairs and stashed them one by one in the nearly inaccessible attic off Marella's room. In three additional trips (making nine altogether between the two men), Grady did the honors with the reams of Stenocraft typing paper—while his disgruntled partner sat slumped behind the station wagon's steering wheel cleaning his fingernails with the blade of his pocketknife. Stevie signed, and the two men left. Only one of them waved as they went around the corner.

"I've got to hurry back to the clinic, kiddo," Dr. Elsa said. "Sam'll say I've been AWOL. You gonna be okay?"

"It's not a practical joke," Stevie assured her. "It's a genuine gift, by way of compensation. Don't worry. I'll be fine."

"Why'd you have those fellas put every one of the typewriters in your attic, then? Looks like you're tryin' to hide 'em away. Shouldn't you have stuck at least one in your office?"

"Not today, Elsa. Go on back to your patients."

The two women embraced, and Stevie spent the afternoon running errands, one of which was finding a handyman to repair the hole in the kitchen ceiling and another of which involved a careful manicure of the mound over Ted's grave and the setting-out of a large basket of penitential roses. That evening, after a trip to the grocery store, she prepared baked potatoes, buttered asparagus spears, and broiled steaks for her happily taken-aback children. The hole in the ceiling still yawned above them, for the man she had found to patch it (a carpenter from Wickrath with whom Ted had often worked) would not be able to come until Thursday, but its portentous presence did not dampen their festivities, and a Good Time Was Had by All.

Later, Teddy and Marella in bed, Stevie listened for the sound she knew would soon begin emanating from the attic. Finally she heard it, a muffled series of overlapping tap-tap-taps. Stealthily, then, she proceeded to Marella's room, stepped down into the sunken closet, and pushed her way through the hatch opening to the source of this rhythmic mechanical music. There greeted her eye—just as she had known it would—an industrious contingent of capuchin monkeys banging away at Seaton's secondhand typewriters and grinding out sheet after sheet of a random simian literature.

'Crets was the fastest typist among the bunch, and it was to him that all the others looked when they had reached the end of a page, created a typebar jam in their baskets, or run short of even the doubtful inspiration of simple nervous energy. 'Crets spurred them on by either example or direct assistance, and soon the temporarily blocked capuchins were busily typing again. Stevie gave them all throat lozenges and read over their shoulders, moving from cardboard box to dusty end table to backless chair bottom cheering them on and monitoring their compositions. Most of it was gibberish, of course, but 'Crets had accidently reproduced the first half of the opening chapter of a contemporary horror novel and the capuchin one plywood island away had composed a limerick in a language suspiciously akin to Dutch or Afrikaans. At this rate, even those monkeys tapping out line after line of ampersands or semicolons would soon be producing salable work, some of it in English, and Stevie would never have to go near a typewriter again.

"Keep at it, fellas," she encouraged them, ducking through the hatch into the closet. "I'll be back in ten or fifteen minutes with a tray of fried-egg sandwiches. Minus the bread, of course."

And she went downstairs into the many, many happy days remaining to her in this life, all of which were of her own composition. . . .

T*H*E E*N*D

A NOTE ON THE TYPE

The text of Who Made Stevie Crye? *was set in the film version of Baskerville, modeled after the original designs of John Baskerville (1706–1775), an Englishman who contributed greatly to the printing industry as a whole through his work with typography, paper, and ink. His type is a classic of the transitional style, with generous counters, a curved vertical stress, and contrast between stem and hairlines. The text extracts were spontaneously composed in American Typewriter Medium by a rambunctious Exceleriter that remained persistently impervious to attempted editorial intervention.*